The Dance

A Novel by Gordon W. Fredrickson

The second book of the Discovery series

BEAVER'S POND
PRESS

Edited by Kellie M. Hultgren
Front cover artwork: Dance Hall at Twilight, acrylic on canvas by Judy Malz, 2024
Back cover: Lyrics for the "Dance Hall Polka" by Gordon W. Fredrickson, circa 1995

ISBN 13: 978-1-64343-547-3
Library of Congress Catalog Number: 2025901493
Printed in the United States of America
First Printing: 2025
29 28 27 26 25   5 4 3 2 1

Book design and typesetting by Dan Pitts

BEAVER'S POND
PRESS

Beaver's Pond Press
526 Seventh Street West
Saint Paul, MN 55102
(952) 829-8818
www.BeaversPondPress.com

Contact Gordon W. Fredrickson at www.gordonfredrickson.com for more information about the author.

I dedicate this book to the musicians who play music for our listening and dancing pleasure. They give our world a special dimension to love.

I especially dedicate this book to the musicians who played in old-time bands of all sizes, traveling from ballroom to ballroom or house party to house party, spreading joy to all, while maintaining and adding new dimensions to their cultural heritage during the decades of the twentieth century. I'm pretty sure they made proud the spirit of their immigrant ancestors, as well as those who stayed in the old country.

Thank you all for your contributions to the world of music and the joy of dancing.

CONTENTS

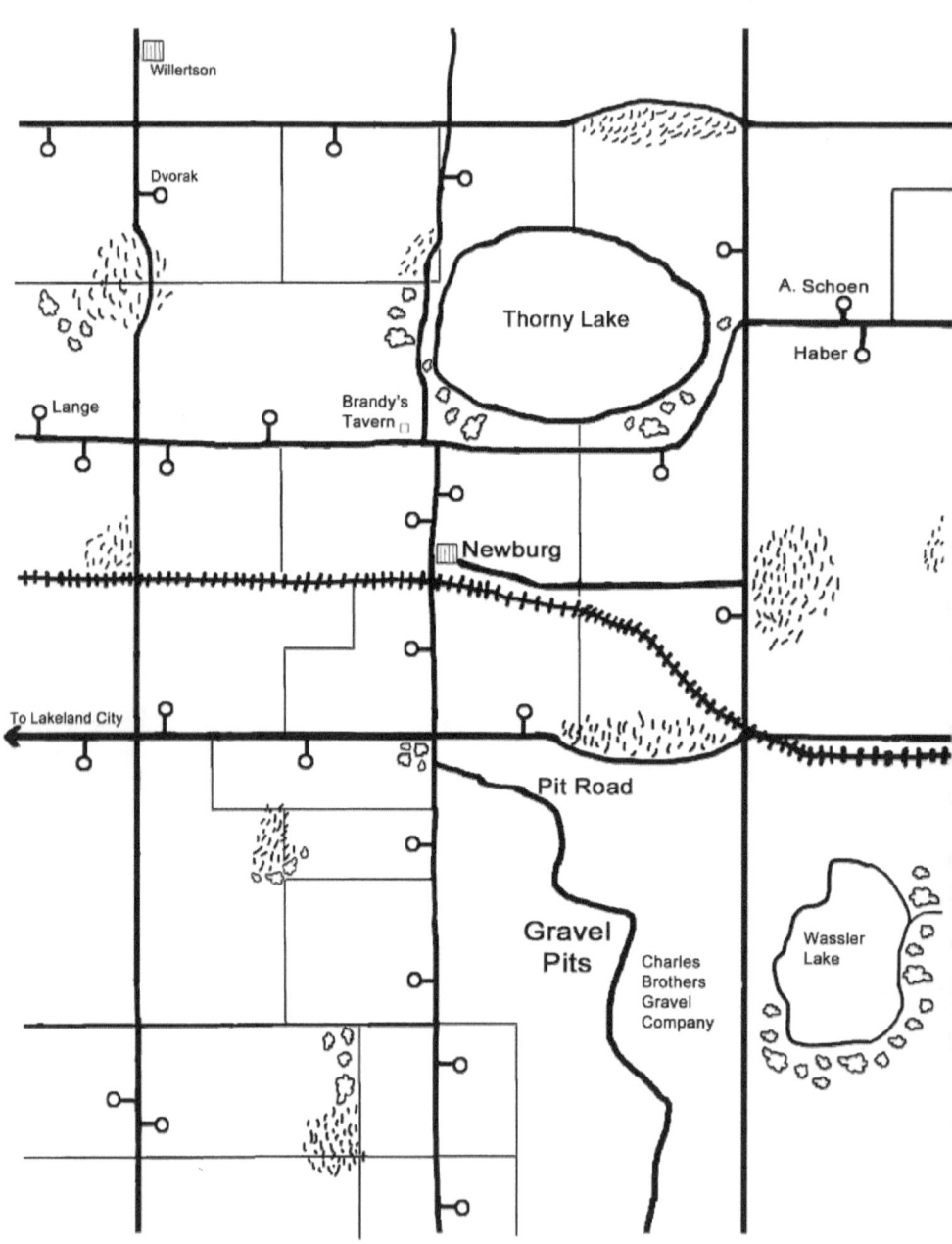

Willertson

Dvorak

Thorny Lake

A. Schoen

Haber

Lange

Brandy's
Tavern

Newburg

To Lakeland City

Pit Road

Gravel
Pits

Charles
Brothers
Gravel
Company

Wassler
Lake

Map of the

Neighborhood

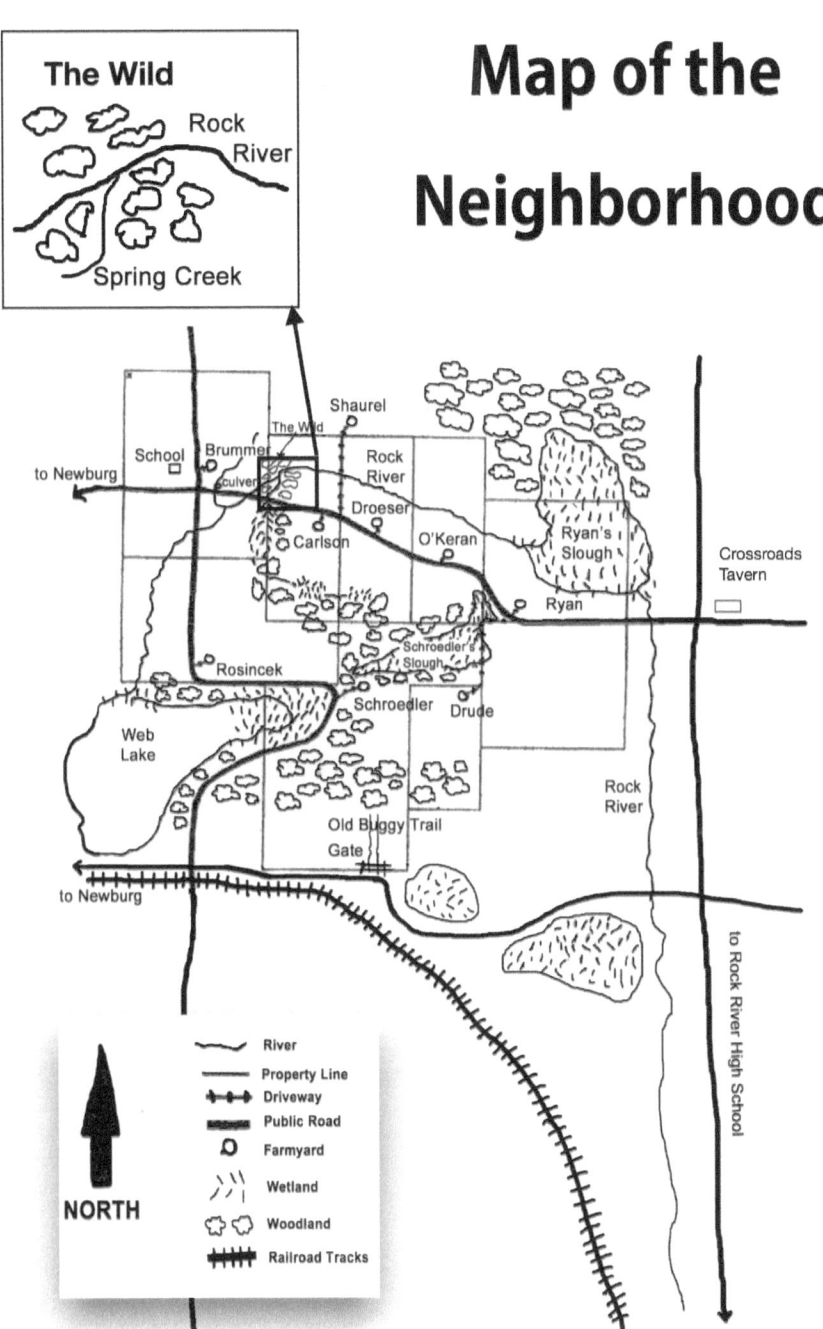

Seating Chart for the Neighborhood Country School, 1950–1951

To enhance readers' understanding of the familiar relationships among the teens and preteens at the Dvorak—Lange wedding dance, displayed below is a seating chart for the neighborhood country school from the fall of 1950, nearly six years prior to the wedding. Imagine the friction and friendships among twenty-six students who have heard each others' lessons daily at school and played together for two recesses and a lunch break every day. Also, many walked to and from school together, attended the same church, and worked together when their families harvested crops on their farms.

KEY

NAME
GRADE IN FALL 1950
DATE OF BIRTH
AGE DURING *The Dance*

LIBRARY

Miss McHone
TEACHER'S DESK

STOVE

Blackboard

TABLE FOR CLASSES

P I A N O

Ann Shaurel
Grade 6
Dec. 3, 1939
Age 16 in *The Dance*

Billy Joe O'Keran
Grade 8
Nov. 10, 1937
Age 18 in *The Dance*

Jack Drude
Grade 8
Mar. 15, 1937
Age 19 in *The Dance*

Jane Shaurel
Grade 8
Feb. 12, 1937
Age 19 in *The Dance*

John Ryan
Grade 8
Aug. 9, 1937
Age 18 in *The Dance*

Mary Schroedler
Grade 5
Oct. 28, 1939
Age 16 in *The Dance*

Jimmy Carlson
Grade 5
May 1, 1940
Age 16 in *The Dance*

Joseph Brummer
Grade 7
May 20, 1938
Age 18 in *The Dance*

Colleen O'Keran
Grade 7
Sept. 12, 1938
Age 17 in *The Dance*

Thomas Ryan
Grade 7
July 28, 1938
Age 17 in *The Dance*

Maggie Carlson
Grade 4
April 30, 1941
Age 15 in *The Dance*

Ralph Schoen
Grade 4
Aug. 13, 1941
Age 14 in *The Dance*

Jerome Schoen
Grade 4
Oct. 21, 1941
Age 14 in *The Dance*

Peggy Ryan
Grade 5
Oct. 30, 1940
Age 15 in *The Dance*

Laura Schoen
Grade 5
June 4, 1940
Age 16 in *The Dance*

Joey Carlson
Gr. 1, Dec. 27, 1944
Age 11 in *The Dance*

Robert Schoen
Gr. 3, Nov. 14, 1942
Age 13 in *The Dance*

Katherine O'Keran
Gr. 3, April 27, 1942
Age 14 in *The Dance*

James Schoen
Gr. 3, Sept. 25, 1942
Age 13 in *The Dance*

Margaret Shaurel
Gr. 3, Oct. 5, 1942
Age 13 in *The Dance*

Caroline Shaurel
Gr. 1, May 30, 1944
Age 12 in *The Dance*

Ronald Schoen
Gr. 1, March 15, 1944
Age 12 in *The Dance*

Elizabeth Brummer
Gr. 2, June 28, 1943
Age 12 in *The Dance*

Mary Ryan
Gr. 2, January 28, 1943
Age 13 in *The Dance*

Helen Rosincek
Grade 2
January 10, 1943
Helen died 12-5-50 of influenza

Seating Chart for the Neighborhood Country School, 1955–1956.

To enhance readers' understanding of the familiar relationships among the students from the country school, displayed below is a seating chart for the neighborhood country school for the last years in session, 1955–1956. During a birthday party in *The Dance*, Joey began to organize a ballgame for the country school students. In the third book of the series, *The Search*, the kids play the game during the summer. The next school year would see them bused to town where their farm neighborhood identity, would be scattered among the masses of students in a larger school.

KEY

NAME.
GRADE IN 1955–1956
DATE OF BIRTH
(AGE during summer 1956)

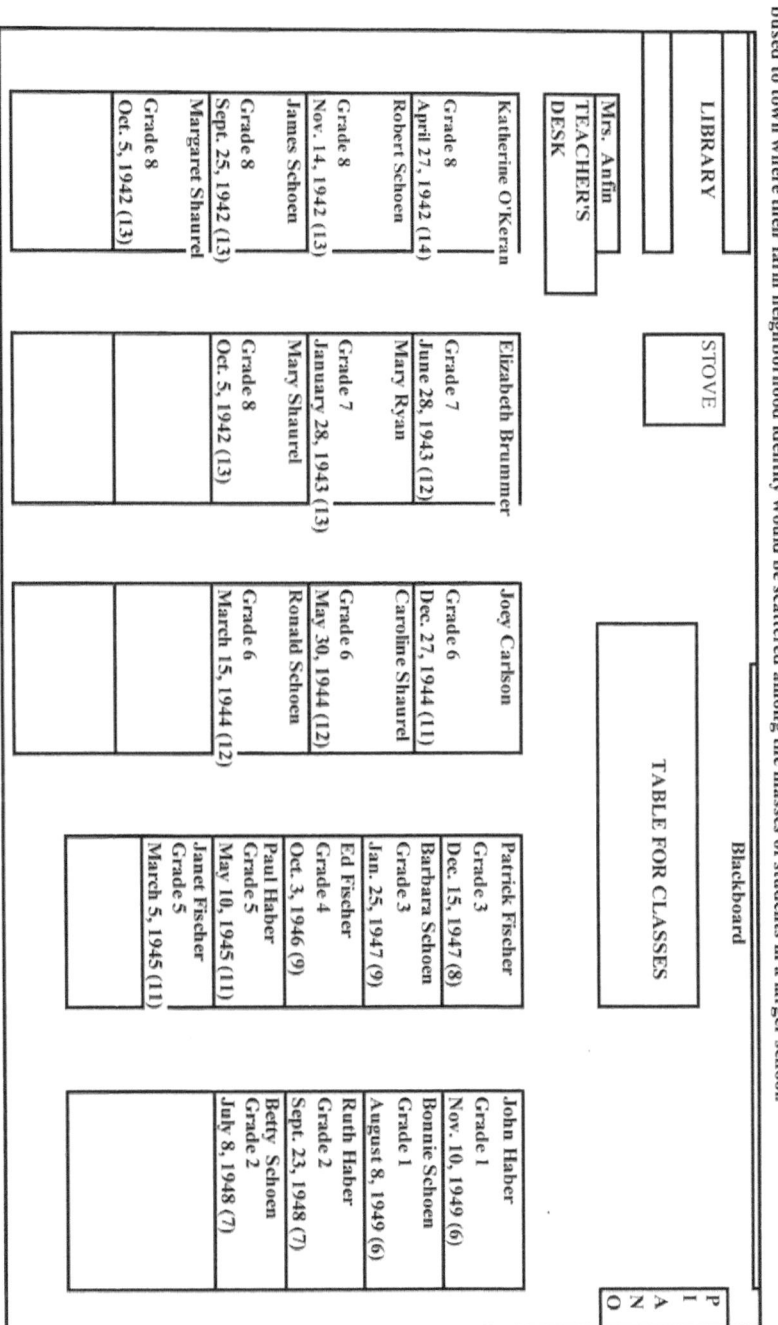

LIBRARY

Mrs. Anfin
TEACHER'S DESK

STOVE

Blackboard

TABLE FOR CLASSES

P I A N O

Katherine O'Keran
Grade 8
April 27, 1942 (14)

Robert Schoen
Grade 8
Nov. 14, 1942 (13)

James Schoen
Grade 8
Sept. 25, 1942 (13)

Margaret Shaurel
Grade 8
Oct. 5, 1942 (13)

Elizabeth Brummer
Grade 7
June 28, 1943 (12)

Mary Ryan
Grade 7
January 28, 1943 (13)

Mary Shaurel
Grade 8
Oct. 5, 1942 (13)

Joey Carlson
Grade 6
Dec. 27, 1944 (11)

Caroline Shaurel
Grade 6
May 30, 1944 (12)

Ronald Schoen
Grade 6
March 15, 1944 (12)

Patrick Fischer
Grade 3
Dec. 15, 1947 (8)

Barbara Schoen
Grade 3
Jan. 25, 1947 (9)

Ed Fischer
Grade 4
Oct. 3, 1946 (9)

Paul Haber
Grade 5
May 10, 1945 (11)

Janet Fischer
Grade 5
March 5, 1945 (11)

John Haber
Grade 1
Nov. 10, 1949 (6)

Bonnie Schoen
Grade 1
August 8, 1949 (6)

Ruth Haber
Grade 2
Sept. 23, 1948 (7)

Betty Schoen
Grade 2
July 8, 1948 (7)

CHAPTER 1

ARRIVALS

Early Friday morning, February 24, 1956

Mary Schroedler lay in her bed in the attic bedroom of Dorothea's farmhouse, thinking of her friends. Only four days ago she had stolen Jack Drude's Model A and left her life behind. She felt safe now in the attic, where the deeply recessed dormer windows prevented her from being seen.

She loved how the morning sun streaked through the east window, illuminating strange patterns formed by the cracks in the plastered walls and showing particles of dust in the air. But she was drawn to the south dormer window, a view that attracted her every morning and many times throughout the day. Sliding out of bed, she grabbed the soft pink robe Dorothea had given her and slipped it on over her flannel pajamas.

She kneeled to look out on a patch where Dorothea had cleared away the snow down to the grass, next to a stone the size of an overstuffed pillow, its surface painted white. Dorothea had promised that in spring, she would get a similar stone to place atop the new grave.

Mary had arrived at her aunt's farm shortly before dawn that day. After feeding Mary vegetable soup, buttered toast, and soft cheese, Dorothea had led her upstairs, past her own second-floor bedroom, and helped her climb the steep stairs to the attic bedroom, where the low ceiling slanted sharply to meet the floor. Exhausted and weak, Mary had slept the fitful sleep of a fugitive and awoken feeling cramping in her abdomen and warm wetness under her body.

Suddenly, Dorothea had been by her side. "Don't worry," she'd said, "you will be fine."

"What did I do wrong?"

"Nothing, sweet child. Nothing."

Mary's sanity hung on the belief that her aunt's statement was true, but guilt chewed at her. Had she accidentally done something to kill her baby? Travel in the cold? Stress? Lack of sleep? Poor nutrition?

"You did nothing to cause this to happen," her aunt assured her.

With a feeble voice, Mary said, "I want to believe you." But a worse guilt tore at her mind—relief. Relief that the pregnancy resulting from her non-biological father's rape no longer grew inside her womb. She was glad she was free from it. She hated herself for the feeling, but it remained, hovering over her like a storm cloud, adding to her feeling of being unworthy of love.

Dorothea had tried to make her feel worthy. "Your job is to rest for the next few days. I'll bring you everything you need and stay by your side most of the day and night. I'll take your temperature often. If you get a fever, you probably have an infection, and I'll take you to the doctor, but I think you'll be fine. You see, the same thing happened to my baby years ago. I told no one about the miscarriage. Only you and I will share this secret."

Undeterred by sorrow, Dorothea had carefully folded the sheet and given Mary time to sob her goodbyes before trudging out into the cold to dig a shallow grave with pick and shovel. Although Mary had slept fitfully during the next days and nights in the attic, the fever didn't come. There was no doctor's visit. Her anonymity remained secure.

Two days had passed before Mary had worked up enough courage to go to the window to see the new grave. She'd checked on the mound every day since, whenever feelings of loss and guilt flooded her mind.

She heard footsteps on the stairs and turned away from the gravesite view.

"It's just me, dear," Dorothea said brightly. "I brought you a couple of things, but I just like to check on you in the morning. How are you today? Did you sleep well?"

"I slept okay, Aunt Dorothea," Mary lied. "But I really am feeling a lot better. I feel a lot stronger too." Though she had physically healed faster than she had expected, nights were an eternity of darkness. Sometimes, closing her eyes simply provided a dark projection screen for horrifying memories of her father's abuse, Jack Drude's violent threats, and even her stepbrothers' abuse when she was a small child a decade ago. If she did drift off to sleep, terrifying dreams sometimes took control. She had hoped that putting physical distance between her and her past would also provide distance from the memories, forcing them to become a smaller part of her life. Instead, the past horrors grew stronger.

"Call me Dory. Everyone around here does."

"I like *Dorothea*. It's so classy. But I'll like calling you Dory," Mary said. "I like my attic room too."

"Good, because you're going to be stuck up here for a long while." After a moment Dory asked, "You've been looking out the window at the burial site, right?"

Mary nodded and turned her eyes to the floor.

"You know, dear, feelings of guilt are normal, but that doesn't make them any less painful. I still feel guilty about losing my little Violet. Yes, I named the child. Not because I knew the sex, but because I just didn't want to be calling the baby 'it' for the rest of my life."

"I can understand that, but is it okay if I just refer to my baby as *Baby*?"

"Of course. And it's okay to look at the burial site. It's okay to feel guilty. I understand. And sometimes having someone who understands is all you can hope for. Here, let me show you something."

Dory handed her a book of poems.

"The poems are written by Robert Frost—probably not a perfect man by any measure, but wisdom seldom comes from those who are perfect." She laughed and then added, "I heard he tried to farm, but he wasn't very good at it. I like that about him."

Concerned that her aunt was overestimating her abilities, Mary said, "I've not read much poetry."

"Neither have I," Dory declared. "Fact is, I don't know anyone who has." She chuckled. "Just think of them as stories when you read them."

"I probably won't know what the poems mean."

"Don't worry about what a poem is supposed to mean to someone else. Just try to discover what it might mean to you."

Dory opened the book to the poem "Home Burial" and gave Mary a note before she explained, "Keep the note in here to mark the page, but go ahead and read it to yourself now."

Dear Mary,

Read this poem when you start thinking about our babies and you feel alone, like no one understands you. Lots of people feel that way, so you are not alone. Robert Frost has lost his wife and four of their six children, one just three days after the child was born. So, he understands loss, and he understands the pain and guilt that come after losing a child. The poem isn't so much about him as it is about anger between a husband and wife who don't understand each other. I want you to know that I understand you, and I think you understand me too. Together, we are never alone.

Love,

Aunt Dorothea

Dory added, "You don't have to finish the poem every time you start. Just read until the pain and frustration fade a little.

"Also, after my miscarriage, whenever I started feeling low, I would write my thoughts down in a notebook. I've kept it up ever since. Oh, I don't write every day." She giggled briefly before she added, "Sometimes my writing is barely legible, but I don't write to read it later. I just write to get it out of me. I find it useful. Want to give it a try?"

Mary reached out to take the spiral notebook Dory offered her. "Thanks. I will."

"A few years ago, I became frustrated because my writing couldn't keep up with my thoughts, so I bought a used typewriter. I like typing better than writing. It's faster and more legible. I keep the pages in a three-ring binder."

"I don't know how to type, but I like to write longhand. Maybe I can learn to type sometime, though."

"Look, dear, today is Friday. You've been here four days, and it's time you got up. Soon we'll get you outside for some fresh air, but we have to be careful. If someone were to see you out in the yard, they might suspect the presence of a guest. For all we know, they may have picture posters out on a teenage runaway and car thief. You're safe here, but we can't risk your being seen. But on Sunday, when the neighbors are in church, we can dress you up warm and roam around the yard. I'll take you to the barn where you can visit all the cats. There must be over twenty of them. The neighbors store hay in the hayloft, but the lower part is just left to the cats. You can visit them during the day if you are careful to avoid Tom when he hauls hay from my barn to his. He'll be starting that job soon. Eventually, I'll have you meet the neighbors. I trust them. Tom and Kathleen Weber. He is German and she is Irish. She was a Walsh. She likes to be called Katy now, but she used to be called Rusty because of her hair color. They have three kids—Jean, who we call Rusty, is thirteen; John is twelve; and the oldest boy, Jerry, is nineteen and will be leaving for the Army in April. Sometime in July the mother is going to have another child. They farm the half section adjoining mine and have a herd of dairy cows. They are fun and honest people. They rent my land, and I help them out with chores and fieldwork regularly.

"My regular garden is out in the open where anyone who drives in the yard could see someone working in it. But this spring I'll till up a special garden behind the shed so you can work in it without being seen, even if someone drives in the yard. You can plant cucumbers and watermelon or whatever you want."

"I'd love that! I miss working in the garden with Mom. Maybe we can make dill pickles this summer?"

"You bet we will. I promise. Now, I've got work to do, but I wanted to check up on you first. Glad you're feeling better, but do not come downstairs yet. Stay up here. It's roomy, and it will stay fairly warm because it's above my bedroom, which has a heat register connecting to the warm kitchen below. I'll bring you some books to read too. Maybe next week you can come down to my bedroom after dark and we can play euchre and listen to the radio. Television reception is poor out here. But day after tomorrow, we'll start with a walk around the place. I think you'll like it here.

"I'll empty your chamber pot now, and I'll see you at noon when I bring you something to eat." Dory stroked Mary's cheek and said, "Bye-bye, for now," before she left.

Eager to make a morning entry in the notebook, Mary checked the calendar on the wall and opened her new journal.

About 8 a.m., Friday morning, February 24, 1956

I seem to be recovering faster than I thought. D said I would get well quickly. Still a little weak, but am sleeping a little better. Feelings of sadness, but D is good at cheering me up. I am so lucky to have found her, to know my real father had such a loving sister. She gave me a book of poetry, which I'll look at later, but she also gave me a notebook to write in today. I like the idea. During the week she brought up cookies and milk and we played checkers for a little while.

Before I ran away from home, I told Maggie I wouldn't write to her, but I really miss her. If I write to her, I can't give her my address to write back! One-way letters won't help ease my loneliness. Sometime I wonder if I could drive the Model A to meet Maggie and Jimmy somewhere safe. I could write to them first to tell them where to meet me. I know it's just a wish that I can't make come true. What if I just surprised them at some event? Or showed up the end of their driveway! Crazy idea. But it would be so great to see Maggie and Jimmy again! I hope they're not mad at me.

CHAPTER 2

PARTING

Late Friday night, February 24, 1956

"You should probably go in," he said softly. "It's late. Your folks might wonder."

"I'm not worried," she reassured him. "They know we have a lot to talk about. Our future together."

He had more he wanted to say, but he was reluctant to take the risk. The dim yard light shining though the car window illuminated her face as he untangled himself from her arms just enough to start the engine of his maroon 1949 Ford.

"What!" she teased. "You're kicking me out?"

"No, no, I thought I'd warm up the car. It's nearly March, but the cold still creeps in." He paused before he repeated, "It's getting late."

"But we've settled nothing."

"We can't solve anything tonight. Our future will have to wait for us."

Her body tensed. "No, it won't," she said. "You talk like it's distant. We have to make decisions now." She grasped his hand in hers, moved her face close to his, and pleaded, "Don't you see? I don't care what anyone thinks."

Her closeness softened him, but he forced himself to speak. "We can't alienate our families."

"The hell with them!"

"You're not serious."

"I am."

"Well, you're making light of a serious topic, then." He realized too late that his voice carried more of an accusation than he had intended.

"No, I'm serious," she countered. "It really doesn't make a difference to me. It did once, but not now. You see, my situation has changed." She inhaled. "You see—"

"It makes a big difference to people close to us," he interrupted.

"You mean our parents! *Especially your mother!*" And she too regretted her accusatory tone.

"Yours too. Your mother too!" he said with more volume than he wanted. He toned his voice down and added, "But you're right, especially my mom."

"Why can't your mom be more like her brother? Martin thinks the folks should stay out of it."

"And why can't your mother be more like her sister? Mary agrees with her husband. They both think the decision is ours and ours alone."

"It's *you* I love!" she exclaimed. "Only you! And I really can't wait any longer. You see, I—"

"I know. I know! All I need in the whole world is *you*. But we have to wait."

"No. Let's just forget about them all. I'm nineteen and don't need anyone's permission. Let's do what *we* want. *I'm* willing to say the heck with what my mother wants. I'll change religion. We'll get married in your church. That should satisfy your mom. Besides, you turned twenty-two last Saturday. I thought that would make a difference. That maybe your mother would let go."

Billy paused to try to arrange hurtful words to sting as little as possible. "I'm afraid it won't satisfy her anymore. Honestly, I don't know what will. At first it was just the religion thing. But now, she blames it all on . . . you—you, personally. She's obsessed with thinking it's your fault, no matter how much I explain that it's me, that I want *you* in my life."

He watched her face change—her full lips pursed. Then he felt her body—which moments before had been softly pushed against him—become frozen and unbending.

"Your mom hates me!?"

"It's not really you she hates. I can't explain it, but her obsession with us has driven her crazy. She's angry at me and at you and at the whole world."

He felt her relax a little as she took deep breaths, and then she abruptly moved away from his side. A coldness entered the car that could not be offset by the warm air from the car's heater. And he feared no words could bring back the warmth between them. *Jeez, I said it. What have I done?*

"You want me to wait? For what? I have to try to win over your mom all over again? Starting now, when she hates me?"

"I need time to reason with her."

"You need her approval to love me?"

"My mom is unstable. I can't risk it. What if she went through with her threats? How would we feel if she hurt herself? Or worse, took her life, as she claims she would do. And you, you mustn't separate yourself from your whole family. Can't you wait just a year—"

"A year! No, I can't! I would leave them all tomorrow. Just ask me. Ask me!" She screamed again, "Ask me!"

"I can't . . . yet. Maybe we need . . . time."

Her eyes flashed. Her tears pooled but held. She inhaled deeply before choking out barely audible words that still hammered at Billy. "You want more time! I can't believe it! I give up."

"Give up? On what?"

"On you!" she screamed. In a whisper she added, "I give up on you, Billy Thorson. I give up on you! Good night."

In disbelief, he uttered, "Good night," as she opened the car door and stepped out into the darkness.

The door of the '49 Ford slammed shut, rocking the car and shaking his dreams. But he managed to flick on the headlights to light her path to the doorstep and watched in horror as she entered her house without turning to wave. For a moment he found comfort in the smooth idle of the engine, but the lingering sweetness of her rose-scented perfume seized his mind. Suddenly, his heart ached. This was the first time in years they had parted without a kiss. Should he run out, knock on the door, and try to talk to her again? But what could he say? His message hadn't changed. They had to wait. He'd call her tomorrow.

Once inside the house, Anna leaned back against the door, her heart racing and her breathing quick. Too angry to cry and yet too hurt to stop, she let the tears flow down her cheeks as she considered rushing out the door to seek a different ending to the evening. *I need to tell him I'm pregnant! How can he not know that I cannot wait any longer, even if I weren't pregnant? If he knew, surely it would make a difference! But I don't want that to be the reason. I don't want to force him.*

She turned to face the door and grabbed the knob, but hesitated. *What if I called his mom? What if I appealed to her personally? Begged her to understand that Billy and I want to marry. Billy is afraid of her reaction. I could plead with her, tell her, "Rose, Billy loves you!" What would Billy think of that idea?* She turned the doorknob and opened the door, only to witness the lights of his car leaving the farmyard.

Trying not to panic, she quietly shut herself in the bathroom and washed her face before creeping up the stairs to her bedroom, where she changed into her pajamas and slipped into bed. Resting on her side, she let her hands stroke her belly. *I said I was giving up on Billy, but it's not that easy. I love him. What if I told Rose that her son and I are having a baby? No, then I'd have to tell Mom and Dad first. Mom would probably want to ship me off to one of those church organizations where girls have their child and then give the baby away. I can't do that. No, I need to convince Rose without telling Billy or my folks that I'm talking to her. And without telling anyone I'm pregnant. Who can I talk to? I don't want to bring my sisters in on it, either. Maybe Aunt Mary? She'd listen. But I think my first move is to call Rose tomorrow morning.* With that plan in her mind, she fell asleep.

Her mother's knock on the door came early on Saturday morning, but Anna was already awake, her nose running and her eyes puffy from crying.

"It's Billy. He wants to talk to you. I left the phone off the hook. Just go pick it up when you're ready."

Anna cleared her throat, blew her nose, and tried to mask her voice before she answered. "Tell him I'm not available."

"Are you sure? He sounded pretty serious."

She breathed in deeply before choking out her answer. "Just tell him to call tomorrow."

"Okay. Whatever you say." But then her mother flung the door open. "You've been crying. Did you have an argument?"

"A doozy, but what do you care?"

"I care about you. You must know that."

Anna softened her response. "I know you do. I know, but after five years of loving Billy, I think I'm giving up on him, Momma." Seeing real concern in her mother's face, Anna added, "Just leave me be for now. Please. I'll be okay, but I'll need to use the phone for some private calls later."

"Your dad and I are going to take eggs to town in about an hour. But your sisters will be home. You'll just have to ask them for privacy. But I'll tell them to stay out of the kitchen when you're on the phone. And I'll go tell Billy your message."

"Thanks, Mom."

Anna planned carefully what she would say to Rose, and an hour later, still in her pajamas, she began to dial Billy's number from the kitchen wall phone. Halfway through the numbers, she hung up in a panic. *What if Billy answers?* She checked the clock. *He and John will be cleaning the barn.* She dialed again and waited. Someone on the other end picked up. There was no turning back now.

"Hello, this is Mrs. Thorson."

Anna took a deep breath before she said, "Hello, Mrs. Thorson. This is Anna Dvorak. I am hoping you have a few minutes to talk with me." *Damn! I should've just started talking. Now I'm standing here waiting for an answer like a fool.*

"Anna. Yes, I'm listening."

Her voice seems like a challenge. Did Billy tell her we had a fight? I'll come clean. "Mrs. Thorson. I want to be totally honest with you. Billy and I had a fight last night. He wants to wait a year before we get married because he is worried about you. He said you threatened to hurt yourself. But please, you don't have to do that. I agreed to change religions."

"What does Emma say about that?"

"Well, I haven't told Mom for sure yet, but she knows and she doesn't like it. But I will go ahead with it."

"Look, Anna, I know your mother, and she never lets go of anything. She still thinks her sister should not have changed religion to marry my brother. You can't tell me otherwise."

"And I won't try to tell you otherwise. Mom may believe as you say, but Mom and Dad are good friends with Mary and Martin. They visit often."

"And they drink too much, from my point of view."

"I only want to convince you that with Billy and me, I am not taking him away from you and your religion. I want to join your family, not separate him from his family."

"You may say that, and you may even believe it, but I know that even though Mary left her religion to marry my brother, my brother ended up changing his ways more than she did. I expect it would be the same with Billy. You would lure him in your direction."

"Lure him?" Anna struggled to keep her composure. "What kind of person do you think I am? I've never lured him into anything."

"Oh, yes you have. On New Year's Day, when John and I went to visit his older brother and his wife at their farm in western Minnesota, you lured Billy to eat dinner at the Carlsons' place with your family. We needed Billy along with our family to show support for Fred and Ida when they were getting back on their feet after lots of bad luck. John's sister Betty and her husband, Pastor Mark, drove all the way from up by Duluth to come to the dinner that day, but Billy felt obligated to be with you and your family."

"Couples try to rotate holidays between each others' parents. Billy was with you on Thanksgiving, and we were each with our own families at Christmas, so New Year's was to be with my family."

"Billy knew it was a special trip. If it hadn't been for you, he would have been with us."

"He never said it was special. I would've told him to go with you if I would've known it was special."

"And it became even more special because two weeks later Fred and Ida were both dead. Killed in a car accident. John's sister was shocked that Billy wasn't there to visit them New Year's Day, and she let him know how angry she was when she met Billy at the funeral."

"That's really sad, and I am sorry, but we didn't know his aunt and uncle were going to die, Mrs. Thorson."

"But he knew New Year's Day was special. I told him, but because you have your hold on him, he wouldn't have brought it up to you."

"My hold on him?" Anna said incredulously. "I don't have a hold on him." And then she exclaimed louder than she had intended, "We love each other! Billy and I love each other!"

"Don't yell at me. I know what you are." And then Rose added in an even tone, "You are a red-haired demon trying to take my son. Well, you can't have him, and that's that."

The click of Rose hanging up sounded like a gunshot as Anna stood alone in the kitchen holding the receiver. She set it gently on the holder before she turned to see all four of her sisters standing in the doorway to the living room at the far end of the kitchen. With her head down, Anna hurried past them to run upstairs to her room and quietly close the door.

CHAPTER 3

VISIT FROM A FRIEND

Saturday afternoon, February 25, 1956

Anna stayed in her room during Saturday's noon meal, but early that afternoon her brooding was interrupted by a visit from her sisters. When Marcella, seventeen, and Helen, sixteen, brought her a small plate of food, Anna responded with gratitude as she closed the door behind them. "Toast and jam and coffee. Perfect. Thank you so much. Now, if one of you will bring me a chamber pot so I don't have to go to the bathroom downstairs, that would be really perfect."

"Sisterly love only goes so far," Marcella joked, "but I'm glad you still have your sense of humor."

"What we heard of that phone call sounded pretty rough," Helen said. "Sorry for eavesdropping, but it got kind of loud and . . . well, we were worried about you. Are you okay?"

"Billy and I had a really bad fight. And after that phone call to Rose, I don't know if things can be patched up."

"But you want to make up, right?" Marcella asked. "I mean, you still love Billy, right?"

A soft knock on the door stalled Anna's answer. After she said, "Come in," the door swung open to reveal her twelve-year-old twin sisters, Janet and Josephine.

"Your identical sad faces make me smile," Anna confessed. "Glad you came. I'll just announce to you all that Billy and I had a bad fight. Yes, I still love him, but after the phone call to his mother, I don't know if we can ever patch things up. And worse yet, I don't know if I want to."

"How can you say that if you still love him?" Helen demanded.

"I could feel his mother's hatred of me through the telephone wires," Anna replied hoarsely as a shudder moved through her body. "I can only imagine what she is putting Billy through. Poor guy. For months—for *years*, I underestimated the crap he was dealing with from his mother. He was too kind to let me share the extent of his problems."

"What are you going to do now?" Marcella asked.

"I don't know, Marcy. First, I'm going to eat this toast and jam and drink some coffee. Then, go downstairs to pee and clean up. You girls can leave with the satisfaction that you helped cheer up your pathetic older sister. Seriously, thanks to you all."

After her sisters filed out of the room, Anna looked in the mirror as she tried to smooth her puffed face. *I wasn't kidding about the chamber pot. I'd like to spend the next two weeks up here where no one could see me.* Satisfied her face revealed as little of her pain as possible, she hustled downstairs to clean up.

Fifteen minutes later, as Anna came out of the bathroom, she was surprised by her mother's voice.

"Are you feeling any better? I hope so. George Lange called and asked if he could stop by to visit us all for a while. I told him Joe was helping the neighbors with some tractor problems, but he just joked and said that he really was more interested in seeing me and my daughters anyway. He'll be here in about half an hour."

"George?" Anna said in disbelief. "You called him, didn't you? Jeez, Mom, I mean, I'm still all puffy from crying. Five years of serious dating with Billy, and now you've called George the morning after I break up! How could you, really?"

"Okay, I admit that I called him, but he was so sweet. He wanted to come, but he was unsure if it was a good idea or if he would be welcome. I told him you and Billy broke up last night."

"But maybe we will get back together, Mom. Did you think of that?"

"Honestly, honey, the way you were this morning, I don't believe you will. And I thought a little attention from George would do you good. Look, just say hello and leave, if you want to, but he is a family friend and neighbor. You don't want to be rude."

"No, I don't, but it's going to be tough to smile."

"His car has just pulled into the yard. You'd better hurry to get dressed."

Anna ran upstairs. *Let's see, pleated plaid skirt. Green blouse, green socks, penny loafers. Casual but classy. Why do I care? Well, he is a nice guy. And he likes me. Need to keep my options open. I've given up on Billy. And I'm pregnant. I can't believe this is all happening to me.* She pulled her hair back into a ponytail and headed downstairs.

Tall and humble, George stood up from his chair at the kitchen table as she entered the room. He grinned as he said, "Hi, Anna. You look great! Definitely worth the wait to see you looking so pretty. I hope you have some time to sit down and talk."

Anna smiled at him. He was so sincere and yet always teasing at the same time. Kind of like Billy. Or like Billy used to be. He was handsome in a rugged way, with a large nose, wavy red hair, bright hazel eyes, and a large, fit torso that would have made some men look clumsy. But George had the grace of a dancer and the bulk of a heavyweight boxer.

He stepped toward her with ease, grasped a chair with his large hand, pulled it out from beside the table, and said, "Please. You don't have to stay long."

Surprised at her own reaction, Anna found herself wanting to sit and to stay a while.

"I'll pour you each a cup of coffee and then leave to catch up on some sewing," Emma said.

Anna listened as George babbled on easily, never reluctant to bring up the most foolish or serious subjects. It gave him a confident demeanor that Anna found attractive. Sometimes he was funny, and sometimes he was philosophical. Other times he was just full of baloney. She giggled to herself. *Mom was right to call him. He is exactly what I need right now.*

"I think we should go for a drive," George said. "Nothing like the bright February sunshine to perk up a person."

Anna laughed briefly. "And you think I need perking up, do you?"

He laughed too but abruptly said, "Hey, throw me a line, will you? I'm doing my best here, but I still seem to be drowning. And I'm a Navy man. I'll come clean. Your mom called to tell me what happened. Not a lot of detail, don't worry. I protested that it was too soon to visit, but she insisted. She said I could work magic. She actually said the word *magic*. Truth is, I don't feel like much of a magician. If you want me to leave, I understand." He backed his chair away from the table.

Anna scrambled to find her voice. "No, don't go. I'm glad you came. And I'd like to go for a ride. Sunshine and more of your magic is just what I need." Anna loved how he beamed at her words. Once out the door, he took her hand as they walked the short distance before he opened the car door for her. As she slid onto the soft cushion of the seat, she struggled to overcome a pang of guilt. *I've only been with one man my entire life. I'm pregnant with his child, and just a little over twelve hours since I split with him, here I am, getting in the car with another man. I must be some slut.* And she smiled at the harsh absurdity of the situation.

He got in and started the car, and as they rolled out onto the road, he talked briefly about his time in the Navy before he said, "I thought I might make a career of the Navy. I reenlisted once. Put in a total of six years. Then, about a year ago, Mom sent me some photos of the farm and the family, and I began to think about how much I was missing. My folks, the farm, and the beauty of a home life. After that I decided to come home when my enlistment was up."

"Are you happy to be home?"

"Absolutely!"

"What was one of the first things you did when you got home?"

"That's easy. Look you up. I hadn't been home for more than a week before I came over to give you that ride last year."

Anna smiled. "You're just saying that."

"And why would I say something like that if it weren't true?"

"You tell me," she said. *How can I answer that without sounding vain?*

"You don't remember seeing me when I was home on leave, but I remember seeing you and your family at church. You must've been about seventeen then. I've had that image in my mind ever since."

"You're embarrassing me. I'm just some Czech farm girl. You're a man who's traveled the world."

"And come back home to find that what I am looking for is right here."

Anna looked at him just as he turned his eyes away from the road for a moment to meet her gaze, which made her simultaneously happy and uncomfortable. She broke the gaze first to look at the road. "My life is pretty confused right now."

"I don't mean to make it more confusing. Look, are you available to go on a date with me on Wednesday? I know it's a work night, but I'll just take you out to supper. I'll have you home by twenty-one hundred." She saw him turn to check her reaction before he added, "That's nine p.m., your time. I'll pick you up at six, okay?" He turned his car back into the driveway as he added, "If you want to think about it, I can call you tomorrow or early in the week to get your answer."

Anna paused; her mind filled with reasons to say no. Then she heard herself say, "Yes, I'll see you Wednesday."

He opened the car door for her, and they walked to the front door. He squeezed her hand and said, "Bye, for now. See you soon. If you change your mind, just call me."

"Goodbye," Anna said.

Her parents were sitting at the kitchen table when Anna entered the house.

"How did it go?" Emma demanded with a smile. "Did he cheer you up?"

Anna stopped short, suppressing a brief streak of anger. Then she asked, "Did Billy call?"

"No, dear," Emma responded quickly. "Did George manage to cheer you up?"

"George was kind and gave me a few fun moments. I'm glad I went for the ride, but, jeez, Mom, you seem to have no understanding of my real feelings about losing Billy!"

Anna ran upstairs and closed the door to her room before she returned to the large mirror above the three-drawer dresser. *Who am I? I was Billy's girl and he was my guy for so long. Who am I now?*

A knock on the door interrupted her thoughts.

"Come on in."

Marcella peeked her head in as she swung the door open. Always lively with speech and gesture, like her mom, she said as she grinned sheepishly, "Helen and I were worried about you. We thought Mom was pushing it to call George, but we were surprised when you accepted the ride. But now"— she held up her hands, palms out, to indicate she could not control her curiosity—"now we're just nosy. So, how did the ride with the old guy go?"

Helen, the more serious and restrained of Anna's four sisters, slipped in behind Marcy and added, "Oh, it's not true that we're just nosy." To Anna she said, "You know we really care about both you and Billy."

Anna sat on her bed and patted the spaces on either side of her with her hands, inviting her sisters to sit down. "The ride went fine. George was kind and entertaining."

"But . . ." Marcy said.

"I still love Billy," Anna said, with a look that tried to express joy and hope.

"What are you going to do?" Helen asked.

"You must call him!" Marcy insisted. "You have history. That must mean something. You share so many things!"

Unaware of her gesture, Anna moved her hand onto her belly and said as if in a trance, "More than you can imagine."

Helen and Marcy gasped simultaneously. As Marcy grasped Anna's hand, she said, "I've noticed you've had an upset stomach in the mornings. Not like you at all."

Shocked at her own revelation, Anna said, "I really didn't mean to burden you girls with this. Sorry. Please don't tell anyone, especially Mom or Dad or the twins. I'd like to keep it a secret until I know how I'm going to handle it. Right now, I don't know what I'm going to do. I've got to think it over. But you're right, Marcy. I've got to call Billy, but I was hoping he would call me first. I told Mom to tell Billy to call me tomorrow."

CHAPTER 4

THE TALK

Sunday night, February 26, 1956

On Sunday night, Maggie Carlson lay awake in her tiny bedroom, staring at the edge of the curtains hanging over the narrow window, dimly illuminated by the moon rising over the trees east of her family's house. She would be fifteen in two months and four days, catching up to her brother Jimmy for a day before he'd turn sixteen on May first. She wanted to convince him to ask their parents for a single birthday gift for the two of them—a phonograph. Then they could buy records of the music they heard played on faraway radio stations late at night, stations from the South that played music local radio stations did not play—music by Elvis Presley, Fats Domino, and Little Richard.

But thinking about the phonograph was just a distraction from what was really keeping her awake. Horrific events of last weekend replayed again and again in her mind. Guilt about withholding information from the law and keeping secrets from her family stole her peace. Could she have done something to change the outcomes? Could she have made a different decision that would've kept her friend safe? Or did fate control outcomes regardless of her own actions? Believing that everything that happens was fated to happen would relieve her of guilt, but she couldn't swallow the idea that her actions had made no difference.

Her parents' bedroom was directly below hers, but she was sure they were asleep by now. After easing herself out of the single folding bed, she grabbed her flashlight from the top of the dresser, wrapped herself in a blanket, and crept quietly out the doorless doorway before turning right to follow the long hallway to a large room where her two brothers slept. Passing through another doorless doorway, she saw Jimmy sprawled on the floor, carefully turning the dial on an electric radio plugged in to a thin brown extension cord, which was plugged in to the socket at the base of the lightbulb mounted high on the wall. His flashlight lay nearby, illuminating a small circle on the floor.

Without looking up, he whispered, "I figured you'd be here soon."

"Couldn't sleep."

"Me either." He flicked off the radio. "Can't seem to get any stations tonight."

Careful not to awaken their eleven-year-old brother, who slept in a bed on the other side of the room, Maggie eased down beside Jimmy, ensuring her blanket made a nest for her on the cold floor. Once settled, she casually reached over to wipe the window and peered into the darkness.

"See anything?" Jimmy remarked with a teasing whisper.

"Nope. No dancing ghosts. No dog. Nothing."

"And no Jack Drude either, I hope."

They both smiled, as people who have survived the same horrific event often do.

"Hard to believe it all happened just a week ago," Maggie said.

"Yeah, I've been trying to make a song of it." He sang in a whisper to the tune of a popular Christmas song, "Nine dead dogs, eight gallons of gas stolen, seven dead puppies, six . . . I'm stuck for six. Five farm kids running, four . . . stuck for four and three, but two shotguns blasting and a thief taken away in handcuffs. For the last one I've got too many choices—one broken wrist or one stolen car or one lost girlfriend?"

"It's not funny, anyway," Maggie protested.

"Not meant to be funny. I just can't get the crap out of my head. Can you?"

"No, and I feel guilty about letting Mary run away and about not telling the law that Jack and her dad abused her. And aren't you afraid of Jack coming after you? I'm sure he's out of jail by now."

"Honestly, I am," Jimmy admitted. "I don't feel safe, but it'll take a few weeks for his broken wrist to heal. I know it was just luck that I came out on top in that fight. Next time, it's hard telling what he'll do to me." He paused before he added, "But it's Mary I'm losing sleep over. Today was going to be our first real date. Now, all I can ever do is imagine how that would've turned out."

Maggie stifled her usual tendency to tease him and simply said, "I miss her too."

She decided to change the subject. "At church this morning, Billy told me he wanted to talk to you. Did he find you?"

"Yes."

"Well, what was the big message? It seemed that it was a big deal."

"All he said was that he wouldn't be coming over for Sunday afternoon training in the hayloft with me."

"Why not? I thought he likes training with you."

"Yeah, I thought so too. He didn't say why he wasn't coming. And he said not to expect him for quite a while and he'd let me know when he could start again."

"He and Anna probably have a lot of planning to do," Maggie said. "Maybe he finally proposed."

"That's what I figured," Jimmy said. "You know, Mags, I think Mary will write to you. She'll get lonely and write to her best friend because she will need to talk to someone. Then we'll use the letter as a clue and go look for her."

"Jeez, you have to give up on it. Maybe you two were never meant to be, you know? Not like Billy and Anna, who are probably engaged by now. Now, *they* were meant to be together, don't you think?"

"I don't really believe in the meant-to-be crap, not when so many un-foreseeable things can happen. People can interfere with things without even knowing they do."

"Generally, I agree with you, but the meant-to-be crap kind of releases people from responsibility. If it's fate, it's fate."

"People should be responsible for their actions."

"Releases them from guilt, then."

"Maybe guilt is a good thing?"

"You're no help!"

Jimmy laughed. "You know I'm just being contrary. It's what I do best."

"I want to look for Mary too, but if we find her, we have to tell no one so she stays safe from Jack and the cops, who suspect her for stealing his car."

"And that's what so stupid and wrong. It's Jack, not Mary, who should be arrested. What he did to her is criminal."

"But if she turns him in, she would be arrested too. We'll just have to wait until she writes to me. I think she will." Maggie waited a moment before changing the subject again. "And then there's school. I want to focus on my classes, but my mind wanders. I'm working on my fantasy assignment for Mrs. Deem's English class. Being a social outcast at school actually seems to help me come up with ideas."

"I think that's Mrs. Deem's plan. But you're only in your first year of being a social outcast. As a sophomore, I'll be completing year number two. I've got one friend, Robert. And he's your friend too."

"Actually, I've made a couple friends since last fall. Anne Busch, for example."

He couldn't resist correcting her. "That's only one, not a couple. But it's more than I've accomplished. Anyway, I've pretty well settled into being a nonsocial being. People expect me to be antisocial. I just want to get good grades and say the hell with the other kids."

"Not a good attitude. I've told you a hundred times that you need to try to get along with people. Instead, you try to irritate them."

"And I practice on you."

"Well, I'm not going to give up on people. A girl has fewer options than a boy does."

"I suppose."

"You know, Jimmy, when Emma and Joe and the kids were over on New Year's Day, Marcella said she got a phonograph for Christmas. I admitted to her that I was really envious, and she suggested we ask Mom and Dad to pool our birthday presents and get us one together. What do you think?"

"Spring is such a strain on the folks' pocketbook. I hate to ask."

"It can't hurt to ask. Remember when you were ten and wanted a sled but were afraid to ask Santa because it was such an expensive gift? Well, I convinced you to ask, and Santa came through, didn't he?"

"What does that have to do with our birthdays?"

"Well, you asked for the sled and you got what you wanted!"

Jimmy smiled and poked Maggie in the arm. "But that was *Santa*! He can do anything."

Maggie shoved him. "Jeez, you can be so . . . exasperating sometimes."

"I try," Jimmy said with pride. "Really, though, I think it's a good idea. Then we could give each other records as gifts. Let's have a strategy. We won't mention it to Dad. You mention it to Mom first. She'll want to know how I feel. Then in a day or so, I'll mention it to her. If we get it, it'll be up to her. We'll look up some suggestions in the catalog."

"It's a plan," Maggie whispered and got up to leave. "Good night."

Before she got to the doorway, Joey turned over and whispered, "You know I can hear you guys."

"You're listening to us?" Maggie asked, astonished.

"I can't help but listen. You might as well let me sit down on the floor with you when you have your meetings."

Jimmy put his hand over his mouth to stifle a laugh. "Yeah, Mom might just as well be mad at you for waking them up as just me and Mags. Besides, I agree with you, Joey. You're not a little kid anymore."

"Okay," Maggie said. "We'll see. But I'm going to bed now."

Satisfied with the night's exchange of thoughts, Maggie shuffled back to her room, eager to crawl into bed and fall asleep. Although guilt about her entanglement with Mary's escape plan hounded her, she found solace in the idea that her friend would write. Her thoughts turned to Jimmy's claim about being antisocial. *Well, I'm not giving up on being more social. I'll bet he really isn't either.* As she imagined herself in social situations, like a dance or a party, sleep took her into darkness.

Jimmy wound his alarm clock and set it for half past four, giving himself an hour to exercise in the hayloft with his rope routine before his folks came to the barn to start morning milking. After shoving the clock under his bed, he crawled under the covers. Unable to relax, he lay there longing for the simple days of childhood, when the biggest question in his life was whether or not Santa would bring him a sled. As he closed his eyes, images of Jack Drude controlled his thoughts. Breathing deeply, he relaxed, embracing the sleep that took him away, despite the violent images in his mind—

> *From the ground, Jimmy looked up into the darkness of the open door of Jack's Model A. Where was Jack? Then he felt Jack's boot kicking him as he tried to crawl under the car. He dug his fingernails into the ground to pull himself away, but he couldn't*

move. Painful kicks to his back made him bounce with each blow. Again, and again and again he bounced.

He awoke with a jolt as his body bounced slightly on his bed. He thought he heard himself groan. He threw the covers aside to feel the cold air. After a moment, he pulled up the covers, turned on his side, and closed his eyes. He'd think of Mary, not Jack. The goodbye kiss, which one week ago had been their first kiss and their last kiss. It had been a sweet fire that he had felt throughout his body. He could feel it still, not on his lips, but in his heart. Was it meant to be? He fell asleep resolving to find her, somehow.

CHAPTER 5

CONFRONTING ROSE

Sunday morning, March 4, 1956

Resolved to confront his mother about her refusal to accept Anna, Billy Thorson sat in church on Sunday morning, unable to concentrate on the sermon. He rolled his plan around in his mind. *I'll drive over to Anna's and tell her I'm ready to abandon my family for her. I'll move out of the house if I have to. We could be married by a judge. We could rent a house in town. I could work out a farming arrangement with Dad. He's always been a reasonable man. Or I could apply for work at one of the shipping companies on the Minnesota River. Or I could work for a farmer.*

When the sermon ended, Billy was relieved to escape the discomfort of the wooden benches as he gladly joined the congregation to stand and sing the final hymn of the morning's service. As he sang softly, he glanced to his left at his mother singing boldly, and to her left his father singing reluctantly. He loved them both, but he loved Anna too. She was his future.

On the way home, Billy sat in the back seat, giving himself some physical distance from his folks. Let them chatter in the front while he contemplated how to broach the topic of getting back with Anna. *I'll ask them to sit at the table right away when we get into the house. I'll announce that I love Anna and we intend to marry right away.* But Rose interrupted his thoughts.

"Well, didn't you hear me, Billy? I asked you a question."

"Sorry, Mom. I didn't hear you."

"I'll repeat the question. How long are you going to mope about that woman? We know you broke up with her. You might as well give up on her and move on."

Taken by surprise, Billy responded with some anger. "No, I'm not giving up on her. I've been calling her every day, but Emma says she won't talk to me. I'm going to call her again today."

"You've been calling her?! And she won't talk to you? Give up! Don't chase after her. That's shameful!"

"I might just drive over there unannounced."

"That's not a good idea. She's been seeing another guy, you know. George Lange is his name."

"I don't believe it!"

"Dvoraks' neighbors go to our church, and they know George. They saw Anna go for a ride with him the day after you two broke up. You need to grow up, son. She's gone."

Billy said nothing as his dad turned onto the driveway and parked the car in its usual spot by the house. Billy jumped out and rushed toward his own car.

"Where are you going?" Rose demanded.

"I'm going over there right now to propose to Anna!"

"Then I'm going into the house to get the kitchen knife to slit my wrists!" Rose warned. "I will not have that red-haired demon running your life."

She strode toward the house, but John restrained her for a moment as Billy ran to her side, yelling, "Don't call her that! It would crush her to know you called her that name."

"Then she's crushed, Billy, because she called me on the phone the day after you broke up."

"And you said nothing to me? Well, there's no reason to ask you what Anna said. You'd probably just lie."

"See, she's already controlling you—making you think your own mother would lie to you."

"Come on, Billy," John reasoned. "This is your mother and dad, here. Let's go in the house and talk."

"No, I'm driving to Anna's."

Rose dropped down to sit on the gravel next to the car. "I'll not live to see you marry that woman!" Without regard for her Sunday clothes, she sprawled out on her back in the dirt and pleaded, "Please don't go, son."

Unable to withstand the scene of his mom on the ground and his dad's terrified expression, Billy said, "Okay, let's go in." He helped his mother to her feet.

"I got a nice roast in the oven," she said, brushing herself off. "We can talk after we eat."

Billy led the procession to the house as John took his wife's arm. As Billy entered the house, the phone began ringing. He grabbed it off the receiving hook in the kitchen.

"Hello."

"Thank goodness it's you, Billy. It's Anna."

"Hello, Anna. I love hearing your voice. Please go on. I've been wanting to talk to you. I miss you so much."

"I miss you too."

Billy lowered his voice after his folks walked in the door. "Can I come over today?"

"That's her, isn't it?!" screamed Rose. "I'll take the knife to my wrist right now if you leave to go over there, Billy. She's seeing somebody else anyway. Ask her about George Lange. Ask her if she's been dating him. Ask her!"

Unable to think of what to say, Billy simply asked, "Did you hear that?"

"Yes, but . . ."

"Is that true? Are you dating already?"

"Billy," Anna pleaded, "it is true, kind of, but it's not what it seems. Really. It's you I love. I need you to listen—"

"So how's the red-haired demon spinning the tale, Billy?" Rose yelled.

Billy looked over and saw his mother holding a knife to her wrist.

"Stay away from me, John. I'll bleed to death before you could get me to any hospital. Hang up the phone, Billy!"

"Things are crazy here, Anna. I've gotta go." Billy hung up the phone.

Rose put the knife down as soon as the receiver disconnected the two young lovers. She ran into the living room, sat down, and began to cry. John moved to comfort her, and Billy said, "This has to stop, Mom."

Without any remorse or empathy, Rose remarked, "Only you can stop it, son."

"No, dear," John said. "Only you can stop it."

"You're taking his side again. I'm always alone in this family. No one understands me. I want you to leave me alone to cry on my own."

Billy followed his father back into the kitchen. "What can we do, Dad? She feels alone. And yet she's telling me what to do. I need to make my own decisions."

"Right, Billy. And we'll deal with that. But first, I think we need to help your mother, and neither you nor I seems to be able to. I'm going to call Betty right away. Your mom and my sister were friends before I met her. Betty can help."

At the other end of the disconnected call, Anna held the receiver, staring at the blackness of the instrument as if it portended her future. She looked around to see if she were still alone in the kitchen. The family had eaten dinner early and were relaxing in the living room. She had hoped to sneak a private call in before her sisters came in to do the dishes. She had succeeded, but the call was a disaster.

I accomplished nothing. He knows I'm dating! I was going to tell him anyway, but now it looks like I was sneaking around. I made a stupid decision. I should've said no to George.

"Hey, we can handle the dishes," Helen said as she appeared in the doorway. "You look like you've seen a ghost."

"I think I am a ghost," Anna said without understanding her own words. "Thanks. I'll be in my bedroom."

In her room, she grabbed a pen and paper. *A letter. Why haven't I thought of writing a letter before now?* She began writing.

My darling Billy, I am pregnant with our child. The decision we made to make love on New Year's Day has blessed us! I wanted to tell you that I was pregnant on that last night we were together, but your concern about your mother was . . . She scribbled out the last part and said, "I'll have to re-write this anyway." She began again: *but you kept interrupting me about your mother . . .*

She stopped writing and said to herself, "The same thing happened on the phone today."

Anna stood up, folded the letter twice, and tore it up into pieces as she whispered to herself, "I need to think this over carefully. He can't change his mother, and she isn't going to change on her own. She just gets worse. I've got a baby in me. I need to look out for myself and my baby, and I've got to start making better decisions."

CHAPTER 6

THE PERMANENT

Sunday afternoon, March 4, 1956

"What did you and Aunt Emma do in the olden days before home permanents, Mom?" Maggie asked from her chair by the kitchen table. Towels covered Maggie's shoulders, back and front, and the ends of her dark red hair were rolled up in curlers.

In her mid-thirties, with no traces of gray in her dark brown hair, Mary Carlson was medium height, only a couple pounds overweight, and appeared strong and youthful, but she grudgingly understood her teenage daughter's narrow perception of the olden days. She said in her normal, understated, matter-of-fact manner, "Just sit still. I don't want to spill any of this solution. The kit cost me a dollar and a quarter. I'm glad you got the Tip Toni so I only have to do the ends of your hair. Only needs half the curlers too. And by the way, child," she added with a hint of sarcasm, "we're only talking about less than twenty years ago."

"But how did you curl your hair way back then?" Maggie persisted, missing the sarcasm.

From a chair across the table from Maggie, Aunt Emma answered, "Well, we didn't go to any fancy beauty parlor. That's for sure." A little taller than her sister and a couple of years older, Emma always spoke with animated emphasis, traits she had acquired as the favorite child of her parents. She took a long swallow of beer out of a bottle before she continued. "If we were going on a date, we washed and rolled our hair in curlers the night before and then slept in the curlers or pins. Our mom got us a curler with a handle that opened a cylinder like a scissors. We could heat the metal cylinder on top of the wood stove, and after we washed our hair or just the part we wanted to curl, we opened the curler so we could grab the hair with it. Sometimes you could smell the hair burn a little if we kept it on too long.

"But before that, remember this, Mary?" she interjected with enthusiasm. "We'd use the flatiron that we used to iron clothes with and heat it on the stove, and then we'd wrap the ends of our hair around some flat piece of metal, and then we'd press our hair with the hot flatiron against the flat piece of metal." She waved her hand in the air to indicate it was all past and laughed loudly before she took another long swig of beer.

Trying to concentrate on the job at hand, Mom laughed lightly before she stepped away from her daughter's chair to grab a thin, flexible plastic cap to fit over Maggie's head. After ensuring it was secure, she said, "Okay, Maggie, we have to let you sit for fifteen to twenty minutes. Change places with Emma." Mary finished her beer and asked, "Please open another one for me, Emma."

Emma had already stood up to wash her hair by the sink. After opening each of them another beer, she dipped hot water from a copper container on the stove and said, "Glad you were able to melt some snow for soft water. It makes such a difference."

"Sure does." Mary sat down to enjoy her bottle of beer.

Emma checked the mirror. "I see a little gray, but I'm planning on coloring my hair so it's more even. That should take care of the gray. I have to wait a few weeks after the permanent, though."

"I don't think I'll ever get used to the smell of this stuff," Maggie said as she settled in to wait.

"The only good thing about the smell," Emma joked, "is that it drives the men away so we women can talk about women's matters."

"Seems to work for that," Maggie said, giggling. "Jimmy and Joey ran upstairs in a hurry."

"Yeah," Mom said. "Martin got out of the house right away. He said he was going to putz around in the tool shed, but I think he's probably using this snowy Sunday to nap in the hayloft. It's not very cold out." The sisters laughed before they took another drink of beer. "He'll be back in to drink some beer after we finish and the smell goes down a bit."

Emma sat down in the chair, and Mary sectioned off strands of her wet hair and wrapped the ends of each grouping with special precut paper provided with the kit before rolling it up in a curler.

"This will take a while," Mary explained. "You got the big kit for a tight curl."

"I like lots of curls," Emma said with a giggle. "I'll take another swig of beer before I tell you some pretty exciting news."

Mary stepped back and took a big drink from her own bottle as she waited for Emma.

"I wanted to tell you as soon as I got here, but I wanted the men to leave first. Then, I thought maybe I should tell only *you*, Mary, and not tell Maggie. I thought that at fourteen, maybe Maggie was too young, but she's almost fifteen, and I realize Maggie is a woman and she's one of us too."

Maggie smiled, liking her aunt's logic.

"Anyway, here it is: Anna broke up with Billy!"

Maggie gasped. "No!"

Mary stepped back to ask, "Are you sure?"

"I'm sure," Emma gushed. "Look, you know I liked Billy, but the religion thing was always an issue, and he would not give it up. Said he was worried his mother would hurt herself if he and Anna got engaged."

Maggie's and Mary's eyes met. "Billy must be heartbroken," Mary said.

"They both must be!" Maggie exclaimed.

"Okay, take that as the bad news, if you want, but I think Anna is ready to move on. The breakup happened after a Friday-night date a week and a half after Valentine's Day. The next morning, Anna stayed in her room. She was crying. Wouldn't talk to anyone. When I went in to tell her Billy was on the phone, she told me that she didn't want to talk to him. She said she had given up on him. Her exact words were 'I've given up on Billy, Momma.' My nineteen-year-old daughter called me 'Momma.' I could've cried right then.

"But I admit it. I called George Lange that very morning, and he came over that afternoon. I told Anna I called him. She didn't like that I did at first, but she agreed to visit with him. He cheered her up, I think. They went for a ride. The breakup was just a little over a week ago, but they've been on several dates already."

The three women were silent while each assessed their feelings. Finally, Emma pleaded, "Things were not progressing with Billy. He had hinted before Christmas that a ring might be coming on Christmas Eve. When it didn't, Anna expected one on New Year's Day. Then Valentine's Day. Anna really hurt every day after that. He kept saying that they had to wait."

Mary lamented, "A girl can only wait so long before she realizes it may never happen."

Heavy footfalls on the stairs announced that the boys were about to arrive in the kitchen. The women took the cue to change the subject.

Mary said, "You won't have to wait much longer before you can remove the curlers, Maggie."

The boys barged through the doorless doorway into the kitchen with smirks on their faces.

"Jeez, how can you stand the smell?" Joey exclaimed.

"Why don't you stay upstairs?" Maggie demanded.

"Well, we got curious," Jimmy said with a sly grin. "Seems to me you all had a permanent last fall."

"Yes, right before Halloween," Emma responded.

Jimmy continued, "Well, how can they be called a *permanent* if you need one every few months? Shouldn't they be called a *temporary*?"

Joey laughed loudly, and Maggie couldn't help but to giggle too.

"I don't want to be going through this mess just to give someone something called a *temporary*," Mary said. "You've got a good point. But I don't think it would sell if they called it a *temporary*."

Emma laughed and joined in the game. "I can hear the announcer saying, 'Get your temporary wave kit now before your last temporary wave leaves your hair straightaway.'"

Giddy from the beer, Mary and Emma giggled more than the humor deserved, embarrassing Maggie, who decided to enlighten her brothers. "Mom was telling us earlier about how they curled hair in the olden days. And many still do it the old way, by putting curlers in every night before bed so they can awaken with *temporary* curly hair. Or they do pin curls, like Mom taught me. You wet and twist some hair around your finger and then hold it in place with crisscrossed bobby pins. That gives me a curl for a day."

"But thank goodness," Emma chimed in, "someone invented the home permanent wave, so now we can do at home what they do at beauty salons."

"So, what makes the curls last longer?" Jimmy seemed serious now.

Mary had just begun the process of dabbing the formula onto each curled-up grouping. "It's this solution I'm adding on now that makes it last."

Jimmy jumped on this. "So, you have a permanent solution." He began to laugh before he added in a pretentious voice, "What's the problem for which you need a *permanent solution*?"

Maggie blurted out, "Straight hair!" And everyone laughed.

"I'd say the problem is it's a permanent stink!" Joey howled.

"And my solution to that," Maggie said, "is for you to go back upstairs." And she held up the box from the product, saying, "See, it says on the box this is a permanent wave. Well, here is my permanent wave to you!" And she held her hand high, flapping her hand up and down in an exaggerated wave.

"Good one!" Jimmy admitted. "We're off to our room. But, Mom, can we take along a few cookies from the cookie jar?"

Mom nodded her approval.

After they each grabbed several cookies, the boys left the kitchen to hurry upstairs. But Jimmy poked his head back through the doorway to add, "By the way, Maggie, we'll be back, which means your permanent wave goodbye is only a temporary wave goodbye."

Once upstairs, Joey commented, "Jeez, Maggie seems like a different person. Like she was one of them and not one of us."

"Who's *them*?" Jimmy asked.

"Grown-ups! I mean, usually she's a kid like us. She's one of us, but now, just because she's getting a permanent, she thinks she's a grown-up."

"Don't be too hard on your sister. In a way, she is in the grown-up group today. And don't pretend you don't behave differently according to who you are with. I know you do. We all do."

"Not me. I'm the same guy no matter who I'm with. No matter what group I'm in."

"So, you're telling me you don't act differently when we are in church?"

Joey stayed silent, but Jimmy persisted. "How about when you are with a friend from school, like Ronnie Schoen? And do you act the same as when you are in the group with those five girls walking home from school? Or how about in the country school, when your class is gathered around the table with the teacher going over the daily lessons?"

"Okay. Okay. You're just like Maggie. You have to be right all the time." Joey took a moment to gather his thoughts before saying, "Somehow, the things you mentioned all seem different."

"That's because they all are different. And that's the point. Different situations call for different behavior. You might be the same nice guy in all those groups, but you are going to behave differently. You'll maybe say things in one group you wouldn't say in another group. That's how we get along with people, see?" *Here I am lecturing my little brother on how to get along with people,* he thought. *When did I become the expert on that? If Mags were here, she'd whack me one and tell me to practice what I preach.*

Meanwhile, in the kitchen, Maggie declared, "Jimmy seems so different when he and Joey are together. Don't you think, Mom?"

"That's the way of the world, dear," Mom replied, smiling.

"But back to the breakup," Emma declared. "I've not seen Anna so happy in some time. I think George has been serious from the get-go. She won't have to wait five years for him to propose."

"And how can she be so sure?" Mary asked earnestly. "I'm happy for her, of course. And I'm happy for Rose too. She can quit whining about losing Billy to another faith. I'm sick about how hurt Billy must feel, but he's young. He'll move on. Eventually."

"It's a leap year," Maggie inserted. "Maybe that'll help, though I guess the year hasn't been too good for him so far."

"I'm glad you can see the big picture," Emma responded. "The way I see it, Anna and Billy weren't meant for each other. It wasn't meant to be."

Mary stiffened. "That is the exact thing you said about Martin and me, remember? You said that if we were meant for each other, we'd be the same religion."

"Did I?"

"You know you did. And I told you we'd make our own decisions."

"And you did. So maybe I was wrong then. And you and Martin were meant to be."

Mary relaxed, sensing the humor in the moment. "So, whatever turns out to be, that's fate, then? But to me, it seems that the kids may have gotten pushed into making certain decisions. Or, in Billy's case, putting them off."

Emma threw up her hand that wasn't holding the beer. "I admit I don't know. But it became clear to me that Anna wanted to move on, and George had piqued her interest from the start. Because he was serious from the start. Billy was serious too, but he didn't follow through."

"Seems like he didn't, and that's his loss," Mary said. "But I know he wanted to. We'll probably never know the whole story."

"Maybe not, but Anna told me she wants to talk to you."

"Wants to talk to me?" Mary was genuinely surprised.

"Well, you are her favorite aunt!" exclaimed Emma. "Yesterday, when I told her you were going to give me a permanent today, she told me to tell you that she wants to come over and bake cookies with you like she did as a kid, but I think she wants to talk about the breakup. You're a good listener."

Mary thought for a moment. She did laundry on Mondays, but if Anna wanted to talk, she'd put laundry off till Tuesday. "The sooner the better. Tell her to come tomorrow afternoon if she can get off work. The kids will be at school, and I'll make sure Martin is outside doing something. We'll have the house to ourselves."

"Didn't Billy try to call Anna?" Maggie asked.

Emma shook her head no but quickly added, "Well, he did call the Saturday morning after, but Anna was not willing to talk to him yet." Then she announced, "You can take out your curlers now, Maggie."

Finished with applying solution to Emma's curls, Mary fitted the plastic cap over her sister's head and said, "I'll wash my hair quick. Can you do me while yours sets?"

"Easily, dear, but I think we both need another beer." She finished hers and opened another for each of them.

Soon after Mary sat in the chair, Emma asserted, "I work best when we sing," and began to sing the first verse of "Green Meadow Waltz" in Czech. Mary chimed in before she got out the first two words, *Louka zelená*.

Suddenly, Dad barged in. "I was getting a little lonesome out there. And I thought about you women in the warm kitchen, drinking beer and having fun."

The women continued singing as he opened a beer and sat down at the table. "I have to hand it to you. You sure do know how to party, even in the stink of this permanent thing. Every time you do permanents, you party. It's like a permanent party!"

The singing sisters began laughing and choking. Mary, nearly in tears, forced words out as she giggled. "Yeah, life is a permanent party!"

The giggling of the three women became uncontrollable, fueled by the blank look on Martin's face.

CHAPTER 7

THE GOOD AUNT

Monday afternoon, March 5, 1956

"Anna is due to arrive about half past noon," Mary said as she cleared the table after Monday's dinner and prepared to wash the dishes. "You agreed to be out of the house so she can feel free to bring up the subject of the breakup or whatever she wants to talk about."

"I thought she came here to bake cookies," Martin said.

"Don't play dumb, Martin."

"Only teasing. I know the situation, and I promise I'll leave for some work in the barn, but I want to be here when she comes so she can say hello to her favorite uncle. That's what she calls me, you know."

Picking up on the chance for some good-natured competition, Mary replied, "I was her favorite aunt a few years before I even met you. You're her favorite uncle by accident."

"Are you calling our firstborn an accident?" he teased, making a clicking sound with his tongue and cheek.

Mary whacked him softly on the arm as she exclaimed, "Oh, you!"

"Don't worry, I'll be out of here like a shot after a short greeting."

Anna arrived a few minutes later and gave a big hug to each of them before she hung her jacket over the back of a kitchen chair, and plopped down in the chair next to it. When she said, "No, thanks," to Martin's offer of a beer, he took it as his cue.

"I leave you to your cookie-baking visit," he said. "I got work in the barn. Good to see you, Anna." He donned his coat and cap in the porch enclosure and left.

Mary busied herself setting out the utensils and ingredients, letting Anna decide what topics to broach. After Anna remained silent for an awkward amount of time, Mary asked, "What kind of cookies should we bake?" When Anna didn't answer, Mary offered, "Chocolate chip, oatmeal raisin, or should we make sugar cookies and decorate them with frosting?"

Anna looked down at her hands, which were folded in front of her on the table. Finally, she looked up to meet Mary's eyes. "You're the best aunt ever," she said sadly. "I hate to burden you with my problems, but I have to tell *someone*. The fact that Billy is your nephew makes me feel even more guilty for dragging you into this."

Mary sat down, expecting that cookie-baking might be postponed indefinitely.

Anna took a deep breath as she ran both of her hands over her ponytail. Pulling her chair closer to the table, she released a volley of words. "I'm pregnant. Billy's the father. I tried to tell him, but he kept saying we had to wait to marry. I left him in a panic. I stayed in a panic. I called his mom the next day. The conversation was a disaster. Then George Lange showed up. We've been kind of dating ever since. I think he's serious." She stopped to inhale and began breathing rapidly, too full of anxiety to cry.

"I'm such an idiot! I don't know what to do! I can't imagine what you must think of me. What everyone will think of me! Going with Billy for five years and then going out with George regularly only days after we break up!"

"First thing," Mary said softly, "I'm not here to judge you. I'll listen. I'll even give you advice if you want it. But you don't have to take it."

Anna sat back in her chair, relieved that the conversation she had been dreading for days had finally begun.

"Who knows about the baby?"

"Just me, and now you. And I foolishly let it slip to Marcy and Helen too."

"Not your mother?"

"No. If I tell Mom, I'm afraid she'll dictate my options."

"Like what?"

"Well, if Billy were Catholic, she'd push for a wedding, but since she doesn't want me to marry him, I'm afraid she'll want to cart me off to one of those places that girls go to have their babies and then put them up for adoption through the church. Katherine Bartletz did that and came back all slim and pure. I don't blame her for the cover-up, but everyone knows about it, but no one speaks about it. I can't do that. I want my child."

Mary drew in a deep breath and exhaled before she ventured to speak. "So, let's start with that for now. You might change your mind later, but right now you want to keep your baby."

"I loved Billy. I'll love our child."

"Do you still love him? I am not trying to talk you into anything, here, but have you thought about making up?"

"Yes, but he only tried to call me once, the morning after we broke up. I wasn't ready to talk then, but what I don't understand is why he hasn't called me since. When I left that night, he was more wrapped up in his mother's issues than our future together. His concern about his mother is wild. And I think she is just using his sympathy, but he can't see it and never will. I called Billy yesterday, but his mother yelled at me while we were talking on the phone. It's hopeless. He thinks she's suicidal. Maybe she is. She threatened to kill herself while I was on the phone. Over the years I've tried to get him past his concern about her. But I've given up." Anna began to cry. "And then," she added as she sobbed, "I made it worse when I called Rose to try to explain things the Saturday after we split. The conversation was a disaster."

Mary listened quietly as Anna explained the entire phone conversation, but bristled at the end. "She called you a red-haired demon!? My goodness, Rose has gone too far! She's not herself anymore. If Billy has to deal with her behavior every day, I can see that any kind of reconciliation with him is probably impossible."

"That's what I thought."

"If reconciliation is out, and taking a vacation to have the baby and give it up is out, are you thinking of raising it yourself? That's a tough road. I know Martin and I will do what we can to support your choice, but the eyes will be on *you*."

"I know. And I'm afraid the hardest eyes for me to bear would be Mom's and Dad's. I can hear the lectures about my being a bad example for my sisters. I can already feel the silence at the table during meals."

"Honestly, I think your mom would come around."

"I don't think so. At least not for a long time. She's harder on her daughters than on her only sister. Well, maybe not, but you don't have to live with her every day."

Sensing the hopelessness of the discussion, Mary tried a little humor. "Well, she likes to sing Czech with me."

Anna smiled. The tension eased a bit. "Maybe I should learn Czech."

"Tell me about George."

Anna smiled again. "I know Mom called him. I was against it at first, but when he showed up and was so kind and funny—I have to admit, I'm glad she called him. We went for a drive that Saturday he came over, and we had our first date on Wednesday, February twenty-ninth. He said having a first date on leap day was meaningful. We've been dating ever since. I really like him. When he came back from the Navy and wanted to date me last year, I liked him then. But of course, I'd been Billy's girl for a long time. I told George then that Billy and I loved each other and breaking up was out of the question." She paused before adding, "And it still would be out of the question if I hadn't got pregnant. What a twist of fate!"

"No lecture from me, Anna, but my words come from experience. Pregnancy can't be blamed on fate. It's always the result of a decision of at least one of the people involved."

Anna nodded. "Of course, you're right. But by fate, I meant the whole situation, really. You see, I think George wants to marry me!"

"Are you sure?"

"He said he's had his eyes on me since we first met when I was thirteen, which was the same age I was when I met Billy. I know, it sounds crazy, but I can feel myself falling in love with George."

Mary nodded, encouraging Anna to go on.

"And I can no longer see myself with Billy. I'm not sure when that happened. But I know when George gave me a ride in his car last year, I felt attracted to him then. He was serious and funny. Childlike, yet mature. I felt guilty about enjoying his attention because Billy and I were so in love."

"So, dating George is serious? Not just a rebound thing?"

"I think he'll ask me to marry him soon."

"And what will you say?"

"Yes!"

"What about the baby?"

"I know I need to tell him. I won't lie to him and pretend it's his and call it an early baby. The question is, when should I tell him?"

"Tell him soon, but the time has to be right. He mustn't think you're just using him. I know you aren't, but he needs to have no doubt that you have chosen him over Billy. He'll probably figure out the child is Billy's, anyway. You need to be ready to be completely honest with him. Com-plete-ly. He deserves that. He's a good guy."

"I'll be ready to tell him everything. He's really easy to talk to."

"He'll understand your situation more than most people will. Josie No-votlik was an unmarried girl of seventeen when George was born. Most people knew who fathered the child. He delivered cattle feed to farms, and when George was born with red hair, people supposed he had been deliv-ering more than feed when he stopped at Josie's folks' place. He was quite the talker."

"Mom told me you both knew George's mother."

"Yes, she was closer to your mom's age than mine, but for some reason Josie and I became really close, especially after she became pregnant. I used to walk over to visit her after school while she was carrying him. I remem-ber, he was born March 30, 1930. I was ten. I'd go over to visit Josie and play with George. He was a fun baby. I decided then that I loved babies and wanted a family of my own one day.

"When Josie married Elmer Lange a few years later, there was no doubt that red-haired George wasn't his kid, but unlike some men, Elmer treated the child like his own. It was only at school that others called him a bastard, and some families shamed Josie even years after Elmer went through the expense of actually adopting him and giving the boy his last name. People can be really mean."

"So, George knows what it's like to be a child out of wedlock," Anna stated flatly.

"More than that," Mary added quickly. "More than that. You see, George not only knows firsthand what it was like to be a child out of wedlock, but also knows what it was like to have a man adopt him and treat him like his own child. Elmer never, ever allowed any shame on the boy and felt nothing but pride for him. George has had a model father in Elmer."

Anna blushed a little as she said, "Here I am checking up on a guy as if I have some right to be picky."

"You have to be," Mary asserted. "Your baby's future cannot include being shamed. George will understand your situation. But I have no clue how it will affect his decision to marry you. I can't lie about that."

"And I won't lie to him. If we get married soon, we could have an early baby and no one would guess. You see, we both have red hair." The two women laughed at the thought.

"And," Mary added thoughtfully, "Billy's mother has reddish hair too."

"The more we talk about George, the more I realize I love him. What he's been through! I know his brothers resent that their dad treats him so well, even though he isn't blood like they are. He told me that. I know it sounds ridiculous to feel this way so soon, and it may seem self-serving, but I think it's real."

"The clock is ticking, but don't marry just to avoid scandal. A bad marriage is a lifetime of scandal. A wrong choice lasts forever."

"Maybe Billy and I were never meant for each other."

"Now you're starting to sound like your mother. Look, you're made some choices and you have to deal with the consequences. And you have to make the best of those consequences for the rest of your life. If it turns out for the best, call it fate or luck or whatever you want, but if it all starts to turn sour, work on making some choices to change things. Never give in to being a helpless victim of fate. You always have options, especially when you are young and smart and beautiful."

"And pregnant!" Anna inserted, making them both laugh.

"Yes," Mary assured her, "and pregnant. Think of the child as a gift."

Mary saw that Anna's face had brightened compared to when she had first come. "You know what we should do now?"

"Make cookies!?"

"Hell, yes!" Mary exclaimed.

CHAPTER 8

SURPRISES

Saturday morning, April 28, 1956

On the last Saturday in April, Anna dressed in jeans, just as George had requested for their morning date. He had said he'd pick her up at nine in the morning. They'd spend the entire day together and eat supper somewhere casual. Anna looked at her full-length profile in the mirror on the back of her bedroom door. She imagined her jeans felt a little tight as she zipped them up to the button at the waist. She picked a loose-fitting green blouse that would look good without being tucked into her jeans.

She inhaled and observed her reflection. *Sixteen weeks. I wonder when I'll start showing. I'm scared as hell. Only three other people know so far, but in a few months everyone will probably know.* Moving closer to the mirror, she stared critically into her own eyes as if to discover something new about herself. *The day of reckoning is approaching, Anna. I need to tell George soon. But I have no plan. And I have no courage. What if I lose him?*

George had said they would be doing some walking, so she should wear comfortable shoes. Taking him at his word, she had polished up the men's work shoes that she used when she did fieldwork on the farm. As she stood outside waiting for him, she felt more like she was going to do farmwork rather than going on a date, but the morning was sunny and she was going to enjoy the time with him. Besides, he had promised a unique surprise.

George drove his 1955 Chevrolet into the yard at nine as he had promised. She had come to like the two-tone green-and-white car that he had bought used from the dealer. "Green is your color," he had said. Anna had reminded him he'd bought the car before they started dating.

She opened the door and slid in beside him before he could get out to open the door for her. After she gave him a quick peck on the cheek, he sped out of the driveway and turned south onto the road.

As George drove, Anna enjoyed watching his profile and listening to him chatter about finishing seeding grain and the beginning of corn planting. But after he turned west toward his folks' farm, she said, "I know you're just stalling. You know I like to hear about the farmwork, but you said there was to be a surprise. How long do I have to wait before you give me a hint?"

"I'll tell you after we get past my folks' place," he said secretively. "And I love that curious look on your face."

Anna watched the landscape of his folks' farm pass by—level farmland, small wooded areas—and as they drove beyond the place, she spotted a two-story white house about fifty yards from the road. George grinned at her as he turned up a driveway and parked in the yard.

"Guess who owns this place," he said with a new pride in his voice.

"My guess would be that older couple coming out of the house to greet us."

"A few months ago, you would have been right. But now, I own it!"

Anna's mouth dropped. "You're moving out of your folks' place?"

"I think I'm old enough, don't you?" He laughed slightly as he added, "Dad helped me buy it. But we can talk about that later. Right now, Ben and Tillie are waving for us to come in for coffee. Let's not keep them waiting."

George made the introductions before they entered the house. "Ben and Tillie, I'd like you to meet Anna Dvorak. Anna, meet Ben and Tillie Kelser."

"We know your folks a little, Anna," Tillie said brightly, "but we've known George his whole life. We remember when his folks moved onto the farm. Come on in now and sit down. Coffee is ready."

George held the porch door open, and Anna followed the couple into the house. They were probably about seventy. Although they walked slowly, neither was frail, but she guessed they had been a bit taller in their youth. He wore a bib overall and she a flowered housedress. Their short sleeves revealed thin, once-muscled arms with sagging flesh. Their hands remained large from fifty years of manual labor on the farm.

Anna let George handle the small talk as she took in her surroundings: a large modern kitchen, an archway to a living room with doorways to other rooms or a stairwell, a bathroom near the entryway, and a door to the cellar in the kitchen. *A lovely place. Neat. Homey.*

"We've lived here since 1906, the year we got married," Ben declared. "Of course, we remodeled more than once. It's been mostly good times, but there were hard times too. Low prices when we started farming, then World War I, then the flu epidemic in 1918. Neighbors getting sick and dying. Prohibition and low prices in the twenties and thirties, drought in the thirties, World War II, the Korean War, and now low prices again. We raised a lot of wheat at first. Then corn and hay after we started milking cows. Farming got a lot more hectic when alfalfa came along. The yield was so much greater than grass hay, and you could get three cuttings in a season! We raised hogs and chickens too, most of our lives here. I can't even begin to tell you about all the changes in farming and in the rest of the world."

"This place has been good to us," Tillie declared. "We raised four daughters and two sons, but none of them want to farm, and the place is too much for us now. Two of the girls are teachers. The other two work in the Cities. The boys went into construction together. It's nice when they bring the grandkids home to the farm, but they have such busy lives that we don't see them that often. Sure, we rent out the land, but keeping up the yard and this big house is more than we want."

"Right, and that will be a lot of work for me too," George said. "But my dad and my brothers will help. Although I own the place, farming it will be a family effort. Or rather a family pleasure. It's a nice farm."

"We hadn't planned on selling," Ben said. "But when George and his dad made us a good offer last December when he came back from the Navy, well, we accepted. He took possession in March so he could put in the crops, but he let us stay in the house until we could find somewhere to live. We bought a new little rambler on the edge of Lakeland City, close to a café and a couple of taverns. Easy to clear out the driveway in the winter. We have to start being a little careful. Hate to leave, but it will be good to know our place is being taken care of."

"I won't let the house stay empty long," George promised. "I'll move in as soon as you move out. Mom said she will help me furnish it. In fact, my folks have extra furniture I can have."

Anna looked at George before she turned to face the former owners. "You have a lovely place here, and I'll bet it's full of memories."

"Yes, it is, but we're not selling the memories," Ben joked. He pointed to his head as he added, "We'll keep those right up here."

Anna smiled as Tillie folded her hands on the table and Ben clasped a hand over hers.

"But enough of our blabbering," Ben declared. "George wants to walk around outside and then maybe come back inside to tour the house."

Anna noticed how Ben and Tillie smiled at her as they tilted their heads. *They're such a cute couple. I envy their lives here together.* Anna's heart was drawn to the nice house, the kindly old couple, and the excitement of the moment, but suddenly she felt panic. *I've been blind! He's going to propose today, and I haven't told him about the baby yet. I kept putting it off. I can't let him pop the question before he knows the truth!*

George stood up before he said, "Let's go walk around, Anna."

Anna followed his lead and thanked their hosts as they left the house. She searched her mind for the next step. *I have to tell him before he drops down on one knee to propose. What can I do? The car. We should sit in the car!*

"George, before you show me any more of this lovely farm, can we sit in the car for a while? I have to tell you something, and I've put it off too long."

"Of course," he said graciously. "Whatever you want."

Once settled in the car, Anna said, "I'll speak only the truth, sweetheart. This is a lovely place. You are a lovely man, and in the short time we've dated, I have fallen in love with you. Truly, I have." She turned to meet George's inquisitive gaze. "Maybe I'm vain to think that you are leading up to a proposal today, which I would immediately accept, by the way, but before I can let you propose, I have a fact to confess." She inhaled deeply and exhaled slightly before she blurted, "I am pregnant with Billy's baby. Nearly four months. We expected to marry, but his mother is suicidal over it, so he delayed asking. Then you came along. I'm sorry I didn't tell you sooner, George. Really sorry. But—"

"Hold on, Anna." George said in an even voice. "Please don't muddle my mind with anything else quite yet. This is a big deal—a big surprise—but I'm not sure telling me earlier would've helped much. Just let me think before you say any more."

Anna stared straight ahead while George sat silently. *What must he think of me? That I'm a foolish girl but foxy enough to take advantage of him as a father for another man's baby!* With desperation she recalled Aunt Mary's words. *George not only knows firsthand what it was like to be a child out of wedlock, but also knows what it was like to have a man adopt him and treat him like his own child. Why didn't I trust Aunt Mary's words? Why didn't I tell him sooner?* She waited less than a minute before she confessed, "I waited too long to tell you. I don't remember exactly when I decided to deceive you." *I must not allow myself to cry!*

"It's my guess you never did—decide to deceive me, that is. One day leads to another pretty damn fast, especially when you're falling in love. Must've been hell for you to keep that secret. Who else knows? No, don't tell me. That shouldn't drive my decisions. Let me figure this out."

Anna remained silent. He put his hands to his head and said, "My first reaction is that I don't care. But that's incomplete. I have to care. With you or without you, I have to care. And I do care, because a baby will change everything." He turned to her and smiled. "Not my love for you, though. That hasn't changed. And the child will have my love."

Anna smiled at his last remark but said nothing.

"Let's go for a walk."

Anna was out of the car before he could walk around to open the door. He took her hand and led her around the barn to open the sliding door to the hayloft. Anna followed him into the massive space, which was empty save for a few scattered bales. George examined the tops of the bales carefully before he turned one over. "We'll put the pigeon shit on the bottom," he joked as he motioned for her to sit down.

Anna sat down, hoping this was still a prelude to a proposal. *Could he accept the news of my pregnancy so easily? He seemed to think it over. Or maybe he is going to explain why he changed his mind. Please speak soon!* She looked up at him and as he stood between her and the doorway, and the light behind him shone as if he too were illuminated.

"Anna," he began, "I'm afraid I am so in love with you that you can do no wrong in my eyes. But wait! I don't mean to say that being pregnant is wrong. It's just human. You said you loved him. You told me that you loved him the day I gave you a ride last year. There was a time I even wondered how two young lovers could date for five years without . . . well, you know." He smiled sheepishly. "In a moment I'm going to ask you to marry me, but before I do, I have a question for you, and your answer will not change what I say next. What were your plans for the baby if I had not come along?"

"Raise the child on my own."

"As my mother intended with me," he said.

"I honestly hadn't made the comparison myself, but yes, that's true."

"Look," he said abruptly, "if I've not made it clear already, you should know that my family's decision to set me up on this farm had nothing to do with you and me, originally. That deal was started soon after I returned from the Navy. So don't feel obligated about anything. But I want to say that nothing could make this place more like heaven for me than if you lived here with me. And your child will be our child. So, without further delay,"—he dropped to one knee, opened a ring box, and held it out to her—"will you marry me?"

Hardly able to contain her joy, Anna exclaimed, "Yes, of course! I'd have said yes even if you hadn't tempted me with the farm."

He slipped the ring on her finger before they both stood up for a kiss and a long embrace. Then George said, "And now, we go break the news to Ben and Tillie. I'm pretty sure they already have guessed, though. Aren't they great?"

"Wait until I can stop my tears of joy," Anna said.

"I intend to make you cry tears of joy for the rest of our lives, sweetheart. Now, let's go back in the house. The deal was that if you said yes, we would come back in to show them the ring."

Ben and Tillie welcomed the young couple back into the house and gave congratulations and handshakes and hugs. They raved at the ring and the beauty of the bride-to-be and wished them all the happiness possible at the farm.

Ben said, "It's too early in the day to drink booze, but we should drink a toast to your happiness with lemonade." After Tillie poured them each a glass, they raised their glasses and clicked them together as Ben proclaimed, "To you, young folks—I hope you have a swell life here on this farm. I hope your life here is better than ours was, if that's even possible." Everyone laughed before taking a big drink. Anna decided she couldn't be happier.

George asked, "Tillie, can I use your phone to call my folks? I need to tell them the news. They'll be expecting us for a special celebration dinner around noon. And, Anna, I think Tillie wants to show you around the house."

An hour later, in the car, George declared, "We have some decisions we need to make before we tell people about our engagement. First, do you want to try to rush the wedding?"

"Yes, but not just because of the baby. I'm ready for married life with you. Marcy and Helen and Aunt Mary know I'm pregnant. I accidentally let the fact slip to my sisters, but I told Aunt Mary when I asked for her advice. But neither my younger sisters, my dad, my mom, nor Billy know."

"Do you want a big wedding?"

"Yes, and so will Mom, but it's hard to get a reception hall and a ballroom on short notice. And I'd sooner get married when I can still fit into a dress."

"After we celebrate a little with my folks, we can stop at your place to tell your mom and dad."

"Mom will know when we can book the church. It would be nice if we could marry without me showing so much that people think that . . ." Anna hesitated to remind her fiancé of the reality—"I mean, that people might guess the truth."

"Shame with our truth is only in the eyes of the beholder," George said boldly. "You and I are solid."

"I don't want Mom to know. After the baby is born, she will just figure you're the father. No, wait. I think I should tell her I'm pregnant. She'll figure it out anyway, and if I tell her before she figures it out, she will have every reason to believe it's ours. I'll tell her I'm due in . . . let's see, from March when we started going out to . . ." She named off the months as she counted to nine. "December. I'll say I'm due in December."

"Just so you know, if it works that way, fine, but if it doesn't, we can handle it."

Anna scooted close to him before she stretched up to kiss him on the cheek. "You are a prince," she said softly as she felt the ring fitting snugly on her finger. *Is this the feeling every woman has when the man she loves proposes? I hope so, but no one is as lucky as I am.* She looked at George. "I love you more than anything in the world, and your folks are grand people. Your brothers treat me nice, and Walter's wife is fun."

"Walter and Jenny both said they liked bowling with us," George said. "Paul is a little harder to get to know, but I'm sure you'll charm him as well."

"You're the charmer in the family," she teased.

"When it comes to winning over your sisters, I think I have my job cut out for me. They were all pretty taken with my predecessor."

Anna pushed at his arm to scoff at the idea. "They'll get over him," she said. "I did."

Once George had parked the car in his folks' yard, the two lovers bounded into the house and were immediately greeted by congratulatory hugs and kisses and handshakes. Elmer was stocky and jovial, and Josie, who was always full of smiles, was short and plump. They had both dressed for the occasion, Elmer in a new bib overall with a white shirt and tie and Josie in a blue dress with white polka dots, with sparkling earrings and a multicolored beaded necklace.

Anna had found the Langes to be easy to talk to from the very first time George had brought her to their farm. Like so many people that her folks knew, she knew about them but didn't actually know them as individuals. Everyone in the area knew the story of Josie's out-of-wedlock child and her marriage to Elmer. Some said he treated George even better than his own sons. With all that attention, George had grown to be an outgoing, friendly boy and then a man everyone seemed to like and seek out as a companion. Anna chuckled to herself as she remembered how George had put it: "I became the special bastard child, and people expected great things of me."

The meal of roast beef, potatoes, vegetables, and apple pie for dessert was a scene of merry joking and special praises for the food and the charm of couples old and young. Although Anna declined Elmer's offer of a shot of blackberry brandy after the meal, she raised her glass of lemonade as Elmer said, "Here's to a wonderful future for the two of you."

"Honestly," Josie said after the toast, "we were a little worried that taking you to the farm for the proposal might have been a little overwhelming for you. I warned him that not every woman wanted the life of a farmer."

"I think he knew that this one did," Anna said. "I'm giving my notice to my boss on Monday. No more office work for me. Pay is low, and they treat women like crap, and I even have a woman as a boss. She's the worst!"

The celebration ended as it had begun, with hugs and handshakes and good wishes. Once the newly engaged couple was in the car and on their way, George said, "Are you sure we shouldn't have called your mother?"

"I'm sure," Anna declared. "My mother isn't like yours. She likes to over-plan things, and she'd be upset we didn't give her a day's notice so she could make a big deal out of it."

"Well, to be fair, my folks knew in advance."

"They do love their firstborn," Anna teased. *Lucky me, to be marrying into*

a family where the son feels free to share plans and dreams with both his parents.
Her heart ached suddenly with sympathy for Billy, and she allowed herself to
feel guilty at leaving him in the clutches of his mother while she had escaped
into a world of love. *Though I'm powerless to do anything about it.*

Anna cuddled up to George as he drove in silence until they pulled into
Dvoraks' driveway. Then he said flatly, "Isn't that Billy's car parked by the
front door?"

Startled out of her perfect world and into reality, Anna glanced out the
windshield to see Billy's maroon '49 Ford. "It's his car all right. And jeez!
He's sitting in the car too! Pull over to the left of it. Stay way over by the
grass. You stay in the car. I'll go talk to him."

"Let me come along. I'll stand behind you for support."

"No! Stay in the car."

"Will you be safe?"

"Of course. Billy is a gentle soul. It's his mom who is dangerous. Stay in
the car!"

CHAPTER 9

MORE SURPRISES

Saturday afternoon, April 28, 1956

Anna jumped out of George's car and bounded to Billy's driver's-side window, where she saw his face turn toward her.

"Hi, Anna," he said with a weak smile.

"Hi, Billy."

He spoke quickly before she could say more. "I called you many times, Anna, but every time I called, your mother told me you didn't want to speak to me. I respected your wishes until today, when I finally came over anyway, but I was just about to leave because your mom said you were out with George. When I saw the car coming down the driveway, I waited because I didn't want to meet a car on the narrow driveway. But I was set to leave. I mean, I am set to leave."

Anna hid her shock. *He called me many times!?* But then she realized she'd put her hands on the bottom of Billy's car window. Seeing Billy's pained expression as he saw the ring, she explained, "George just gave it to me this morning. We came here to tell my family. I would've called to tell you today. As it turned out, you found out before my folks."

"Not much comfort in being one of the first to find out," he said bitterly, raising his gaze from the ring to her face. "Took you only two months after we split. Must be some kind of record." He slapped the steering wheel with the palms of his hands.

Anna understood that the truth of his remark was too real to easily digest, and she briefly felt a strong urge to tell him the truth—that she carried his child. *And I would've told him earlier if Mom had given me his messages! If I had known he was calling me! My God, what have I done? All because of Mom's lies!* For a few silent moments, she inwardly exploded with anger that her mother had crushed her future with Billy. But then she flashed back to the phone call with Rose. The words *red-haired demon* hit her like a hammer. *No. Billy has no control over his life. George is the right choice for me and my baby. I truly love him.*

Still, her heart ached to see Billy in pain, and she watched with growing concern as he gripped the steering wheel, his knuckles going red and then white. But she did not want him to leave angry. Trying not to accidentally signal to George that things were not going well, she searched for the right words to give Billy a bit of comfort—but she found none.

"Good thing too," he said with sarcasm. "Now, you don't have to dread talking to my mother when you call, or dread talking to me either anymore."

Anna could have taken the cue to leave, but she persisted, hoping he would cool down before he left. She'd known him for a long time, and she was not ready to abandon him in this state. He, too, seemed reluctant to leave. Finally, she offered an olive branch.

"Last time when we had a conversation in this very spot, I left in anger. I don't want either one of us to leave in anger this time, okay?"

Anna watched as he slowly loosened his grip on the steering wheel. He said, "So, I'll just say congratulations to you and the lucky guy. Seriously, I wish you all the happiness in the world."

"Thanks," Anna said. "I know you mean it too." She saw Billy look down and expected he was about to leave, so she backed away from the car, adding in spite of herself, "How are you doing, Billy?"

Billy turned to look at her. "Yeah, I'm doing okay. Maybe not as well as you, though. Oh, yeah, and don't worry about me calling you anymore. Your mother told me she was sick of answering all my calls. Goodbye, Anna."

He backed the car up, turned, and glanced toward her before he drove down the driveway and out of her life. She felt sad for Billy, and then her anger resurfaced. *My mother was sick of answering all his calls!? She said he only called me once. She manipulated me with her lies! Maybe he didn't want to give up on me, but after he saw the ring, he gave me up pretty easily. I gave him up pretty easily too, now that I look back on it. But he still has to deal with his mother, poor guy. My mother is a pain, but his is impossible. I can't be sure*

Billy and I could've ever patched things up, even if Mom had told me about the calls. No, it's best that we split.

After Billy's car cleared the yard, Anna waved for George to come to the front door, where she knocked once before briskly entering, pulling a willing George behind her with her right hand while flashing her left hand in front of her so the new diamond was leading the procession. *One day I'll confront Mom about her lies. But not today.*

"Guess what happened this morning!" Anna exclaimed. "What do you think?"

Emma and Marcella looked up from cleaning and packing eggs by the kitchen table. Emma exclaimed, "I didn't know you two were here! Wow! Look at that. Come here, daughter. Hug your old mom. And you too, George."

Marcella joined the line for hugs as she joked, "If the diamond were any bigger, you'd have needed a wheelbarrow to get it out of the store. You've set a pretty high standard for your four younger sisters, Anna."

"Joe is seeding, Helen is dragging a field, and the twins are somewhere outside, or maybe in the barn playing with kittens. They'll all be in for supper, so if you can stay, I won't bother to send the twins out to get them."

"Dad isn't expecting me home for chores," George said. "Anna and I were going out, but for my part, I'd sooner stay here for supper."

Anna caught his glance to check for her approval. "Me too," she said.

Marcella teased, "Tell the truth, my beautiful sister Anna—you knew he was going to propose today, and you figured you'd wear the ugliest outfit possible so you'd know for sure it was true love."

"That's just mean," Emma said, though she smiled as she went to the refrigerator to fetch some beers. She handed one to George and took one for herself after Anna and Marcella declined.

"Well, the truth is," Anna explained, "if I had thought there was a possibility of a proposal today, I would have had my hair done and bought a special dress for the occasion, but my choice of wardrobe was based entirely on George's recommendation. You see, he took me out to Ben and Tillie Kelser's farm to show me around because he is the proud new owner. He proposed in the hayloft."

"Pretty romantic, I'd say," Marcella said with a laugh. "And smart too. That way he discovered if you were game to be a farmer."

"So, you bought the Kelser farm!" Emma exclaimed. "Nice place. You know the key to Anna's heart. Say, do you have a date set? I hope you're not one of these long-engagement couples."

"Nope," George asserted. "The sooner the better."

"Wow!" Emma gestured with her free hand before she took a swig out of her bottle of beer. "I'm one of the mothers that helps schedule things for Father Fenn at St. Michael Church in Willertson. The Bartilik-Cavenaugh wedding is off. She just called the secretary today. I don't know the details about why yet—the rumors are just getting started—but I could call right now to book the date. And they were to have their reception at Hilda's Hall and the dance at the Lakeshore Ballroom. Maybe you could step into their whole plan. I don't remember the exact date, but I know it's on a Saturday in June."

"Perfect!" Anna exclaimed.

Emma made the calls immediately and returned, announcing, "You're on for Saturday, June ninth. We've got six weeks to plan the big celebration. When Joe gets back from the field, he'll be shocked as heck."

"Mind if I use your phone to call Hilda's and Lakeshore?" George asked. "I know Hilda's requires a deposit, and with Lakeshore we have to pay for the band."

"I'll look up the numbers," Anna said.

After a few minutes on the phone with Hilda's and another few minutes with the owner of Lakeshore, George returned to the table, bragging, "It's all set. Six weeks from now you'll be stuck with me for life, Anna."

"Whoopie!" Emma exclaimed. "That's worth another beer! Now, Marcy, get that ham out of the refrigerator and we'll heat it up for supper. Good thing we're done packing eggs, but we'll use a bunch to scramble for supper. Then set the water boiling to cook some elbow macaroni and we'll add some cheese and frozen peas. Hope you don't mind a quick supper, George."

"It all sounds great. Both Hilda's and Lakeshore said they want me to get the deposits to them tomorrow morning. I told them I'd be there right after morning mass."

"So, do I get Anna's room?" Marcella asked. "Is it too early to divvy up her property?"

Although everyone laughed at the question, no one doubted the seriousness of the request, and Anna understood that Marcella not-so-secretly hoped that Billy might be available for her to claim. She made a note to herself to warn her sister about the dangers of his mother, for even now, as Anna gleefully celebrated her engagement to a man she loved, she knew that if it weren't for Billy's mother, she and Billy would've been engaged last Christmas.

Supper at Dvoraks' home was both casual and special. Joe and Emma were thrilled about the upcoming wedding of their oldest daughter, and Helen and the twins listened carefully to every detail of the plans.

Emma asked, "When are you going to tell Martin and Mary?"

"Let's go over there tonight, George," Anna said.

"They're having a birthday party for Jimmy and Mags tomorrow after-noon," Marcella said. "I'm sure you could come to that and announce your engagement then."

"No, I don't want to call attention to us at someone else's party," Anna said.

"Very noble of you, really," Marcella said seriously. "So, have you picked your maid of honor yet, hint, hint?"

"We haven't talked about it much. But yes, you'll be maid of honor."

"Walter will be best man, and then Paul," George said. "That's really all I have. My cousins from St. Paul will be invited, of course, but I hardly know them well enough to put them in the wedding."

"This will work out perfectly," Anna remarked. "Helen can stand up with Paul, and then we can have Jimmy and Maggie as a couple. They will be thrilled and so cute. And they're both ready to partake in some big social function. Well, Maggie is, anyway. Jimmy will pretend to scoff at it, but he'll love it."

"We've got chores to do," Joe said. "Which of you girls are with me to-night?"

"Me and Janet," Josephine said. "Let's get started. I hate to miss all the wedding talk, but you have to promise to fill me in on it later, Marcy."

"Sure thing."

After Joe and the twins left for chores, Anna said, "We'll wait to leave for Carlsons' place so we know they'll be done milking when we get there. I want them all to be together in the house. Don't want to launch this surprise on them one at a time."

"Good," Emma said. "That'll give us time to do some wedding planning."

Anna looked at George. "This will be boring for you, honey," she said gently. "Why not go visit Dad and the twins while they milk? I'm sure Dad would like to talk to you. The twins too."

"Hey, I can take a hint, Anna," George said. He smiled and headed for the door.

As soon as he left, Anna said, "Mom, I need to tell you something, and I may as well tell my two sisters at the same time." She smiled at Emma on her right and then turned her head to smile at Helen and Marcy on her left, with a wink of her left eye, hoping they would go along with the partial truth she was about to reveal to her mother.

"I'm pregnant," she announced boldly. "George and I expect our baby in December."

She focused on Emma's reaction, but out of the corner of her eye she was glad to see her sisters reacting as if they had just heard the news.

"That was fast," Emma blurted before she added quickly, "Oh, I'm not judging you, honey. Not at all. And you look so happy. So did George."

Emma stood up to hug her daughter. Helen and Marcy came over for hugs too, whispering their congratulations.

Anna explained, "I tell you this now so that you hear it from me instead of some rumor. Look, I want to tell you that George and I loved each other from the start. He talked about marriage from the very beginning."

"Who else knows?" Emma asked.

Anna hated how one lie led to another, but she answered without hesitation. "The three of us and George." *Aunt Mary will say nothing, and my sisters know the whole truth and will say nothing.* "You can tell Dad later, and even the twins when we get closer to the wedding date, but for now, let's just keep it between us, okay?"

"Right," Emma said. "I'm so glad you told me this early, because when we buy your wedding dress, we will have to take your expected growth into account." Emma smiled. "You'll be less than three months along at the wedding, but some women show earlier than others. And since you aren't very tall, you may be one that does."

"I never thought of that, Mom."

"That's what mothers are for, child," Emma joked. "On a Saturday, we'll have Dad drive us up to those new stores at the Hub in Richfield, and we'll pick out dresses for all the girls—we'll bring Maggie along too—and then we'll get the right dress for you. I think an empire-waist style will be perfect. The waistline is under your bust, and the dress flows out from there. Growth will not affect the fit."

"Thanks, Mom. I'd never have thought of that until it was too late."

"I'll tell Dad about the situation tonight, and we'll plan a Saturday to drive up. We'll want to take the whole family, so we might need two cars. I don't think it would be bad luck to have George drive up too. If you and the girls ride with him, Mary and Maggie could ride with us."

"George would love that!" Anna exclaimed.

"Of course, it's up to him to arrange the fitting for the tuxedos for the men. Be sure to let him know that."

"I will. I'm so glad I talked to you right away. Here we are, planning my wedding! I couldn't be happier!" And she meant it too. *Mom sure knows how to organize things in a short time. And manipulate too. I'm still angry about the lies, but I won't let that get in the way of my happiness. To think, less than twelve hours ago, I hadn't told George or Mom; I was with child, without a fiancé, and full of doubts.*

Anna and George drove into the yard at Carlsons' place at about half past eight, and as they were exiting the car, Anna said, "Someone just flicked on the yard light. They know we're here."

"They probably don't recognize my car."

"Well, they'll know who owns it soon."

Eager to share her joy with the Carlsons, Anna also hoped she could get a private moment with Mary. *She will be thrilled to learn that I've told George the whole truth before he proposed.*

The family shut off the television and moved to the kitchen, excited to visit with the young couple. Although everyone knew each other, Anna stated boldly, "Hi, everyone. This is my fiancé, George Lange. I know you all know who he is, but I want to introduce each of you because he is not familiar with most of you, and you are my favorite relatives."

George shook hands with each of them as Anna introduced them.

"Joey is eleven, George, and not just a little kid. Call him one and he'll let you know otherwise. Also, you should never forget Joey's birthday"—Anna paused to intercept George's curious look—"because it is the same day as mine!"

"On December twenty-seventh," George said hurriedly.

"You've trained him well," Maggie commented.

"Oh, and this is Maggie. She will be fifteen on Monday. Wouldn't you agree she's cute enough to be in our wedding?"

"Absolutely!" George exclaimed.

Maggie jumped up and down, turned to look at her mother, and pleaded, "Can I, Mom and Dad?"

Anna waited until her aunt and uncle nodded their agreement before she continued. "George and my dad will take Maggie and Aunt Mary, along with all of our family, to buy dresses and shoes and things for the wedding at the Hub in Richfield on a Saturday soon. We need to set a date."

"That would be nice for us," Mary said.

Anna continued, "But where will we find someone to stand up with Maggie? He must be young, handsome, and debonair. And, of course, totally trustworthy. George, this is Jimmy. He will be sixteen on Tuesday. What do you think?"

"If Jimmy agrees to be in our wedding," George piped in as if he and Anna had rehearsed the bit, "they will be the envy of all who attend." He reached over to grip Jimmy's hand; Jimmy glanced over to see his folks nodding their approval.

"And George, meet two of the best people in the world, Aunt Mary and Uncle Martin."

George hugged Mary. As he shook hands with Martin, Mary asked, "Do you have a date set?"

Anna explained their incredible luck at booking everything immediately because of a cancellation while each member of the family took a turn at examining and praising her ring.

"And what a surprise George pulled on me!" Anna began.

Mary interrupted her. "And we want to hear every detail, but first, we need to toast to your engagement. Martin, open a few beers for us."

"Kool-Aid for me and the kids," Anna said immediately.

After drinks were in hand, Mary said as they clicked their drinks, "May your life together be long and happy."

"Thanks," George said. "And I'm pleased to have you two as my aunt and uncle. Anna thinks you guys are the best. She's told me all sorts of stories about the good times her family has had visiting you."

"And you proposed to her anyway?" Martin joked.

"Let's hear the details of the day, Anna," Mary said.

As Anna told her tale of the early morning date that lasted all day and into the evening, she enjoyed how George and the members of the Carlson family felt free to interrupt to insert a joke or a comment, creating a fun atmosphere where laughter reigned.

Even as she spoke, though, Anna noticed Mary watching her intently. *How can I let her know I told George? Mary is smart. She'll figure out a way.* Anna watched Martin and Jimmy too. *They're taking George's measure, trying to discover what kind of man he is. Probably comparing him to Billy.* She was certain Maggie was comparing him to Billy. *Both of them are good-looking, Billy in a boyish way and George in a more manly way. I'm only nineteen. I've been so lucky and unlucky too.* She looked at Joey, whose eyes were riveted on George. *My fiancé has definitely won over Joey.*

After Anna finished, Joey said to George, "Tell me some things about the Navy!"

"What do you want to know?"

"Everyone I know has gone in the Army. So, how is it different?"

George paused a moment before he began. "Let me tell you some ways they are the same. You have to follow orders from those who outrank you."

"What does outrank mean?"

"Rank is a person's position of authority and their pay grade. You earn rank by how long you are in the service and how well you perform at your job or if you graduate from a certain school or training. As a sailor goes up in rank, his pay goes up too. People with more rank get to order around those with less rank."

"Should I join the Navy or the Army?"

In an attempt to save her new fiancé from too many questions, Anna interrupted, "Hey, Joey, there are other services too, like the Marine Corps and the Air Force. You can't join for a few years. Check them all out to see what you want to do. Go to the library and do some reading. I'll bet George will answer all of your questions if you get more background on your own."

"Sure, anytime," George said, smiling at Anna with relief. Then he added, "It's been fun tonight, but we should really go. Thanks for letting us barge in on you like this."

"Wait a second," Mary said, eyeing Anna with a hinting nod. "I can have a quick lunch ready in no time. Might as well eat a sandwich and some cookies with a cup of coffee or another beer."

"I admit that I'm hungry," Anna said as she caught her aunt's hint. "I'll slice some bread for sandwiches."

"Maggie, put on the coffee. Jimmy and Joey, set the table," Mary directed. "I'll show Anna which loaf to slice."

In the small room adjoining the kitchen, Anna stood by a cupboard table with the breadboard in front of her and the bread knife ready in her hand. Mary leaned toward her to dig out a loaf of homemade bread from the bread box.

"Well?" Mary asked.

"I told him today, right before he asked me. No hesitation."

"He is a prince," Mary whispered. She walked to the door, then turned back to Anna to add, "Slice up the whole loaf. There's more in the bread box if we need it." Turning back, Mary almost ran into Jimmy. "Whoops!" she exclaimed. "I'm sorry, dear. I'm just excited about the news—the engagement, you know."

Jimmy stood still and smiled. "Well, Mom," he drawled, "that's old news, and you're first getting excited now?"

Only Maggie and Jimmy seemed to notice their mother's slight embarrassment. Maggie said, "Don't worry, Mom. Jimmy's just jealous because you picked someone else to slice the bread. He thinks that's his job."

Mom opened the refrigerator to grab the summer sausage, exclaiming, "What did I ever do without a refrigerator! Come on, everyone, pull up your chairs and dig in. We've got bread and butter and cheese and summer sausage, cookies, and milk or coffee. Oh, yes, and I almost forgot the pickles," she added as she reached into the refrigerator to grab a quart jar and began fishing out the pickles to put on a special long blue-and-white pickle dish.

At about 10:00 p.m., after everyone had left and the kids had gone upstairs, Mary and Martin sat at the kitchen table, finishing their beers. Mary said, "Bridesmaid's gown and shoes for Maggie, rental tux for Jimmy—and he'll need new dress shoes—and I'll need a new dress because I have nothing fit to wear to a wedding. We may as well rent a tux for you and Joey too. No, if it gets too soiled, we'd have to pay for it, and I don't trust either one of you not to rip it or something. We'll have your suit cleaned and get Joey a new sports jacket. He'll just outgrow a suit."

"Fine with me," Martin said. "My suit is only a few years old."

"And we'll need to give them a really nice present," Mary added.

"Red Bessie is two months late getting bred. Let's put her on corn for a couple weeks and ship her to South St. Paul. She's big so she might bring enough money. If not, we'll ship another one."

"And we were set to get a little ahead this summer." Mary smiled and shook her head.

Martin laughed a little. "It's only money, darlin'. That's why we raise the young stock. We have plenty replacements coming up." Then he added the usual joke as he hoisted his beer up to clink it with hers. "That's living and that's farming, and we love every day of it!"

CHAPTER 10

THE BIRTHDAY PARTY

Sunday afternoon, April 29, 1956

"I don't know what I was thinking, Maggie," Mom joked. "No, I'm pretty sure I wasn't thinking at all when we planned this birthday party for you and Jimmy on a Sunday afternoon. If everyone shows up—and we hope they do—there will be over twenty kids here. Our house isn't that big!"

"We set up chairs and stuff outside on the lawn, just as you said, Mom."

"Right, we'll manage. It's nice outside. I'm comfortable wearing this light jacket. Probably get to the high sixties this afternoon. They'll be okay eating outside on the lawn north of the house."

"The kids will wear jackets if they need to," Maggie offered. "I decided to not dress up too much and just wear jeans. Jimmy tried to shame me into wearing a party dress, but I told him that everyone knows the party is outside so no one is dressing up. He never does."

"And I'm glad," Mom said. "Dress slacks cost too much."

"Jimmy and I decorated the picnic tables with some crepe paper, and we ran an extension cord out the living room window from the plug-in off the living room lamp. The kids know that Jimmy and I got a phonograph for our birthdays, so they will be bringing records for gifts. We'll play them, and the kids will hang around the lawn to listen and eat all afternoon."

"I hope so," Mom said as she and Maggie walked outside to a picnic table. "I've put out several decks of cards and board games, but I didn't plan any other games. We'll have several drawings for prizes, though. Remember to give everyone a number when they come, and then we'll draw out of a milk pail for the winner."

"What are the prizes?"

"There's that foot-tall brown-and-white teddy bear I won playing the shuffleboard machine at Crossroads. I never took it out of the plastic bag. There's a used hardcover of *Little Women,* and I bought a new book called *The Indian Mummy Mystery.* There's a big bag of butterscotch hard candies too. I'll put them out on a blanket by the house with a *Prizes* sign."

"Good work, Mom," Maggie said as they walked out to the lawn where Jimmy and Joey were working.

"The picnic tables only seat six people each," Jimmy told them, "but Joey and I raked the lawn and picked up the old chicken droppings from last fall. Kids can sit on the grass like we do when you serve a meal at threshing, and we can bring out blankets to spread out on the grass too."

"Nobody will mind," Joey added. "As long as there is plenty of food. Kids like beans and wieners and Jell-O and potato salad."

"And we have two big layer cakes and two pans of fudge," Maggie added. "I made lots of popcorn to snack on, and Jimmy helped me put syrup on about half of it. We'll need a pan of water out here and a couple of towels to take care of sticky hands."

"Sticky hands!" Joey exclaimed. "I'll bet that will help me throw my curveball if Ronnie and I play catch."

"Don't play catch by the house," Mom warned. "We don't want any broken windows or cracked siding. Play out in the calf pasture if you are going to throw stuff. There is plenty of room to hit balls in the calf pasture too."

"Too many rules," Joey complained. "What if they don't listen?"

"They will, if you ask nicely. It's nothing their own parents wouldn't ask of them. Besides, too late to change things now," Mom said. "I see some kids walking up the driveway."

"Looks like it's Peggy and Mary Ryan and Katherine O'Keran," Maggie said to her mother, then hollered, "Hi, girls! Come on up."

"Where should we put our gifts?" Katherine demanded. "Should we take them inside? They should not be left in the sun or they might warp."

"I like the sound of that," Maggie said. "We've been expecting these round, flat objects, and we have a lower shelf on a table in the shade. And Jimmy and I plan on opening the gifts early so we can all enjoy them. Hey, it was your birthday Friday. We're both fourteen for a few days."

"I catch up to you for three days until you turn fifteen. Then you catch up to Jimmy for a whole day before he turns sixteen. It's always kind of fun every year." Katherine turned to Jimmy to demand, "Hey, Jimmy, did you invite Mary Schroedler?"

Shocked, Jimmy became a bit defensive. "I'd love to invite her, but what makes you think I know where she is? I don't, and neither does anyone I know."

"B. J. and I write to each other every week," Katherine bragged. "He says you and Maggie probably know where she is."

"News to us," Maggie said. "But who is B. J.?"

"My brother, Billy Joe. Since he started school in the Missouri Seminary, he started calling himself B. J."

"Calls himself B. J., eh?" Jimmy commented. "I like it. He used to come home during the summers when he started there, didn't he?"

"Not anymore. I'm not even sure he's still in school. Since he turned eighteen, he doesn't come home much, but he writes to me, and we are closer than we've ever been. I'll tell him Mary wasn't invited to your party in my next letter."

"You do that," Maggie said as she urged her toward the gift table. "Place the gift here, please. And thanks. Pour yourself some lemonade if you want."

Jimmy made a mental note to pick up the conversation with Katherine later, but now he turned to greet Peggy and Mary Ryan, which was not something he looked forward to. Peggy was in his grade, but they had never got along that well. Mary was okay, and since she was thirteen and a grade ahead of Joey, she seemed to prefer to pick on him instead of Jimmy. They were both always critical and uppity, but Mags had told him he must try to be outgoing and not expect her to do all the greeting. *I'm already regretting that I agreed to this party. But I'll try to be social.*

"Hi, Peggy and Mary. Glad you came."

"You said that like you really mean it," Peggy remarked.

"Yeah, Mags had me practice with her," Jimmy said, never missing an opportunity for a smart remark.

"I'll tell her you did well," Peggy said, matching his sharp tone. "Don't you think, Mary?"

"Let's put our gift on the table and get some lemonade," Mary said. "You can argue with Jimmy. I'll go talk to Joey."

"Mary's kind of grumpy," Peggy said. "She was looking forward to attending the country school for another year. As eighth graders, she and Liz would've ruled. So she's been upset ever since Dad came back from the school board meeting and told us they were closing the country school after this school year."

"What did you tell her about being bused to the big school?" Jimmy asked.

"I told her it wasn't so bad. That she would probably have lots of classes with her best friend, Liz Brummer. I told her I missed the closeness we had in the country school. But I think what really upset her is that Liz is looking forward to it. Mary likes everybody to agree with her."

"Who doesn't?" Jimmy joked.

"Certainly not you or me!" Peggy said with a smile.

At the sound of an approaching tractor, Jimmy announced, "That looks like an Allis-Chalmers WD. That'll be the Shaurel girls—I bet Ann is driving. Excuse me, Peggy, I want to greet the newcomers as they jump off the wagon."

"I'll find you later," Peggy warned. "You'll not get away that easily."

Jimmy could've waited until the girls had reached the lawn, but he enjoyed the short walk to where Ann had parked the rig. It was a reprieve from Peggy's clutches. As Ann shut off the tractor's engine, the other three girls jumped off the wagon. At thirteen, the twins were cute and gangly, and Jimmy called to them, "Hi, Mary and Margaret. Glad you came. Sorry to ask, but which of you has the pigtails and which has the ponytail today? I'm not going to pretend I can tell you apart."

"I'm Mary, and I've got the ponytail today," Mary said with a giggle.

"And I like it when you don't pretend to know who's who," Margaret added.

"And greetings to you too, Caroline. Glad you came." Then he added, "Isn't your birthday in May?" *Am I smooth, or what—remembering birthdays.*

"I'll be twelve—older than Joey, even though we are in the same grade."

"He's looking forward to seeing you today." *Joey didn't say so,* he thought, *but I had to say something.*

"I'll bet he didn't say so. He usually ignores me at school," Caroline remarked flatly.

Trying not to react to the twins' snickering, Jimmy asserted, "Well, none of us will ignore you today. Why don't you girls put your gift on the table and get yourself some lemonade." *Jeez! I broke Maggie's first rule: Never lie just to make small talk.*

Ann had dismounted the tractor, and Jimmy said, "Hi, Ann. Glad you came. I'll catch up to you in three days. Hope to get my driver's license this summer." Ann was usually kind and friendly to him. *I'll practice being social talking to her.*

She wore jeans and a white blouse. She tossed her light hair to the side and smiled as she spoke. "I'm taking my test next week. Wish me luck, Jimmy."

"I do wish you luck," he answered sincerely. *She's so humble compared to the Ryans.* They walked side by side back to the lawn.

"Without making a big deal out of it," she said in almost a whisper, "have you heard from Mary Schroedler?"

"I haven't. And I don't expect to hear from her, either."

"I just wanted to ask you directly. Some kids are saying that you and Maggie really do know where she is."

"Let me guess," Jimmy joked. "Could 'some kids' be Katherine O'Keran?"

Ann laughed. "Did she ask you already? I'm sorry to bring it up again."

"It's okay that you bring it up, because you believe me when I say I haven't heard from her. Katherine seems to doubt my answer."

"Why would you lie?"

"If I did know, there would be plenty reason to lie. I would be an accessory to the theft of Jack's car. But I assure you that neither Maggie nor I knows where she is."

"But if you did know, you wouldn't tell me anyway."

"Okay, you got me there, but I don't know. Really."

"I believe you, Jimmy. I'm just glad Jack is restricted to his folks' place. He's dangerous."

"Sooner or later his probation will be lifted, and I do not look forward to the day."

They both quit talking as the roar of a Model H Farmall, pulling a hayrack carrying six kids, drove past them to park next to Ann's Allis-Chalmers WD. Jimmy said, "Looks like both families of Schoens have arrived. And Ralph stopped to give Liz Brummer a ride too. Mary Ryan will be glad Liz is here, as are Maggie and I, of course."

"Yes, Liz is nice. Everyone likes Liz."

"Yeah, even Joey, who has trouble getting along with most of the girls. He says even Mary Ryan is nice when she's with Liz."

"Here come Joey and Maggie to greet the Schoens," Ann said.

"Maggie should be out here," Jimmy declared. "Most of them are in her grade or one grade below, and Ronnie is Joey's best friend."

In an effort to put Ralph at ease, Maggie walked directly to him as he dismounted the tractor. "Glad you came and brought the whole group. Picked up Liz too. That was nice of you."

She waited for him to say something, but he just smiled and nodded. *I'm going to have to ask him a question to get him to talk.* "How did you decide who would drive?"

He looked down and then to the side and muttered, "Well, the H is kind of my tractor. If the Oliver had been hooked to the rack, Laura would've driven. She likes the Oliver."

Maggie smiled and said, "Oh, I get it." Expecting he would say no more, she added, "Let's all go up to get some lemonade. Great to see you all. Thanks for coming. Now that the kids from west of the school are here, that's pretty well the whole neighborhood, except for the little kids."

"Mags," Jimmy said, "don't forget Dvoraks will be coming, and Robert too." Then, turning to the group getting off the hayrack, he added, "Hi, Laura. Thanks for coming." Jimmy liked talking to Laura, but her good looks and kind manners were a little intimidating. Her sincerity kind of scared him. Always finely groomed, she wore tan slacks and a green blouse today, and her blond hair fell to just below her ears, a shorter cut than most girls.

"Well, happy birthday, Jimmy!" Laura exclaimed. "But I suppose I'm not the first to say that to you today."

"Actually, you're the first."

"It's a few days yet. That's probably why. I suppose you'll be taking your behind-the-wheel test soon. Dad says I have to wait till I'm sixteen before I can even get a permit."

"June fourth, right?" Jimmy asked. *More social points for me, remembering birthdays.*

"You have such a good memory. Better than mine. You were saying that Robert and the Dvoraks were coming—I figure you mean Robert Plathe, and I know him from school, of course, but I don't remember the Dvoraks."

"You've not met them. They're our cousins, and some of them stayed here during the summer when we threshed with the neighbors, so only the neighbor kids we threshed with would've met them."

"And those neighbors all live east of the schoolhouse. We live west of the schoolhouse. There's that old invisible demarcation for social interaction." She laughed at the absurdity of it. "But it is true. We only saw each other during the school year at the country school, never during the summer. I always envied the east-siders."

"Can't imagine why," Jimmy said as he laughed. "I always envied the Schoen families west of the schoolhouse. It was like a Schoen dynasty over there! You're all so blond and good-looking." *Jeez! Did I really just tell Laura that she was good-looking? Thank goodness Marcella just drove into the yard.* "Hey, the Dvorak girls just drove in. I'll introduce you."

As the girls piled out of the car, Jimmy said, "Laura, this is Marcella, Helen, Janet, and Josephine. Marcy is seventeen, Helen is sixteen, and the twins are twelve. As you can see, they are identical, but I can tell them apart, usually. Today, Janet has the red ribbon in her hair and Josephine has the green one." He paused briefly before he added, "Cousins, this is Laura Schoen, our neighbor from west of the schoolhouse."

"Oh, I love your hair!" Marcy exclaimed. "You have the courage to wear it short, but of course, you're blond, so everyone loves your hair anyway. I have this plain dark hair."

"I'm sure you'd look great in any kind of cut," Laura assured her.

Figuring the girl talk was a good reason to move on, Jimmy said, "I'm going to go talk to your brothers, Laura."

"Wait a minute, Jimmy," Laura teased. "I'll bet you and Robert spend as much time fixing your hair as we do fixing ours."

"Maybe so," Jimmy agreed, and he laughed along with the others, but was glad when Maggie said, "I like the looks of that flat gift you have in your hand, Marcy. Follow me to the gift table where you can drop it off. We'll open presents early so just in case we get some records, we can play them for everyone to hear."

Soon all the partygoers were gathered on the lawn, eating popcorn and drinking lemonade. Jimmy announced that the first drawing would be held as soon as he checked that everyone had a number. Maggie put numbered slips of paper in the milk pail, and Joey drew the number.

"He'd better not draw his own number," Robert kidded.

"Jimmy, Joey, and I are not eligible," Maggie said. "We don't have numbers. We're getting gifts from the rest of you."

"Not Joey," Ronnie complained. "Joey should have a number."

"I'd sooner be an official person who picks the winner," Joey assured his friend as he mixed the pieces of paper. While looking the other way, he drew out the number, and then he read aloud so everyone could hear, "Fourteen."

"It's me!" Liz exclaimed. "I have number fourteen! I usually never win anything."

"Give me your number, and you'll get your choice of prizes," Jimmy said, waving her to the prizes on the blanket.

Liz immediately picked up the copy of *Little Women* and exclaimed, "I love this book and always wanted my own copy!"

"Wow, that's really nice!" Peggy exclaimed. "All of the prizes are. I could be happy with any one of those prizes."

Mom came out to announce, "Wieners and beans, potato salad, and Jell-O are in the kitchen. Get your plate and fork and come out here to eat, please. We'll bring the cake and fudge out here so we can all see the birthday boy and girl blow out the candles."

The two sets of twins were the first to get up to go to the kitchen, and as others followed, Ann Shaurel commented, "If the birthday kids are going to eat last, why don't you two open the gifts so we can be listening to music while we eat?"

"Great idea," Jimmy said. "Agree, Mags?"

"Yes! Let's get started. Here's paper and pencil. You record names and gifts, Jimmy. I'll open them. This one first. 'To Maggie and Jimmy from your Dvorak cousins.'" Maggie ripped the paper off the album and exclaimed, "*Elvis Presley*! His first album! Just what Jimmy and I both wanted. Thank you so much."

"Perfect for us both," Jimmy added. "That's only been out a month or so!"

Guests chanted for her to play it, and soon the group was listening to Elvis's rendition of "Blue Suede Shoes."

"These gifts are from Katherine O'Keran, Liz Brummer, and Peggy and Mary Ryan. Elvis's single 'That's All Right'; Johnny Cash's single 'Cry, Cry,

Cry'; Chuck Berry's single 'Maybellene'; a single by Little Richard, 'Tutti-Frutti'; and two singles from Bill Haley and the Comets, 'Rock around the Clock' and 'Shake, Rattle, and Roll.' Wow! You did a lot of shopping."

"Thanks so much," Jimmy said. "I'll bet you had some trouble finding these."

Peggy explained, "We got my brother Tom and Liz's brother, Joe, to take us around to places searching for them. It was kind of a fun trip. People called me to say which records had been purchased so we didn't double up on any. Your mom told me your cousins were buying the Elvis album, so we all knew we couldn't get that for you."

"Thanks," Maggie said. "You really went through a lot of trouble."

Maggie continued, "An album from the two Schoen families, *Moanin' the Blues* by Hank Williams. So many great songs on this one."

"Yeah," Jimmy said. "And he won't be making any more. He died young. He wasn't even thirty. Thanks for the album, you guys."

"An album from the Shaurel family," Maggie said after opening the next package. "Wow! It's Hank Williams's *Memorial Album*! Perfect."

"Now we have two great albums by the man!" Jimmy exclaimed. "Thanks."

Maggie read the next one more slowly. "From Robert to Jimmy, 'Honky-Tonk Man' by Johnny Horton."

Robert explained quickly, "The song has some wisdom on dating for you, Jimmy."

"Funny guy," Jimmy teased. "But really, thanks."

"Also, two singles from Robert to Maggie and Jimmy, 'Blue Suede Shoes' by Carl Perkins and 'Ain't That a Shame' by Fats Domino."

"Those are a couple of my favorites, Robert," Jimmy said. "Thanks."

"From Robert to Maggie," Maggie read, and she blushed a little when she opened the box. "A beautiful bracelet. Thank you, Robert."

"What?" Jimmy complained. "I don't get to wear the bracelet?"

"Shut up, Jimmy," Maggie said with a smile.

He laughed and stood up. "Let's thank the kids, Maggie. I'll start." Jimmy raised his volume a little to be heard over the record player and announced, "Thank you all for coming! And thanks for the great gifts! Lucky for us it's a nice day. Spring jacket weather. Lots of fun to be had yet. Some drawings and good listening. We'll play the records today in no special order so you'll all get to hear the songs. As you know, we just got the phonograph, so your gifts are our first records we've played on it. And we can move a lever to adjust to any one of three speeds so we can play any size record. Thank you all for coming and for the terrific gifts. Now, here's Mags."

Maggie began with a smile, but her face turned serious after the first few words. "So wonderful that so many people showed up to celebrate our birthdays. Our dear cousins, thanks for being here, and thanks to our special friends from the country school, which will be closing after this year. I can't imagine my life if I had not had the chance to meet my neighbors and play with them and learn with them in the little school on the crossroad. Thanks to you all. Now, please stay to eat more and listen to music and watch me and Jimmy blow out candles."

As she finished speaking, Mom and Robert came out of the house, each carrying a two-layer birthday cake. Joey carried the pans of fudge. Mom lit the candles, and the birthday kids each made their silent wish before they blew them out. As guests clapped their hands, everyone joined in singing "Happy Birthday."

"Jimmy and Maggie will cut their cake," Mom said. "And Robert and I will put it on your plate as you come through the line. No rush. Plenty for everyone. Get a piece of cake and a piece of fudge."

At first the partiers grouped together as they would have at a school recess, with Jimmy and Maggie missing Mary Schroedler as they sat with Robert on the picnic table with the cake. Robert got up to tend the phonograph as necessary. At the other picnic table, Mary Ryan, Liz Brummer, and Caroline Shaurel sat with Joey and Ronnie.

Deciding to give Robert and Maggie some alone time, Jimmy left the table to saunter toward the kids sitting on the grass. The four Dvorak girls sat with the three remaining Shaurels, and Peggy Ryan sat nearby with Katherine O'Keran and Laura Schoen. The four Schoen boys, too shy to push into a group, sat between but alongside the two groups of girls until Marcy said, "Hey, let's just make one big circle instead of three little ones. I want to get to know everyone."

The two groups moved around until they faced each other, which inspired Laura Schoen to remark, "That's better. What do you think, boys?" To the girls she said, "My brothers and cousins are really very friendly. They're just kind of shy."

Jimmy laughed and commented, as he sat down next to Ralph, "Except for Ronnie."

"Yeah," Ralph added, "but everyone wishes that Ronnie was shy."

They turned to look at Ronnie sitting at the table with the others and laughed, drawing Ronnie, Joey, Mary, Liz, and Caroline over to join the others in the big circle. Robert and Maggie came too.

"Hey, everyone," Marcy began, "our sister Anna is getting married on June ninth. Helen and I are in the wedding, and so are Maggie and Jimmy. The dance is at Lakeshore Ballroom. Her fiancé doesn't have many relatives, and the married couple gets lots of free tickets to the dance, so wouldn't it be fun if all of you came to the dance? I could try to get as many free tickets as possible and pass them out to you all. It's mostly adults at the dance, but there will be kids of all ages there, and we could dance the night away. The band will play mostly old-time music, but it's fun, and they play some modern sets too."

"I'm in for that," Laura responded immediately.

In the next second or two everyone was either saying "Me too" or nodding in agreement.

"Good! I'll see how many free tickets I can get," Marcy promised.

Ann Shaurel asked coyly, "If Jimmy's in the wedding, doesn't that mean he has to dance with everyone who asks him?"

All eyes turned to Jimmy, who looked up at the sky and then down at the ground. Finally, he spoke. "I've never heard of that rule. Have you, Marcy?" He looked around for support. "Has anyone?"

The laughs were loud and long. Marcy waited until the noise subsided before she said, "I think I have, now that you mention it, Ann. I know it's true about the bride and the bridesmaids, so it must be true about the groomsmen as well."

"You'll be an outcast if you don't," Helen said.

"Well, I'm already a social outcast," Jimmy complained. "So, no change there."

"Come on, Jimmy," Josephine added with enthusiasm, "you can do it."

"We will disown you as a neighbor if you don't," Laura said.

"My sister and I will never speak to you again," Peggy declared.

"That's motivation for me not to dance, Peggy," Jimmy joked.

"Don't be mean, Jimmy," Katherine said. "Be nice. We're not so bad."

"Never said you were, but does that mean I have six weeks to learn to dance? I'm starting to wish I'd used my birthday wish to wish I could dance."

"Heck," Maggie teased, "we can both learn how to dance in six weeks, but I don't know if I can teach you to be nice. I've failed so far."

Everyone laughed at that, especially Robert, who added, "Looks like everyone is rolling on you, Jimmy. Time to be a man. If you can break Jack Drude's wrist, you sure the heck can ask a few sweet neighborhood girls to dance."

"So, I only have to ask the sweet ones?" Jimmy teased. "Not many of those around."

"See what I mean, girls, about trying to teach him to be nice?" Maggie groaned.

"Okay, okay," Jimmy said, relenting. "I would be happy to take up the challenge. Honestly, I'm just a bit shocked anyone would want to dance with me."

"Don't get a big head about it, birthday boy," Peggy said abruptly.

"I'll make sure he doesn't," Maggie promised.

The pause was only long enough to hint that Jimmy was no longer the butt of the joke, but his joy was cut short as Katherine remarked, "Even if we don't get the free tickets, we should all try to go. I think most of us know the groom, Billy Thorson. He used to help thresh grain at Carlsons' place a few years ago, right?"

The moment became instantly strained. Maggie glanced at Jimmy, and Marcy's jaw dropped while her three sisters stared. But none of the other kids had a clue that Katherine had dropped such a bomb. Maggie would've stepped forward to say something, but she saw Marcy open her mouth to tell the story. But Peggy got the first word in to stoke the fire.

"Your sister is Anna, right? She and Billy have been going out for years. That's who she's marrying, right?"

Marcy said, "Actually, no. Well, Anna is my sister, yes, but she and Billy broke up last February. A friend of the family, George Lange, came back from the Navy last year and started dating Anna after she broke up with Billy. As it turns out, they fell in love and were both ready to settle down. He proposed yesterday. They got the dance hall on short notice because there was a cancellation. That's why the wedding is so soon."

Although the west-side kids did not know Billy because none of them had ever threshed at Carlsons' place, Maggie noticed that they seemed to sense the discord, and they joined the combined sigh of surprise at the news that Billy was not the groom-to-be.

Ann Shaurel muttered, "And they were such a cute couple too."

Maggie heard Katherine whisper to Mary Ryan, "I've got to write to B. J. tonight to tell him the news. He'll be as shocked as I was."

"Honestly, we were all pretty surprised when they broke up," Helen said. "Anna was crushed for a while, and I'm sure Billy was too. But things happen. The religious issue was a big deal. We all felt really bad about it."

"That's for sure," Marcy said.

Maggie added, "But Mom said that Billy is young and will eventually work through it."

"I'm surprised one of my brothers didn't know about it," Peggy said. "Billy was friends with both John and Tom during those days when we threshed with your family, Maggie, but they haven't been close for years. How's Billy doing?"

As if on cue, a car pulled into the yard and Maggie said, "I'll go ask him. He just drove in."

"I'll stay and tend the record player," Robert said.

"I'll join you in a minute," Jimmy added.

"I'll go with you, cousin, if you don't mind," Marcy said.

"Me too," Peggy added as she jumped up to follow.

Maggie hurried toward the yard, and by the time Billy parked by Schoens' rig, Maggie was there to greet him with the two other girls close behind her.

"Glad you stopped by," Maggie said with enthusiasm. "But I want to forewarn you that this group has just learned that you and Anna broke up. They're still kind of reeling at the news that she's marrying someone else."

"I know the feeling," Billy said seriously, but with a big grin on his face.

Marcella stepped forward to explain, "I'm so sorry Mom was so abrupt with you yesterday. She was just plain mean."

"That's okay. I don't blame her. She's had issues with me from the beginning,"

"But we all liked you so much, Billy. You must know that," Marcy said.

"I do, and thanks. Look, I don't want to mess up the party. I just stopped by to drop off this gift for Maggie and Jimmy." He handed Maggie a small box wrapped in bright blue-and-red paper just as Jimmy arrived. "It's not a record. I didn't know what records the others were giving you, so I bought you a new needle. It's a diamond needle, the best kind. It tells you in the instructions how many hours it's good for. When yours goes bad, replace it with this one right away so you don't damage your records."

"Very thoughtful!" Maggie exclaimed. "Thanks."

"Perfect!" Jimmy added, "I'm sure we will be playing the phonograph often, and we'll need a new needle before we know it."

"Remember me?" Peggy asked Billy as she moved to the front of the group.

Billy flashed a smile. "Of course. You're Peggy Ryan. I used to see you when I helped Carlsons during threshing. I remember the year Billy Joe O'Keran and Jack Drude got in trouble for throwing a sack full of snakes at someone. But you're Jimmy's age, right? I don't think we met until the next year when I met your older brothers, Tom and John. Haven't seen you or them for some time. Good to meet up with you again. Say hello to your brothers."

Maggie noted that Peggy was blushing, clearly flattered that Billy remembered her, but she managed to say, "You should come to the dance and say hello to them yourself. The whole neighborhood will be there."

"I don't know how welcome I'd be. I think Emma would sooner I didn't come, and I don't want to mess up Anna's big day."

"You should come," Marcy said. "You should definitely come. It's a big place. You won't bother anyone. You should come and dance with all of us. Now that Anna is in your past." She added, rashly, "You need to get out among people again. I'd sure like to see you come."

"Me too," Peggy added.

"We should get back to finish the drawings, girls," Maggie said.

"Is Uncle Martin in the barn?" Billy asked. "I want to say hello to him before I leave."

"Yeah," Maggie said. "He wanted to stay out of the party, and he said he had drinking cups to fix. After you see Dad, stop by the lawn for some cake."

"I'll do that. Say, Jimmy, I'd like to start coming over on Sunday afternoons to train again if you're interested."

"Heck, yes!" Jimmy exclaimed.

"Okay. See you next Sunday then." He left for the barn.

When he was out of earshot, Peggy said, "What a dreamboat."

"Back off. He's closer to my age than yours," Marcy said.

"Give the guy a break," Maggie said. "He's got some healing to do. Let's go back to finish the drawings. We should do them right away while we are all still finishing eating."

The drawings went fast: Ronnie Schoen picked the butterscotch candies, and Janet Dvorak picked the mystery. When Peggy Ryan won the final drawing, she picked up the teddy bear and exclaimed, "This would have been my first choice anyway."

As Hank Williams wailed "Moanin' the Blues," Katherine asked Maggie, "Do you think Anna will be inviting Mary Schroedler to the wedding?"

"Jeez, Katherine," Maggie replied. "Anna hardly knows Mary. They may have met a couple times at our place, but even if they were friends, please remember that I told you no one knows where Mary is!"

"B. J. thinks otherwise," Katherine said smugly. "And he also thinks that Jack Drude will probably not stick to his probation requirement of staying at home. Is Jimmy afraid of Jack?"

"Well, if he isn't, he should be. Jack is a danger to everyone."

"Jimmy's so brave. Peggy just told me that he trains with Billy in the hayloft every Sunday afternoon. Is that true?"

"Yes, and he gets up early in the mornings to train before milking." *Darn! I shouldn't have told her that, but she is so exasperating.*

"Wow, do you suppose he would show us what he does in the hayloft? I'll bet lots of us would like to watch."

"I don't know, and I suggest you don't ask him," Maggie said bluntly. "I've got to go. I think the record needs changing."

Meanwhile, in the calf pasture, Joey and Ronnie tossed a ball back and forth while James and Robert Schoen did the same.

"I don't see why we can't play catch in the yard," Ronnie grumbled.

"Cars and tractors and people are all over," Joey said. "We could break something or hit somebody. Besides, there isn't enough room to bat the ball if we want to play workup."

"Too many rules take the fun away from the game," Ronnie complained.

"Without rules, there is no game, little brother," James proclaimed.

"We don't have enough for workup anyway," Robert said.

"And if we did," James continued, "we would have to follow the rules."

"I don't like so many rules," Ronnie said.

"That's why you get into so much trouble, little brother."

"The four of us should meet up at the school ball diamond for a game sometime," Robert suggested.

"Better yet," Joey exclaimed, "let's set a date and time and ask all the kids from this year's eighth grade and down to meet for a ball game in July!"

"Great idea!" Ronnie exclaimed. "Do you think the kids would come?"

"Sure," Joey answered. "Look at how many came to the party."

"The party has music and food and stuff," Ronnie remarked. "The girls wouldn't come to a ball game."

Joey was optimistic. "They might. We could have everyone bring some food."

"I'd be like a recess with food," Robert said. "Only it could last all afternoon instead of just fifteen minutes or so."

"It'll be like a last recess," Joey said. "Let's start by asking Liz and Mary and see if they'll come."

The four boys raced toward the lawn to tell others about their plan.

CHAPTER 11

MARY'S COMPLAINT

Sunday evening, April 29, 1956

"Dory," Mary said suddenly, "tomorrow is Maggie's birthday."

"Your head's not in the game, dear. I thought you enjoyed our regular Sunday night euchre games."

"I do, I do!" Mary assured her. The two of them sat at a small table in Dory's upstairs bedroom, isolated from the outside world. After a moment of silence, Mary added, "She'll be fifteen."

"Here I thought you were pausing to figure out what card to play. Should've known better." Dory put a trump on the last trick, raked the cards in, and said, "I got my three tricks." As she moved her marker to ten points, she added, "I'm out. Want to play another one?"

"Sure."

"My deal."

As Dory began shuffling the cards, Mary said, "Then, on Tuesday, Jimmy will be sixteen. He'll catch up to me."

Dory put the cards down on the table. "I seem to be playing two-handed euchre by myself. Look, if you don't want to play, we can just talk."

"I wish I could've sent them a letter before their birthdays. We always used to give each other something. Like a piece of candy or a piece of paper folded over with *Happy Birthday* written inside. One of the first things Jimmy gave me for my birthday was an apple he'd picked from a tree in their orchard. A Haralson. He said that they ripened late in the fall and stayed firm a long time. I saved it by my bed for weeks before I ate it."

"Honey, you really need to quit torturing yourself with the past. Think about your life here. You can't go back there."

"The next year, Jimmy gave me a Wolf River apple. It was nearly the size of my head, but he told me it wouldn't be very tasty, so he gave me a Haralson too. That was the same year Maggie gave me a piece of fudge for my birthday."

"Didn't you hear a word I've said?"

"Sure, I hear you, but you talk about my life here as if I have a life! Sorry, Dory. I know I'm safe and you care for me, but I am so alone most of the time. And my attic room seems to be getting smaller and smaller. If I could just write to my friends and if they could write back to me, I could feel like I was close to them again."

"And that might work for a couple of months. But you'd be putting them at risk of being charged along with you if anyone found out."

"They can keep a secret."

"A secret is only a real secret if you and only you know about it. The fact that I know about you is risky enough. No, I don't plan on telling anyone, but secrets have a way of getting out."

"But you said that one day I could write to them. Why not now?"

Dory said, "You may as well write to Jack Drude himself as write to your friends now. That's how risky it would be. It's way too soon. Please, understand."

"I did write to Jack once."

"Yeah, you told me. You pretended you wanted to run away with him. It fooled him into parking his car where you could steal it and run away. I am very grateful you accomplished that, Mary. And I applaud your courage. You need to remember that you told me how close that it came to going all wrong. What if you had ended up in his clutches? Look, I'm grateful you are free of him and all of that. I am grateful you are here with me. Just be patient."

"Go ahead and deal," Mary said. "I've got nowhere else to go."

"Neither do I. And I'm not even running from the law. Not yet, anyway."

Although they both laughed at Dory's joke, Mary found it disturbing to hear the phrase *running from the law* applied to herself and to her aunt. She found it hard to think of herself as a criminal. She was more a victim of Jack Drude than he was a victim of her. But he would be the one who would try to get revenge. What revenge could she possibly get on him?

"Let's not play anymore tonight," Dory said. "I've got the feeling you want to talk."

"Yeah, tell me more about our neighbors."

"I've got nothing but good things to say, but here's a bit of news. I told you Katy was Irish, remember?"

"Yes. Her maiden name is Walsh."

"Well, her cousins by the last name of Cavenaugh told her their son's wedding is off. He and the Bartilik girl had an argument and they broke it off."

Mary was sincere but dispassionate. "That's really sad. Dreams and plans canceled forever. Sorry to hear it."

"And to make it worse, they were about to lose their down payment on the band and the reception hall, but Katy told me just today after she got a call from her cousin that another couple were just engaged and booked the spots, so they're off the hook."

"Lucky break!"

"I think the names of the new couple were Dvorak and Lange."

Mary's head tilted upward with sudden interest. "Maggie and Jimmy have cousins named Dvorak. I've met them."

"Well, now the Dvorak-Lange wedding will be June ninth, not the Bartilik-Cavenaugh wedding," Dory said. "Katy was sad about the breakup, but I told her it was probably for the best. Better to break up now instead of later."

"The Dvorak I knew was going with a Thorson, not a Lange."

"Funny thing about that too," Dory said. "Katy told me the girl was a red-haired beauty and had just broken up with a guy after five years of going with him. Katy thought that maybe breaking up went in streaks. I told her that maybe it was contagious."

The two women chuckled at the thought, but Mary said nothing as she yawned and stretched to hide her interest in the wedding couple.

Taking the hint, Dory commented, "You look tired. Maybe it's time for bed."

Once in bed, Mary lay awake. *The redhead is Anna. I know it is. Jimmy and Maggie and the whole family will be at the dance! What a fun time it would be if I could be there too. But I'm stuck here. Can't go outside unless I'm very careful. Can't be downstairs in the house unless I'm very careful. Can't go near the windows unless I'm very careful. Can't make a lot of noise. Can't go to town. Can't ride in a car. Jeez! I'll bet Jack has more freedom than I do.* She thought about how she had fooled him into thinking she wanted to run away with him. She giggled to herself when she thought of how he'd brought extra gas along because she had suggested it. And yet, it was that very desire for her that made him so dangerous. *Wouldn't it be great if I could fool him again to my benefit? Maybe get him arrested again while I got away! That would be sweet revenge for me. Something to think about. Maybe I'll ask Dory if I can start up the Model A again, just to keep it in working order. Wouldn't Maggie and Jimmy be surprised if I pulled into their yard driving it one day! Or if I showed up at the dance!* With the images of her two friends fresh in her mind, she wondered if they were thinking of her on their birthdays.

CHAPTER 12

THE LETTER

Friday afternoon, May 18, 1956

Jack Drude did not agree with his neighbors who thought that the law had been too easy on him. Okay, so he'd stolen some gas, a few tools, and some chickens, but Mary Schroedler had stolen his car. *My Model A is worth a lot more than that small stuff, and they got their stuff back. I didn't get my car back. And then, with a couple of lucky moves, Jimmy Carlson broke my wrist in a fight. Lucky little shit. I'll break his neck if I see him again. And Mary Schroedler's neck too!*

He hated being confined to his folks' farm to serve his probation. No more prowling at night or stalking the neighborhood for things to steal and trade for cash. And he'd sooner be locked in a jail than be in the house with his family. He'd been ostracized by his mother, ruthlessly bullied by his four older brothers, and only tolerated by his father for as far back as he could remember. He'd felt his mother's coldness toward him grow every day since he was a child; when he was ten, his father had helped him move a folding bed into an empty horse stall in the barn. From that time on, he was only allowed in the house to eat supper a few times each week, and often his mother was absent from the table.

He usually avoided seeing her too, but after Jimmy had broken Jack's wrist, his father had insisted he needed special care to get better and had him eat three meals a day in the house, forcing him to see more of his mother than he had for years. She gave him no sympathy, and he didn't expect any. He didn't want any. Sympathy was for wimps. At nineteen, Jack felt more alienated from his family than ever. He looked forward to getting his cast off and making his own meals in the barn, where the cats and cows welcomed him.

Eager to leave the house after the noon meal, he decided to see if the mail had come. As he strutted through the yard toward the quarter-mile driveway, he touched his wrist and ranted silently, *Damn Jimmy Carlson. And damn Mary Schroedler for lying about wanting to run away with me and then stealing my car and leaving without me. Me, bested by a kid and then jilted by a wench who's damaged goods anyway.*

His mind went blank for a few strides as he cycled back to his situation at home. *No one really seems to think I belong here, and neither do I. So, this really isn't my home.* He vowed to himself aloud, "I'm getting out of here as soon as I can!"

At that promise, he heard the familiar *squeak* of the mailman's brakes, and he hustled toward the end of the driveway. *Even when I get the mail, I'm violating my probation.* He grinned at the thought as he crossed the dirt road and opened the large country mailbox. Jack grabbed the daily newspaper, and as he opened the fold, he was pleased to discover several letter-sized items placed neatly inside. Getting the mail had always been the highlight of Jack's day, not because he expected mail for himself, but because he liked to sit down on the grassy road bank and rifle through the bills and read the newspaper before anyone else saw it. It made him feel as if he had some control in his life.

Plopping himself on the two-foot-high ledge of the road bank, he set the bundle of mail on the grass and began to sort through his treasure. To his surprise, the third item was addressed to him. The envelope was even typed. *Strange. Must be from the county or something about my probation.* But there was no return address. *A letter from the county would have a return address.* Suspicious, he turned the envelope over, and although he was eager to solve the mystery, he enjoyed delaying the discovery. He was sure the anticipation was more enjoyable than the contents. He took out his pocket knife, folded out the smallest blade to insert in the corner of the envelope, and carefully sliced across the edge.

Unsure of what to expect, he unfolded the single page, glancing first at the name typed at the bottom. *Mary Schroedler.* He scanned the page for a return address but found none before he read the letter to himself.

Tuesday, May 15, 1956

Dear Jack,

Sorry I had to steal your car. I had to get out of there even though you couldn't be with me. I hope your broken wrist has healed. I learned how to type, so I decided to practice by typing a letter to you instead of writing. I put no return address on it because I do not want you to know where I am yet. Here's my plan. On Saturday, June 9, Anna Dvorak will marry George Lange, and many people from the neighborhood will attend the dance at the Lakeshore Ballroom on Saturday night. Lots of people we know will be there. Jimmy and Maggie are even in the wedding. Get a good car and meet me near the east end of the Lakeshore Ballroom. Show up only after the dance, when most people have left. Won't we feel good when they see the two of us drive off together in a nice car, never to return. The ultimate revenge! You can live with me. There's plenty of room where I am staying.

I won't be there for the dance, and I can't tell anyone how I'm getting there, either. I'll only get there at the very end, so if you don't see me right away, just wait in the park, east of the ballroom. Don't tell anyone about this plan. Be sure the car is full of gas.

See you then, Jack. I know you won't let me down.

Mary Schroedler

"Wonder how she knows about the wedding?" he muttered to himself. "Or about my wrist? She must be writing to Maggie or Jimmy, the little shits. I should go to the dance just to slap them around some."

He put the letter down on the grass for a moment as he looked around at nothing in particular. Then he roughly grabbed it again, exclaiming, "Wait a minute! She ain't going to sucker me with a letter this time! Why should I believe her?"

He reread the letter carefully. "Well, she's right about one thing. She had to take the car to get away. And the cops had me, so she had to go alone." He shuffled to get more comfortable on the grass. *She'd better be careful showing her face around here. Wonder how she's getting down here. Maybe she'll drive my car. Naw, she's wanted for stealing my car, so she wouldn't dare. She must be getting a ride that Saturday. Maybe from someone going to the wedding.*

He set the letter down and shuffled through the rest of the mail before he picked up the newspaper. Losing interest in the front-page headlines, he let the paper lie on his lap as he returned to the fortuitous letter. *She seems to have a place to live. Why is she writing to me? She must want to be with me. I knew it all along. And she hasn't finked to the cops about the little secret we share. I might've caused old Matt's death, but she was the one who planned the cover-up. Yeah, she did a good job on the cover-up.* He stared around the driveway again, looking at familiar tips of the large rocks that poked through the surface of the driveway. Finally, he whispered, "There's nothing for me here. Never was. Might as well chance it."

Finding a car to steal would be easy, even if he had to hot-wire it, but he had an idea where he could get a really nice one, including the keys. Ziton might still be out with his horse-drawn camper, peddling his goods to customers until five or so on most Fridays. *On the Friday before the wedding, I just need to get to Berris's barn before Ziton stores his horse and camper and leaves with his Caddy to stay at his Minneapolis home for the weekend. If he's had a good day, I might get something from his cashbox too.*

CHAPTER 13

JOHN'S REQUEST

Friday morning, May 25, 1956

"We finished spring fencing yesterday," Billy said to his dad as he sat down for breakfast, "so are we going to put the cows on pasture today or wait until June first like we usually do?"

Rose spoke before her husband could answer. "Let's say grace before we start any farming discussions." She poured coffee before she took her place at the table. "Whenever you are ready, John."

After each family member bowed their head and folded their hands, John prayed, "Come, Lord Jesus, be our guest, and let Thy gifts to us be blessed. Amen." And without a pause, he continued, "Let's put them on pasture today. The weekend is coming up, but we're not going anywhere, and we'll be home to keep an eye on them, except on Sunday when we're at church."

Rose commented quickly, "It's so nice to have our son home again on the weekends."

"Don't forget. I'll be gone on Sunday afternoon for a few hours to train with Jimmy."

"When did you start that up again?" Rose asked with a disapproving tone.

"I'd talked to Jimmy about it at his and Maggie's birthday party. We started training together again the following Sunday."

"I didn't know you'd gone to the party. Did you know, John?"

"Yeah, Billy was a little late for milking that evening, and he told me about it then. Said lots of people at the party wanted to talk to him." John added with pride, "It seems, Rose, that all of the Carlsons' neighbors remembered our son from the days he used to help Martin and Mary thresh. They even urged him to come to the Dvorak-Lange wedding dance."

"Why didn't you tell me about it, Billy?"

"I didn't want to bring it up during a meal," Billy said, "and that's really the only time I'm in the house during the day."

"Why not? Are you avoiding talking to your mother?"

Billy was silent for a moment before he answered, "No, Mom, but I didn't want to set you off about Anna again."

"Set me off!" Rose exclaimed in a huff. "She wasn't there, was she?"

"No, she wasn't."

"But you went there hoping she would be?"

"No, I was pretty sure she wouldn't be there."

"Were her sisters there?"

"Yes, they were, and they were very nice to me about everything. They said that they wanted me to come to the dance."

"I'll bet," Rose said sarcastically. "I know that the one next in line is after you, son. Stay away from them. And don't go to the dance."

Billy spoke with more passion than he intended. "Mom, I want to go. I need to get back out there and let people know that I'm okay."

"I forbid you to go!"

"You've got to quit trying to run my life! You wonder why I don't tell you stuff. It's because you just want to tell me what to do!"

John said calmly, "Don't yell at your mother, son."

"I'm sorry, Mom, but you need to let me do as I please when it comes to my social life."

"As long as you're under my roof, I have a right to guide you, and I don't want you near that red-haired demon's family."

Holding back his anger, Billy paused before he turned to face his father. "Dad, you know how much I love this farm, but I think it might be best for all of us if I moved out and got a job somewhere. After the party, Tom Ryan contacted me and said they're hiring where he works during the summer at the river docks."

"Where would you live?" Rose demanded.

"I could temporarily move into one of Berris's small cabins. I'd have to leave most of my stuff here until I got something more permanent. I could still help you with some fieldwork, Dad, and even help with the milking some of the time, but I wouldn't be staying here or eating my meals here. I'd be on my own. I've been thinking about this for a while."

Rose stood up to exclaim, "My son is deserting me!"

John stood up slowly before he said, "Billy, I hate to see this happen. I thought the farm would be yours one day."

"Maybe it still can work out, but now I think I should be on my own a while. Maybe I can move back in after . . . time passes."

"So, you think it would be better if I was gone!" Rose screamed. "Is that what you mean? You'd all be better off if I was dead! Well, I can arrange that, you know."

Billy hesitated briefly before he said what he knew he had to say to calm down his mother. "Mom, please. Don't threaten to harm yourself again. I'll stay, if that's what you want."

"Of course, it's what I want, son. All I really want is for my family to be together."

"And you have that, but why not just ease up on me a little now that Anna and I split? You've won. We broke up. You got your way. What more do you want?"

"I want you to be careful. I want you to make the right decisions."

"And every time I make a decision you don't like, I suppose you're going to threaten to harm yourself. I can't live like that, Mom. I need to make my own decisions!"

"If I had let you do that, you'd have given Anna a ring last fall."

"And she would be marrying me, not George Lange. I would be happy now. Would that have been so bad?"

"She and her family would have lured you away from me. You would spend more and more time with them until we wouldn't see you at all."

"But that's over. Now, I just want to go to the dance. I don't need your permission, Mom. So, I will be going whether you approve or not. If I have to move out, I will, but if I stay, you need to let me make my own decisions."

"If you go, you'll break your mother's heart." Rose ran out of the kitchen.

"I'd better go talk to her," John said. As he hurriedly left to follow his wife, he turned back to add, "This was hard news, son. Hard on me and her."

Billy got up from his chair, gazed out the window toward the farmyard, and whispered, "Hard on them? Hard on me too. I love my mom and I love my dad. I love this farm, but I'm still ready to leave it all." Then, as he walked out the front door, he added, "And I loved Anna. Now I've got nothing."

On Friday morning at the Carlsons' place, breakfast was over and the kids had left for school. Mary and Martin sat at the kitchen table, each reading a section of yesterday's newspaper and enjoying a few minutes of peace before hustling off to do after-breakfast chores. Today's newspaper wouldn't come until noon.

A sharp rap on the porch door brought Martin to his feet to peer out the door's window.

Mary heard him say, "It's John," before he stepped into the narrow porch to open the door for his brother-in-law.

Mary rose quickly. "Come in. Come in. Sit down. I'll pour you a cup of coffee."

"I'd appreciate that, Mary. Thanks." John took a chair at the table, and after Mary poured the coffee, the three of them settled in before he spoke. "I know you are busy, so I'll get right to it."

Concerned about what possible issue could warrant this early visit and unusually somber demeanor, Martin and Mary nodded, eager to listen.

"I need to let you know about Rose. You know how she was dead set against Billy and Anna's marriage. The last year or so when they were dating, she moaned daily about losing her only son, and Billy and I witnessed her change. What had been an honest concern about her son changing religion became some kind of mission to control him in every way. She had to know where he and Anna went, why they went there, and his plans for the future. Last fall, I told you Billy wanted to give Anna a ring for Christmas, but when Rose got the news out of him, she went wild. She actually threatened to hurt herself. She's made threats a couple of times since. Once she even put a knife to her wrist."

Martin and Mary gasped, and Mary recalled Anna's words during her cookie-baking visit. *Rose threatened to kill herself while I was on the phone with Billy.* Mary solemnly said, "A suicide threat should never be dismissed."

"Do you think she'd actually go through with it?" Martin asked, amazed. "I mean, I know she can be wild and headstrong. When we were kids, she always fussed until she got her way."

"And she still does," John said. "I don't know if she would hurt herself, but she's convinced Billy she would."

Mary said nothing for a moment. *Anna told me about Rose's. Convincing Billy was Rose's goal. Stall Billy's proposal, and the problem would go away. Anna would give up on him.* Mary shrugged. *Rose got her way. Was her suicide threat just a bluff? A loving son wouldn't take that chance. No one who loved Rose would.* Finally, Mary broke the silence and repeated, "A suicide threat should never be dismissed."

"That's what Billy and I thought too. So, we tried to get her to understand Billy's love for Anna. All that seemed to do was to convince Rose that Anna was some evil person out to steal her son. Then she dragged Emma's name into it, saying it was some kind of plot to get back at her. The whole thing got way out of hand. Billy hoped she would get better, but she kept getting more nervous and sadder and angrier."

"Was she happy about the breakup?" Martin asked.

"*Happy* isn't the word I'd use. She was glad but used it as an excuse to say she was right all along. That Billy and Anna weren't meant for each other. She talked about God's will and fate and evil. Look, she was always strict with her religion, but this is different. The breakup only seemed to make her surer that Anna was evil. She has this 'I told you so' attitude toward Billy, and it's been really hard on him. He's such a great son. He loves his mother and doesn't want to hurt her."

"And Rose knows that," Mary heard herself saying. *Damn. Shut up, Mary.*

"Of course," John agreed. "And she uses that."

"Do you want me to talk to her?" Martin offered.

"Definitely not," John said. "It would just bring up the old squabble about you and Mary getting married and how she quarreled with Emma. Rose brought that up a couple of times. The scab isn't healed on that after over sixteen years. But thanks for the offer."

"What can we do to help?" Mary asked.

"First," John said, "I want to tell you that after an argument with Rose last March, I telephoned my sister. She and Rose were close friends in high school and were like-minded in their faith. I asked Betty to write to Rose to kind of reach out as a friend. I figured it couldn't hurt. Betty must've sent a letter the next day, but Rose only shared it with me this morning after the argument. Read it aloud, Mary."

Mary took the letter John handed to her and began reading.

"March 6, 1956. Dear Rose, Pastor Mark and I are doing fine, and I hope you are doing well, but my concern for your wellness is why I am writing. You are my oldest and dearest friend, and I hope you know that I will do anything to help you deal with whatever challenges you face in life. I know your faith is strong, but I think sometimes the Lord wants us to reach out to our sisters and brothers, and that He intends to work through us to provide comfort.

"Of course, I am writing this letter to you as a friend and sister in Christ, but I did not conceive of the idea on my own. John called me and asked me to reach out to you as a like-minded friend and Christian. He said that you seemed to feel alone and that he and Billy were helpless to provide relief to you. He also told me that you had threatened to hurt yourself more than once. I urge you to not do any bodily harm to yourself. Of course, you know it is against God's law, and I personally beg you to think of all of us who love you. You can do so much good on earth.

"When John and I talked on the telephone, I volunteered to come down to get you and have you stay at our place for a week or two. John agreed that you might like a vacation from farm life. He said the decision was yours. So, I invite you now to come up to stay with us soon. I need very little notice. Whether or not you decide to stay with us, telephone me soon. Or write. I desperately want to keep in touch with you regularly.

"Love, your friend in Christ, Betty."

Mary remarked, "This was written weeks ago. Did Rose call or write back?"

"This morning when she showed me the letter, Rose told me that she called Betty every week and wrote to her several times. Betty did the same. I was glad to hear it, and I think it put Rose on track to getting better."

"So, you came here bearing good news," Mary said with hope.

"Not exactly. At breakfast this morning, Rose discovered Billy had been to Maggie's and Jimmy's party and that kids had convinced him to go to the wedding dance. Rose forbade him to go, Billy threatened to move out, and Rose threatened to hurt herself if he did. It all ended badly with Rose crying in the living room and telling us to leave. When I went in to see her, that's when she showed me the letter."

"What can we do to help?" Mary asked again.

"I came here to ask you for a favor. Billy is determined to go to Anna's wedding dance, and Rose has forbidden him to go. I thought if you could ask him to check up on your cows that day and do your chores that night, he would be distracted and maybe too busy to go to the dance."

Martin exclaimed, "Then we wouldn't have to come home after the reception, change clothes, milk cows, clean up, and drive back to the dance! That would be nice."

"And he'd gladly do it for you. He'd feel proud that his favorite aunt and uncle trusted him with the milking. He knows good dairy families don't trust just anybody to milk their precious cows."

"Okay," Martin said. "When should I ask him?"

"He'll be over on Sunday afternoon to train with Jimmy," Mary offered.

"That'll work. Remember, I was never here. It was all your idea, Martin. No, maybe it would be better if it was Mary's idea. He's got a soft spot for both of you, but especially for his Aunt Mary."

Mary blushed a little, looked down for a moment, looked up to meet John's eyes, and said, "I'll take credit for it."

John took a sip of coffee before he said, "I'd better get back before I'm missed." He moved his chair back to stand and added, "Thanks a lot. This should help settle Rose. Maybe after the whole wedding thing is over, Rose will go back to being her old self, which sometimes was still a challenge, if you don't mind my saying so, Martin."

Martin laughed before he said, "You've lived with her longer than I have. You're the expert. But her old self could be pretty nice."

After John left, Mary commented, "Sounds like this courtship and breakup has caused real trouble. I hope it's all over soon."

"I think it will be all right in the end," Martin said.

"I hope so," Mary said, and added cautiously, "but she never lets go of anything. The squabble when we got married started out about religion, but it soon became about me and Emma, remember? And when we got married in your church, she seemed to accept me, but Emma remained a villain to her. I wonder if she isn't taking her anger at Emma out on Anna. All Anna is guilty of is loving Billy."

"Rose seems to want to control everything, especially her kids. I hate to judge my own sister. We might have similar problems with our kids. Ever think of that?"

"Every day," Mary said. "Every day."

CHAPTER 14

THE WORKOUT

Sunday afternoon, June 3, 1956

Maggie glanced out the kitchen window to see Billy's maroon '49 Ford parked by the barn. "How long has Billy been here?"

"He pulled in a few minutes ago, just before I sat down to read the paper," Dad answered from his chair.

"We're done packing eggs, right, Mom? I want to go talk to Billy."

Mom nodded as she stood to pull her chair away from the egg case and push it under the table. "Martin, the egg case is full. Can you carry it to the porch, please? We can take it to town next week." She took a chair at the table to read the paper. "Maggie, I'm sure Jimmy has already told Billy to stop by to talk to us before he leaves, but you be sure to remind him. I need to ask him about checking on our cows on Saturday afternoon and doing our evening chores during the wedding."

"I'll be sure to remind him," Maggie said. "I want to watch them exercise." She left the kitchen to put on her raincoat, but dawdled on the porch. She was curious about how Billy was managing the fact that Anna was getting married soon, but she was also curious about what her parents had to say.

"I feel a little guilty leaning on Billy to do our chores on Saturday," Dad said. "But John was pretty convinced Billy needs something to keep his mind off the wedding and keep him away from the dance."

"I'm pretty sure your sister is terrified that Anna could still mess up Billy's life, even after the ceremony."

"Sure. You're right. But I'd sooner do our chores ourselves than be part of his mother's scheme to 'protect' Billy. I mean, we could easily do them. We'd just have to get home fast after the reception to make it to the dance by nine. We've done it before."

"I'd even already arranged for Jimmy and Maggie to tag along with the wedding party as they barhop between the reception and the dance so they won't be late for the wedding march at nine fifteen, just in case we returned late."

"Rose may be right, though," Dad admitted. "Seeing the whole wedding party dancing—seeing Anna in her wedding dress—may be tough for him. Maybe keeping him busy is best."

"Well, it's too late now, anyway. We told John we'd ask, and I'm sure Billy will be glad to do it."

Satisfied that she understood her parents' motives, Maggie dashed out into the light rain but found the drizzle refreshing, so she slowed to a walk after a few steps. She liked rainy days, as did the whole family, especially in early June when the crops were all planted and they could delay cutting hay.

When Maggie opened the door to the hayloft, she announced, "Hi, guys. I came to watch," and she climbed up to sit on a small stack of bales in the corner where she could easily hear any discussion.

Winter feeding had nearly emptied the space of hay, leaving an open area for two ropes to hang from the rail fastened to the peak. Jimmy climbed one and Joey struggled to climb the other. Billy lay on his back, holding the rope steady as Jimmy climbed without using his feet. He greeted Maggie with a wave and a quick, "Hi," and then went back to talking to Jimmy.

"At the time, you know, late last fall, I felt pretty cocky about knowing how to treat a woman. I felt I was the experienced guy. That I could give my young cousin advice on what to do. On what to say."

Maggie remained silent as she watched Jimmy let go of the rope near the peak of the hayloft and rotate his body twice before doing a rolling landing on a thin padding of loose hay that covered the wooden floor. Without acrobatics, Joey climbed back down and sat next to Maggie.

"Your advice was right, though," Jimmy said. "You told me that a girl expects some progress in your attention. I did that with Mary. It was the right advice, but there were too many other things going on in her life. Things she couldn't control. And neither could I."

Billy gave a scornful laugh. "That's probably true with everybody. But it's too bad I didn't take my own advice." He used the rope to lift himself to stand. He and Jimmy walked a few yards to sit on some bales near Maggie.

This was better than Maggie could have hoped for—they were going to talk guy-talk right in front of her! She'd best keep her mouth shut and listen.

"I got distracted," Billy continued. "I lost sight of the most important thing in my life: Anna."

"Yeah, you told me if you wait, someone will beat you to it," Jimmy said, "but then you put off asking her to marry."

"That's what happened, all right. I can't blame her. She felt ignored, even while we were dating. Isn't it true, Maggie, that if a guy pays attention to you—no, I mean if he gives you his full attention when you speak—that you are drawn to him?"

"Sure, it is." Maggie was reluctant to say too much. She wanted Billy to talk.

"And if he carries on like he's thinking of something else, you lose interest in him?"

Maggie nodded but winced when Joey announced, "I ignore Caroline Shaurel all the time. So, when is she going to lose interest? Soon, I hope."

Everyone laughed, a break Maggie hoped wouldn't set them on a different path of discussion.

Billy said, "Someday it will. And then you might just wonder if that's what you wanted. Hey, I know you're only in the sixth grade—"

"Seventh, next year," Joey interrupted.

"Okay, seventh. You might want to be a little more interested in her. Maybe you'll end up liking her, even just as a friend. Don't rule it out. Don't do stuff you'll regret later."

Joey said nothing, and in the silence that followed, Maggie scrambled for the right question. "Why didn't you call Anna?"

Billy seemed surprised at her question. "I did. I did. I called her the next day and Emma said she wasn't ready to talk to me. I thought I'd wait a day, but I called her every day for the next seven or eight days! Each time Emma said, 'Anna doesn't want to speak to you.' About the third time I called, I told Emma I was going to drive over, and Emma told me that Anna had explicitly told her to tell me that I 'definitely should not ever come over.' You might imagine how I felt."

Maggie swallowed a gasp. Had Aunt Emma lied to her? Why would Billy lie about it? She could see the hurt in Billy's face as he told the story now.

Billy added, "At the end of one call—I don't remember which one—Emma said that maybe we weren't meant for each other. That it was fate. I didn't say anything in answer to that, but personally, I think I made some stupid decisions."

Maggie hid her anger. *Fate helped along by more than a few of Emma's lies.* But there was nothing to do now. The wedding was less than a week away. She might tell her mom—not that it would do any good, but it might help her understand that Billy tried to hang on to Anna. Would he have lost her without Emma's help? No one would ever know.

"Hey," Jimmy said, "we both lost our girls, but I'm not yet giving up. I don't know how, but I intend to find Mary."

Joey said suddenly, "On the way home from school, Katherine O'Keran told us she heard Mary was coming to the dance on Saturday. She said her brother told her."

"I'm so sick of her spreading that BS!" Jimmy exclaimed. "How would he know, anyway? Mary wouldn't write to Billy Joe O'Keran!"

"And even if she did," Maggie explained, "she wouldn't show up at a public dance where there are cops. She stole a car! And she doesn't want to see her neighbors, either."

Joey responded quietly, "Well, I didn't say I believed her. But I thought you might want to hear what I heard."

Recognizing that Joey seemed hurt by her and Jimmy's protests, Maggie consoled him. "You did right by telling us. Thanks. Really, we needed to know."

"Yeah, little buddy. Thanks for the heads-up," Jimmy added. "I just hope the rumor doesn't bring Jack to the dance."

"But he isn't allowed to leave the farm for now," Maggie countered.

"Rules never had much effect on Jack's behavior," Jimmy said, sounding concerned. "If he showed up, he'd spoil a good time. He'll probably be drunk too."

"Avoid him," Billy suggested. "If he's drunk, that's in your favor, but be careful. Drunk guys are slower than they think they are, and they often stumble, but they also have some dangerous false courage that can lead them to take bold risks. Don't let the bold risks work in his favor. Don't let him get in a lucky blow because you underestimate him."

"Right. No chance, I'll never underestimate Jack."

Billy stood up. "I need to stop by the house to talk to your folks. Aunt Mary said she wanted to talk to me."

"Okay, but can you help me with something else first?"

"Sure, what?"

Jimmy grabbed a thick piece of old wooden siding from a small pile near the end of the barn. "This siding was taken off the house before we put the new siding on a few years ago. There's a mountain of it piled in the weeds east of the house. I've been using it for making birdhouses and pens for ducks and geese." He handed the board to Billy. "I've seen pictures of guys breaking boards with kicks, and I thought I'd try it. Will you hold it for me?"

"Sure. I've seen this done too."

"I want to try to kick it while I'm lying down. There's good chance I'll end up fighting from that position." Jimmy laughed lightly, and Billy smiled.

"When I fall, I'll try to take position where one leg is straight and the other is bent at the knee at a forty-five-degree angle, with the ankle resting on the other knee, like this." Jimmy took the described position. "If the opponent is standing near my feet, I want to be able to kick with the bent leg, using my knee as the pivot point."

"I see," Billy said. "And you want me to hold the board?"

"Right. And keep holding it, because I may try to kick many times."

Billy kneeled and held the board firmly, calling out, "Ready!"

Whack! Whack! Jimmy kicked twice, the first sending Billy back a bit and the second hitting the board lightly.

"Sorry, I moved. That first one was a good hard kick!"

"That's okay. I need to be able to move my body closer if the target moves back."

Billy took his position again. "Ready!"

Whack! Jimmy's kick cracked the board.

"Good one!" Billy hollered. "You broke it against the grain!"

Jimmy remained on the floor as Billy brought over a couple more boards. Jimmy cracked one on the first try. For the second one, he delivered three kicks in swift succession, each time inching toward the target as necessary before delivering the next blow. The third kick split the board.

"Your leg was going so fast it was a blur!" Billy exclaimed. "I nearly fell on my ass."

Seeing Jimmy grin, Maggie said, "Nice one, Jimmy. And Billy's bigger than Jack."

"But, you know, cousin," Billy kidded, "the experts do this barefoot."

"Not me!" Jimmy countered. "We farm kids like our shoes."

As Maggie helped Jimmy collect the broken boards, Billy suggested, "Before I go, let's take a few runs at each other. My advice about fighting worked out for you, Jimmy. So, let's work on that."

"Let's do it."

Maggie and Joey watched as the two took turns attacking each other, jostling for control and struggling to throw the opponent down. Billy was taller and outweighed Jimmy by about twenty-five pounds, but both men had swift and decisive moves. Joey cheered, "Wow, they're so fast!" And Maggie found enough joy in watching to distract her from angry thoughts about Emma's lies.

After about fifteen minutes, Jimmy stopped. "You know, we'll miss you at the dance if you don't show up."

"Yeah, I haven't decided yet, but it's probably better if I stay away. I don't want to ruin anything for Anna or Emma."

"Well, Maggie and I have decided to make a real effort to mingle. I decided to quit being antisocial. To dance with the neighbors and some strangers too. We're out to charm."

"*Charm* was your word, Jimmy, not mine," Maggie said flatly. "I just said I wanted to dance with as many people as possible for practice. Mom says I can date when I'm sixteen next year. I can go to a movie matinee or something. Not having a boy take me home after the dance or anything. Mom said I'm too young for that."

"Well, that's fine for you. But I'm all out to charm the girls. I lost one girl I thought was mine, and I need to be more confident. I'm going to work on it. I'll dance with all the neighbor girls and practice meeting new girls too. I don't want to leave everything to chance. I want to be able to say the right thing at the right time. A guy needs a plan."

"Maybe I should ask Caroline Shaurel to dance," Joey said thoughtfully. "Think I should, Billy?"

"Heck, yes."

"Way to be," Jimmy responded.

But Maggie remained silent, wondering what would've happened if Emma hadn't interfered, wondering if fate controlled outcomes or if the decisions people made did. As they started to leave, Maggie said, "Don't forget to stop by the house, Billy."

"You bet!" he exclaimed, and he headed for the house.

Before Jimmy could follow, Maggie grabbed his arm. "What if Mary really does come to the dance?"

"I've started thinking the same thing," Jimmy said. "I can't really figure out why she would. Pretty risky, I'd say. I mean, if she just wanted to see us, why not come to our place some Sunday afternoon or evening? Why show up at a public place?"

"Maybe that's where her ride is going," Maggie suggested.

"Possibly. But really, how would B. J. know about it?"

"Katherine seemed pretty sure about the whole thing," Joey added. "She talks a lot, but why would she lie about that?"

"Well," Jimmy admitted sadly, "I have to admit, Mary's not exactly kept me in the loop on most of her plans."

"Me either," Maggie said. "Me either."

"Hey, let's catch up to Billy," Jimmy declared as he led the three of them outside into the light drizzle and to the shelter of the porch, where they shed their wet outerwear just as Billy entered the kitchen.

"Glad you stopped in, Billy," Martin said. "We have a favor to ask. Got time for a beer?"

"Sure."

Maggie hoped for an opening to ask Billy about the calls to Anna. Having him tell her mother that he called would be far better than hearing it secondhand. As Martin opened the bottles, Mary asked, "Would you check on our cows on the Saturday afternoon of the wedding and come back to do our chores in the evening? It would sure help us get to the wedding march on time."

Billy paused only a moment to consider. "Of course."

"Thank you so much!" Mary exclaimed.

Martin followed with "I need to tell you about the fresh cow. She calved this morning. Maggie called her Popcorn."

"She has puff-like splotches of white on her black belly that look like popcorn," Maggie explained.

"The kids take turns naming cows when they get bred," Mary said. "It's more fun than giving them a number."

"I agree," Billy said as the kids each took a chair by the table. "I can't stay long."

Martin continued, "Anyway, Popcorn is pretty nervous. She kicks a lot. I'll milk her by hand again tonight and tomorrow morning. Usually I put the bucket on the second milking, but she has a cut on her right front quarter that's pretty tender. I'll probably put the bucket on the other quarters tomorrow night and just milk the right front quarter by hand. She could be healed by the Saturday of the wedding, but if the cut is scabbed over, I suggest you milk her by hand and put it in a separate pail. The calves need the milk anyway. Jimmy will write feeding instructions for the calves on the notepad in the barn."

"And thanks again for doing chores for us," Mary said. "Rushing home after the reception and supper on Saturday to do chores and then cleaning up and getting to the dance in time for the wedding march would be tough for us."

"And it would interrupt our party time," Martin said with a wide grin.

Billy smiled. "It's best if I stay away. Every time I called Anna after the breakup, Emma answered and made it clear that Anna didn't want to speak to me."

Maggie saw her chance. "Did you call her many times?"

"Yes, I called her every day for over a week, but I never got to talk to Anna."

Maggie met her mom's gaze as they shared a moment of discovery. She saw the pain on her mother's face turn to anger, but neither said a word to follow up on Emma's lies.

Instead, Mary said, "Billy, you'll be fine. We all loved both you and Anna like our own kids, and we still love you like a son. You will discover another great girl for you out there somewhere. I know you will. You're such a handsome young man and so kind."

"Thanks, Aunt Mary. It's great to feel like I'm part of your family, I mean it, but I should get going." He finished his beer with a couple gulps before Jimmy walked him to the door.

The family rose and shouted their goodbyes out the porch door as he walked to his car. The kids stayed at the door to wave as he drove down the driveway.

After the kids returned to the table, Mom sadly admitted, "I'm sure we all realize that what Billy said contradicts Emma's story that he only called once."

Each family member looked down, as if ashamed to know the truth.

"Billy would have no reason to lie about it," Dad said.

"No," Mom said. "he wouldn't, but it does us no good to know now. No use telling Billy, either. We must all say nothing."

Mary waited until everyone around the table voiced their agreement. "In time, I'll confront my sister, but I will pick the time and place. I can't fix it between Billy and Anna, but I think Emma should know the gravity of her actions."

Maggie smiled. *Mom's right. Nothing to do about it now.*

CHAPTER 15

THE POWER OF WORDS

Friday morning, June 8, 1956

Although Jack had made his decision to meet Mary after the dance the same day that he received her letter, he reread it many times in the days that followed. Her words reassured him that there was a place for him. They offered an escape from a place that never felt much like home. Also, her words offered more than just a place to live. She seemed to be offering herself, and as he reread the letter, he loved to find phrases to reinforce that belief—*Won't we feel good when they see the two of us drive off together in a nice car, never to return. The ultimate revenge! You can live with me.* He had memorized the sentences.

After morning chores, Jack made a couple of cheese sandwiches to stuff inside his shirt, and he filled a quart jar with water. He gathered up a heap of twine strings from the pile that had grown huge from bales broken open to feed hay all winter. After stuffing them in a gunnysack along with the jar of water, he was ready to go. *Can't take the chance there will be enough twine at the barn at Crossroads.*

Leaving his folks' farm was a probation violation, so he couldn't let anyone see him walking to Crossroads Tavern, and he couldn't go in to visit Berris, a man who had tolerated his presence at his place regularly before his arrest. Ziton and Berris had been the closest things to friends Jack had known. Now they treated him like a leper.

With Mary's letter safely stored in his shirt pocket, Jack began his trek to Berris's. He had to stop at Schroedlers' farmstead first because his plan included parking a stolen vehicle there overnight. *I need to make sure the place is still vacant. Wish that damn judge hadn't taken my binoculars.*

Viewing the Schroedler farmstead from the safety of the bushes, he noticed no movement and risked knocking on the door, waiting several minutes for someone to answer. Satisfied the place was empty, he moved on, backtracking along the edge of Schroedlers' slough and then following his folks' driveway. From there, he looked both directions to ensure nothing was coming before he ran across the road to the shelter of the trees along O'Kerans' and Ryans' property lines. It was June, and farmers would be cutting hay, but the volunteer trees and bushes that grew on the property lines between the two neighbors would give him plenty cover. Feeling secure for the moment, he let his mind wander as he walked on the O'Kerans' side of the fence. *Yeah, Billy Joe's still my friend. He helped with a lot of pranks and even stole chickens from his own folks so I could trade them to Ziton for binoculars. I had to slap him up sometimes to get him to do what I wanted, but he always ended up seeing it my way. Too bad he's at that school in Missouri. His folks want him to be a priest. Ha!*

Jack followed Rock River east and used the tall slough grass for cover as he skirted around the south side of Ryan's slough. He had about a hundred yards of open area before he crossed the road to the shelter of trees that led to Berris's barn, where Ziton stabled his horse and stored his camper during the weekend. He had to be very careful now. *Me carrying a gunnysack would look suspicions as hell to anyone who knew me.*

It was a little after noon, and Berris would probably be in the tavern serving a few customers, but sometimes on Fridays, Ziton would quit early. If today was an early quit for the old man, Jack's plan would be totally foiled. With utmost caution, he opened the small side door to reveal the Caddy parked inside. *Good. Ziton is probably still out on his rounds. I can wait.*

He passed the time unpacking and untangling the twine and braided about twenty feet to make a rope. He laid out the others so he could easily access them in a hurry and then used a slipknot to tie three strands to the hammer loop on his jeans. He was ready. He didn't want to hurt Ziton, but he would do what was necessary.

He sat on the floor near the door where Ziton would enter to get his car after unhitching his mare from the camper and stabling her on the other end of the barn. Resting comfortably, he felt some pain in his wrist as he checked details—braided rope with a slipknot noose hung over his shoulder, loose twine strings hung from his side, and a large red handkerchief hung from his belt. All he had to do now was to wait.

In less than an hour he heard the large barn door open on the other side of the wall. Ziton talked to his mare as he unhitched and then curried her. "Nice job today, Sarah. I think the lady really liked those buttons, and she gave cash for the used dress." Most of the comments were muffled by the noise of movement. Jack was beginning to get impatient when he heard the peddler say, "Well, good night, then. Berris will take good care of you over the weekend. I'll be on my way. See you Monday."

The door slowly swung inward, and Ziton sauntered through the opening, tired after a hard day's work. Jack struck like lightning. He stepped up behind the old man and tossed the rope over his head as he bear-hugged him from behind, forcing him to drop the cashbox he carried. Jack pushed him to the floor, placed his knee on his back, and pulled the rope tight, securing Ziton's arms to his body. Ziton barely had time to open his mouth to holler, and when he did, Jack gagged him with the large red handkerchief. "There," Jack said. "I'm glad I didn't have to hurt you. But you can be sure I would've if I had to."

He sat on the old man as he tied his feet and hands with twine. Not satisfied that his job was complete, he knotted a strand around Ziton's arm and wrapped the twine around his body from his shoulders to his feet until the old man resembled a mummy. Then, after dragging him to a center post, Jack rolled his back to the post, looped a slipknot around his neck, and brought the twine around the post to tie to his ankles.

"There, I think you'll stay tied. I really don't want to hurt you, but I need you to stay here for tonight and tomorrow until after the dance while I borrow your car and use some of your money. I'll get you a blanket from your camper for a pillow. Might not believe it, but I want you to be comfy." He returned with the blanket, folded it, and placed it under Ziton's head. After stuffing the contents of the cashbox into his pockets, he opened the big door, drove the car out, closed the door, and sped off north to avoid driving past Berris's tavern, just in case he peered out the window to wave to his friend.

Jack had to be careful. He wanted to fill the car with gas and buy several bottles of whiskey, but in some areas either he or Ziton's Caddy could be recognized. Once he crossed the Minnesota River, he turned west and soon stopped at a small gas station in one of the southern suburbs of Minneapolis. When the attendant came running out to pump the gas, Jack powered the window down and hollered, "Fill it up!"

"Yes, sir."

Jack followed the young man in his side mirror. *Damn! I hope he knows where the gas cap is. I don't. Not too late to look in the book.* Jack reached into the glovebox for the book and began flipping pages as he checked his mirror to monitor the attendant's progress.

After a moment he heard the attendant shout from the back, "Okay, sir. I give up. Where's the gas cap in this classy Caddy?"

Jack's throat started to feel tight just as he flipped to the right page. "I was wondering if you were going to find it on your own. Try the left taillight."

The attendant set the nozzle on to begin and came around the front. "You need oil checked or anything else?" he asked as he began cleaning the windshield.

"No, that's fine. Just the gas." *My luck I've got to get a blabbermouth. Lucky no one knows this car is stolen yet.*

"This is the first fifty-six I've seen. Real sharp. Had it long?"

"No. I'm still getting used to it," Jack answered. *Did he see the manual on the seat?* He held up the manual. "That's why I keep the manual handy."

"Not many guys as young as you have a car like this, sir. I'll bet you're the envy of all your friends," he said as he walked back to top off the tank. Returning to the window, the attendant said, "That'll be two ninety-five, sir."

"Yeah, everyone loves a Caddy," Jack said as he handed him three ones. "Keep the change, sport." He sped off. *Didn't want to hang around and have the damn attendant think I wanted to visit with him. He'll remember this car, though. I've got to be more careful.*

Following the highway southwest until it gradually headed south, he crossed the river and found a municipal liquor store where he was sure the clerk wouldn't know he was only nineteen. His size and build usually deterred clerks from checking his ID. He parked on a side street where the car wouldn't be noticed. *No use taking a chance. If they check my ID and then see me drive off in a Caddy, someone might get suspicious. I've gotta be careful. Don't want to mess this up.*

He bought two quarts of whiskey and three pints of brandy. He also bought a half-pint because it was easier to carry and he could refill it from the other bottles. He stashed the liquor in the trunk and walked to a small grocery store to buy a loaf of sandwich bread, some luncheon meat, Twinkies, and several bags of potato chips.

Satisfied with his progress and pleased that the approaching darkness was giving him cover, he sped back to the farm neighborhood, following the road south past Brummers' corner and the schoolhouse, around Rosinceks' curve, and to Schroedlers' driveway.

After parking the car behind the barn, he removed the bottles of alcohol and groceries and hid them in the hayloft under some old bales. "If someone finds the car, they won't find my booze too," he said. "Tomorrow I'm gonna have a real party." He took the meat with him to store in the milk cooler overnight. Then, sure that his father would be done with evening milking, he hustled back to his folks' farm.

CHAPTER 16

WEDDING DAY

Saturday morning, June 9, 1956

"Quit counting, Mags," Jimmy said as they practiced waltzing in the living room at seven forty-five on the morning of the wedding. "You know, we're going to have to dance without counting aloud."

"One-two-three, one-two-three," Maggie continued, stopping only long enough to say, "My counting is better than your humming."

"Now you're just doing it to bug me."

"Okay, I'll stop. We'll need to practice having a conversation while we dance too."

"I don't know if I can do that. And we don't have much time to practice."

Just a few feet away, the door to the small master bedroom remained open as Mom sat on the bed in her white slip, fastening her nylons to her girdle. "You kids are doing just fine, but here's some advice: When you dance with someone, don't just start stepping off and turning. Take your dance stance by holding each other, and while you are facing each other and before you do any turning, do your steps to the left and right a couple times so the girl knows what the boy is doing, and she can follow. Jimmy and Joey, if you end up dancing with some old lady, like anyone older than me, they will appreciate you doing that because they know how to dance and they will help you out at that stage. Maggie, give the guy a chance to try this before you take off dancing."

"I'll remember that, Mom," Jimmy said. "But I'm mostly worried about everyone watching when only the wedding party dances or even when we're just standing in church."

"Don't be nervous about being in the wedding. You'll do fine," Mom assured him. "Besides, everyone will be watching the bride." She looked at Joey, who was sitting on the couch. "And Maggie, be sure to dance with Joey too."

As if on cue, Dad yelled from the kitchen, where he stood by the sink, shaving, dressed only in his underwear, "Hey, Jim, empty this drain pail, will you?"

"Here's your big chance, Joey." Jimmy gave Maggie's hand to Joey and moved quickly to the kitchen as he replied, "Be right there, Dad. Good thing I haven't put my tux on yet. Wouldn't do to spill dirty water on it. As a groomsman, I need to look neat and clean. People will be looking at us all."

In the kitchen, Jimmy waited while his dad pushed the red-and-white-checkered cloth skirting on the sink aside before he reached for the handle on the five-gallon pail placed underneath to catch drained wash water. "Got it," he said, and left for the back door. "It's always easier if it isn't running over yet."

Maggie hollered after him, "They won't be looking at you much, anyway."

Breaking away from dancing with Joey, Maggie swirled around once in her light-green bridesmaid dress, exclaiming, "Everyone will be enamored with the beauty of the bride and her stunning bridesmaids!" Looking at herself in a small mirror hanging on the wall, she muttered sarcastically, "Well, some of the bridesmaids will be stunning, anyway. Marcella and Helen will look great. They have beautiful dark hair."

Maggie heard her mother call from the bedroom, "The green dress really goes well with your auburn hair, Maggie." Before Maggie could reply, her mother added, "You look great, sweetheart!"

"Thanks!" Dad said as he hurried into the bedroom. "And I haven't even put on my suit yet."

"You smell of shaving soap," Mom said.

"And you smell of lilac perfume," Dad said as he leaned toward her.

There was little modesty in the Carlson house, and Maggie and Joey watched unabashedly as Dad slapped Mom's thigh lightly and made a clicking sound with his tongue against his cheek. "I sure like those silkies, though."

"Oh, you!" she exclaimed, brushing his hand away. "You know they're nylons. Silk stockings are from an earlier time. And don't talk like that. Maggie and Joey are watching."

"They're always watching," Dad countered. "And why shouldn't they be? We've nothing to hide. Even if we did, the house is too small."

"Hey, Maggie, come here," her mother commanded. Maggie obeyed. "We won't have much time to talk today, honey. I just want to tell you to have fun at the wedding reception and the dance. But at the dance, don't go outside with any boys. You're a pretty girl. Enjoy dancing and meeting people, and help us keep track of Joey."

"Sure, Mom."

As he pulled on his socks, Dad added, "She's telling you to stay out of the back seats of cars. Lots of things can happen in the back seat of a car. One thing can lead to another. In fact, that's probably why Emma got married so young."

Maggie listened with interest, but she had heard most of it before.

"Martin, don't. We know Emma had Anna seven months after she was married, but that happens to lots of good people, even us." Maggie saw her smile as she gave Dad a wink.

"I know. I know, and Emma and Joe are great people. Like my own brother and sister to me. And Anna turned out great, as did all their girls. Too bad the religion thing stopped Anna and Billy from hooking up. Anyway, at least there was no big grudge when we got married. No promises about the kids being raised this way or that way, and no anger about someone changing. Neither of our parents gave a shit by the time it got to us."

"Emma never quite got over it, though," Mom said bluntly. "And neither did your sister."

"Well," Dad said. "Rose can be a real pain."

The kids listened intently, piecing the mysteries of life together from adults' talk.

Maggie heard the door slam as Jimmy returned with the empty pail, bragging sarcastically, "I didn't even get any on me!"

"But now you'd better take your turn at the sink and hurry to wash up and get dressed in your tux," Mom prodded. "We've got to leave in about twenty minutes."

"Yeah," Maggie teased, "don't make us late. Joey and I are already dressed and ready to go."

"And Dad and I will be ready soon too," Mom said.

While Jimmy took his turn at the sink, Maggie listened to her dad talk as he and Mom dressed.

"Hard to believe," he said, "that Billy and Anna seemed so in love when they visited us on New Year's Day. Only five months ago they were all over each other, but now, she's marrying another guy and Billy is doing our chores. But it's going to be a great day!" Dad stopped to put on his shirt. "They get married at ten in the morning, and we eat a dinner with the wedding party around noon or so and celebrate at the reception the rest of the day before they feed us again with a grand supper. Lucky for us, Billy will do our evening milking so we don't have to come home for chores. After supper, we can do a little barhopping before we go to the dance at nine. What a day! Sure, I hate to waste a nice day in June. Plenty of work to do, but jeez! We can't miss the wedding of your godchild, Anna, though I know her relatives never would've settled for us to raise her, if something had happened to Emma and Joe."

"I need to remind you," Mom said, "that when I stood up for my older sister's first child, they had no reason to think then that I'd marry a Lutheran. And you're *some* Lutheran."

"You may have married a Lutheran, but this Lutheran drinks beer and dances too," Dad said as he thumped his thumb hard on his chest for emphasis.

And as he raved on about the day ahead of them, Maggie mused that her dad seldom babbled as he did on this morning. In fact, farm men were normally silent, grunting their approval or disapproval, keeping opinions to themselves, hiding feelings, knowing that their lives did not provide a freedom that would allow for others to read them. But it seemed her dad was looking forward to this day of celebration, a day he could set aside all worries of money and cattle and crops. And Maggie sensed her mother's growing uneasiness.

Finally, her mother said, "By the sound if it, Martin, you're ready to celebrate today. Well, so am I. Believe me! But I need to remind you that it will be a long day of celebration, and they'll be passing around pints of brandy to hit, I suppose—"

"Don't worry, darlin'," he interrupted her, "I'll stick to beer. I want to last for the dance tonight. But I will be drinking plenty of beer."

"The best advice to you kids"—Mom raised her voice a little—"is to drink absolutely no alcohol today, but I know that when you're in the wedding party, sometimes the more you refuse, the more some will take it up as a challenge to get you to drink. If they pass a bottle of something, just put it to your lips, pretend to drink, and then sputter as if it tasted bad. You won't have to pretend. But under no circumstances let yourself consume much of it."

"I don't plan on drinking any booze, Mom, no matter how much someone pressures me," Maggie asserted. "Did you hear that, Jimmy?"

"No booze for me either," Jimmy hollered back from the kitchen.

Joey said nothing.

Jimmy finished washing, went upstairs to dress, and returned in time to ask Maggie to dance. "I need more practice. Not just the steps, but I need to be able to talk and dance at the same time."

"Planning to meet someone?" Maggie loved to tease her brother.

Ignoring the question, Jimmy tried to talk about something else as they stepped off. "My dress shoes are so pointy. It was easier dancing in my work shoes. Why do they make dress shoes pointy? No one's toe fits up in a point that sharp. It adds inches to my foot. Makes it more likely I'll step on my partner's foot."

"Don't worry," Maggie said. "I'll watch out. Or maybe you're thinking of dancing with many new partners?"

"I admit it. I told you before that I'd like to meet and dance with some new girls tonight," Jimmy shot back at her. "I suppose you aren't fantasizing about meeting some prince charming!"

"Maybe, but I'm only fifteen. I really am not that keen to find any steady boyfriend. Anna just turned fourteen when she and Billy started dating. Maybe I should wait."

Jimmy ignored the comment. "I think we're doing pretty good, talking and dancing at the same time. Don't you?"

Maggie ignored him right back. "So, if you still plan on dancing with the neighborhood girls, I'm sure Shaurels will be there. And maybe Ryans and O'Kerans."

"I wish Mary would be there. That would make the night perfect. According to B. J. O'Keran, we know where she is. If I did, I'd go get her."

"No, you wouldn't. We both know it's best if she isn't at the dance."

"You're right. And you know how I hate to say that to you."

"And you don't say it nearly as often as you should."

"But we are doing a good job talking and dancing. Don't you think?"

"Now you're just trying to get me to agree with you."

Joey stepped toward them and said bluntly, "If Caroline Shaurel is there, I'm going to ask her to dance right away to get it over with."

"Good idea, little brother," Jimmy said as he stopped dancing. "But will you dance with her before or after you and all the young boys run and slide across the floor like running on a snow slide?"

"After," Joey answered, and giggled. "But it was you who taught me how to do that, remember? I was about five."

"I remember." Jimmy smiled as he gave Maggie's hand to Joey. "Your turn to practice with Maggie."

By a quarter after nine in the morning, the family had piled into the blue 1952 Ford and begun the drive to the Church of St. Michael at Wellerston, happy in the certainty that chores for the morning were done and Billy would handle their evening chores. What lay ahead of them over the next sixteen hours would be a ceremony of the essence of life itself, celebrating love, food, drink, and dance. Dressed in their finest, the family was eager with anticipation for the perfect day ahead of them.

Only a few minutes after ten in the morning, with the guests all assembled inside the church, one by one the bridesmaids inched down the aisle: Marcella with dark hair and wearing a light-blue gown, Helen with dark hair and wearing a light-pink gown, and Maggie with auburn hair and wearing a light-green gown, each young woman the picture of beauty and virtue in the holy surroundings of an ornate church.

The bride followed the fanfare of music, and all stood to view Anna, in her shiny empire-style white dress with lace overlay and a veil covering her light skin and flaming red hair, appearing as a goddess next to her somber father as they marched slowly down the aisle for all to see. The ceremony was truly a treat for the eyes.

The words were a treat for the soul, but they were also practical words to live by. *To love, to cherish, to honor, to sustain each other in sickness and in health, to be true to each other in all things until death alone part you. All* those truly listening were moved by the grandeur and gravity of the moment that followed, when the bride humbly walked alone to the side of the altar to kneel at the feet of a statue of the Virgin Mary, where she prayed and offered the Mother of God her bouquet. Hardly a dry eye was left in the church.

The mass required communion be given to the wedding party, who had dutifully fasted in preparation, and after they completed the holy sacrament, communion was offered to all those in the church who had spiritually prepared themselves.

The ceremony was one of wondrous solemnity, but a joyful applause burst out after as the bride and groom were introduced to the audience for the first time as "Mr. and Mrs. George Lange." Everyone stood, smiled, and applauded. The crowd spilled out of the church onto the wide entrance sidewalk, forming a line to congratulate the entire wedding party, who were already assembled in a neat single file to greet them.

After hands were shaken and hugs and kisses exchanged with each of the guests, members of the wedding party were swept back into the church for photographs, a long and tedious process that challenged the limits of their patience after fasting since last night. At half past noon, the wedding party sat down to their special feast, stomachs growling but still in good humor thanks to the groom's outgoing good nature and constant light dialogue with anyone he talked to. And he made a point to talk to everyone. Truly, if his goal was to charm the whole world, he had made a good start.

Only the wedding party were served the noon meal. Other guests were left on their own until the reception began at two in the afternoon. Except for the parents, George and his brothers, Walter and Paul, were the only ones in the wedding old enough to be served alcohol. Jimmy and Maggie clearly looked like teens, and although seventeen-year-old Marcella and six-teen-year-old Helen looked more mature, mistaking them for twenty-one would be a stretch. But none of the teens ordered alcoholic drinks, much to the dismay of Paul, who was paired with Helen.

He and Walter ordered rounds from the bar and sneaked shots from pints they carried in their suitcoat pockets, all the while urging the und-eraged party members to join them. Walter's wife, Jenny, was pregnant, so the brothers did not expect her to take any shots, but they expressed loud disappointment that Jimmy didn't take a swig and that none of the women, including the bride, were drinking any alcohol. The two Dvorak girls did leave an opening by replying, "Maybe later." But the brothers were mostly disappointed that their new sister-in-law, who seemed so fun and was so beautiful, had committed herself to staying dry her entire wedding day. However, the day was still young.

CHAPTER 17

ZITON FOUND

Saturday morning, June 9, 1956

"I trusted that kid for years! And yesterday he grabs me from behind, binds me up, takes my money, and drives away with my car!" Ziton exclaimed in a hoarse voice as Berris removed the gag at about ten on Saturday morning. "I gave him good deals! Then in February I find out he's been trading me stolen goods. And now this!"

Berris nodded. "He came here often. I trusted him too before he got caught stealing. I even let him stay overnight in one of my cabins sometimes during off season. I let him use my phone to call you in Minneapolis. It was long-distance, but he'd pay. You can just never be too sure of people."

"What's driving that boy?" Ziton tried to clench his bound fists. "That look in his eyes! He's just wild!"

"Take it easy, Ziton," Berris said. Although the two men had been friends and had done business with each other for decades, they were known to each other, as they were to everyone in the countryside, by their last names only. Not a sign of disrespect, but quite the opposite. "Wait until I untie you," Berris said. "These twines are wrapped and knotted pretty tight. Not easy to get loose. There will be plenty time for you to tell me what happened, but first we got to see if you're okay."

"I just need some water. I've been sucking on this gag all night."

"Don't talk more until I get you a drink." Berris brought him a dipper of water before he said, "Now, slow down. Tell me the details, and then I'll call the sheriff."

"My brother would not have thought it too strange when I missed synagogue on Friday, but I know he will be worried about me when I don't show up this morning."

"We'll call your brother too." Berris focused on loosening the twines.

Ziton was known for his smooth voice and low-pitched, comforting cadence, but today, he was so angry that he stuttered and spit as he told his story. After he finished, Berris called the sheriff to report that Jack Drude had attacked Moses Ziton and stolen his car. After getting a detailed description of the car for the local police, the sheriff said he'd be right out.

Sheriff Kaeler and Deputy Schultz arrived at Berris's tavern nearly two hours later to find the two men seated at a table. Ziton sipped water from a glass and assured them that he was feeling better. Berris asked if they had found the car.

"The Minnesota State Patrol has the information on the vehicle, but he's probably clear across the state by now," the sheriff explained. "But don't worry, Ziton, we'll get him. The important thing is that you're okay. What more can you tell me about the incident? Let's start with what Jack was wearing."

After the deputy recorded that answer and several more in his notebook, the sheriff said, "Now, is there anything at all you can remember that might give us a hint as to where he was headed?"

Ziton paused. "I don't think he knew Berris would discover me as soon as he did. Drude said he needed me to stay tied till after the dance on Saturday."

"Wow!" Deputy Schultz exclaimed. "Dumbass Drude gave it away. We know where he'll be tonight!"

"Maybe," the sheriff said. "Let's not underestimate him, though. I'll call Lester Grossman. He usually does cop duty for the ballroom on Saturdays. I'll give him descriptions so he can keep an eye out. We don't want to have a big show of police cars there. It would just scare Drude away, and I know ballroom owners always prefer if our presence is subtle for business reasons."

He turned to his deputy. "We'll park a couple police cars in alleys nearby so we have backup. If we spot him, I don't think he'll give us much trouble, but he broke his parole so he must figure he won't get caught."

"He'll be desperate, right, Sheriff?" Deputy Schultz seemed to almost drool in anticipation of the arrest. "I arrested him just last February. This'll be twice in just a few months. And this time, we got him on some serious charges."

"We don't have him yet," the sheriff said thoughtfully. "In fact, right now, we have no idea where he is. I doubt if the state patrol will spot him. Drude will probably stay off the main roads. In the meantime, can we call his folks from here to see if he came home?"

"They don't have a phone," Berris said. "Drude used to come over to use mine."

"Well, it ain't that far," the sheriff said. "Better if we go over there anyway." He looked at his watch. "We can get there by a little after noon." He turned to Ziton. "Where can we get in touch with you?"

"My brother is coming to get me, so I won't be here much longer. You have my home number, and you can always call Berris."

Sheriff Kaeler paused on his way to the door. "If any of you think of anything we should know, call my office. I'll be checking in regularly." Deputy Schultz rushed to open the door for him, and both men exited to the parking lot.

Berris and Ziton sat at the table in silence for a few minutes. Ziton finally said, "He had me fooled. Sure, I was surprised when the cops told me he was stealing from his neighbors, but that was nothing compared to this. He attacked me. He said he didn't want to hurt me but he would if he had to. I believed him too!"

"Something is driving him, that's for sure," Berris said.

"You know," Ziton said suddenly, "maybe he has a girl he wants to see. Last spring, he bought a nice necklace and bracelet from me. Maybe he has a girlfriend."

"He was after that Schroedler girl, but she's the one that ran away."

"Took his car too!" Ziton exclaimed. "I guess that's why he needed mine."

Unaware that Ziton had been found and the sheriff was looking for him, Jack did not hurry to leave home. He retrieved the luncheon meat from the cooler, filled a couple of quart jars with fresh water, and stuffed all of it into a pillowcase along with some clothes, several chunks of cheese, and a box of crackers. Careful not to signal that he planned to never return, he avoided being spotted by his family as he carried out his baggage. By noon he was clear of the yard, and he raced to Schroedlers' place with a vision of new freedom in front of him—freedom from a home where he wasn't wanted and a family where he didn't belong.

He found the car parked safely where he had left it, and he stored his clothes and food in the passenger seat before he went to get the booze. It was half past noon before he sat in the driver's seat of the Caddy with a half-pint of brandy in one hand and a meat and cheese sandwich in the other. After taking a couple of long swigs from the bottle, he inspected the car, admiring its fine leather upholstery.

"She's gonna love this car!" he exclaimed to no one as he took a letter out of his breast pocket to read again. *I know you won't let me down.* The words made him smile as he stuffed the letter back into his shirt pocket, leaving the empty envelope on the seat beside him.

Inspiration from Mary's words added to his good humor, and he began to hum "She'll Be Coming 'Round the Mountain When She Comes" as he finished the sandwich and the half-pint in short order. "Good thing Ziton had some cash on him. More than I expected. I'll have a party while I wait. She'll crap when she sees this car. First-class buggy, this Caddy. Let's see if I can figure out all these controls."

Jack didn't drink alcohol often, not because he didn't want to, but because it cost money and he was always short of cash. But he never questioned his tolerance to drink all day and drive to the dance. He just knew he could handle it. But when he opened a quart of whiskey, he started to think of things that could go wrong with his plan. *What if someone drove into Schroedlers' yard by mistake? Maybe I should drive somewhere else to wait. Somewhere closer to Lakeshore Ballroom.*

He started the Caddy, intending to drive out of the yard, but as he fiddled with the dials to turn on the air conditioning and roll up the power windows, he nearly ran into a tree near the driveway. Slamming on the brakes, he hollered, "Wow, I love this power shit, but maybe I gotta adjust stuff before I take off driving." Sideways in Schroedlers' driveway, he set the air-conditioning before he sped off—only to stop at the end if the driveway. *I'd better turn south to avoid going back toward the neighborhood. And I'll stick to the small gravel roads on the way to Lakeshore Ballroom.*

"He was here last night, and he did chores this morning," Jacob Drude told Sheriff Kaeler. "I didn't see him leave, but he ain't here now. Search the place if you want."

"Check the house, Schultz," Sheriff Kaeler ordered. Then, turning to Jacob, he asked, "Do you have any idea where he could've gone?"

"He's been gone for an hour or so. I know he ain't supposed to leave the place, but he does, once in a while, walk over to Schroedlers' place through the trees there." Jacob pointed west. "I hope he won't get in trouble for breaking probation. I didn't mean to tell on him."

"Don't worry about it, Jacob," Sheriff Kaeler said. Then, turning toward the house, he hollered, "Schultz! Finish that up and get out here!"

Deputy Schultz appeared in the doorway. "Yes, Sheriff?"

"Drude might've parked the car at Schroedlers' place overnight. You go through the trees, and I'll drive the car around to the yard to meet you." As he hurried to the car, he added, "Maybe we can catch him before he leaves."

Unaware that Sheriff Kaeler was about to turn south toward Rosinceks' and Schroedlers' farms, Jack sat in the Caddy at the end of Schroedlers' driveway for less than a minute, considering his route. "I'll avoid Newburg too," he said, and he turned to take the road south. "Those folks might recognize Ziton's Caddy." After he turned west onto the road to Lakeland City, he took a long swig from the whiskey, and then an idea hit him. "I know exactly where I can party until after the dance starts! The gravel pits!" In a few minutes he turned south onto a narrow, curvy road where boulders embedded deep below the roadbed protruded above the surface. He slowed to a crawl as the washboard-like surface challenged even the fine suspension of the Caddy. The road wound uphill to overlook a mile or so of poor farmland on the left and deep abandoned gravel pits on the right, their surfaces overrun with tall sweet clover plants. "That stuff will grow in plain gravel," Jack said, smiling, "and it grows tall." He turned right into a steep driveway that descended about thirty feet into the pit before the grade leveled off to a flat bottom. Jack drove swiftly over the loose gravel surface, causing yellow blossoms to whip the side of the Caddy and infuse their sweet odor into the warm summer air. He slowed the car to avoid hitting any large rocks left on the flat bottom of the pit. This was not his first visit there, but he knew the steep sides could slide, rolling rocks into new areas.

"The woods are clear, Sheriff," Deputy Schultz assured his boss when they met at Schroedlers' yard.

"He was here, all right," Sheriff Kaeler said as he examined the tracks on the dirt surface. "But he's not here now, and I don't know for sure when he left or where he might be headed."

"Should I check the house?"

"Yeah, and I'll check the barn. Meet back here as soon as possible, and we'll make a quick drive to Lakeland City. Maybe he decided to get a good parking spot behind the ball field and wait for the dance to start."

In less than ten minutes, the sheriff and his deputy were speeding toward Lakeland City. Upon their arrival, they scoured the parking lots and the small roads used by trucks to restock the concession stand. They found nothing. Frustrated, Sheriff Kaeler said, "I know all the nooks where kids park their cars to drink and make out, and we've covered them all. Any ideas, Schultz?"

"We should check again later."

"Right. And we should relay the ideas to the city patrol car too. After we stop to talk to the city police, we'll check back at the office for messages. Then we'll get ready for a long night."

"Will we be coming back here, sir?"

"If we don't find him first, we'll station ourselves around here after the dance starts."

Thirty yards or so into the floor of the gravel pit, Jack turned right to drive parallel to the rough road that had led him to the pit, and, after covering another fifty yards, he parked, satisfied the big black Caddy was not visible from any direction but the sky. After he turned off the air-conditioning and powered down the two front windows to encourage a cross breeze to blow through, he shut the engine off and grabbed his quart of whiskey, a bag of potato chips, and a couple of Twinkies. He kicked his shoes off and stuck his feet out the window. With the sweet smell of clover tickling his nostrils, the breeze cooling his feet, and the taste of whiskey burning his tongue and throat, he exclaimed, "This is the life!"

He didn't examine his feelings, but at the moment he felt exhilarated. He had an afternoon and evening to get drunk, and if he were lucky, he might get a chance to get even with Jimmy Carlson. Most of all, though, he expected to meet Mary, and the two of them would drive away in Ziton's Caddy. He felt triumphant from every angle.

Jack emptied the first bottle sooner than he expected. He tipped the bottle up, tilting his head back to catch the last drops, and tossed the empty bottle out the window. He had plenty more booze and plenty more food too. But now he felt a bit uneasy. He needed some air. The sun glared into his face as he crawled out of the car door to stand, but his legs let him down and the soft sand surface came up to greet him abruptly. He tasted the sand, rolled on his back, and laughed at the bright sky. He slurred, "Screw it all! I'm gone from this place. This place of cold stares and beatings from brothers!"

He struggled to get up but fell down again near the car. Grabbing the open door, he managed to roll on his side, get his knees under himself, and stand. The world spun, but he waited till it stopped before he climbed the steep bank of sandy gravel, each step punching a deep hole and causing the sand to slide, slowing his progress. He pulled on the strong stems of sweet clover to aid his climb, sometimes uprooting them and falling back a few feet before he recovered his balance. Near the top, he turned his face to the wind to inhale the fresh air he desperately needed to settle his stomach. He had a jar of water in the car, but wishing for it was not the same as tasting it. His stomach roared like an engine on full throttle, and he had no choice but to let it go. Taking a step down the hill, he felt himself falling forward as his stomach spewed out its mixture of alcohol, potato chips, sandwiches, and Twinkies. His retching continued even as his face met the sand. At last he felt empty, and although his head throbbed and his parched throat cried for water, he pulled his sweating body into the shade of a large tuft of clover a moment before his mind went dark. With his legs stretched uphill on the sandy surface, exhaustion and alcohol swept him away to a deep sleep.

CHAPTER 18

RECEPTION

Saturday afternoon, June 9, 1956

As the Carlson family entered Hilda's Hall promptly at 2:00 p.m., Mom commented, "This is *the place* for a wedding reception. They're known for their homemade rolls, poppyseed kolackies, and large portions of everything. Emma told me everyone will be served roast beef and chicken with potatoes, gravy, and dressing. I'm sure there'll be vegetables too. Usually corn and coleslaw."

"Where should I put the paper plate with the brownies you made, Mom?" Maggie asked.

"On the small table by the wedding cake. They'll move it to where they want it. We won't be eating until five, anyway. Until then we have three hours of free drinks."

"Pop too?" Joey asked.

"Yes, pop too," Dad said. "But don't drink too much just because it's free."

"Be sure to take your own advice, Martin," Mom remarked seriously. "Three hours for free drinks is a long time."

"I'll stick with beer," Dad promised. "No hard stuff for me."

"And you kids will stick with pop, right?" Mom said.

"Pop is my first choice," Jimmy said.

Maggie added, "Same here."

"Me too," Joey said. "And I plan on starting right now."

With two bartenders drawing beer from kegs, pouring whiskey to mix drinks, and opening and serving bottles of pop, there was little waiting at the bar, mainly because no money was collected. Jimmy and Maggie walked around greeting others but soon settled down at a table with Marcy and Helen.

"How did you like the ceremony?" Marcy asked.

"Beautiful, but long," Maggie said.

"What was the deal with Anna taking the flowers over to the statue?" Jimmy asked.

"It's the Virgin Mary," Helen said.

"Oh," Jimmy answered, pretending to understand, "I get it."

"Don't you think St. Michael is a beautiful church?" Helen asked.

"Yeah," Jimmy responded. "Lots of ornate walls, and even the ceiling had designs on it. I liked the stained-glass windows."

Maggie agreed before she said, "I wish I had worn my new shoes before today to break them in a little. Although they're better now than when I started the day."

"That's good," Marcy said, "because you want the shoes to be comfortable for the dance tonight." Then she leaned her head in and gestured them all to do the same. "Look, Walter and Paul are planning to steal the bride and want us girls to steal the groom. It's my job to explain the plan to you, and I will do that, but first, Jimmy and Maggie, I need to tell you a secret that is bound to get out soon anyway. I want you to know ahead of time, but you mustn't tell anyone. It's a big deal. Are you ready?"

Jimmy looked at Maggie, and they both nodded.

Marcy whispered, "Anna's pregnant. She and George figure the baby will be due in December, maybe around Anna's birthday."

Jimmy hid his surprise as he looked at Maggie, who said nothing.

"Anna figures no one will be too surprised at her having a baby six months after the wedding, right? What do you think?"

"Well," Jimmy said. "Congratulations to them both. But why are you telling us?"

"And," Maggie asked solemnly, "does Anna know you're telling us? Or George?"

"Yes, because George wants you, Jimmy, to look out for Anna when they steal her. Anna does not know about the steal. George kept it from her because he figured she wouldn't go along with it and his brothers are dead set on doing it. Tough choice for him, but that's why your help is so important. Anna will refuse to drink, and you need to be on her side."

Jimmy shifted uncomfortably in his chair but answered boldly, "Anna can count on me. Whatever it takes."

Maggie said, "Be careful. Walter is pretty good, but Paul is kind of a jerk."

"Right," Helen said. "I'm paired with the jerk."

"Okay," Marcy said. "I'll outline the plan, but don't tell anyone, not even your folks, until the moment it is set to happen."

"Right," Jimmy said as Maggie and he nodded their agreement and leaned forward for instructions.

Time passed swiftly as old friends and newly acquainted guests mingled with each other, and about four forty-five, Emma and Mary urged the bridal party to take their places at the head table, which faced the three hundred or so guests. Attendees lined up in one swift-moving line that split to either side of the large buffet table. Soon the hall hushed as the priest said grace, and conversation remained low as the clanking of silverware against plates echoed in the large serving hall.

As people finished their meal, the usual speeches of praise and thanks were given, with the best man delivering entertaining tidbits about his brother and the maid of honor contributing a few anecdotes about her older sister. During her delivery, Marcella was an animated personality, moving about with quick gestures, tossing her hair to the side with a smooth flick of her head, and rising to the balls of her feet to emphasize a point. She joked, "Anna had always been Mom and Dad's favorite. She was the prettiest, the most talented, the smartest in school, and the most perfect child in every way." After a short pause she added, "We'll be *sooo* glad to be rid of her!" And the audience roared with laughter, understanding that the sad truth can be funny in the right context.

Walter's speech was less animated, but not without entertainment value. He, too, raved about his brother's home status, saying, "George made hard work look easy, which made the rest of us have to work harder. He could reach the top shelves without the ladder, which means the rest of us had to fetch the ladder. His handsome appearance drew girls to him, which made Paul and me have to try harder, and he was always Mom and Dad's favorite." After a pause, he added, "You guessed it. He pissed us off!" The audience loved it.

Walter went on, "But we missed him when he joined the Navy. We learned how much he did for all of us. We missed his constant bad jokes. We missed his unwavering can-do, positive attitude. And we missed kidding him about his thick red hair, which was central to his identity everywhere he went. Clearly, he found no female match for himself while in the Navy, for after six years of dating girls in every port, he rushed home to marry a beautiful bride with thick red hair to match his. And it only took him seven months after he returned from the Navy to bring her to the altar. And I, for one, think they make the loveliest of couples. Please give them a hand as they stand. Then clink your glasses until they kiss!"

Mary listened to the speeches with love, humor, and some discomfort. Most guests knew that George was not Elmer's biological son, and they didn't care, but was Elmer still sensitive to it? Had Walter intended to call attention to the difference in appearance among the brothers? Had he intended to show some resentment? Short, stocky, and with a neck like a workhorse's, Elmer sat in his chair, smiling and taking it all in stride. His two sons were built like him and had his dark hair as well. They were handsome, but in a different way than tall, red-haired George, who had the athletic grace of a dancer and the outgoing personality of an honest salesman.

Mary had been aware of the sister-rivalry in Emma's family. It was no less or more brutal among the four girls than in any family. But it seemed Marcella had made an effort to show her pain as well as praise her sister. *Good job, Marcy. I love Emma's girls like my own. Gee, I wonder if Maggie feels slighted. I'll have to watch out for that. How do Joey and Jimmy feel about it? I should talk to Martin about it.*

With the meal finished and the free drinks turned off, guests vacated Hilda's Hall by six thirty, meeting in the entryway or the parking lot to say, "See you at the dance." If they didn't have to go home to do chores, they made plans to meet up at a particular bar to kill time until the dance started. The Carlsons prepared to hang out with the wedding party.

"Meet us at the car," Mary said to her kids as they left Hilda's Hall, but Jimmy and Maggie had a surprise for her.

"I gotta help steal the groom," Maggie said without much enthusiasm.

"I gotta go help steal the bride," Jimmy admitted foolishly.

Mary was skeptical. "Why must they do stuff like that to break up the celebration? I'm pretty sure Anna will not want to be separated from George.

Where are they going to take them?"

"Bowling!" Maggie exclaimed. "Only to different places. The guys will take Anna to the BB&B, Bottom's Bowl and Bar, down on the river bottom. Jenny will drive so they can continue drinking. She's pregnant, so she won't drink anything. We girls will take George to the one in Lakeland City. We plan to meet up at Jim's Corner Bar before we all go to the dance."

Mary shook her head. "I suppose they'll do it no matter how much Anna objects." *Bowling in her condition is not ideal.* "George's folks are headed to Jim's, so Dad and Joey and I may as well go there now. We'll see you there later. Be careful, and don't drink any booze!"

Maggie's first job was to stay with George as he waited for his bride outside the main entry, where Walter was to pick them up in his car. Instead, Walter's wife drove up in Marcella's car. As George stooped down to look through the window, Marcella grabbed him by one hand and Helen grabbed the other, and Maggie opened the back door. The three girls pushed him in, with Marcella and Helen crowding into the back seat on either side of him.

Maggie waited by the car door for further instructions, marveling at her cousin's ability to take charge.

"I'll be just a minute, Maggie," Marcella said before she turned to George and purred in a low, sultry voice, "No use struggling, dear boy. You're under our spell, now. Besides, they've already taken your bride. May as well enjoy the company of us young women. It's your last chance."

"What do I do now?" Maggie asked.

"You take my place," Marcella said as she hopped out of the car. "I'm driving."

Jenny exited the driver's seat, saying, "Got other places to be."

Marcella quickly slid into the driver's seat as Maggie climbed in the back with George and Helen.

"Let's go, Marcy," Helen yelled to the driver.

As Marcella drove away, she said, "Sorry, George. We lied to you. Anna has not yet been taken. I told Jimmy to wait for her outside the washroom. Jenny's driving Walter's car and should be picking her up any time now."

Maggie commented, "Your new sisters-in-law seem to have a good plan."

"I never had a chance," he said.

Minutes later, as George and the girls were lacing up their bowling shoes in Lakeland City, Maggie emphasized, "This will be my first time bowling. Jimmy's too."

"Really?" Marcella teased. "I can't believe you and Jimmy have never bowled before. Does the Carlson family live in a cave or what?"

"No, but kind of. I can't imagine Dad and Mom bowling. Can you?" Maggie replied. "They are always working, except when they go to town or go to church. And, honestly, they'd sooner work than go to church. They go for our benefit, I think."

"Our folks have taken us bowling a few times," Helen offered thoughtfully.

"Our folks take us to the county fair if we ask them to," Maggie said, marveling for a moment at the contrast between the two sisters. Unlike Marcella, Helen was seldom animated. She liked to joke, but her face usually remained deadpan, as it was now. Maggie continued, "And they take us to some summer festivals. We never miss a Fourth of July celebration in town. They let us come along to McShane's to listen to the jukebox and the customers as they BS while they take turns buying rounds of beer. Listening to them can be pretty entertaining, and everyone's so generous. They always say, 'Give the kids what they want.' Sometimes I get so full of ice cream and pop, I pass. Then they say, 'Hey, take a candy bar to eat later.' They insist, so I do. I feel a little guilty about it, but I take the candy bar."

Helen nodded. "We'll teach you to bowl tonight. You'll want to know how for when you start dating."

"Maybe next year, if someone asks me."

"Oh, someone will, all right," Helen assured her. "Jimmy told me his friend is interested."

"Come on, girls," George said. "Let's get going on this bowling game. I don't want to miss my own wedding march."

Maggie followed them all to their lane. "I'll go last so I can watch you all."

"George goes first," Marcella insisted.

And as he stood ready to deliver, Maggie looked him over with her cousins. "He's a good-looking guy. And he is fun to be around. He treats everyone so nice too."

"Yeah, I like him fine." Helen said quietly. "But when I see him standing there, I think, 'What if it had been Billy?'"

Marcella sighed and whispered, "If we'd have stolen Billy, I wouldn't return him. We'd be driving off into the sunset about now."

Although shocked to hear her cousin's confession, Maggie giggled along with Helen. But she stopped laughing when she saw that Marcella had leaned back in the seat, crossed her legs, folded her arms, and closed her eyes. Smiling, as if in a dream world, she said nothing and didn't watch as George's ball knocked down all but the ten pin.

In a few long strides he was beside them, saying, "Anna is probably kicking everyone's butt wherever they're bowling. She's the best. One thing we used to do for fun is deliver the second ball with our left hand. Want to do that, just for the heck of it?"

Marcella jumped up from her dream. "Heck yes! Sounds like fun."

Helen nodded to agree as Maggie said, "But I'm left-handed."

George roared with laughter. "Then you bowl with your left first, and if you need another ball, you use your right. You've got a lot to learn, but this is the perfect time. You have three good teachers here, right, girls?"

"Right!"

George picked up the ten pin with his left-handed delivery, causing the girls to yell that he was "Just lucky!"

Maggie eagerly watched to learn as Marcella left two pins standing and missed her left-handed pickup. Helen left half of the pins standing but miraculously picked them up with her left-handed delivery.

"My turn!" Maggie exclaimed. And she took her ball and stood up to bowl.

"Listen, Maggie," George said seriously. "Anna and I learned this bit of wisdom doing left-handed pickups. Whatever foot we start out on when we bowl right-handed, we start out on the other foot when we bowl left-handed. So, since you bowl left-handed, you don't want to copy the way we do it right-handed. Got it?"

"Yeah, I'll copy the way you do it left-handed." She imitated George's stance and took a few runs without delivering the ball as George and the two girls coached her.

Confident, she declared, "I'm ready!"

Her first ball left only one pin standing, and she easily picked it up with her right-hand delivery. "Actually," she said with pride, "I do a lot of things right-handed too."

"Ha!" George exclaimed. "Don't get cocky. The game has just begun. But seriously, those were some excellent deliveries. Hard to believe they're your first."

"Jimmy and Maggie are both pretty athletic. I hate them," Marcella joked.

"Yeah, I know what you mean," Helen added before she slapped Maggie on the back, saying, "Good job!"

As Maggie watched George bowl, she mused how lucky she was to be among such fun cousins as Marcella and Helen, and to be part of a wedding, where although she hardly knew the groom, he was turning out to be a really great guy. Happy for Anna, her thoughts turned to Billy. *Will he decide to come to the dance?*

Time passed swiftly for the bowlers, who were all having fun. George enjoyed the attention of the young women and easily fell into joking about everything without ever being crude or insulting. He led most of the way, and when the final score was tallied, it was George, Helen, Marcella, and Maggie.

"Thanks for letting me beat you, Maggie," Marcella teased, "although I barely did. I'm so bad at games and such."

"I was doing my best! I thought I had a chance of winning with this left-handed pickup thing. But I kept getting confused with my steps."

"That's what makes it fun," George said. "I like to bowl with people who do it for fun. Serious bowlers bore me."

"Let's go to the lavatory before we leave," Marcella said, pulling on Maggie's hand.

"I'll meet you at the door," George said.

Once in the lavatory, Helen proclaimed, "That was really fun. Anna said that George is fun to dance with too." She and Maggie took the first turns in the two open stalls as the girls continued talking.

"I'm sure we'll get a chance to find out tonight," Maggie said.

Marcella looked in the mirror to check her lipstick and hair. "I wonder if Billy will be at the dance."

"I doubt it," Maggie said from the stall. "He told Jimmy and me he thought it best to stay away."

"Well, if he is," Marcella cooed in a deep, sultry voice, "I will make it very clear to him that number-two sister is *very, very interested.*"

"How are you going to do that?" Helen asked, returning from her stall.

"I don't know yet. I might just say, 'I'm yours, dreamboat,' or I might ask him to dance and kiss him."

Maggie exited the stall and took a spot at one of the washbasins. *Marcella throwing herself at Billy could be awkward. Seems a little soon. Might embarrass Anna. And what makes her think her mom is going to be less against her dating Billy than Anna dating Billy?*

"Why not just call him up in a couple weeks?" Maggie suggested.

Marcella smiled as she entered the stall, saying, "I don't believe in wasting time. Anna wasted five years! What a dummy! No, if Billy's there tonight, he will know how I feel. And I intend to muster up all the charm I can to make him mine. I don't give a damn what Mom says."

The girls met George at the door to the parking lot, and as he held it open for them, he joked, "Now listen, you lovely ladies. Don't tell Anna that I had such a good time. Tell her I seemed to have a horrible time. Tell her I was mopey, reticent, and talked only of my bride and how lucky I am."

The girls laughed, but Marcella punctuated their laughter with "I think you know you can't bullshit Anna."

"Don't I know it!" George roared. "Seriously, girls, I had fun, but I am anxious to get back to my bride."

Maggie was just as glad that the bowling was over. They piled into the car and headed to Jim's Corner Bar.

CHAPTER 19

ANOTHER STEAL

Saturday evening, June 9, 1956

When Anna came out of the lavatory at Hilda's Hall, Jimmy met her head on, saying, "Sorry. I'm just following orders." He grabbed her purse as Walter and Paul stepped in on opposite sides of her. Each firmly took a hand and walked her to Walter's car, which Jenny had parked near the exit.

"They've already taken George, so there's no use looking for him," Paul said as Anna strained to look for her husband. Jimmy opened the back door, and after Paul pulled Anna in behind him, Jimmy climbed in next to her.

"We're set to go back here," Paul said.

Walter got in on the front passenger side and said to the driver, "We're ready to take off, Jenny." As the car started, Walter added, "Make sure she doesn't try to jump out." And the car sped off, heading for the river bottoms about fifteen miles away.

Jimmy felt Anna's hand holding his as tightly as if she actually had been kidnapped. She asked in a high-pitched voice, "Where are you taking me?"

Imitating the voice of a villain tying the heroine to the railroad tracks, Paul said, "We take you to a fate worse than death!" He pretended to twist a mustache while he laughed.

Her grip on Jimmy's right hand tightened. "Take me back to George!" she yelled.

Jimmy was confused. Was she acting? Playing along with the joke? Her fear seemed real, but why would she be frightened? He moved his left hand to the top of hers so her hand was firmly set between both of his. She turned to him. In the darkness of the back seat, he felt her body relax as he assured her, "We'll only be gone a short time. Walter told me that we're just going to bowl a game at that new bowling alley on the river bottoms."

"Damnit, you guys!" Paul exclaimed. "I had her going there. Just having some fun."

"Not fun for her if it's only fun for you." Jimmy realized what he said made no sense, but he was not comfortable with Paul's behavior. He seemed to enjoy being mean! Jimmy was relieved to hear Walter's supporting voice from the front seat.

"Lighten up, Paul. Jimmy's right. If she's not having fun with your villain act, knock it off!"

"We get to have fun with her now. She gets her fun tonight. Although with the rush put on this wedding, I think they've had their fun already." Paul laughed at his own crude remark.

Jimmy felt Anna stiffen as she said curtly, "You wouldn't talk like that if George were here."

"No, you wouldn't!" Walter yelled from the front. "And you shouldn't talk like that when he isn't here, either. Damn it, Paul, why do you turn into such an asshole when you drink?"

"Booze brings out the best in me, I guess." Paul laughed as Jenny drove into the parking lot of Bottom's Bowl & Bar. "Hey, park way in the back area."

"I have no choice. The lot is crowded. Hope some lanes are open."

The car stopped in a dark area. Paul reached in his suit pocket to pull out a pint of blackberry brandy. After peeling back the seal, he offered it to Anna. "Here, you get the first drink before we go in to bowl."

Jimmy felt her grip tighten on his hand. "I'm not drinking today," she said softly.

Paul waved the bottle in front of her face, moving it closer until Anna turned away. "Come on! Just one drink."

Jimmy grabbed the bottle. "Give me that. I'll take a drink for her, and then we can go in." "Good idea," Walter said as he got out of the car to open the back door for Jimmy.

Jimmy put the bottle to his lips and tossed his head back as if he were drinking, and then he handed the bottle to Walter.

"Hey, boys, that's mine."

"Not anymore!" Walter exclaimed. "At least not until after we bowl."

Without releasing Anna's hand, Jimmy crawled out of the car, pulling her after him as he said, "Let's get this bowling shit over with. Can you bowl?"

"Yes, George and I bowled here with Walter and Jenny a few months ago."

"I'm a damned good bowler," Paul proclaimed as he caught up to them. "Let's have a bet on who is high scorer. The lowest two scores have to drink the brandy on the way back. The whole bottle."

"I've never bowled before," Jimmy confessed.

"And I'm not bowling," Jenny declared.

"Okay, we'll take you two out of the running. Make it the low scorer of us three has to finish the bottle on the way back."

"I'll take you up on that," Anna announced with some confidence. Jimmy felt her squeeze his hand.

Walter stepped up to Jimmy and whispered, "Don't worry, Jimmy. Anna always beats George, Jenny, and me. And we'll teach you how to bowl tonight too."

As Paul took another pint of brandy out of his coat pocket, he said to Jimmy, "I had this one hidden in the car."

"Keep that bottle in your pocket or you'll get us all kicked out," Walter told Paul before they entered the bowling alley

"What did you do with my other one?"

"It's in Jenny's purse. You'll get it back when we leave."

Paul laughed. "And I'll give it to Anna to drink because she's going to lose the bet."

"I'll order beers and pop after we get our shoes," Walter said. "It should take us less than an hour to bowl, and we'll be on our way back in plenty time to meet everyone at Jim's for a drink and get to the dance by quarter after nine."

"Hell," Paul muttered, "they won't have the wedding march without the bride. They'll wait."

"I want to be there in time," Anna said decisively as she led the way to pick up shoes.

At the lane, Anna said, "I'll go first, then Paul, Walter, and Jimmy. And, Jimmy, watch the footwork as it coincides with the backstroke. Watch how we start with our feet and how the arm gripping the ball swings back as the feet step forward. We'll give you a couple dry runs before you actually bowl."

Jimmy nodded, and he watched as Anna delivered her first ball. "Wow. You knocked them all down!"

"It's called a strike, Jimmy. It will be the first of many tonight. I know that Walter is really good." Aware that other bowlers had been watching her, Anna bowed to them as they cheered her first ball.

"And yet, you always beat me *and* George *and* Jenny."

Paul took his place and began his delivery, knocking down all but the nine pin.

"How did that little bastard manage to stay standing?" he yelled. "Must be rigged."

Jimmy noticed he easily knocked it down with his second delivery. Anna showed Jimmy how she scored it. "Nice pickup, Paul," Anna proclaimed. Then turning to Jimmy, she said, "That's called a spare, and I may have underestimated my opponent."

Jimmy watched Walter bowl another spare, knocking down the seven pin with his second ball. "My turn," he said with more enthusiasm than he felt. He listened to Anna and Walter as they monitored his approaches several times. When he delivered his first ball, it bounced down the alley, striking the one pin directly.

"Not a bad delivery for your first time, Jimmy," Walter said. "Even people who are experienced bounce balls sometimes."

"I hit it in the center! Why didn't the pins go down?"

Paul gave a forced, derisive laugh and said, "This ain't shuffleboard, kid."

"What do I do now?" Jimmy asked as he stared at the standing pins.

Walter counted off, "Seven, eight, and ten."

"Hey, you can do this, Jimmy," Anna encouraged. "You seem to throw hard and straight, which isn't necessarily a good thing, but you can use that now. Deliver the ball so that it hits the seven pin and just clips the eight pin, making it fly over to knock down the ten."

"Do people really do that?"

"All the time," Walter lied convincingly.

"Drinks are on me if he does it," Paul offered. "And I hope he does."

Nervous but excited, Jimmy found that he had started caring about the stupid game. *Who am I turning into? A town kid?*

His delivery was smooth and fast. The four bowlers watched the ball hang close to the gutter before it ripped into the seven and sent the eight flying to the right, knocking the ten pin out like a bullet.

Jimmy heard a cheer go up, not just from his companions, but from by-standers behind them and nearby lanes. He heard shouts of "Nice job, kid!"

Even Paul admitted, "That was a pleasure to see, even if it's gonna cost me a round of drinks."

"Beer for me," Walter said, "and Cokes for the others."

"Seven Up for me," Anna corrected him as she slapped Jimmy on the back. "Don't expect to do that too often. Better yet, avoid leaving those pins. I'll explain later about how to avoid that." Jimmy felt her grab his sleeve as she whispered, "Do me a favor and taste my drink. I'll leave it sitting on the table, and when Paul isn't looking, take a swallow. I don't trust him, and I don't want to risk hurting my . . . hurting myself."

Jimmy understood and prepared for the clandestine taste test.

Paul and Walter returned with the drinks. Conveniently, Paul then went back to the lavatory, leaving Jimmy plenty time to taste the drink.

"Negative," he said to Anna.

"Positive?" she asked.

"No, I mean, it's negative. No booze."

"And I meant, are you positive it's negative."

They giggled like children at the unintentional wordplay, which flooded both of them with memories. Jimmy felt a warm closeness to this favorite cousin, a cousin who was now a married adult. Joy and sadness swept over him.

When Paul returned from the lavatory, Walter smelled the booze on him. "Can't you slack off a little until we finish the game? The night manager is watching you."

"Let's get the ball rolling," Paul commanded as he accidentally kicked into the side of the bench. He fell forward and sprawled out on the floor while his pint of brandy skidded across the alley and into the left gutter.

Close behind him, the manager retrieved the bottle. Handing it to Walter, he said, "See that this stays in your pocket till you leave. If there is no more trouble, I won't be calling the cops."

"Thanks," Walter said.

The rest of the game continued without incident. At the end Anna announced, "Highest scorer is me, then Walter, Paul, and Jimmy. Just as I would've predicted, although Jimmy came close to beating you, Paul."

"I'm ready to drown my sorrows on the way back."

Each of them stopped at the lavatory before they left for the car, where Paul crawled in the back seat. Anna grabbed Jimmy's hand, saying, "Let's sit in the front with Jenny."

Walter sat in the back with his brother, who quickly located his bottle and began drinking. Soon he was singing all the words he knew of "Home on the Range" as the car sped toward Jim's Corner Bar.

At Jim's Corner Bar, Mary sat with her back to the wall at a long table filled with cocktails, beer glasses, and bottles, but she agreed with George when he smiled across the table at her and said, "All this toasting to the bride and groom would be more fun if the bride were here."

Noticing the sad expression behind his smile, Mary said, "They should be back any time now." To her right were Emma, Marcella, and Helen, with Maggie and Joey crowded around at the end of the table. To Mary's left was Josie, with Elmer at the end. Across from Mary were Martin, Joe, and George. In the past hour or more, the group had shared boisterous joking, stories of past weddings, and tales of exaggerated deeds.

George stood up and announced, "We've got plenty time for another round."

Mary waved her hand from side to side, exclaiming, "No more for me!" With a full glass of beer in front of her and one with a swallow or two left in it, she had lagged behind the others in beer consumption. Martin, Joe, and George had just downed the contents in their glasses.

"None for me either," Emma said. "I'm about ready to float out of here."

Martin eagerly fed his regular straight line to his wife. "In your drinking, you girls are a little *be-hind*."

To which Mary replied, "I'd sooner be a *little be-hind* than a *big ass!*"

The exchange was as well known to the group as any Burns-and-Allen comment, yet everyone howled with laughter as if the joke had been improvised just now and not a decade earlier.

"Okay, ladies." George turned to the others at the table. "Bourbon on the rocks for Joe, beers for Dad and Martin, plain Seven Up for Mom, and a Pepsi each for Marcella, Helen, and Maggie. None for me this round. I have to remain respectable for my dear wife." He smiled at Joey, saying, "Come up to the bar with me and help me carry this stuff. Then you can tell me what you want."

Just then the back door to Jim's burst open and the rest of the wedding party entered, led by Paul, who exclaimed, "Looks like my generous brother is buying! Make mine a double scotch on the rocks!" He slurred his words a little as he stumbled toward the table and crashed into Joey's empty chair.

"Careful," Walter said. "You may want to slack off a little. You've downed a pint of brandy just since we left the bowling alley."

"Hey, mind your own business. I'm twenty-one and this is my first big *shelebration* since my birthday."

"Yeah, but tomorrow is my birthday," Walter said. "And I want you to make it till then so you can help me celebrate, especially since George will be gone on his honeymoon."

George ignored them all. Upon seeing his bride enter the place with Jimmy at her side, he had rushed to pick her up and twirl her around and around as they kissed.

Walter put money in the jukebox and played Johnny Cash's new hit "I Walk the Line."

"I got mighty lonesome," George said as he held her. "And they're playing our song."

"Let's dance, honey. I got lonesome too, but Jimmy and Jenny took good care of me, though. And so did Walter."

Jimmy recognized George's reaction to the omission of Paul's name. Walter stared at his brother, adding, "Give him the damn double scotch on the rocks."

Martin interrupted. "George, go dance with your bride. I'll get this round, and my boys and I will bring them to the table."

Mary was proud of her husband. *He may be drunk, but he usually tries to do the right thing.*

After the dance, George and Anna sat in chairs facing Mary, still looking into each other's eyes.

"I was worried I was going to have to go on my honeymoon alone," George joked in a sad tone.

Elmer hadn't said much all evening, but suddenly he spoke. "So, tomorrow you're off to Duluth, then?"

"Yes, I know it's not exotic or anything," Anna said. "But George has been there before, and he said the city is magical—the lake, the docks, the aerial lift bridge—and we'll probably go up to Two Harbors, which is a unique town."

"And you'll no doubt be spending quite a bit of time in your hotel room too," Emma asserted with a grin. "That's why they call it a honeymoon."

Anna smiled and looked down. "Well, yes, we're staying in the Hotel Duluth, which has a reputation for elegance. I expect we'll be doing more leisure than travel."

"Spoken like a devoted newlywed," Mary interjected. She listened intently, curious to discover any hint of what others knew of Anna's condition.

Paul and Walter had taken chairs next to Elmer, but Paul stood up on unsteady legs to demand, "So, how come you ain't drinkin' a little, Anna, to shelebrate the occasion? Marryin' my big brother ought to be worth a drink or two." He leaned on an empty chair. "Come on, I'll go get you a Tom Collins or a Seven and Seven. Tasty drinks."

"Maybe she wants to stay sober for her wedding night."

Josie interjected, "But really, Paul, it's none of our business."

"Come on, Ma, don't butt in here. This is between me and my new sister. We're just talking, you know." Paul involuntarily lurched to the side, putting his hand on Walter's chair to keep from falling.

Walter steadied his brother while Elmer stood up and grabbed Paul before he fell. "I got you, son. Let me help you sit down."

"I don't need help! I just wanna know why the bride ain't drinkin' any booze. Are you too good to drink? Did you ever drink any booze?"

"Well, she's not twenty-one," Emma said bluntly. "But she's had some wine or beer in the past."

Mary asserted, "It's her choice, isn't it? Anna could drink a cocktail now, if she wanted, but it's her choice if she prefers not to drink on her wedding day."

Walter said, "I'm fine with toasting the couple when she's drinking pop. It's fine with me. There's only one reason to drink—that's because you want to."

"You're a damn wimp!" Paul exclaimed.

"Maybe, but I'm not the one Dad had to help sit down."

Paul lunged at Walter, and his dad held him back. Martin returned with the drinks just as George said, "Hey, hey! What's going on? I told you to behave yourself today, Paul. Come on, this is my wedding here."

"I was just trying to get your bride to drink a real toast with a drink instead of pop."

"She told me she wasn't going to drink all day. It's her decision," George said firmly.

Mary hoped Martin would say nothing. He was drunk, and often alcohol increased his smart-ass tendencies. To her delight, Martin said nothing, but Joe, who might have been drunker than Martin, shocked everyone by commenting, "Come on, Anna. You drink at home sometimes, and I've seen you and Billy drink together many times."

At the mention of Billy, silence washed over the table, as if someone had switched off the sound. Mary watched the Langes, who knew about Billy and Anna but were not aware of details, nor did they want to be. Would the mention of his name evoke unwelcome images for them, and for Anna's side of the family? Joe was a fun-loving guy who never intended to embarrass or hurt anyone, and yet he had unwittingly released a party-killing cloud over the room.

Paul persisted, "I wanna hear more about this Billy guy. What kind of an asshole is he, anyway?"

Mary feared what Martin might do, but she relaxed when he simply said, "Hey, Paul, he isn't even here. No use talking about him when he isn't here."

The statement seemed innocent enough, but Paul became enraged. "You stay out of it!" With a wide swing, he threw a punch with his right fist, connecting sharply with the left side of Martin's jaw. *Smack!* Everyone froze.

Martin staggered to his right a step. He smiled as he saw the second punch coming, ducked beneath the blow, bent down to cradle Paul's crotch with his elbow, and picked him off the floor. Raising him high in the air, he twirled around several times before setting him firmly in a nearby chair.

Meanwhile, Walter had run into the men's room and grabbed a wastebasket. He held it out near his brother just as Paul turned his head, grabbed the basket, and threw up several times.

Walter grinned, saying, "I know my little brother."

Mary looked at George. *Will he slug Martin to defend his brother?*

With physical and personal grace, George moved to his brother's side. "You just slugged my favorite uncle. He was easier on you than I would've been. You're lucky he got to you first." He slapped Martin on the back. "Nice move, Uncle Martin. You must have a jaw of stone!"

"Oh, I can feel it some," Martin said, slowly rubbing his jaw.

The owner was there in an instant. "It better be all over, George. I don't want to have to call the cops."

"I'm sorry, Jim. My brother lost control, and we had to settle him down, but he's okay now."

"Looks like no damage was done. Best wishes on your honeymoon, buddy."

"Thanks, Jim." George turned to announce, "Let's drink up, everybody, and be on our way. We have an audience to impress."

Mary sat back in her chair, relieved at the smooth resolution after the outburst of violence. Martin was always unpredictable, but she was proud of him tonight. Yet she dreaded the thought of more than five hours of celebrating to go. *A lot can happen yet. How are Josie and Elmer feeling about it? I'll talk to them tonight. Try to smooth things over. Their son was just drunk. That's all. But why the crude behavior toward Anna?*

Jimmy, too, was proud of his dad. Proud that he was able to physically handle the younger man and even prouder that his dad didn't overreact. *Maybe I'll listen more closely to the old man's advice on fighting.*

Martin's voice interrupted his thoughts. "Jimmy, carry this six-pack to the car." He smiled wide as he handed Jimmy the carton. "I bought it for me and your mother. We'll need it tomorrow morning. Give it to Mom when we get to the car. She'll know what to do."

Jimmy took the carton. "Okay, Dad." *Some things never change.*

CHAPTER 20

THE GOOD NEPHEW

Saturday evening, June 9, 1956

On this warm Saturday evening, when the interests of most young people had turned from serious matters of the day to *more* serious matters of the night, searching for romance wherever their imaginations led them, Billy Thorson found himself milking cows. His muscles had been made hard by repetitive work and training, giving him the strength and balance to make difficult tasks look easy. His movements were both forceful and graceful. His bright disposition made him the delight of all around him. His face usually sported a broad smile, revealing the boisterous love of life that burned within him. But tonight he allowed himself to brood more than a little as he finished up the evening chores for Martin and Mary.

He tugged at the leather strap attached to a timepiece in the watch pocket of his bib overall. "A little short of half past eight and only one left," he said to himself, "but I'm going to have to milk her by hand."

"Easy, now," he said in a low, calm tone as he rested the palm of his hand high on Popcorn's thigh. "Your cow friends have all been milked and all but two released to the pasture, but I left these two locked in their stanchions to keep you company."

He repeated "Easy, now" several times as she shifted her weight from her left leg to her right and then back again and again, creating a kind of dance step. "I hear that you're called Popcorn. Look, young lady," he continued in low, affectionate tones, "I'm not taking you to the dance tonight no matter how cute you move those hips." His laughed softly and then repeated, "Easy, sweetheart. Easy, Popcorn. Easy, now."

The smooth talk seemed to work. The young Holstein slowed her dance, and Billy slipped his body between her and the cow in the next stanchion. In one motion, he squatted onto his three-legged stool, hugged the small milk pail between his knees, and squeezed her right back teat, using just his thumb and forefinger. First, he used the milk to moisten her teats and his hands, and only when they were slippery did he began to milk her in earnest.

"Uncle Martin warned me about you," he said gently. "I know you calved two weeks ago for the first time, and normally all this would be routine to you by now, and I'd be milking you with the machine, but that nasty gash on your right front teat keeps you jumping. Some blood will get into the milk if that scab comes off, so I'll milk you by hand and use the milk for the calves. They don't mind a little blood. I'm sorry, but I gotta get the milk out. I'll be careful, though. And gentle. It ain't so bad. Tomorrow Uncle Martin will be back, but tonight it's just you and me."

Although he continued his friendly banter while milking Popcorn, he struggled to keep focused on the job. She could move or kick or stand back down into the gutter, only some of the many cases where he would have to grab his pail and stool. But the rhythm of the milk squirting into the pail was familiar, and he became lost in the comfort of it all. Fortunately, Popcorn did not challenge him. Only when the milk foamed toward the top of the pail and the squirts from all four of her teats became dribbles did his trance break.

Then he uttered, "Well, she's married, then. And to someone else. How in the hell did I ever let that happen? If I had a mirror, I'd look in and see the biggest dumbass in the universe."

He divided Popcorn's milk among several pails, pouring the majority of it into a pail to feed her baby. To the other pails he added cold water, and he fed the mixture to the older calves. With the aisles cleared of pails, he released the last of the cows, and after carrying the last of the milk up the stairs to dump into the strainer on the bulk tank, he washed the equipment.

Although done with chores, he was not ready to leave for home—but without work on which to focus, his mind took him away to recall times with Anna. Glorious Anna! Going nowhere in particular, he walked into the barn entryway and peered into the dark hayloft and sat on a stack of bales nearby. Head in his hands, he saw visions of Anna—her radiant smile, her red hair, her lovely face, her whole self dressed in green on New Year's Day after they left dinner at Carlsons' place, telling everyone they were going to a movie. Her idea. And later, nude in bed with him. How he adored her! And how she had looked at him with love and adoration! He looked up at nothing and lamented, "How the hell did I lose her?"

Comforted by the surrounding darkness, he mused how he and Jimmy had used the open area in the hayloft to practice judo and karate moves every Sunday afternoon last winter. Eager to learn about how to understand relationships with women, Jimmy had listened to his advice. *Always move forward. Love doesn't pause. A girl expects progress in a relationship. Let her know how you feel. Never let her wonder. Some expert I turned out to be! My advice was good. I just didn't follow it. A short time ago we had belonged to each other for five years. When did it stop? When she left me after that last date in February, why didn't I pursue her?*

He spoke aloud to the darkness. "Well, she's married now. I've lost my chance, but I can't even imagine life without her. I need to see her, not close, but from a distance. I need that. Everyone told me the best thing was to stay away from the dance tonight, but a glimpse of her from a distance won't hurt anything. I want to see her on her happy day. I'm a fool, I know."

He looked at his pocket watch. "I can get to the dance by half past ten." He took long strides toward his car, climbed in, and sped home to get ready for the dance.

CHAPTER 21

THE GATHERING

Saturday evening, June 9, 1956

Jo Anne Shaurel drove her family's black 1954 Chrysler Imperial carefully out of the yard, fully aware that her father was watching out the kitchen window. The car's roomy interior easily accommodated all five of her sisters—Jane, nineteen; Ann, sixteen; twins Mary and Margaret, thirteen; and Caroline, twelve.

"I think the old man would've even let me drive to the dance," Jane said to her older sister from the passenger side of the front seat." Then, leaning forward to avoid Caroline, who sat in the middle, she added with a hint of sarcasm, "But you are his favorite."

"Until baby Audrey came along unexpectedly a couple years ago, maybe. But Dad knows I am the oldest and wisest of his brood," Jo Anne remarked matter-of-factly. "And at twenty-one, I'm old enough to supervise all you wild Shaurel girls at the dance."

The comment was met with a flurry of giggles from the three girls in the back seat before Ann remarked, "I'm just glad they had baby Audrey. Otherwise, he and Mom would've come along. We'll have a much better time without them."

"And I'm glad he got rid of the old Plymouth and bought this used Chrysler!" Jo Anne exclaimed. "He said he bought it just so that he had a car big enough for all of us. Mom was worried about the price, but when she sat in it and felt the roominess, she was sold too."

"There's probably room in this big boat for us to take a couple boys home with us!" Jane giggled.

"More room for them in the back seat with us," Ann asserted.

"We can joke about it, but when we're at the dance, try not to fight over guys, little sisters," Jo Anne ordered. "It will not work out for any of us. Besides, the matchups will sort themselves out."

"How do you figure that?" Ann asked abruptly.

"Easy," Jane answered for her sister. "Jo Anne and I are clearly older, so real young guys will look toward Ann. Jo Anne is too tall for many boys, so the shorter ones will eye me. Mary and Margaret and Caroline are too young anyway."

"Not so!" screamed the twins.

"Well, you can dance with boys, but do not leave the dance hall with one, and if they ask to take you home, you must refuse."

"I just want to dance, anyway," Mary said.

"And talk," Margaret added. "Dance and talk."

"I want to dance and talk with Joey Carlson," Caroline said dreamily.

"I thought you were done swooning over him after last Valentine's Day, when he gave you and Mary Ryan the same valentine," Margaret teased.

"I'll forgive him if he asks me to dance," Caroline proclaimed.

"Fat chance," Mary said. "He's only eleven."

"He'll be twelve in December. I'm only seven months older. And he's big for his age."

"That's right," declared Jo Anne. "Don't give up easily. Things can change. I've had my eyes on Billy Thorson ever since I met him during threshing at Carlsons' farm years ago, but he's been dating Anna Dvorak for over five years. Now she's marrying someone else, the stupid girl. So, Billy is free."

"Think he'll be at the dance?" Jane asked.

"If he is, you stay clear, little sister."

"He is quite the dreamboat," Jane teased. "Thor-son, son of Thor. He looks like a Norse god, that's for sure."

"I doubt if he'll be there tonight, but if he is," Jo Anne said shamelessly, "you girls are walking home because I want the back seat of this big boat to myself and Billy!"

"We can all fit in the front while I drive," Jane added to be helpful.

The sisters all laughed with joy at the lustful images stirring in their minds.

"But you're right about things changing," Ann said warily, as if unwilling to share her hopes with her sisters. "I've always liked Jimmy Carlson, though he's a grade below me in school. Mary Schroedler was his sweetheart since first grade. But she ran away last February, and Jimmy will be at the wedding dance tonight. If he doesn't ask me to dance, I'll ask him. As a neighbor and country-school friend, a girl can do that. Don't you think?"

"Absolutely!" Jane exclaimed.

"He'll see how charming I can be," Ann explained. "And I've got this new perfume."

"And I saw you tuck some tissue paper down your bra too," Margaret teased.

"That will help more than the perfume," Mary added.

"Unless he goes for second base." Jane giggled.

Ann blushed in the darkness. "Jimmy's a gentleman. He won't try that on the dance floor!"

"And if he did?" Jane teased.

Ann stammered, "Well, he won't! He probably won't even notice."

"If you dance with him, he'll notice all right. They'll be poking his chest!" Jane laughed before she continued, "Sixteen-year-old boys notice! Especially if you pay attention to them."

"Gee, I've been paying lots of attention to Joey," Caroline complained. "Why doesn't he notice me?"

Jane laughed at her sister's ignorance. "The boy is eleven. *E-lev-en!* When boys are young they ignore girls, and as they get older, they pretend to ignore them, but soon they can't take their eyes off the girls. I'll give him less than two years and he'll be noticing you, especially if you fit into the dress Ann's wearing tonight."

"You're making me feel like some kind of tramp," Ann said.

Jo Anne came to her rescue. "Don't worry. You look lovely. Jane is just being *Jane.*" After a brief pause, she continued, "I shouldn't say this in front of my little sisters, but whatever Billy Thorson tries on the dance floor is fine with me. I'd just invite him into this big car of ours."

"Remember," Jane added, "you younger girls are not to go outside with a boy."

"We get it," Mary said. "Rules are different for you old maids."

As the girls in the back snickered, Caroline spoke from the front seat. "I just want to dance with Joey."

Silence reigned for a moment before Caroline added wistfully, "I heard Mary Schroedler was going to be at the dance. Katherine O'Keran said her brother, Billy Joe, told her."

"I heard that too," Ann remarked. "But I don't believe it! Dad says the sheriff is looking for her because she stole Jack's car and she's under eighteen and her brothers are seeking custody. I think she'll stay away. At least I hope she does, even for her own good."

Jane jumped on the chance to tease her sister. "And maybe just a little for your own good? Giving you a shot at Jimmy."

"Maybe so," Ann admitted, blushing in the darkness of the car.

"We're coming up on Lakeland City now," Jo Anne said.

Like the other dance-seekers, the Shaurels didn't need to drive through the neatly kept Czech-German town of Lakeland City. Instead, they turned south on the east end of town, passing a fine baseball field before continuing south through the park, where towering American elms and broad oak trees formed a high canopy over an outdoor bandshell and an ornate white gazebo north of the ballroom and the lake. Finally, the road led to Lakeshore Ballroom, where Jo Anne parked in the east parking lot.

As they walked to the entrance, Jo Anne exclaimed, "I love this place! Look how the yellow-white lights hanging from the eaves make the place look so romantic. And the summer breeze is causing small waves on the shore of Wild Rose Lake."

"Yeah, the night is beautiful," Jane declared. "And the dance attracts people from all over. Look, there's a guy with a suit on, riding a bicycle. Hope he didn't have to come from too far away. He's actually kind of cute."

"It's a popular place," Jo Anne said. "They have Friday- and Saturday-night dances for the public year-round. Friday nights have a modern band—swing or country—and Saturday night's band plays old-time music in the Czech, German, or Polish tradition. And believe me, it's *the place to be* on New Year's Eve."

"We've got our tickets already," Jane said. "But let's hurry in to see if we can rent a booth. Even if I dance all night, I'm going to need a place to sit down once in a while."

Everyone agreed, and the sisters hurried in, excited about the night's prospects.

The Carlsons arrived too late to get a parking spot near the dance hall. Mary declared, "I don't mind parking in the ballpark lot. The walk to the pavilion is pleasant."

"I love the park!" Maggie exclaimed. "In the twilight the trees look romantic. Don't you think, Jimmy?"

"Not the word I'd use. More like they look a little creepy."

"Come on, Jimmy. You know I'm right."

"Sure, sure. I'm just kidding."

"You need to start getting out of your skeptical mood and into your social one if you're going to have fun tonight."

"Don't worry. I've got another twenty yards or so to work on it. You know I'm committed."

After they entered the ballroom, they walked past the coat check, the ticket booth, restrooms, and a twenty-foot bar, where Mary stopped to dig into her purse as she remarked, "I know you have your own money, but here is a dollar each. If you get hungry later, you can order hamburger on a bun and add ketchup, mustard, pickles, and onions at the table nearby. The thing can get a little messy, but they wrap it in cellophane-like paper that prevents some of the grease from dripping on the floor. The sandwich is really tasty."

"I'm still stuffed from supper and all the pop I drank after supper," Jimmy admitted.

Mary motioned for her kids to look at a middle-aged man near the ticket check. "See the big guy in uniform? That's Lester Grossman. He's a foreman at the flour mill, but he's worked as a cop here for years on some of the dance nights. He's a nice guy. You can trust him."

Tickets in hand, the family nodded to Officer Grossman as they went on through to the ticket check, where each person with a ticket got their hand stamped to allow reentry if they left the dance hall.

"The booths for the bridal party are at the far end of the dance floor," Mary explained. Might as well go over and get a seat."

Walking past the elevated stage, Maggie commented as the band members were setting up, "I didn't realize the band was so big. There's at least eight of them."

"And most of them play more than one instrument," Mary said. "Look, they've got a concertina, two saxophones, two clarinets, a bass horn, two trumpets, drums, and a piano."

"So," Jimmy said, "I'll bet they can play all kinds of music."

As they reached the booths, Maggie glanced back at the entry. "See those guys standing to the left of the ticket-check line, eyeing all the girls as they come in?"

"Yeah, the girls are doing the same thing on the other side."

"Not quite, Jimmy. The boys are staring and the girls are at least trying to be nonchalant."

"Girls are looking for Prince Charming and the boys want to be Prince Charming."

"Most of them aren't exactly behaving like princes, though."

"Go easy on them, Mags. We're all just kids, you know. I plan on working on being charming tonight, though."

"I think that's probably the place the girls stand if they are available to dance."

"I'll check it out later," Jimmy assured her.

"There goes Joey, sliding across the dance floor," Maggie said. "I knew he couldn't resist."

"Heck, it's hard for me to resist," Jimmy said. "With a short run, you can glide fifty feet or more past the bandstand. A few very young girls are out there too, but they won't last. Girls like to pretend they're young ladies. Boys, on the other hand, never want to rush into adulthood."

"Are you speaking for yourself, older brother?" Maggie teased.

"Yes, but I'm also describing all mankind." Jimmy laughed and added, "Look at Joey and Ronnie go!"

After a particularly long glide, Joey ran up to Jimmy to exclaim, "It's just like gliding on slippery snow. If you have new overshoes with good grips, you can't slide. Here, if you have rubber soles, you can't slide. My new shoes and Ronnie's have leather soles."

Ronnie remarked, "I'll bet none of the neighbor girls will join us, though, like they did on our snow slide. I see Liz Brummer and Mary Ryan over there thinking they're so smart. Too good to glide."

Before he took another run at it, Joey said, "Heck with them. How often does a guy get a chance to glide on a floor this big!"

"I'll just pretend I don't know them," Maggie said to Jimmy. She looked around and added, "Everyone from the wedding party is here except George's two brothers and their bridesmaids. Well, they've got fifteen minutes before the wedding march begins."

"I thought they left Jim's Corner Bar the same time we did," Jimmy said. "I saw Jenny driving, but I'll bet Paul had her stop at the liquor store for couple of pints."

"Meanwhile," Maggie joked, "we can be entertained by our little brother and his friends doing their ice follies imitation. You taught him this when you were ten and he was five."

"Yeah, I have to admit it, I am a little envious. I had a pretty good career doing the dance-floor glide. I got all I can do to resist going out there now to show those kids up."

"Go ahead. I know the little boy in every male is just a bit below the surface."

"And it's our best part, probably. Say, here come a couple of our neighbors."

Maggie turned to see Mary Ryan and Liz Brummer.

"I think the whole neighborhood is here!" Liz exclaimed. "And, Maggie, you look great in your pretty green dress. It's perfect."

Mary agreed. "You'll be turning boys away left and right."

"I'm not sure she'll be turning them all away," Jimmy teased.

"Shut up, Jimmy," Maggie commanded and turned to face the girls. "Thanks. You girls look great. I'm glad you could come. It should be fun night with lots of dancing."

"Doesn't look like Joey's ready for dancing yet," Mary said. "He seems to be in the gliding group."

"He may surprise you," Maggie said. "We rehearsed dancing in the house before we left this morning. Jimmy too."

Jimmy seized the moment to work on being social, and, using an overly gallant manner to mask his discomfort, he announced, "I'll be asking you ladies to dance tonight, if you'll have me." And at that moment the band began with a waltz. "They'll play a couple sets before the wedding march," Jimmy said. "Care to dance one with me now, Mary? Maggie and Liz can dance, and then we'll change partners when the tune changes."

Mary was pleased but sarcastic. "That way we'll all get to dance with Jimmy. Lucky us."

"Like that's some big deal," Jimmy joked. "Be careful, I've got my pointy shoes on." Mary was his neighbor, but he discovered as they clumsily took their places to dance together, knowing her from the country school did not make things less awkward. Having his arm around a thirteen-year-old neighbor girl who was closer to Joey's age than his own made Jimmy a bit uncomfortable, and to make things worse, their legs were bumping as they stepped. He stopped and readjusted his hand on her back to lead better. *I should've followed Mom's advice—lead your partner in a step in each direction to see how you move together before you waltz into the crowd.* "Hey, Mary, let's just start again," he offered. She giggled nervously but agreed. They tried a few steps first, and then they waltzed smoothly into the crowd. "There. We're going good now."

"Are you expecting Mary Schroedler to come tonight?" she asked.

Jeez, I'm gonna have to talk too. And this was my idea? He struggled to talk and do the steps at the same time. "No, but I don't have any idea where she is. You know that, don't you?"

"I guess so. You're a good dancer, Jimmy."

"Nice of you to say, but thanks. You're better than I am."

"Nice of *you* to say. I didn't realize the band would have so many instruments. So many horns and stuff. Do you think Joey will dance later?"

"Pretty sure he will. Are any of your brothers here?"

"Yeah, John and Tom are both here. John brought his girlfriend, Jeanette. Liz and her brother Joe came with Tom and me and Peggy. Mom made him bring us. He didn't want us tagging along, but when Dad agreed that we could go, Tom didn't have a choice."

"Well, hope you have fun." Then, trying not to sound too worried, Jimmy asked, "Say, Tom isn't still sore at me about that that haircut episode, is he?"

"No, but he really never told us much about it. He was never mad at you, anyway."

"Good to hear." Jimmy let the subject drop as he saw Maggie and Liz approach just as the music stopped. "I enjoyed the dance, Mary. And if Joey doesn't ask you to dance, ask him. But don't tell him I said so. I know he wants to dance, but he may be a little unwilling to risk asking. You look really nice. Ask him."

He left Mary to step toward Liz as Maggie and Mary prepared to dance. The two couples twirled into the crowd.

Liz started the conversation. "Maggie looks so mature and beautiful tonight, and her hair is so perfect. You both look so nice together."

"I hope you told her that. Not about me but about her. If you did, she will be your friend for life."

"What do you mean?"

"She's kind of touchy about her hair. Kids in school have teased her about it all her life."

"But it's so pretty!"

"Like I said, tell her that."

"Kids must be even more mean to each other in high school than they are in the country school."

"True, I think, but not true of all families. The Brummer kids are always nice to everyone. Your folks taught you right."

Liz giggled. And Jimmy twirled her around the floor with renewed confidence.

Maggie and Mary danced easily together as Mary asserted, "Liz is really nuts about your hair and how nice you look tonight. She said you and Jimmy were the best-looking couple here."

"She's just being nice. She's always nice. Joey said he has fun with the two of you sometimes at recess."

"Yeah, Joey's fun. He's with Ronnie Schoen tonight, though. Boys can be so different when they're with their friends."

"Girls too," Maggie replied, without having anyone in mind.

"We've got the whole neighborhood here tonight. I saw six of the Shaurel girls in the parking lot getting out of their big Chrysler. Jo Anne is such a beauty! I hope Jack Drude doesn't show up."

The music stopped as Maggie said, "I think he's still under probation. He's not allowed to leave his folks' place."

Mary held on to Maggie, pleading, "Can we do one more? They aren't ready to play the wedding march yet."

"Sure," Maggie agreed, and she stepped into another waltz.

A few turns later, Mary asked, "Do you think Mary Schroedler will come tonight? I heard she's coming, but I know if anyone knows for sure, you would."

Maggie tried to say as little as possible. "I really don't know."

"Katherine O'Keran says B. J. told her."

"How would her brother know? Isn't he in Missouri or someplace?"

"Maybe from Jack Drude. B. J. hates him, but I think they still communicate."

"Sorry, it's hard for me to picture Jack writing to a guy studying to be a priest."

"He dropped out, but he still goes to school there."

"Well, I don't know anything about where Mary is or if she is ever coming back. I promise you, I don't." *And I don't, but why do so many others think they do?*

The music stopped, and the girls smiled at each before Mary said, "Good talking to you, Maggie. I'm sure you have to get ready for the wedding march soon. You're so lucky to be in the wedding. Have fun."

"You too."

CHAPTER 22

THE WEDDING MARCH

Saturday night, June 9, 1956

The stream of people funneling into the entryway continued even after the orchestra began playing at nine. But by nine fifteen, after people had danced to several waltzes, the orchestra leader spoke into the microphone to announce the wedding march. Everyone quickly sought a spot along the perimeter of the ballroom floor to view the couples in the bridal party as they marched in a big circle, while the orchestra played an old-time version of "Here Comes the Bride." Viewers commented on the bride's beauty, the tall and handsome groom, and the boisterous state of the groom's youngest brother, who weaved from side to side as the couples paraded to the music. The beauty of the bride's two dark-haired sisters and their eloquent manners escaped no one, as the two teenagers managed to walk alongside the rowdy brothers of the groom, each of whom often punctuated a musical moment with a loud "Ahh-haa" or Yaa-hoo!" as they stomped their feet hard on the floor in their own version of a jig. Jimmy and Maggie drew many comments on their poise and appearance as members of the crowd passed on the knowledge that they were teenage sister and brother.

After the couples had completed two parade laps, the orchestra began a waltz, signaling the couples to dance with their partners. Then the bride and groom separated to dance the next waltz with each of their attendants. George and Anna easily moved down the line to dance—first breaking up Marcella and Walter, then Helen and Paul, and finally Maggie and Jimmy.

George reached his hand out to Maggie, bowed his head, and asked, "May I dance with yet another beautiful redhead at the ball?"

Maggie smiled at his compliment, responding in like manner, "Of course, George. I rather like being called a redhead when you put the word *beautiful* in front of it."

They stepped off together in a swirl, and Maggie felt she was floating in his arms. His height made conversation a challenge, so she said nothing. But he dipped his head close to her ear to say, "You and Jimmy make me so proud. Thanks for being in the wedding. I hope my brothers, especially Paul, haven't been big jackasses by trying to get you to drink out of the pints they pass."

"No, it's been fine. I just refused most of the time. One time I put it up to my lips and pretended to drink just to shut them up."

"Did it work?"

Maggie laughed. "No, but just the bit on my lips confirmed my resolve to not try more."

George laughed loudly. Maggie honestly liked him. She was happy for her cousin Anna. What had happened between her and Billy was in the past and none of her business.

Jimmy took his turn with the beautiful bride, admitting, "I'm a little worried about stepping on your dress."

"Don't worry about it. You wouldn't be the first, and I'm sure you wouldn't be the last." After a moment she added, "Thanks for sticking with me during the stealing-the-bride thing. I don't know why I was so frightened, but I was. You holding my hand helped a lot."

"The whole thing was kind of crazy," Jimmy said. He kept further thoughts to himself. *Those jackasses were scary.*

"You waltz pretty smoothly, Jimmy."

"Thanks. Practicing with Maggie helped. I think we both evolved past counting our steps."

Anna chuckled at the truth of his joke. "Later in the evening, I want you to ask me to polka. Tell Maggie to let us do the first one, and you should cut in. I want to polka with Maggie like we used to do when we were kids."

"Sure thing," he promised. *Is it okay to polka when you're pregnant?* Her face beamed with joy, as it should on her wedding day, but he couldn't block out images of her and Billy together on New Year's Day, just a bit over five months ago. How happy they'd seemed then. To counter his thoughts, he said, "George is a fun guy. And he seems to be having a good time today."

She laughed, throwing her head back slightly. "George always has a good time." Jimmy felt like she'd read his mind when she added, "He's a good man, Jimmy. He is fun and kind. And we love each other."

"That's what counts."

"He can be quite a rascal, though. I'm pretty sure he will be dancing a polka with you and Joey and Martin before the dance is over. He can be smooth as a dancer, but he loves to be wild sometimes. He told me he was going to dance with every member of the Carlson family because I said you were my favorite relatives."

"I'll look forward to it," Jimmy said. Then he felt George's tap on his shoulder, asking for his bride back. As the bridal party returned to their original partners, the crowd took the signal to join them, and instantly the ballroom floor filled with people eager to dance the night away. When the music stopped, the dancers applauded and cheered as the orchestra took a quick bow before resuming play.

"Let's dance another one," Maggie said. "I really love this place. And I love the sound of the orchestra. Saxophones, horns, and a concertina." And she took her position as Jimmy began.

"Sure. It's fun." Jimmy answered as he gave his sister an extra fast turn. "Anna and her sisters are good dancers, but we aren't bad either, eh?"

"No. Not so bad." She waited a few steps before she added, "Dancing with George's brothers wasn't much fun. They're too drunk. Glad I don't have to dance with them again. George is a good dancer, though. And he's fun. I think he appreciates Anna—not that Billy didn't, but it's none of our business what happened between them. I think she's happy now." Maggie continued earnestly, "Mary Ryan asked me if Mary Schroedler was coming to the dance."

"She asked me the same thing. What the heck!"

"She said Katherine O'Keran had said her brother told her she might."

"How would he know?"

"I told her I heard nothing about it."

"That's what I told her too."

"I just hope it isn't true," Maggie confessed.

"Me too," Jimmy agreed. "I sure would like to see her again, but not here. Not tonight."

Jimmy felt a tap on his shoulder. He turned around to see a tall boy with a big smile and a pretty girl standing next to him.

"May we cut in?" he asked. He continued in a tone of heightened formality, "I hear you two are brother and sister. Well, Annette here is my cousin, and she would like to dance with you, and I'd be delighted to dance with your pretty sister."

Maggie felt goosebumps on her back when he crooned, "I'm Tony. May I know your name?"

"Maggie," she heard herself say as she fitted herself into his arms. They twirled away into the crowd of dancers. She kept silent, enjoying the music and the ease of waltzing with him. He was smooth. Good-looking too. And he held her in his arms like she was special. *The dance has just begun, and I've found Prince Charming.*

"Hello, I'm Jimmy. I'm pleased to meet you, Annette." He aimed to keep the introduction simple, but repeating her name made him more apt to remember it. And he would need help concentrating. She wasn't just pretty. She was stunning. With her dark-brown hair hanging to the front of her left shoulder, her right shoulder was bare. Jimmy barely avoided staring at her smooth skin and instead caught her gaze before he stepped closer to put his right arm around her. As they waltzed, she danced close. He felt her squeezing his hand. *Could the night be more perfect?* He began to feel too warm. *Take a deep breath. Say something. Keep it short.*

"Maggie and I are the bride's first cousins. Our mothers are sisters." *So lame! Ask about her!*

"Tony and I are George's cousins from his mother's side, but we don't see his family very often. We both live in St. Paul. He's a couple years older than I am, but we kind of grew up together because our folks visited each other often."

Good so far. Now ask her a question. "Have you been to this ballroom before?"

"Never. I like it a lot, though. The view of the lake is really beautiful. As I said, Tony's older, but he is kind enough to take me to dances sometimes, even if he has a date. There's a lot of old-time music played around our neighborhood and some modern dance music played in the roller rinks. I love to dance. I love to roller-skate and go bowling too. Do you?"

"Dance, yes, but I've never roller-skated, and tonight was the first time I bowled when we stole the bride."

"Really? What do you do for fun?"

Jimmy let the question hang in the air as he guided her around other dancers. *Whatever I say will mark me as a hick, which I am. May as well tell the truth and disappoint her right away.* "My family farms. We don't really have a lot of leisure time. If it rains in the summer and we can't work outside, we might pack a picnic lunch and go fishing. On Sunday afternoons we might go to a baseball game in town."

"Well"—she smiled wide—"I've never been fishing or to a baseball game or on a picnic. I like the sound of it all, though. I help out at a grocery store when I'm not in school and find time to go out when I can. There's not much to do around our house. Not like on a farm."

Satisfied he had not put her off by the farm confession, Jimmy let the music sweep them away. She seemed happy dancing with him, and he thrilled to be holding her in his arms. When the dance ended, Jimmy thanked her for the dance and was glad she answered before he said something stupid.

"Walk me part way to my friends' booth so you know where it is. Then you can stop by to ask me to dance later, if you want to. I'm here with friends. We all like to polka."

Jimmy broke out in a wide grin. "Absolutely! See you later." And he left her with her friends, relieved that he had not bombed with the beautiful Annette.

Spotting Jimmy returning from escorting Annette, Maggie hurried toward him. "Hey, let's take turns dancing with Mom, Emma, and Josie. I think Dad and Joe are past dancing. I saw Emil and Caroline here too. There they are! Let's cut in."

Maggie found that Emil's polka was quite a challenge of twirling energy. *Gosh, he is fun! Hope he's not getting a backache bending down to dance with me. Heck, I think I'm taller than Caroline!*

The music stopped, and as they clapped he said, "Don't suppose you heard from Mary?" He moved his head to indicate they should walk back to the side where Caroline and Jimmy waited.

"No, and I doubt that I will." Careful not to say something that would reveal her prior knowledge of Mary's plans to run away, she said, "That note to you made it pretty clear she was going to stay hidden. I really miss her."

"So do we," he said as they approached Caroline and Jimmy.

Caroline reached out to grab Maggie's hand. "What a couple of sweet kids you are," Caroline declared. "Asking your old neighbors to dance."

"Maggie said she hasn't heard from Mary," Emil said.

"If I do, I'll let you know," Maggie heard herself say without thinking. *Damn! If I do hear from her, I can't let her know. Shut up, Maggie.*

"We just worry about her. Let us know how she's doing if you hear from her," Caroline said. "Thanks for the dance." And the two left Jimmy and Maggie standing there.

Maggie whispered, "Those two are probably the nicest people on the planet. I hate lying to them."

"And I'm starting to wonder what I would do if Mary actually showed up tonight."

"Ask her to dance," Maggie joked.

Jimmy was about to say that they needed to look for Mom, Emma, and Josie when he noticed Ralph and Laura Schoen approaching. Ralph, a shy, soft-spoken boy in Maggie's grade, said nothing, but his sister said, "Mind if we dance with you two before we have to stand in line? You both are the neighborhood celebrities, you know. And you both look great!"

"So do you both," Jimmy said. "It's amazing how we farm kids can clean up, isn't it?" Everyone chuckled briefly before he added, "Yeah, glad you came. Let's dance."

He and Laura took a moment to sync their feet before joining the crowd of dancers. They moved easily together. Like all the Schoen kids, Laura was really friendly and kind. None of them, male or female, was the least bit uppity. *Maybe they just take being good-looking for granted.*

"I'll bet you miss Mary Schroedler," she said. "I do too, but I never got to be as close to her as you and Maggie did."

"That's because you lived way out west of the school, right?"

"Sure thing," Laura joked. "Now that Mary's gone, you finally pay some attention to me. Seriously, though, it's too bad we didn't get to know one another very well, even though we spent eight years in the same grade. Now, in high school, it's not the same. We have different classes. But it's good for the neighborhood country kids to stick together. Don't you think?"

"Yes, I do," Jimmy said, "And I just thought of one big advantage you west-side-of-the-school kids had over us east-siders." He paused a moment. "You didn't have Jack Drude!"

They laughed together at the truth of it. Then the music stopped, and they clapped and laughed some more.

"Thanks for the dance, Laura."

"Thank you. I have a confession to make. Of course, I wanted to talk to you, but the main reason I came over is that Ralph wanted to dance with Maggie, and he was too shy to ask her on his own."

"Really?"

"Yeah, despite the fact that he is one of those good-looking Schoen kids."

"You're fun. Too bad you live west of the school. I hope they got along. We'll find out soon enough. Mags will tell me."

"Let me know, will you? Ralph won't say. See you later." She waved as she left.

Jimmy stood at the side of the dance floor. *What a nice girl. I always knew it, but Maggie and I never really got to know her. Strange. Life zips by and you miss out on stuff. And on people. Maggie always said I need to try harder to get along with others more. She was right. And I am getting more social. Maye I'm a grown-up? Ha! No chance.*

Maggie tapped his shoulder. "Hey, let's go to their booth and ask the folks to dance. I'll take Emma, and you dance with Mom. Stay close and we can switch before the number ends. When we take them back, we can dance with Josie and then the twins. We'll stay close and switch off."

"Okay. You've got it all figured out. Mom said we should try to dance with everybody."

When they got to the booth, Maggie explained her plan to Emma, Mom, and Josie.

Emma said, "Great idea. Let's all go out there at once and switch around. It's an odd number, though, so I'll grab Helen to even it up. This will be fun. Don't you agree, Mary?"

"Heck yes. You get your girls, and I'll dance with Jimmy first before he backs out on dancing with his old mother."

"Never happen," Jimmy said.

They took their places, and Jimmy led a few steps before they danced into the crowd.

"Good job," Mom said.

"I had a good teacher."

"Isn't it fun? I mean, the dancing is a way of life for some. I wish Martin and I'd come more often, but he didn't grow up with it like I did."

"Yeah, his church, our church now, was against it."

"And that makes no difference to us now, but it just isn't in his blood, if you know what I mean."

"I suppose it isn't." Jimmy liked to just listen to his mom. She said more if he just shut up and let her talk, especially when she was drinking beer.

"Here's what I mean, Jimmy. See that couple dancing to your left? He's thin on top, wearing the blue dress shirt with the sleeves partially rolled up. She has the navy polka-dot dress."

"Yeah," Jimmy answered.

"Those two were a young married couple when Emma and I used to come to these dances as teenagers. Now, they have kids, farm two hundred acres, and have a big herd of dairy cows. Work like dogs. But they're here nearly every Saturday night, letting off steam."

Jimmy said, "They dance so smooth together."

"And look, he looks just like your father with his sunburned forehead below a line of white where his cap covers his head when he's in the field. And her arms are white because you know she wears long sleeves outside in the sun, like I do."

The music stopped, and as they clapped, Mom said, "Their names are Charles and Emily Rezachky. I'll bet they're nearly fifty years old."

Emma came over. "My turn with Jimmy."

"Did you see Emily and Charles?" Mom said. "I was telling Jimmy about them."

"I saw them, and I'll continue the story," Emma yelled as she danced away with Jimmy into the crowded floor.

"There's a story?" Jimmy asked. "I like stories."

"Oh, it's the same old story of so many young lovers. We'd see them cling to each other all night and dance as one during the last dance of the evening. Your mother and I only went to dances for a couple years together. Neither of us dated much then. We just liked to dance. But we recognize many of the older couples here tonight that used to be young lovers back then, or in their thirties. Now they're old and still dancing."

"Seems there's people of all ages here," Jimmy said.

"And most of them are busy farmers or laborers who work hard all week and come here on Saturday night to celebrate life. Some of them drink too much, but you can be sure they're milking their cows Sunday morning and going to mass too. There are dozens of old couples like that here tonight and lots of young couples who will grow old dancing together. It's in their blood."

"That's what Mom said."

"Really! Did she?"

"Yeah, I'm new to it all, but I can see how that happens. When the orchestra plays and the people start dancing, it brings us all together into one."

"Wow!" Emma exclaimed as the music stopped. She threw up her hands and said, "I see the Czech blood you got from your mom ain't been a-wasted!"

After switching off to a few more partners as Maggie had planned, Jimmy realized he was the only male in the group. *I must be a weirdo. But it's fun.*

CHAPTER 23

MINGLING

Saturday night, June 9, 1956

"That was fun!" Jimmy exclaimed as he finishing dancing a polka with Helen.

"Mom said she was so proud of you and Maggie."

"Tell her not to be too proud yet. The night isn't over."

"You're just like your father. Always a smart-ass."

They laughed together in the way that Jimmy loved to laugh with his cousins as the band leader announced, "Let's play a number to get everyone dancing. It's called the circle dance."

"I'm going to go find Joey," Jimmy said. "We talked with Mom about doing this one."

The leader continued, "All women and girls of all ages, gather at the center of the floor. Men, form a circle around them by joining hands. Women, join hands and form a circle inside the men's circle. Don't worry about being alongside someone you've never seen. This is all about meeting other people. It's all about making tonight all one big party, not hundreds of little ones. Okay, there's still time to join the circle. Folks, let these newcomers join. Those of you still seated, there's still time to get in the circle."

Jimmy and Joey found their place in the circle just as they saw Maggie and the Shaurel girls across the dance floor.

"Wonderful," exclaimed the leader, "the circle is way out to the perimeter of the dance floor. Lots of willing male dancers out there! Great. Okay, here we go."

And as the music started, he called out, "Girls hold hands, face the center of the circle, and move to your left with the music. Boys, hold hands, face the center of the circle, and move to your right. Everyone, keep dancing as you move. When the music stops, ladies turn to face out and dance with the gentleman in front of you."

Jimmy started out in the circle with Joey at his side, but as others joined, they were separated. Jimmy was glad that Joey didn't seem to care. They circled for about thirty seconds before the leader called, "And stop. Find a partner and dance. You don't have to date them, ladies and gentlemen, but you do have to dance with them in the spirit of the dance. Have fun!"

The polka "Just Because" rang out throughout the dance hall. The orchestra members sang too, and many of the dancers joined in as they polkaed swiftly around the floor with partners they'd never seen before. Jimmy saw tall old ladies dancing with short boys of ten or younger and old men dancing with ladies they'd probably never met, some young and others old. Chubby men and women danced with skinny partners, and short men and women danced with taller partners. The clumsy danced with the graceful, and sometimes good dancers passed on their skill to the less skilled. Teen girls and women of all ages danced with each other if there weren't enough boys to go around.

No one judged a partner to be unacceptable, whatever flaws he or she might have. This was the circle dance, and no one cared. At least that was the theory. Of course, the practice didn't always match the theory.

"Ready to dance?" the short, chubby lady asked Joey when the music stopped.

"Yes, but I'm new at it all."

"Of course, you are, dearie. I was new at it once too."

Joey leaned in to lead, and the lady fit herself in his arms and waited till he started.

"You've done some practicing," she said.

Joey was surprised at how smoothly the old lady moved. *She must be over fifty!*

"I'm Madeline."

"I'm Joey. My brother and sister are in the wedding."

"That cute brother-and-sister couple! Wonderful."

They moved smoothly around the floor. Madeline was only a little taller than Joey, making conversation easy. Maggie had told him to practice talking as he danced. "I'm eleven."

"Well, I'm much older. I have a grandson a few years younger than you. He won't dance with me yet, but I hope he will soon."

When the music stopped, Maggie found herself opposite a short bald guy in his forties who said, "Hello, I'm Joseph. You're stuck with me unless you'd sooner not dance."

Maggie saw his smile and said, "I'm here to dance." And he whisked her away like a feather.

He was a really good dancer. She was glad she'd agreed to dance. Her high heels put her face a little above his, but he managed to lead and talk easily to her.

"You and your brother looked great in the wedding party."

"How does everyone in the whole place know we're brother and sister?"

"My wife found out from her friend. Not much gets past her."

"Your wife or your friend?"

"Ha! Beauty and wit. Just like my wife."

"And you are kind and can dance. I like it." Over his shoulder, Maggie spotted Jimmy dancing with a fine-looking woman with lovely black hair and a great figure. "Wow, looks like my brother is having fun dancing too."

"Coincidence! He's dancing with my wife. She's a great dancer!"

The music stopped, and his wife came over to talk. Jimmy followed.

"Hi, I'm Shirley. Did my husband behave himself?" She was clearly kidding.

"Did my brother?" Maggie quipped.

"Unfortunately, he was a perfect gentleman," she joked. "Have fun, kids. Time to circle up again."

"Boy, was she a good dancer!" Jimmy said as they moved to different circles.

"So was he!" Maggie added.

Next time the music stopped, Maggie found herself facing a tall, dark-haired young man. He said, "I'm not a very good dancer, but I hope you don't mind."

"Not here to judge. I'm Maggie." She took her dancing posture as he moved toward her and the orchestra struck up a waltz.

"I'm Albert." His voice vibrated above her hair. Maggie adjusted to his slow pace. She smiled as she detected a faint whiff of barn odor mixed with sweat. *Nothing I haven't smelled before.*

"Sorry, I move kinda slow. You're only the third person I've danced with. Thanks for putting up with me."

Call me a sucker, but I like this guy. Such honesty! "You're doing fine! It's hard to believe I'm only your third dance partner."

"Well, the first only lasted about half a minute before she said she didn't want to dance with me anymore."

"Heck with her, then. There are lots of other girls here, tonight. Besides, isn't it fun just to dance?"

"Yeah. I'm glad this one is a slower one, though. I can keep up and talk too."

Maggie giggled in spite of herself. "I'm not laughing at you. It's just that my brother and I were practicing dancing and talking at the same time this morning before we left for the wedding."

Albert said, "Ha! Now I don't feel so bad. I only practiced with a broom before tonight. It's much more fun with a real girl."

"Thanks. I think. Say, I think my brother knows who you are. Your family lives south of town, right? Our cousin is Billy Thorson. His dad bought some cows from your dad when he got sick."

"I remember Billy. Big husky guy. Nice fella."

At that moment, as they neared the perimeter of the floor, the leader announced, "That's all for the circle dance. Let's begin a round of polkas, starting with the 'Charming Katie Polka.'"

Maggie felt a tap on her shoulder. She turned to see Jane Shaurel.

"Hi, Maggie. I was hoping you'd introduce me to this young man."

Maggie stammered, "Well, I hardly know him myself. I know his name is Albert. So, Albert, this is Jane, my neighbor."

"Hi, handsome."

Albert's mouth dropped open a bit as she took his hand. "Why don't you come over to sit with me and my sisters? We'll dance later." Before she left, she added, "Thanks, Maggie. You're a real friend."

Jimmy came up to her and said, "You were dancing with Albert."

"Yeah, nice guy. A little shy, but nice. Funny thing, though, Jane Shaurel just came here and took him away like he was a real prince."

Jimmy said dramatically, "My hope is that every guy gets to be some girl's real prince."

"You've been reading too much fiction."

"More like your kind of fiction, Mags."

"Look they're squeezing him in the booth with all six sisters. Say what you want, Jimmy, but they are a good-looking bunch of girls."

"I won't deny it, but most of us guys squirm at their aggressive approach. I'll dance with Ann later, but I don't know if I have the courage to walk up to the booth to ask with all five of her sisters there. Jo Anne always embarrasses me."

"If you dance with Ann, you'd better not try to watch your feet. That low-cut dress she's wearing would distract a monk."

The two laughed as the music played. They were about to move to the side when Katherine O'Keran joined them. "Mary Ryan said you wanted to dance with all the neighborhood girls, no matter if they were younger than you. Well, I'm fourteen. Is it a good time to dance with me now?"

"Perfect," Jimmy said as he moved into place.

"I'm not real good, yet, but Mary said you were real easy to dance with."

"Nice of her to say, but I'm new at it too."

Jimmy felt at ease with his younger neighbor as he enjoyed the music and the dance, but he had to know one thing. "Is Billy Joe coming home this summer?"

"No. Not everybody knows this, but B. J. was glad to get away from here. You see, Jack Drude used to bully him an awful lot."

"I thought they were buddies. They used to do all kinds of mischief together, didn't they?"

"All Jack's idea. If B. J. refused to join, Jack would punch him until he agreed. It was horrible for him!"

"I didn't know that. So he isn't really the Drude accomplice I thought he was."

"You have such a way with words, Jimmy. All of that mean stuff B. J. did in the country school was Jack's idea, and he made B. J. join in. I miss him now, but I like it better when B. J. is away because he is free from Jack. My brother is such a nice guy, really. In my last letter to him, I kidded him about his bad penmanship, and yesterday I got a typed letter from him saying he learned how to type and he decided to practice by typing a letter to me so I could read it easier. He's so smart."

"Teaching himself to type. That's pretty impressive. I remember he was smart when he was in the country school. But Jack Drude got in the way of anyone getting to know him."

"Hey, I see Peggy Ryan coming. I told her I'd hand you off to her. She was afraid to ask you herself."

"Are we talking about the same Peggy Ryan?" Jimmy was honestly incredulous.

"She acts kind of uppity, but it's just a coverup." She yelled at Peggy, "Hey, Peggy. It's your turn!"

"Hi, Peggy," Jimmy said once she arrived, trying to think of more to say. "Glad you're here, and may I have this dance?"

"Very impressive, Jimmy. Such manners. I probably don't deserve it."

"Why would you say that?"

"We haven't been the best of friends, but I'm glad we're dancing."

"I'm glad too. And the past is all school stuff. Besides, if I only danced with best friends, I'd be alone most of the night."

"Me too, I guess."

"Look at it this way. Here we are at a nice dance with great music. We are here to have fun." Waltzing was easy with Peggy, and he figured that would be the end of the chat.

But she wanted to talk. "I'm not familiar with this kind of music. A few of my relatives play fiddles. I like Irish music, don't you?"

"Sure, but I haven't heard a lot of it, I guess," Jimmy admitted. "But I do like listening to violin music. Four of my mom's brothers had a small band—two fiddles, a button accordion, and a bass fiddle they used instead of a drum. The waltzes were sweet with the two fiddles. They did mostly Czech tunes."

When the music stopped, the band introduced a polka.

"Gee, I can't polka," Peggy confessed. She made an effort to let go of Jimmy's hand.

"I think you can. And you and I are going to polka like we know what we're doing. Hang on!"

"Okay. I'll follow best I can." It sounded like Peggy was surprised at herself.

The couple twirled into the crowd. Jimmy giggled to himself that for once he had told the pushy Peggy Ryan what to do. *This is not the same girl as the bossy kid at the country school!*

After two polkas, Peggy was smiling like Jimmy had never seen her smile. He escorted her back to the side and said "Thanks" as she headed for her group of friends. The next set started with a waltz. He looked around for Maggie but found Joey along the perimeter.

"Hey, buddy. Are you ready for the big test?"

"What's that?"

"Well, I've been trying to work up the courage to ask Ann Shaurel to dance, but she's with all her sisters and Albert, and I have trouble walking up to a table filled with so many girls. So, I wonder if you could come with me and ask Caroline. You said you wanted to, remember? No time like the present."

"But it's early yet."

"Yeah, get it over with so you don't have to worry about it. If it doesn't go well, then it's over. And if it does, you can dance some more."

"What do I say?"

"Just say what I say to Ann."

Joey nodded, and they headed for the booth.

Ann sat on the outside, and Caroline sat next to her. Next was Jane and then Albert squeezed into the middle. Across from Ann were the twins in the inside and Jo Anne on the outside.

Jimmy said, "Hello neighbors. Good to see you all here. You all look great." Then he turned to ask, "Care to dance, Ann?'"

Jimmy noticed she controlled her smile before she answered. "Of course, Jimmy." She stepped out of the booth, and Joey moved to ask Caroline.

"Care to dance, Caroline?" Joey asked a little too loudly.

She grinned wide and slid out if the booth.

As the two couples were about to leave, Jimmy heard a loud voice.

"Not so fast, you two Carlson boys," Jo Anne commanded. "Just what are your intentions with my dear innocent sisters?"

Joey froze, but Jimmy had expected to get some flak from Jo Anne. He responded quickly, "We intend to have some good clean fun dancing with your two lovely sisters."

"If there are any shenanigans going on out there, dear boy, I expect it will be my sisters who start it. Ha! If you weren't five years younger than me, I'd start it with you myself!"

Jimmy smiled as the girls all giggled. Joey and Albert seemed a little tense, and even Ann and Caroline appeared embarrassed.

"You have my permission to go dance," Jo Anne declared. "Glad you came by, Jimmy and Joey."

The couples walked to the dance floor. Jimmy decided to let Joey handle it on his own, and sure enough, they were dancing before he and Ann began.

In her heels she was his height. Before he stepped toward her to take the dance position, he glanced at her feet so he wouldn't step on them as he moved forward. *Yes, the neckline is a distraction. I'll not look there again.*

He lifted his eyes to her hair and then her eyes and they began dancing. "This is a nice waltz—'Blue Skirt Waltz,' and you happen to be wearing blue."

"You're not going to tell me that you planned it."

"No, I'm not that clever."

"My sister says you are. Jo Anne was only half kidding back there, you know."

"Which part?" *Damn, why did I ask?*

"The part where she said if you weren't younger than her, she'd start something herself. She always called you cute and clever."

"Mr. Clever here has no comeback for that."

"Good. We don't need to talk. Let's just enjoy the dance."

She moved in closer, changing the position of her left arm. He felt her breasts against his body, and in the next moment, her head rested on his shoulder. He smelled her hair. Her perfume. Not too strong. Tasteful. *Who is this girl? This isn't the Ann Shaurel I thought I knew.* Their bodies moved together as one, gliding across the dance floor as if they'd been partners for years. Maybe it was the music vibrating through them, but no, he felt the beat of her heart. Maybe it was his. *What's going on?*

The waltz ended too soon. He felt her step away to applaud, and he said, "Thank you for the dance."

"I enjoyed it, Jimmy. Did you?"

His mind raced. *I enjoyed it way more than I thought I would.* But he said, "Very much."

"Let's continue then."

"Yes, let's continue. As long as you want."

The band began the "Helena Waltz." He found himself hoping she would take the same position. When she did, he positioned himself to encourage her closeness. They waltzed in the same manner until the leader announced, "It's polka time! And we'll begin with the 'Round and Round Polka'!"

They paused to look at each other.

"You like to polka? I do," Jimmy said with a big grin. He could see a small crease on her cheek where she had been holding it against him.

"I do too." She smiled and looked down before she met his eyes again. "It won't be the same, though."

He knew what she meant, and he was sorry for it as they moved into position and swirled into the crowd of dancers.

CHAPTER 24

ROSE'S PLEA

Saturday night, June 9, 1956

Home from doing Carlsons' evening chores, Billy filled the bathtub. Deciding to attend the dance had put him in a cheerful mood. He was no coward. He would face the people he knew, and they could judge him as they pleased. He would not dance with the bride. He would stay clear of her whole family and just visit with some neighbors and maybe the Carlsons. If he got the chance, he would wish Anna well. He would cause no trouble.

He soaked in the tub long enough to get rid of the smell of barn, but he hurried to clean up as fast as he could. He wanted to arrive at intermission, which gave him only about an hour to clean up, get dressed, and drive the twenty miles or so. He'd tell his folks he was leaving on his way out. He expected his mother to try to talk him out of it. But he was determined to go.

He dressed in a lightweight navy-blue suit, white shirt, and red-and-white-striped tie. His folks were watching television as he stopped in the living room to say goodbye.

"I decided to go to the dance," he announced. "Anna only gets married once, and I want to be at the dance to celebrate for her and her new husband."

"I'd advise against it," his father cautioned, "but you have to do what you think you must, I suppose."

His mother stayed silent for a moment before she said, "Don't go, son. Please don't go. I know you loved the girl, but that's why you shouldn't go. No use causing more heartache for either one of you. You know I'm right on this."

"I agree with your mother, Bill. And that hardly ever happens."

Everyone smiled at that, but Rose turned off the television to prepare for a discussion and the room stayed silent.

Billy rubbed his face with his hands. "I've thought about this a lot. I have one chance to see them together on their wedding day. If I see them together and Anna appears happy, then I can rest. I want her to be happy."

John noted rationally, "You will probably see them together at family functions many times in the future. We have some of the same relatives. You'll see them then."

"It won't be the same. It's today that matters." He turned to leave.

Rose jumped up, and with agony on her face and her voice cracking, she pleaded, "Please don't go! That girl has caused you enough trouble. She's not for you!"

"Her name is Anna, Mom. And she and I were in love for five years. We were committed to each other. We wanted to marry. We would have married but for your objections. I'm not interested in blaming anyone but myself, and I realize it's over, but I want to see her happiness for myself. That's all."

"I know you blame me!" Rose exclaimed. "I know you think it's all my fault, but I could not bear to lose you to her. And I wouldn't have been able to bear it. I couldn't have lived with it. I couldn't have." She sobbed as she sat back down on the sofa.

John moved to sit beside his wife, comforting her as best as he could.

"Well, we didn't marry, and that's what you wanted. So, now we can go on with our lives. It was hard for me at first, but I've accepted it now. She's married. I just need a little piece of the celebration. And I need to let people know I can still dance." He smiled at the metaphor for life. "Carlsons' whole neighborhood will be there, and I know many of them. It should be fun for me." Billy turned again to leave. "I'll probably stay until the end of the dance, but don't worry. I'll be ready and eager for morning chores, and I'll plan to go to church at ten. Goodbye, Mom and Dad. See you tomorrow."

"See you tomorrow, Bill," he heard his dad say over his mother's sobs.

Billy waited by the door for a response from his mother.

Suddenly she stood up again, wailing, "I won't let you go! I can't bear the thought of you seeing her again. I don't want you with the family that tried to steal you from me!" She ran to her son, kneeled at his feet, and wrapped her arms around his legs. "I will hang onto you all night if I have to."

"Look, Mom, you promised you wouldn't hurt yourself if we broke up. Well, we broke up. I thought you'd respect my independence after I turned twenty-one, so I put off proposing again and again, but after I turned twenty-two last February, you were even more set against her, so I put off proposing yet again. She gave up on me, Mom. She gave up on *me*. Now I need you to let go of me. Instead, you try to control my movements. How long will this go on?"

"Why are you so obsessed with going? Let it be over with that red-haired demon!"

That was it for Billy. "I can't come back to this, Dad! I can't make sense of anything anymore. I may be back for chores tomorrow morning, but if I'm not, you can manage without me. Maybe I'll rent one of Berris's cabins at Crossroads and take a week off."

John pleaded, "Please, Rose, let him go."

Billy stood still as John forcibly peeled Rose's arms away from her son.

She hoarsely sobbed, "Don't leave me, Billy." Then she turned her anger on her husband and screamed, "You always take his side! I'm all alone here. Everyone here hates me!"

Freed from his mother's arms, Billy said, "Goodbye, folks," and left.

Standing with the other groomsmen in a corner of the ballroom, Jimmy listened as Paul complained, "So, she drinks a cocktail with *Billy*. With *Billy!* But we ain't good enough!"

Walter said, "Look, I can see why you're mad. I am too, a little, but, you know, there could be other reasons that she won't drink."

Ignoring Walter's hint, Paul yelled, "Bullshit! I know one thing. If this Billy boy shows up, I'm gonna kick the hell out of him. And if I can't do it, you and George should help. The cocky SOB goes out with a girl for all those years and then drops her. Poor kid. She meets George right after and marries him four months later. It doesn't make sense. We need to teach him a lesson."

"His lesson is that he's lost the girl. We should just celebrate."

"Right! But she's too good to celebrate with us!"

Walter put his arm around Paul, and putting his face close to his brother's ear, he whispered, "Look, I don't know for sure, but Jenny thinks Anna is pregnant. That's why she won't drink. Now shut up about it."

Paul rocked back on his heels. "Well, why didn't she say so? Okay, so she can't drink because she's pregnant, but that's another reason for us to celebrate. We are going to be uncles! But I'd still like to kick the shit out of Billy-boy if he shows up."

Suddenly, George's voice boomed from behind them. "You will leave him alone. Or else!" They turned, and he held their gazes for a moment, waiting for their reply.

"Right, George. We'll leave him alone," Paul muttered.

Then George turned to Jimmy, bent down, and whispered, "Thanks for taking care of my bride when they stole her. We'll have to take you and Maggie bowling sometime."

CHAPTER 25

SISTERS

Saturday night, June 9, 1956

As the clock neared ten, Josie leaned closer to Mary in the booth and said, "We'll miss George, of course, but he's only been back from the Navy since December. We've been without him for six years."

Mary nodded, eager to bring the conversation toward a discussion about George. "We didn't see much of him the years before he went in, but now I see he's such a kind, good-humored man. You must be so proud."

"We are. There seemed to be a natural bond between George and Elmer from the very beginning. More than our other two boys even."

"Really?"

"It takes a certain kind of person to bring out the best in Elmer. George has been able to do that ever since he was a little boy. The other boys are different. Brothers can be so different from each other."

"Sisters and siblings too."

They paused to look at Elmer, standing a few yards away swapping stories with Emil, Martin, Joe, and Emma, who, upon seeing the two women smiling at her, charged toward the booth.

"I've never seen Elmer more wound up. He's so funny!" Emma waved her free hand and set her drink on the table as she slid in next to Mary. "Do men never talk of anything serious? Do they make a joke out of everything?"

Sensing the question was rhetorical, Mary waited for her sister to continue.

"Elmer's telling us how he castrates hogs. Said he uses a single-edge razor blade, and when he set it down, he sticks it into a potato. I asked him why he used a potato. He mumbled something about it keeping the blade clean but he emphasized that he had to stick it into something. He said that if you set it on a flat surface, it's hard to pick up without cutting yourself. I asked him why he needed to put it down at all and he said, 'Sometimes I have to scratch my nose and I don't want to do that when I have a razor blade in my hand. My one-eyed uncle did that.' We all laughed. But then I asked, 'Why not scratch your nose with your other hand?' And he says, 'I don't want to set down my beer!' We're all busting a gut by that time, but he waits a beat or two before he adds, 'You can't stick a bottle of beer into a potato!' He got us all in tears. And he was so quiet earlier in the day!"

Josie smiled and said, "I'm so glad he's having a good time. He seldom lets loose like this. He must feel comfortable around you guys."

"Good to hear," Mary said. "I was worried that little incident at the bar might ruin a good time for your family."

"I could've kicked Joe for opening his big mouth," Emma said, waving her hand. "He hardly speaks all night and then he comes up with that."

"I wouldn't worry about it," Josie said frankly. "We know about Billy. The main thing is that George and Anna are good with it. At George's suggestion, we had him and Anna over on Sunday afternoon when Walter and Paul were gone. They told us all about Billy and Anna. I don't think the boys found out until tonight, though. But they would've sooner or later anyway."

Mary watched the faces of Josie and Emma, wondering if "all about" meant everything. At this point she was unsure if Anna had told Emma about the baby. *Well, Anna will tell me if she wants to. None of my business otherwise.*

"Before you came over to the booth, Emma," Josie said, "Mary and I were talking about how different siblings are from each other. I used my boys as an example."

"And my girls too! I swear it's hard to believe the five of them grew up in the same house with the same parents." Emma waved her free hand and held on to her drink with the other. "Anna is so sensible and Marcella is so wild and Helen is so *not like* either of them. She's quiet but deep, yet willing to express herself when she needs to. And the twins! God knows, I adore them, but having identical twins in the home is nothing short of crazy. Sometimes they are like one person and other times they are contrary to each other on purpose, I think."

Never quite as willing as Emma to spill her thoughts about her family to others, Mary thoughtfully commented, "When you think of it now, I imagine the fact that Anna had a steady boyfriend from the ages of fourteen to nineteen had quite an effect on her sisters in their teenage years." *I hope I put that delicately.*

"You ain't kidding it did. It was like a damn soap opera in the house! Where are Anna and Billy going? When will they get engaged? When can I date? The whole house was always about them. No wonder that Marcella screams for attention all the time and Helen gave up on it. I love my Anna, but I am so glad she's married off to a wonderful man like George." Emma reached over to put her hand on Josie's. "Thank you, dear Josie!"

Josie smiled and said, "Elmer helped George buy the Kelser farm a few miles away. Elmer is thrilled to have them close by. He and George were always such pals. I told Anna not to worry about having her mother-in-law live so close. She said she wasn't worried, and I told her five miles away is the right distance for a mother-in-law. Within driving distance but beyond walking distance."

Emma stayed silent as Mary mused that Emma lived farther away from the newlyweds and that was for the best.

Suddenly, Emma put down her drink and, bubbling with enthusiasm, raised both hands as she exclaimed, "I just love this band! The trumpets and the piano with the vocals are so fun. And the guy on the concertina is just the best!" She took a big drink of beer before adding, "Hey, Mary, I think we need to dance this set of waltzes, like we used to do when we were kids. As you can see"—she jerked her head to where Joe, Martin, Emil, and Elmer were still drinking beer and laughing—"I think both our hubbies have done all the dancing they're going to do for the night. And it's not even ten thirty. And, Josie, cut in when you feel like dancing."

"I think I'll be fine just sitting. Go ahead and dance, you two."

Mary seized her chance to talk privately with her sister about Anna. "Yeah," she agreed. "I got two dances out of Martin. That's about his limit."

Emma took lead, as she had when they were children, and they moved to the dance floor in a flourish. Patience would be Mary's strategy. She'd let Emma lead the conversation, as well as the dance, and sooner or later the subjects of her curiosity would arise.

With tongue in cheek, Emma asserted with pride, "We do pretty good for a couple of old married women with kids."

"We do, and I love this band too."

"George and Anna were lucky to step into a cancellation. The Dick Traklic Band was booked for the event over a year ago, as all of the best bands are. Some of the early posters still show it as the Bartilik-Cavenaugh wedding dance. I feel bad for the couple that had a fallout, but it sure worked out for my Anna."

Mary said nothing, hoping Emma's loose tongue would continue to waggle.

"At first I didn't know why they were in such a hurry. I mean, I knew they were in love, but when George proposed in April, they were both immediately determined to have a June wedding."

"June weddings are nice," Mary said, trying to be cordial. "And Anna looks so beautiful! That empire waist flatters her figure. Did you help pick it out?"

"Yes," Emma boasted, "and I recommended the empire waist."

The music stopped, and they applauded the band as Emma suggested, "Let's keep dancing. We haven't really had time alone to talk during all these wedding preparations, and today there's always so many people around all the time."

The orchestra began the "My Village Home Waltz." "Oh, good!" Emma exclaimed. I hope they sing it in Czech." When she realized they weren't singing it at all, she added, "Okay, easier to talk, then."

"Right," Mary agreed.

"Okay, I may as well tell you this now, in strict confidence. You'll find out anyway. Anna is pregnant. She hopes the child is born around her birthday in December. That's about nine months after they started dating. That's fast, but I'm not criticizing Anna, and I know you won't judge her."

"Absolutely not. Babies can arrive any time. All babies are a blessing." Mary smiled to herself. *She doesn't know! Emma is convinced George is the father.*

Mary stopped dancing and held out her arms to hug her sister. "Congratulations, Grandma! You are a lucky woman. And I'm happy for you."

They hugged for a moment before Emma confessed, "I'm sorry about all the secrets. I should've told you when we went dress shopping."

Mary managed to say, "No need to apologize. Not at all."

"I don't think anyone can tell," Emma said. "It's the perfect dress."

"But I don't think it's any big scandal," Mary said for support. "They're young and in love and married." *Hurray for Anna!*

"I've talked to Josie many times, and she always says what you heard her say a bit ago. She's thrilled for her George. Of course, I told her how thrilled we were to have him in the family. She didn't say this in so many words, but she indicated that marrying into my family eliminated any need for her to explain George's heritage. We all know and have loved the guy from the day he was born."

"A day we both remember," Mary added.

"And they can start the marriage with no secrets. George's past is in the open."

Mary nodded. *Glad Anna was able to tell George the whole truth. Hope Emma never finds out unless Anna tells her.* "I know I've told you a hundred times, but the wedding really has been perfect in every way."

"Thanks. I was afraid there would be more tension, you know, with Billy being so close to your family and to ours too, really. I asked Anna if Billy was coming to the dance. Said she didn't know. I hope he doesn't. It'd be awkward. She hasn't heard from him, but I suppose you see him regularly."

"He told me he wasn't coming, but later he told Jimmy he might. We asked him to do our evening milking, so if he comes it will be late. We see him nearly every Sunday when he comes over to train with Jimmy." *So, dear sister, you're not admitting the reason Anna and Billy didn't talk is because you didn't pass on his phone calls. Would I be mean to bring up the phone calls now? Well, now or never.*

"Emma," Mary started talking slowly. "Remember when we did the permanents and you told us Billy only called Anna once? I know he called many times and you told him Anna did not want to talk, and I also know you didn't tell Anna he called."

Emma stopped dancing, and the two sisters stood facing each other on the dance floor as couples waltzed around them. Looking up slightly to meet the eyes of her older sister, Mary remarked, "I wasn't going to bring it up today, but you were talking about secrets—Anna's pregnancy and George's background—so I thought I'd get this off my chest."

Emma said bluntly, "I confess I lied to Anna, but I'd appreciate you not telling her. It's too late for her to know anyway. No good would come of it."

"True, of course, but you may want to consider telling her yourself. I won't tell her. It's not my secret to tell, but I'm guessing she will probably figure it out if she hasn't already. Besides, I can't argue with the idea that it all turned out for the best, it seems."

"Billy called many times, and I didn't tell Anna. In the moment, when the calls came, you know, she seemed resolved already. Resolved to give up on him. I thought a phone call would just confuse her. Worse, though, when Billy wanted to come over, I told him Anna said she didn't want to see him. Once I started lying to her and it was working, I didn't see any reason to stop. I feel pretty guilty about the whole thing, but I'm not sorry about how it turned out."

Mary looked away as she softened her feelings about her sister's actions. She looked back at Emma and smiled as she remarked, "Anna told me she had given up on Billy when she came over to bake cookies. I think she was already falling in love with George then. I don't think your lies changed her decision, Emma. I think that, in the end, she would've picked George anyway, and the whole process would have taken more time and been more painful."

"Thanks," Emma said. "Glad you brought it up. One less secret I have to keep."

"Let's dance," Mary said, and they began to waltz again. *But I must keep the secret that Billy is the father of Anna's baby. Not my secret to tell.*

After a moment, Mary sensed what she needed to say. "Truth can be a steep hill to climb. I don't blame you for holding back the truth about the calls that day we did the permanents. It wasn't the time to confess then. And I won't tell Anna. It's your confession to make if you want to make it." Then Mary found herself confessing, "Billy had told us he tried to call, so Maggie and I both knew. I told Maggie I was going to ask you about it."

"I hate to think what Maggie must think of her old aunt Emma for lying about the calls."

"I think it'll be fine," Mary said. "I'll explain your side of it to Maggie so she'll know why you did what you did. She'll understand."

"You can be so understanding. No wonder Anna loves you so much."

Discussion ceased, and the two sisters held each other a little closer as they waltzed. When the music stopped, they clapped, and as the orchestra leader announced, "It's polka time!" the sisters looked at each other and nodded.

They polkaed easily together, each holding the other at elbow length, neither leading, and singing along to the "Barbara Polka." Spotting Emily and Charles Rezachky dancing side by side instead of in the conventional embrace, Mary broke her song to say, "Look how they do all those steps and arm movements, Emma. They're so good. They were doing that ever since we were kids."

"They've added a lot of hand and arm moves. Pretty fancy."

"Decades of rehearsal," Mary commented before they both began singing again.

After two more polkas, the sisters paused along with all the dancers to applaud the band as the leader announced, "It's waltz time. Stay on the floor for the 'Faded Rose Waltz.'"

As the music began, Marcella and Anna approached them.

"I've danced with Mom and Uncle Martin, but I haven't yet danced with you," Anna said as she moved in next to Mary. Marcella and Emma waltzed away, and Anna smiled and added, "And we have some things to discuss."

Although Mary led the dance, she waited for Anna to begin the conversation, thinking, *I really need to know if she told George everything.*

"I loved to see you and Mom dance. She's told me of the days when you and she went to dances without escorts. You rode with your brothers to the dance. Not really looking for a guy but just loving to dance."

"We always had our eyes open for finding Mr. Right. We did okay with it, I think. Martin and Joe are good guys, although they may not be on their best behavior tonight."

Anna laughed lightly before her expression grew serious. "I took your advice. As you already know, I told George everything. It wasn't easy for him at first, but I convinced him I was over Billy, even though I told him I loved the guy. I told him before he proposed, and he only took a moment to think it over before he proposed a few minutes later."

"Did he say anything about the baby?"

"Yes. He was so honest. I loved him even more after he told me he wanted me and the child and that the child would be our child. I cried when he told me that, like I'm crying a little now when I tell you."

Mary felt her eyes tearing. "Yeah, we always knew he was a swell guy."

"And I realized I lucked out because I was in love totally with Billy, but he couldn't bring himself to abandon his mother in her situation—but then I found George, who I fell in love with and who was ready to commit in spite of my circumstances. Truly, I am a lucky woman."

"You are, but you deserve to be happy."

"Everyone does. Which is why I don't think I'll ever tell Mom. Only you and George and Marcy and Helen know the baby is Billy's. A few others just know I'm pregnant and think I'm due in December."

"The secret is safe with me."

The bride and her favorite aunt twirled, both smiling at the revelations. Mary had nothing to add. *Lovely bride, lovely wedding, lovely groom. Billy has lost so much. But you can't lose what you never had. Or is it "You don't know what you got till it's gone"?*

Anna said, "I want to tell Billy. About the baby."

"Oh, dear, I can't advise you on that one. Do you think it's wise?"

"I don't know *wise*, but George and I agree that if he comes tonight and if I can pick the right moment, I should tell him. George is convinced he'll do the right thing and stay out of it and keep the secret. It's that or I live in fear of his figuring it out somehow, or suspecting and trying to find out."

"Wow, you and your mother take this truth serum seriously." *Oops!*

"What did Mom confess?"

"Nothing, really," Mary lied. "Just some fantasies we had as kids."

"Billy and I had something together. He deserves to know. George agrees."

"This husband of yours is measuring up to be even more of a special guy than I thought. Well, you know Billy best, and what I know of him is that he is the most kind and serious and decent person I know. If that's your decision, do it!"

CHAPTER 26

THE SIX-PACK

Saturday night, June 9, 1956

"Hey," Ronnie said as Joey came off the dance floor, "dancing ain't that much fun for me. It's intermission soon, and I wish we could get some beer. Then we'd have some fun. Everyone seems to have more fun when they're drinking beer, don't ya think?"

"My folks sure do," Joey admitted.

"Mine too! We need some beer."

"Have you ever had it?" Joey asked.

"Sure. Lots of times. Dad lets me swig out of his. Mom don't like it, but that just makes Dad more willing to let me take another swig."

"Really?"

"Yeah, one time at a party, I drank part of a bottle that my dad left sitting on the table when he went outside to pee."

"How was it?"

"Real good. I felt it too."

"What do you mean?"

"I got dizzy. In a good way, you know. Wouldn't it be great if we could get us some beer tonight?"

Joey saw the image in his mind. He'd seen Jimmy give Mom a six-pack. She'd wrapped it in a towel and put it on the floor behind the front passenger seat. He heard himself say, "I know where we could get some."

"Where?"

Joey pulled Ronnie toward him to whisper, "My folks have a six-pack in the car. It's probably even still cold. They wrapped it in a towel so it wouldn't move around on the floor of the car."

"Do they lock the car?"

"Never."

"Let's go!"

Like a bullet out of a barrel, the two boys raced out of the ballroom, eager to experience new adventures.

As Joey led his friend to the car, though, he began to have doubts. He wished he hadn't volunteered the beer. But there was no turning back now. He couldn't tell Ronnie that he'd changed his mind. How would that sound? *Gee, Ronnie, I'd better not take the beer. He'd call me a chicken. I'd never live it down.*

"How far away did you guys park, anyway? We're nearly to the ball field."

"Yeah, well, when we got here, the close parking was taken." Joey cut across a corner of the park to arrive at the spot where his folks' blue Ford was aimed east. "Dad likes to park so the car is heading home, so he doesn't have to turn around." Joey stopped suddenly and whispered, "Holy cow! That's the sheriff's car on the end of the lot!"

Without speaking, the two boys turned to walk in the other direction. Ronnie stopped and ducked behind a tree. "Look, they can't see us in the dark here. Where is your car?'

"Two rows this side of the sheriff. I'm not gonna get caught!"

"Neither am I, Joey, but they don't know we're here, and I'm sure they're not even looking for us. You can go to your car. There's no law against that. And they won't be able to see you carrying two cans of beer in the dark."

Joey thought for a moment. Deciding he didn't want to appear cowardly, he said, "You wait here by the tree."

Trying to walk casually, Joey approached the car and went directly to the back door. He'd never taken anything out of his folks' car that he wasn't supposed to take. This was his first time breaching their trust. A strange feeling gripped his stomach. He recognized guilt, but he couldn't back down now. As he reached for the door handle, he turned to glance at Ronnie next to the tree. *I could pretend the door is locked. But what if he checked it?* He grabbed the handle and hesitated with his thumb on the release button. As if his thumb had a mind of its own, the button was pushed and the door latch released. *Darn!*

He reached down, unwrapped the towel, removed two cans, and set them on the edge of the back seat. He carefully rewrapped the remaining four cans in the towel before he straightened up, grabbed the two cans, and stepped away, closing the door quietly behind him.

When he reached the tree, Ronnie said, "Wow! You got them. I was watching the cops. They didn't pay any attention to you. And there is a city police car parked on the other end of the lot too, but he can't see you either."

"Are there always this many cops here?"

"I don't know. Probably not. Maybe they're expecting some trouble."

Joey handed the cans to Ronnie, who sat with his back against the tree. Ronnie said, "Let's sit here and open them up." He put his hand out to Joey. "Hand me the church key."

"What?"

"That's what they call a can opener. Boy, you are green."

"I didn't bring one."

"How are we gonna open them?"

Could I be any dumber? Wait, maybe I can still get out of this. "Well, I guess we might as well put them back if we can't open them."

"No, I'll find a way. Say, my folks keep a church key in the glove compartment. Maybe yours do too! You have to go back to look."

Joey nodded reluctantly. He retraced his steps to the car to open the passenger-side front door. After a moment of digging in the glove compartment, he found the opener, backed out of the car, shut the door, and, with as much calmness as he could muster, walked back to meet Ronnie.

"The cops never moved," Ronnie assured him.

Joey ruefully sat down by the tree. Ronnie opened the two cans carefully. "Don't want to shake them. The big puncture is to drink out of and the small puncture across the rim is to let air in as you drink. See?"

"Yeah, I know. Sometimes I open the beers for my folks. Give me the opener and I'll put it back so we don't forget."

When Joey returned, Ronnie was standing. His friend handed over a can, saying, "Here, pal, have a nice big drink to start."

Ronnie put his can to his mouth and tilted his head back. Joey heard him gulping as he drank. Joey took a sip and kept a straight face despite disliking the taste.

"Yeah, it doesn't taste that good at first, but you get used to it," Ronnie insisted. "Let's drink as we head back."

Ronnie took another long swallow as Joey sipped a little more. Ronnie gulped again and then emitted a long burp before sitting down again with his back against another tree.

Ronnie said slowly, taking care with each word, "See, I told you I could drink beer."

"I never said you couldn't."

"But *you* can't." Ronnie put the can to his mouth, tilted his head way back, and finished his beer.

Dim park lights shaded by trees lit a pathway a few yards away. At their spot, the light showed the blank expression on Ronnie's face as he said, "I can drink yours if *you* ain't gonna."

"I'll drink it."

"Drink it, then, or let me have it."

"I'm still drinking." He began to worry about his friend. *I wonder if he can walk. He seems so loose. I don't really want mine. But should he drink it?* "Hey, maybe we should walk back to the ballroom."

"I told *you* I could drink beer." He grabbed Joey's can, sat on the grass, and gulped half of what was left.

"And you did. Now, let me help you up."

"Don't need help. I'm almost finished with this beer. Wish I had another." He leaned forward to put his hand on the grass to get up, repeating, "Don't need help." Then he toppled forward and turned on his side. His stomach groaned a moment before liquid spewed from his mouth, making a small, yellowish puddle on the grass.

Joey grabbed his arm and pulled him to the side to prevent him from rolling in the puddle, then darted away to avoid Ronnie's next eruption. He offered Ronnie his handkerchief, but Ronnie seemed unable to see it or understand the offer, so Joey put it away.

Joey was worried. *Do I go get help? Or just stay here and keep watch? My folks don't get sick like this, I don't think. Why is he so sick? What can I do?*

He moved closer to Ronnie, who lay still on his back with his eyes closed and his hands at his sides. Putting his ear next to Ronnie's mouth, Joey heard him breathing. Then Ronnie suddenly rolled onto his left side, put his hands palm to palm under his head for a pillow, and pulled his knees up toward his chest. *Maybe he just needs to rest.*

For a few minutes, Joey watched Ronnie rest on his side, breathing deeply, sometimes making a snorting sound. *I'd like to get back to the dance, but I can't leave him like this. First thing I'm going to do is get rid of the evidence.*

He rose from the grass, found the empty cans, looked around for witnesses, and tossed them as far as he could into the park. *Don't like to litter, but I can't be seen walking around looking for a garbage can.*

After checking again that Ronnie was breathing, Joey settled himself down, leaned against a tree, and closed his eyes. Sleep took him away in seconds.

CHAPTER 27

THE RIDE

Saturday night, June 9, 1956

"Hey, Mags," Jimmy kidded as they stood outside the front entrance, "your boyfriend Tony just got out of that 1955 Ford Crown Victoria. Looks like he's coming over to see you."

"Nice car, Tony!" Jimmy called to him as he approached the ballroom.

"Too bad it's not mine. Belongs to a guy from town I just met. Name is Benny. He asked me to come along for a game of bumper tag. I told him I didn't know what he meant, but it sounded like fun when he explained it. You two can get in the back. I'll ride up front with Benny. It's just a fun game where drivers hide from each other in town, and they have to tag the other car by touching the other guy's bumper with theirs. Benny said we only have time for one game if we want to get to the drag race in time."

They hopped in the back of Benny's car, and Tony introduced his new friends to each other. Benny had short, light hair and sat tall in the driver's seat. He grinned all the time, even when he talked. "They're hiding already and took off to the south. Rules are you have to stay in the city limits, so I'm gonna head west because they'll have to cut north to stay in bounds."

Benny glanced out the window as he said, "Oops! I'd better slow down. That's the third cop car I've seen parked near the ballroom. Wonder if they're setting a trap for someone."

Jimmy turned to Mags, trying to see her reaction as the car passed under street lamps. *Could they be waiting to catch Mary?*

He felt Maggie's hand touch his before she leaned over to whisper, "Maybe Mary is really coming and the cops are waiting for her. We should warn her, but I don't know how."

Jimmy whispered, "Me either."

Benny continued, "Eddy is driving, and he's a chickenshit driver, so he won't park in anyone's yard unless it's a long driveway. I'll check a couple alleys." Benny sped through a stop sign, and the back end of the two-door coupe dipped as they crossed the intersection. "I'll stop twice for that next time," Benny joked. "There's a lot of cops in town tonight, so I gotta be careful. But that's what makes it fun."

Jimmy looked at Maggie in the darkness. *What did I get us into now? Scary, but kind of exciting.* Maggie's face was expressionless.

Benny cut his lights and coasted past a one-way street, then took a left at a dead end without braking. "Don't want him to see my brake lights," he explained to the novices.

He did a U-turn and backed into a private driveway. "These folks are over seventy and always in bed by now, and neither Adeline or Jeanette can hear much anyway." He cut the engine. "Okay, now, everyone, duck down out of sight."

Only a minute passed before Benny said, "There goes Ed! His lights are off, but he's too chicken not to brake, so we'll follow him and watch for his brake lights." He sped out to follow. After bouncing another intersection, he shouted to the backseat passengers, "Don't you love what those dips do to your stomach?! Are you two doing okay back there?"

"Okay," Jimmy choked out, unsure of Maggie's feelings on the matter.

"See his brake lights? He's pulling into Fishers' long driveway. He'll park under that big spruce, I'll bet. I'll shift down and make that turn at a crawl and creep up on him."

Jimmy listened to the soft crunching of the tires meeting the dirt driveway as they coasted down a small hill. Suddenly, Benny braked slightly, and *Thump!* The bumper of the '55 Ford met the bumper of Eddy's green Plymouth.

Eddy jumped out. He was heavyset and tall, with black hair combed into a ducktail. "How the hell do you do that? You got me in less than ten minutes."

Jimmy and Maggie whispered to each other at the same time, "Seemed like an hour!"

The yard light came on, and yelling came from the house, "Out of here, you hoodlums!" But Benny was already backing down the driveway faster than anyone Jimmy had ever seen.

"I don't play tag with anyone whose bumper isn't a good match. This car is too sweet for that. And to show you how sweet it is, I just filled it with premium before I picked you up, and now that it's all mixed good, we'll zip over to the flat stretch west of town to see if I can get her to the limit. Then we'll see who's in on the drag race."

Hearts beat fast in the back seat as they sped west out of the city limits. Benny was up to eighty in a few minutes and then ninety and then one hundred. Jimmy looked over Benny's shoulder to watch the needle on the speedometer bob as it climbed slowly. The car lurched up and down like someone was pumping a swing to get more height. In a few minutes they hit one hundred fifteen. Jimmy thought, *Well, that's good enough for me. We don't need to go faster.* But he remained silent. He put his hand on Maggie's arm. It felt ice cold.

Benny encouraged his Ford, "Come on, baby. You've got some left in you. I know it!"

Jimmy lurched with the car like a rocking swing as the sharp snap of the tires over the concrete seams became a single continuous click. *Why don't I say something before we die? How did I let this go this far? Now if I say something, he might brake, or do something stupid. What if a tire blew? Holy shit!!* He looked at Maggie, who stared straight ahead as if frozen. *Damn! I'm responsible for letting her ride with this maniac!*

The speedometer was bobbing at one hundred eighteen. Jimmy breathed out slowly as he felt Benny let off the gas. "That's the best we can do tonight, boys and girls. We'll try again next week."

Benny let his speed decrease to eighty-five—it seemed like they were crawling. And when Benny slowed to turn off to a road where he could turn around, Jimmy could've kissed the ground—if they'd let him out of the car. But he was pretty sure his legs would be too weak to hold him up.

"We gotta go back eight miles to turn off to the drag site. I'm pretty sure it'll be Jerry's fifty-four Chevy. I got more horse and a newer car, but he's got the short stroke and it's souped up. He won't say what engine he has in the four-door sedan. In past drags, I beat him sometimes and he beats me sometimes. He can't do my top end, but his car is hot."

Jimmy felt himself sweating and didn't like the smell of it. Maggie was still not saying anything. They crested a hill and drove onto a flat stretch of the highway where cars of all makes, models, and vintages were parked along the road and in the ditches. Jimmy had never seen so many teenagers in one spot. With bright headlights illuminating the night and car radios blaring country western music or rock 'n' roll, the event took on the atmosphere of a carnival, but with an exciting, lawless nature. Teen spectators mingled with those in their early twenties. Some of them were drinking beer from cans or brandy from pint bottles. Jimmy thought he recognized Annette surrounded by a group of kids.

Benny pulled over. "I'll let you guys off here. Hope you enjoyed the ride, kids. Cheer for me, eh?"

"Yeah," Jimmy said. His voice had a squeak to it that he didn't recognize. But he felt obligated to add before Benny drove off, "Thanks for the ride. It was really fun!"

"When he's done with the drag race, he'll take us back to the dance," Tony said.

"Not on your life!" Maggie exclaimed. "Never will I ever get in that car again! I thought we were all going to die. Jeez! I've never been so scared. I couldn't even get my head together to pray!"

"Full agreement here," Jimmy said, "but we're less than a quarter mile from the ballroom. I know the way back if we have to walk."

"Good," Maggie said. "We can walk if we have to."

"Okay," Tony said. "Eddy is here—you know, the guy who lost the bumper tag. He'll take us back, but while we're here, we might as well see some drags, okay?"

Maggie smiled and said, "No, I'd sooner go back. If we leave now, we won't miss any of the dance."

They walked to Eddy's car, feeling safe in the knowledge that he was not a maniac.

Eddy said, "Get in and we'll wait for Tony. He has to check in with his cousin, I think."

Once they were in the back seat, Maggie poked Jimmy in the ribs and whispered, "Isn't that Annette passing around pints with those kids? Okay, Tony's coming back."

Maggie was flattered when Tony opened the roadside back door and squeezed in next to her. As he put his right arm around her, she wasn't surprised at the strong odor of whiskey on his breath. She had expected no less. But she liked Tony, and he had been so polite and nice to them both. The car jerked forward a few yards but then skidded to a halt, jolting the backseat passengers forward. The curbside back door swung open, and a fourth passenger climbed inside.

"Hi, everyone," Annette said. "Mind if I join you?" She squeezed in close to Jimmy. Her voice was husky as she said, "There. Now I'm comfy. Are you?"

The green Plymouth sped off as Jimmy inhaled the sweetness of brandy on her warm breath. He smiled, but had no chance to speak as her lips met his softly before taking firm command of his first experience with French kissing. He liked it. And he liked Annette.

Maggie thrilled as Tony kissed her gently, his hands gently holding her face close to his. That her brother was seated next to her did not dull the romance of the moment, which took her away to a place of dreams. But then Tony's kisses became firm, pushing her lips apart, and she no longer felt in control. Unable to breathe easily, she pushed him away as she exclaimed, "Hey, back off! Stop the damn car! Let's get out of here, Jimmy!"

The sudden braking of the car forced her against the back of the front seat as she reached for the door handle. Then, quickly stepping over Jimmy and Annette, she opened the door, grabbed her brother's hand, and lurched out of the car, pulling him after her.

They landed on their backsides on the side of the road and watched the green Plymouth speed away. Maggie jumped up quickly, but Jimmy remained seated on the gravel shoulder.

"That was just crazy!" Maggie declared. "I had to get out of there fast. I'm still shaking." She paused to look at Jimmy, still sitting on the side of the road. "Are you okay?" she asked, offering him a hand up. "Are you hurt?"

"No, but I am a bit surprised. One moment I'm sitting on a soft cushion kissing a beautiful girl and the next second I'm sitting on gravel."

"I felt trapped. I had to get out of there before things got out of control. Tony was really drunk, although I didn't realize it right away."

"You're right, Mags, Annette was pretty drunk too. I wonder if she even knew what she was doing. I didn't think of that until now."

"That was just too crazy to forget," Maggie said as she started walking. "Let's go. We're not far from the ballroom."

"I won't forget it soon myself," Jimmy said as he rose and hurried to catch up.

Adopting a swift pace, they walked in silence for about fifty yards, each reviewing the events of the evening. Then Maggie broke the silence.

"What gets me, though, is that you can just chalk that up to experience. Something to add to your accomplishments."

"So can you."

"Not the same thing for a girl."

Jimmy sensed that Maggie was seriously upset about something. After a moment he said, "It is different for a girl. I agree. But . . . can you explain how is it different for a girl? And what exactly are we talking about, here?"

"I maybe can't explain it, but I think you know what I mean. If I had gone along with him—let him continue to do what he wanted—then I become an easy target for other guys. I get a reputation."

"Well, I'd get one too, a reputation, I mean."

"But for you it's bragging rights among the boys."

"Wouldn't it be bragging rights for you among the girls?"

"I don't honestly know. But I can't see myself bragging in school saying, 'Hey, I went to the dance and made out with this guy I just met.' Yet you can go to school and say to guys, 'I went to the dance and this girl and I . . .' whatever you did."

"First of all, I wouldn't talk about what a girl and I did, but I know some boys would and I think some girls would too, although they might put it a different way, like they'd say they made out with this really cute guy."

"Okay, I've heard girls say that."

"Good." Jimmy laughed. "I was just guessing."

"But don't pretend you don't know what I mean. I think you do."

"I do. I do! But it's hard to put it into words."

"A guy will get a reputation of getting girls in the back seat . . ."

Jimmy interrupted her. "And girls will get a reputation of being easy to get into the back seat."

"And the difference is the reputation is a positive for boys and a negative for girls."

"I see what you mean, and I agree, but there's another way to look at it. Maybe it's the attitude toward the deed more than the deed itself. The reputation for a boy only works in his favor for the boys. Whether or not the boy's reputation works in his favor for girls is up to each individual girl. It's a girl's choice if that boy's reputation makes her more eager to go out with him. And it's a boy's choice if a girl's reputation makes him more eager to go out with her. And, of course, that applies to either a positive or negative reputation."

"I'm with you on that all the way, Jimmy, but you mention the word *reputation*, and I think that's the key. People have different expectations for what is a good—no, *acceptable*—reputation for a boy and a girl."

After some thought, Jimmy continued, "I don't know what it was like in the past, and I don't know what it will be like fifty years from now, but now, in 1956, I'd say girls condemn other girls more readily than they condemn guys, even though they are both involved in the same behavior. It's not just the behavior. It's a difference in attitude of boys toward boys versus girls and the attitude of girls toward boys versus girls." He paused before adding, "Sorry, my explanation wasn't very clear."

"Clear enough. Yes, we girls are hard on each other when it comes to reputation. I was quicker to see Annette as a slut than I was to see Tony as a—we don't even have a word like *slut* for a boy! That kind of proves my point."

"I can think of a few choice words, but none of them condemn him like *slut* does to Annette. I wouldn't call her that, by the way."

Maggie exclaimed, "Ha! Just more of the same."

They'd never slowed their pace. Jimmy was not totally satisfied with their conclusions, but he could think of nothing more to say.

But Maggie had wrestled her thoughts into something profound. "But have you ever heard the term *damaged goods* applied to a man in the same way it was applied to Mary Schroedler?"

Jimmy stopped so suddenly that he skidded on the gravel shoulder. After rubbing his face with both hands, he said, "Jeez, Mags. You nailed it. You nailed it, for sure."

The sorrow in their hearts for Mary reawakened as they walked on in silence, each with their own special memories of their dear friend.

CHAPTER 28

BILLY AT THE DANCE

Saturday night, June 9, 1956

Billy had to park on a gravel side street west of the ballpark, about two blocks south of the main road and two blocks west of the ballroom, but the night was warm, with a soft breeze that cooled his skin, making the walk through the park's majestic trees exhilarating. As he approached the ballroom, he was still unsure if he should've come, but he was positive about one thing—he ached to see Anna. He wanted to capture in his mind an image of her dressed in her white wedding gown. Though the lasting memory of her would bring him more pain than joy, if he didn't risk seeing her now, the chance would be gone forever.

He'd arrived during intermission. As he purchased his ticket, he'd never felt more alone. For five years he and Anna had been a couple. Entering dances or parties together had become natural. Without her, he was lost. She had been his girl since he was sixteen. He had no pre-Anna dating experience to fall back on. Should he stop at the bar to have a drink or go up the two steps to the ballroom to turn his ticket in and get stamped?

The bar was crowded. He went to get stamped instead, but when the man stamped his hand, he saw the folly of entering the ballroom during intermission. The orchestra was just returning from break, and the dance floor was empty. People were gathered around the booths, talking and drinking, and everyone could see him as he entered. He felt naked. Everyone now knew that Billy Thorson had arrived at the wedding dance of his former girlfriend. Were they wondering why he didn't have the good sense to stay away? He was beginning to wonder that himself when he heard a friendly female voice call his name from behind him.

"Billy! I was hoping I'd see you here." Jo Anne Shaurel's voice was both friendly and seductive. "Are you free to dance with me when the music starts?"

Glad to no longer be alone, Billy gave her a big smile. "Would you believe I was hoping to see you too?"

"No, but I like that you're willing to lie about it." Jo Anne was pretty, flirtatious, and eager for fun—all qualities appealing to Billy's lonesome mood. She was also blunt. "I hope you're here to have fun and not to mope, but either way, I'm ready to comply."

For the second time that night, the orchestra introduced the "Blue Skirt Waltz." Billy asked, "Care to dance?" When she smiled, he fit her into his arms and they twirled away.

She was taller than he remembered. Light-brown hair and a figure most girls envied. Like her dad, her behavior was gruff, but as Billy moved easily across the floor with her in his arms, he could not have imagined a better start to the evening.

He and Anna had often danced to the "Blue Skirt Waltz," but there was hardly a tune he hadn't danced with her. It didn't trigger any specific memories until the vocalist sang, "I dreamed of that night with you," making Billy envision Anna and misstep.

"I'm sorry, Jo Anne. Did I get you?"

"No, I'm pretty fast. Don't worry."

Aiming to block further memories, Billy held her tighter, and they finished the waltz set and applauded the orchestra, who took a quick bow before they introduced the "Dance Hall Polka."

Jo Anne was joyous. "I love this tune! There are no words to it that I know of, but I'm ready to polka. Are you?" She grabbed his hand.

"Hell, yes!"

Anna had been among the first to notice Billy as he entered the ballroom, and she immediately tugged on George's lapel. "Don't turn to look, but Billy just came in."

"Okay, you were kind of hoping he would. Do you still want to go through with your plan?"

"Yes, if you are sure you're okay with it."

"I've thought a lot about it, and I think that if he's the man you say he is, then you should do it. I'll find Marcy and tell her to watch for when you quit dancing with him. You told her your plan, right?"

"She knows I'm taking her with me. I think Billy and I will both be more comfortable if we are not alone together. I'll wait until these polkas are over. I need to waltz with him, not polka. Hey, there's Maggie. I want to talk to her too."

As Billy twirled Jo Anne around the floor for the next three polkas, they moved through the crowd like professionals. Occasionally they opened their embrace to polka alone while holding hands, coming together again as he twirled her under his arm. She was great fun to dance with, and he felt his spirits rise above his circumstances. For the moment he felt only joy. But when they stopped and applauded the polka set, he heard another familiar voice near him.

"Excuse me, Jo Anne," Anna said kindly. "I'm wondering if I could borrow Billy for a few dances. George and I might be leaving soon, and I don't want to miss the chance to dance with him. I'm so glad he came."

"Sure. It's okay. Our booth is in the far corner, Billy, so you know where to find me. And if we miss each other tonight, promise you'll give me a call sometime soon. My number's in the book."

"Yeah, it may get hectic tonight, but I promise I'll call you next week."

As Jo Anne left, Billy declared softly, "You look great, Anna."

"Thank you. Jo Anne was very gracious. I wasn't expecting that. And honestly, Billy, I hated to break in, for more reasons than I can even name, but I need to talk with you privately."

Anna smiled. Billy stood still a moment to take in her beauty: red hair, white dress, smooth complexion. Memories rose until she spoke.

"I thought we should dance. One last time."

Her smile made him weak. "Yes, let's dance," Billy said, managing a wide smile that hid his pain.

The music started, and they began to dance.

"After a couple of waltzes, I want you meet me on the north side of the gazebo. Don't worry: George knows. Marcy will be with me, but I want you to come alone."

Billy said, "Okay, if that's what you want."

"Look, you know we all really liked you, Billy. And you and I, we were in love."

"Yes."

"So, this dance is my public goodbye to you. I want people to see we parted on good terms, for the sake of us and both of our families. I'll explain it all when we meet outside. After you dance with me, you'll do a quick dance with Josephine and one with Janet. They'll be thrilled. Then, I just talked to Maggie and she wants to dance with you too. Dance with Maggie for a whole waltz, excuse yourself to leave, and then go out to the gazebo, but take the long way so no one follows you."

"Okay."

"Right. I'll be looking for a time to leave without anyone seeing me go sometime after we part dancing. I need time to get away without being seen. I'll take the long way so no one follows me. George will help distract others. If he can get away, he will want to talk to you too."

"Really? I don't understand."

"Don't worry. He has no grudge against you. He says he's grateful for your stupidity at not marrying me, though." Billy sensed a slight laugh.

"Here's Josephine. See you shortly, Billy. Make sure you are not followed."

Anna tugged the skirt of her gown up a little as she moved swiftly toward the booths. She spotted Marcy, grabbed her hand, and said, "Can you help me go to the washroom?"

Marcy nodded and led the way to the women's restroom, where Marcy helped Anna manage her dress before taking her own turn at the facilities. "Better take advantage of this opportunity," Marcy said. "No telling how long we'll be outside."

After exiting the restroom, the two women walked west and then north around the pavilion to the gazebo, which was dimly lit in the front. "Let's go around back," Anna suggested. "The light won't reflect off my dress if we stand north of the gazebo, but we'll still be able to see each other."

With their backs against the gazebo, the women waited for Billy, and Anna rehearsed in her mind the words she wanted to say to him.

Billy tried to show the twins a good time as he danced with them one at a time. They were fun kids. Sweet kids. All of Anna's sisters were.

He'd managed to maintain a cheerful front for Josephine and Janet, but he was relieved to dance with Maggie. *How much does she know of Anna's plan?* Maggie usually told him everything. He decided to fish.

"Wow, quite a string of beauties I got to dance with. And they saved the best till last."

"Nice of you to say. I was surprised that Anna wanted you to dance with her. Maybe she wanted to put good feelings on display. It would make sense. Lots of people were surprised you showed up here tonight. I thought you told Mom and Dad you weren't coming. But I'm glad you came."

Billy relaxed and enjoyed the rest of the dance with Maggie. Clearly, Anna's plan only included a few.

"Look," Maggie said as the band started to play a polka, "George is going to make good on his promise to dance with our whole family. He's already danced with Mom and me, and now he and Jimmy and Dad are going to jig to a polka. Joey's supposed to be in the dance too, but we can't find him. See you later, Billy. I want to watch this."

Standing near his dad, Jimmy was more than a little surprised when George approached them to jig to a polka or two. He had practiced dancing with Maggie, but he had no idea what kind of steps the three of them were about to perform. He was relieved when his dad shouted, "Hell, yes! Mary warned me about this, and I'm ready and able."

Jimmy watched as his dad and George stomped the soles of their shoes one at a time hard against the floor to every other beat of the music, each trying to make the stomp ring out as loud as possible.

Jimmy commented to himself, "Seems that missing a beat or two or being off a beat doesn't much matter." He laughed and added, "I'm ready!"

"Time for you to join in!" George yelled above the music.

Jimmy nodded, and the three men formed a circle as each tried to do the loudest stomp possible in time with the music. Jimmy felt a real exhilaration with each aggressive stomp, as if the three of them were one team. Too bad Joey was missing this, because it was more fun than sliding on the floor. Now he was in the company of adults, but they were adults who had tossed all decorum out the window, squelched all embarrassment, and risen above all shame.

Glancing around the crowd of onlookers, Jimmy recognized Billy, who lifted his hand high to wave to him. Jimmy enthusiastically waved back, curious about his cousin's thoughts on the dance. *Would Billy have led a dance like this if he'd been the groom tonight?* A foolish thought. George and Billy were two very different people. According to Billy's religion, he wasn't even supposed to attend a dance. Seemed strange. But their minister forbade Jimmy's family from going to dances too. He wondered if Aunt Rose danced.

Jimmy felt especially uplifted as more people gathered around to clap in time, and he was really proud when his dad and George each took a turn at doing a special jig of their own. Not that they were very good at their lone jigs, but the crowd loved it and even the orchestra recognized the special moment and increased the polka to almost twice its normal length.

When the music stopped, Jimmy found that he was sad the dance was over. He glanced around for Billy, hoping to share his exhilaration with his cousin. *Is that him leaving? I'll try to catch him later.*

In that moment, Jimmy found himself swept up by the enthusiasm of his dad and George, both of whom were laughing and slapping each other on the back as all three of them went back to the booth, exhausted and sweating. Martin and George each grabbed their beer and took big gulps until the bottles were empty.

Jimmy took a glass of soda that Maggie handed to him, and even though he did not totally understand his mother's statement, he laughed along when she said, "See what I mean, Maggie? How men behave when there are no women in the group."

CHAPTER 29

SECRETS REVEALED

Saturday night, June 9, 1956

Billy watched Martin, Jimmy, and George dance a jig to "The Beer Barrel Polka." He saw the joy as they stomped hard on the floor. George flung his arm around each one separately and noisily polkaed a few turns before switching to another partner. Great fun.

He caught Jimmy glancing his way and waved high in the air. Jimmy waved back. He could see his cousin's grin even from a distance. *I'll find Jimmy and talk to him later. Now I'd better get going. I have a date with Anna.* The unintended irony stung a little, but he brushed it aside. *George seems like a hell of a guy. Good for her.* Leaving the scene quietly, Billy headed outside.

He turned east outside the dance hall and then turned north toward the park. Passing by oaks that loomed large in the darkness, he enjoyed strolling through the cool night, uninterrupted by anyone. The world was like magic. Dark, mysterious magic. He had no idea what he was walking into. Why would Anna want to meet with him?

His thoughts were interrupted when he noticed the figures of two youngsters on the grass near a tree a few yards ahead of him. When his footfalls caused one to stir, he yelled, "Hey, you guys okay?" He recognized his cousin sitting with his back against a tree. "Is that you, Joey? It's me, Billy."

Joey rubbed his eyes a little before he said, "Billy!"

"Looks like your little buddy got sick. Beer or brandy?"

"Beer."

"And you?"

"I only had a sip. He drank a can really fast. Then he drank mine."

"That'll do it. How old?

"Ronnie is twelve."

"So much for age bringing wisdom, heh?" He laughed a loud "Ha!"

Ronnie rolled over, and Joey stood up next to the tree. "I must've slept. Don't know how long."

Ronnie tried to stand up but only made it to a kneeling position.

"Well, judging by the deep wrinkles on your buddy's face, he's been in the same position for a while."

"We came out here before intermission," Joey offered.

"I got here during intermission," Billy said. "The band just started up again when I walked in. Intermission's been over a long time."

Sensing that Ronnie was better, Billy tossed him a handkerchief, and the boy began wiping his face.

"Look," Billy said with some sympathy, "I can leave you alone if you want. Or I can help you and Ronnie to somewhere so he can lie down where mosquitoes won't bother. They're just starting to get nasty."

Ronnie muttered, "You could help me to my brother's car, if I'm clean enough to get in."

Billy took out another clean handkerchief, and he and Joey wiped Ronnie's face clean.

"Your clothes look good, and I think you'll be fine. Lean on me and we'll walk you to the car."

After about ten yards, Billy said, "Put your arm around my neck." Then he reached under the boy's legs to swoop him off the ground and carried him the next fifty yards to the car.

Ronnie climbed into the back seat, saying, "Thanks for the help." He made himself comfortable and added, "You can go, Joey. Go dance. You're better at dancing than drinking beer."

"He must be feeling pretty good," Joey said to Billy as they smiled. "I suppose you gotta tell my folks."

"I won't say anything about this to anyone. I'll keep your secret till I die."

"Thanks, Billy."

"So, you did some dancing. Good for you!"

"I did. It was fun."

They arrived at the spot where Billy had found them, and Billy said, "I have to leave you here. I was headed out to meet someone. Keep that a secret for me. Okay?"

"Deal!" Joey said. And he rushed toward the ballroom.

Billy found Anna and Marcy standing in the darkness with the light spilling from a nearby light pole dimly illuminating their faces. Although they both appeared uncharacteristically stern, Anna's soft beauty ripped at Billy's heart, even though her whole body seemed tense as she leaned against the gazebo.

"I've been waiting a while. I was afraid you weren't coming."

"I apologize." Billy smiled. "I took the long way here so no one would know where I was headed, and I met Joey in the park. His friend was in kind of a jam, so I helped him out. It took longer than I thought."

Billy saw Anna's stern look soften into a smile. "Joey. What a great kid. No, a young man, really."

"Yeah, Martin and Mary's kids are all great kids growing into young adults."

He noticed her body relax. She smiled as if she were about to say something funny but then stiffened. The stern look returned. "I can't do this."

"Can't do what?"

"I can't let myself get involved in . . . in a friendly discussion with you, Billy. My heart is too fragile." She stood tall against the white gazebo and turned to Marcy, who moved closer and took her hand.

Anna forced her words out quickly in a sharp whisper. "Thanks for coming. No small talk. I'll get right to it."

He had a million questions, but he said nothing.

"This may seem harsh, Billy, but I'm just going to blurt this out."

She dropped Marcy's hand and took one of his in both of hers.

"I'm pregnant. It's yours. George knows. He's okay with it." She turned her head as she began to cry. "I don't want to cry," she sniffed. Billy reached for a handkerchief, but he had given all of his away. His mind raced with questions. *Was she seeing George when we were dating?*

Marcy put her arm around her sister's shoulder and handed her a handkerchief. "Take your time, my brave sister. Billy will wait."

She began again. "I was pregnant, and you wanted to wait. Your mother was suicidal, so you never asked. I was *pregnant*. I couldn't wait. I tried to tell you, but you seemed wrapped up in your mother's behavior. After our last date—after we fought—Mom sensed our breakup was final, and she called George to come over. He'd tried to date me after he got back from the Navy, but I told him that you and I were serious. He never called again until Mom called him. I'm glad she did. We love each other now. I still love you, Billy, but I think our split was for the best. Best for both of us."

Even in the dim light, Billy saw her tears find paths down her cheeks. She inhaled and exhaled deeply. He felt himself doing the same, but for the opposite reason. Anna had just relieved herself of a burden, and he had just taken one on. *How could this all have happened? How could I have let this happen?*

Billy shook with surprise and emotion, but he steadied himself. "Well, you're married now. I'm devastated by it all, but I wish you happiness. I truly do. And I'll do whatever you want me to do for the child. For our child."

"I'm glad you brought up the child. I know you are a good person, Billy, and I don't want to sound mean, but please never refer to the child as ours again. He or she must be mine and George's. George doesn't want a child to grow up with the stigma of not belonging to the family, a feeling heaped on him in his childhood. So, in answer to your question about what you can do for the child, the answer is nothing. You must do absolutely nothing! No one must know. You must never hold the child, give a birthday gift, or look upon him or her in a special way, even from a distance. We may end up meeting at family get-togethers because we have the same aunt and uncle, but you must be only casually friendly to us and treat the child like any other child. Maybe even appear cold. It's a lot to ask, I know, but please, Billy, please, do it for my sake and for the sake of the child."

He could see she was relieved to have gotten the words out. She relaxed a bit, leaned back against the gazebo, and slid down to sit on the grass. Marcy moved to sit beside her, and Billy sat near her other side. Marcy hugged her as tears streamed down her face.

Billy's own tears blurred his vision of her, even as the dim light reflected her red hair. He breathed deeply before he said, "Of course. I'll do as you say." He heard himself say the words and he meant every one of them, though his heart did not want to believe the truth of the promise. It was a terrible moment for both of them, but Billy did not want it to end. Because an end offered no hope.

After a moment, Anna regained her composure. "I've got to leave, and we won't meet again. I think it's best if you stay away from our whole family. Please don't blame Mom for that. It's my idea, Billy."

Marcy stood up first and helped Anna up from the ground. Then Anna bent to kiss Billy's forehead as he remained seated. "We all liked you too much. Loved you, really. Still do. Goodbye." And the two women walked into the darkness.

Billy felt the sweet touch of her kiss until the gentle night breeze dried his skin.

He struggled a little to stand and then leaned back against the gazebo. Still reeling from Anna's revelation, he tried to sort out events but remained confused.

Suddenly, from the darkness came a firm but compassionate baritone voice. "That was a lot for you to take in. But it wasn't easy for Anna either." A tall figure wearing a wedding tuxedo stepped forward. "I'm George Lange, Billy."

Billy shook George's extended hand. The grip was firm, and for a moment he wondered if the groom had some violence in mind. He saw his height, his fit torso, his confident demeanor. None of it scared Billy, but he knew he had not the stomach to fight with the man who had wedded Anna and was going to raise his child. Maybe he'd just let George take a few punches and fall down and stay there.

George must've read his body language. He said, "Look, I'm not here to fight. I'm here to talk to you about the future."

"Is there something Anna missed?"

"I'm sure she covered it all, but I want to get an honest feel of your reaction. I need a promise from you, man to man."

"Go on."

"Believe me, if I thought you were a jerk, I wouldn't be here. I'd let my two brothers try to kick your ass, though I think I did them a favor by telling them to leave you alone. They don't know the child is yours, by the way. They just didn't like it that you showed up tonight. But Anna and I are glad you did.

"Anyway, I'm here because everyone, especially Anna, tells me what a good guy you are. Well, I'm glad to hear it. I heard the end of what Anna said to you, but I just want to repeat some of it, because I know that sticking to the promise to not see a child you fathered will be harder *because* you are a good guy. I can help. You and I will see each other at family gatherings because, as Anna said, Martin and Mary are your favorite aunt and uncle. They're Anna's favorites too. And they are now my favorites, as well. I do not want to deprive any of us of seeing them or their kids, either. So, you and I need to be friendly, cordial. We can't let things be awkward, you know."

"Agreed," Billy answered.

"And just treat the child like any other kid. Do I have your word?"

"You do." Billy grasped George's hand for the second time that night, and the two men shook hands with a firm grip.

Billy watched George disappear into the darkness near the back of the ballroom. *He and Anna are probably leaving the dance early. Most brides and grooms do.* Feeling empty yet full and disappointed but relieved, he listened to the mellow sounds of a waltz wafting through the short, wide windows of the ballroom, which opened outward ten feet above the park grass. He thought how lucky he had been to have had Anna's love. How totally and completely she had loved. How stupid he had been to think he had deserved her love.

He did not want to go back to the dance. As enticing as the thought of dancing with Jo Anne was, he was not in the mood for fun. He'd call her next week. He was in the mood to be alone. He wanted to think.

Finding the orchestra music soothing, he walked the short distance to the back side of the ballroom, sat down with his back to the wall, and tried to relax. After the waltz set, the orchestra leader announced, "I know we already played this one, but we have guest singer Yvonne David, who would like to sing the words she has written for the 'Dance Hall Polka'! Let's all give a hand to welcome Yvonne! And have everyone out on the floor!"

For a moment, Billy wished he were inside the ballroom. The crowd roared its approval of her appearance, and the orchestra played several bars of introduction. Her voice was lovely and clear as it rang out in the soft night air, and Billy leaned back, closed his eyes, and enjoyed her voice as she sang.

> *In the twilight of a Saturday night,*
>
> *near towns or lakeside country roads,*
>
> *dance hall lights beam yellow and bright,*

making summer evenings so romantic!

Oh, how vividly I can recall

the dance halls of those happy days,

and how I wish I could return once more

to feel my spirit soar.

And if I could I know

I'd choose to stay

to dance my life away!

Dancers swirling, twirling,

their bodies free of strife.

Accordions play

sweet chords of life!

Feeling breezes of the

skirts moving through the air.

No one has a care

at all.

As couples hop and step

and twirl again,

emitting shouts of joy!

Tubas pumping out a

lusty, heart-pounding beat,

moving hundreds of

couples' feet.

As they hop and step and twirl

and twirl again,

emitting shouts of joy!

Oh, I know that I would

never feel poor,

if I could dance those halls once more.

CHAPTER 30

DREAMS UNFOLD

Saturday night, June 9, 1956

Although the orchestra would play until one, the dancing grew more intense as the clock neared midnight. The music became sweeter to the dancers as young women made crucial decisions about who would be their sweetheart for the night, and young men became either decision-makers or procrastinators.

Jimmy spotted Jo Anne Shaurel hurrying toward him. "Where did Billy run off to? I was hoping to have some more dances with him tonight."

"I hardly saw him myself. He was here for about half an hour right after intermission. But I haven't seen him since."

"So, he got away from me again. Ha! Last time he got away he was out of circulation for five years. He said he'd call."

"Then he will," Jimmy asserted. Emboldened by dancing with the neighborhood girls, he added, "Who wouldn't jump at the chance to call you? I would."

Jimmy felt her glare at him, just long enough to make him think he had gone too far with the kidding, before she smiled and said, "Look out, young lad. I'd take you home with me right now, but it would break my little sister's heart." Jimmy blushed as she pinched his cheek.

She continued, "But the night's not been a total loss. I'm honestly happy for Jane's successful conquest of Albert, but I couldn't help tease her about having to ride home on the handlebars of his bicycle. I let her stew for a moment on that before I told her not to worry. We'll stick the bike into the trunk of the Chrysler, and she can make out with him in the back seat all the way to his place."

"Not a lot of privacy with all your sisters in the car," Jimmy offered.

"Heck, I told her we'd put Ann and the twins up front with me, and Caroline can be in back with her and Albert. She'll be asleep by that time anyway, dreaming about when she danced with Joey."

"Did you already tell Albert?"

"Yeah, she went to stop him from starting out for home with his bike. She caught him in plenty of time, and he was glad to be able to stay till the end of the dance. They're over at our booth now. Come on over."

Jimmy saw no way out of it and followed her to the booth. *I'll talk a while and then dance with Ann and then escort her back. It's early yet.*

The booth was a couple rows back, and by the time they arrived, the orchestra leader had introduced a schottische.

"Doing the schottische as a couple is fun, but doing it as a group of four is easier and even more fun," Jane said. "How about Albert and me and Ann and Jimmy?"

"Never done this," Jimmy said.

"Me either," Albert said.

"We can teach you," Ann insisted.

"Let's go," Jimmy said, and within seconds they were on the dance floor. Jimmy saw other groups stepping and hopping with the music. "Looks like a challenge."

"Just watch for a moment as Jane and Albert demonstrate," Ann said. "He's new at it too. See, it's one, two, three, lift/hop; one, two, three, lift/hop. Watch how they come down with the same foot for the one count after pausing with it. Let's you and I try it."

Jimmy was skeptical, but Ann's guidance made it pretty easy. After two tries, he nailed it.

"Now let's hook up to make a foursome. We hold hands with the other couple in front of us. Albert reaches back with his other hand to hold mine and Jane reaches back with her other hand to hold yours. And we do the same steps we did as a couple. When the music plays the special part, the front couple lets go of each other's hands but holds on to the hand of the other couple as they do the one, two, three, lift/hop all the way around to take the second row as we take the front row."

Jimmy ran into his partner a couple times before he got it right.

"Goofing up is all part of the fun," Ann encouraged him.

Jimmy was having fun. For some reason, dancing with another couple made it more fun. *What the heck! Am I becoming social?*

Jimmy agreed with Ann when the orchestra started another schottische and she said, "Good, they're going to play several. Too often they only play one and by the time we all get going, it's over."

From ahead of them, Jane turned and shouted over the music, "Hey, look! Mary and Margaret are dancing with your twin cousins, Jimmy. Now, if that foursome isn't worth a double take, I don't know what is."

Jimmy looked to his left to see them. "Two sets of identical twins. People would pay to see it."

"And they're drawing lots of attention too," Ann added.

"The little show-offs!" Jane exclaimed fondly. "My sisters are thirteen, but what flair the four of them have! Look how they switch so that sometimes the identical twins are on each side, so if you see them from the side after seeing them from the front, you might think they're identical quadruplets! They do that switch in step. Did they just make that up?"

Jimmy watched them, but his foursome kept dancing, unlike many other groups who stopped to watch the phenomenon of two pairs of identical twin girls dancing the schottische.

When the set ended, the orchestra leader announced, "You're already in groups, so let's see if you're game to try 'The Bunny Hop.'" As the music started, suddenly Jo Anne and Maggie were beside them, with Jo Anne saying, "I can do this. Stand behind me and put your hands on my hips, Jimmy, and Ann, stand behind him and put your hands on his hips, and so on down the line. Follow my lead."

Fun chaos followed as the group attempted to kick to the right and then to the left in time with the music. Just when they seemed to have mastered the movement, it was time to hop—forward once, backward once, and forward three times to the music. Few groups stayed in sync with each other or the music, and people bouncing off others was more common than not. When any one group mastered the dance, they'd hook up to another skilled group, making the chain of dancers longer and the synchronization more challenging.

When the music stopped, the dancers laughed and applauded the orchestra and reveled in their own enjoyment of the moment. Jimmy was glad to hear the leader announce, "We'll be back with some waltzes in a few minutes, folks."

Jimmy and Maggie shared their feelings of exhaustion with the Shaurels, who followed Jo Anne back to their booth. "I need a beer," she said. Jane, Albert, and Ann followed, but after he thanked Ann for the fun, Jimmy hurried with Maggie to the bridal party's booth to see if they had some soda to drink.

Jimmy heard a girl's voice behind him say, "Hey, Maggie, how about introducing me to your brother?"

"Anne, meet Jimmy. Jimmy, meet my friend and classmate, Anne Busch. Sorry he looks a little more scraggly than usual, Anne, but he's been busy dancing with the neighbors."

"I noticed that. I suppose you're all tired out, then," she said as she tilted her head and smiled up at Jimmy.

Jimmy liked her voice and her looks, but he liked her teasing manner even more. He responded with mock dignity. "I've got a couple of waltzes in me for my dear sister's lovely friend. If you would do me the honor."

Anne grinned and said, "Aha," before turning to Maggie to add, "I see he's not too tired to BS. Can't say you didn't warn me, Mags." She placed her fingers in Jimmy's extended hand, and he led her to the dance floor.

"She lets you call her *Mags*? I call her that to irritate her."

"She actually likes it, but she won't tell you that. I know you two are pretty close. She's told me *all about* you."

"And you still accepted my invitation to dance. My high opinion of you is dwindling."

After a brief trial of steps in place, Jimmy led her into the crowd of dancers.

"And there's that self-deprecating humor she warned me of."

"And you have a vocabulary to match Maggie's. No wonder you're friends."

"So, spill it, Jimmy. What has Mags told you about me?"

"Not enough to prepare me for this meeting, apparently."

"Come on. She must've said something."

"Well, I don't want to embarrass you—"

"Try me."

"Mags said you were fun, modest, kind, and genuinely friendly, even as you love to kid around."

"All true. Your sister is astute."

"There's that vocabulary again. She also said people like you, even though the girls are all envious of your figure and personality and the boys are . . . well, boys."

She laughed. Jimmy liked her laugh.

"Mags warned me about your bluntness too. But I like it. Mags and I became friends when we found ourselves comparing our lives filled with chores at home to the lives of the privileged. We both love our home life, mostly, but some others in class get under our skin. It came up when Mary Schroedler was absent from gym class last fall. Mags said you and Mary used to be sweethearts."

"Yeah, in a grade-school kind of way. She ran away a week before our first official date." Jimmy laughed. "That didn't come out the way I intended."

Anne laughed too before she looked up at him and said, "Gee, I'd never do that."

The music stopped, and as they applauded, Anne commented, "There's Mags with Tom Ryan. Nice guy. Graduated this year. Your neighbor, right?"

Jimmy nodded.

"Looks like another neighbor is asking her for the next dance, though. Joe Brummer. Classmate of Tom's and another neighbor of yours, right?"

"You seem to know everyone. Do you work on it?"

"Absolutely! Knowing people is important to me. I like to be sociable, don't you?"

"Aha! So, Mags has told you about my being unsociable too?"

"I said she told me everything. But I find you totally sociable and fun to talk to."

"Thanks. Mags said you bring out the best in everyone." Jimmy felt her punctuate his comment by moving closer as they danced. Conversation was over for a while. *What an amazing girl is Anne Busch!*

When Tom Ryan asked Maggie to dance, she was thrilled. Handsome, athletic, and polite, Tom had black wavy hair, though he kept it quite short. She'd always had kind of a boy-next-door crush on him, and the fact that he was three years older than she was had made him extra attractive when she was a girl in the country school. The girlhood crush was over years ago, but when he embraced her to dance, goosebumps tingled down her spine. *If the girls at school could see me now. Dancing with the football hero of Rock River High.*

Glad she had rehearsed dancing and talking at the same time, she ventured to speak. "So good to see so many neighbors here tonight."

"Yeah, my family knows both bride and groom, and we wanted to see you and Jimmy in the wedding. The country-school kids clean up pretty nice."

Maggie felt him pull her closer, as if he didn't want to talk. Feeling his hands take a firmer grip on her back made her spine tingle again. *Hey, I admit it. My knees are a little weak. He smells so nice. Now this is romantic!* She decided to stay silent and enjoy the moment. *I know it's just a dance, but a girl can dream.*

The dance ended, and he released his embrace before he said, "Here comes Joe Brummer. I promised him I'd turn you over to him after one dance. Thanks, Maggie. That was fun for me. You are so easy to dance with. Here's Joe. Thanks again."

"Any time," she heard herself saying, and after she felt Joe tap her shoulder, she turned to greet him.

"Hi, Maggie. You look really nice tonight."

"Thanks, Joe." *Gee, Tom didn't tell me I looked nice. Never hurts to start with a compliment.* "You look good too." She felt his arm firmly on her back before they clasped hands and began to dance.

Although a bit taller than Tom, Joe lacked Tom's athletic build. He was a smooth dancer, though, and he led them around the floor with a unique graceful sway that made dancing with him thrilling. *No goosebumps with Joe, but dancing with him is more fun. The tingling with Tom was just from girlish fantasies. I hope Joe asks me to polka.*

The waltz ended, and suddenly Joe said, "I'd like to dance some more with you, Maggie, but I promised Ralph Schoen he could cut in after one dance. I really hate to . . . well, thanks for the dance. Here's Ralph."

"You're welcome, Joe. Thank you." Maggie turned to see Ralph standing close to her. He wore a foolish smile and glanced down at his feet.

"Would you please dance with me again? I know I'm not very good, but I'm better than I was earlier tonight. I learned the moves from you, and then I practiced with some neighbors."

Momentarily put off by his lack of self-esteem, Maggie shook it off and exclaimed, "Well, I was hoping you'd ask me again. Dancing is like life—it's one big learning experiment." *Jeez, where did I dig that up?* And she moved forward to fit into his dance embrace.

The touch of his hand on her back was light, as if he were afraid to hold her close. She moved closer to him to follow more easily, and though his touch became firmer, his hand still seemed unsteady as they began waltzing to the music. His steps were rudimentary, but he had improved greatly since earlier in the night.

"Oh, yes, practice makes perfect," Maggie heard herself say. *That was dumb. As if I'd recognize perfection.*

"Thanks. I didn't want to ask you to dance again unless I was better at it than before."

"Well, you are, and I'm glad you did." *There's that twitch of his hand on my back again. Weird.* And then Maggie had a revelation. *Is his hand twitch the equivalent of my spine tingle when I danced with Tom? Oh, my gosh!* And at that moment, Maggie realized the power of a pretty girl to render a boy weak at the knees, just as she had become weak at the knees in the arms of her girlhood crush. Her empathy for Ralph increased as she felt torn between feeling good about the boy and feeling a bit scared. Smiling to herself, she decided to enjoy the attention and treat him as she would like to be treated by her crush. She squeezed his hand and said, "Dancing is so much fun. Don't you think, Ralph?"

"I like dancing with *you*," he admitted.

The music stopped, and they clapped and listened as the orchestra leader announced, "I know we already played this one, but we have guest singer Yvonne David, who would like to sing the words she has written for the 'Dance Hall Polka'! Let's all give a hand to welcome Yvonne! And have everyone out on the floor!"

"I'll see you later," Ralph said. "Thanks for the dance."

"You're welcome. Thank you." Maggie watched him walk away. He seemed to have a spring in his step. *Jimmy was right. I like the romance in life.*

Jimmy was ready to polka with Anne, but she said, "Let's walk back to where Mags is standing alone. Her last dance was with Ralph Schoen, and he has a big crush on Maggie. I'm sure he left because he won't dance the polka."

"Don't you polka?" Jimmy asked.

"Love it, but I want to hear this singer."

The three of them listened as she sang. Jimmy whispered to Mags, "Have you seen Billy lately?"

"Haven't seen him since you danced with George and Dad."

"I wanted to find out how he's doing." *And to see if he's okay—I know George told his brothers to give up on teaching him a lesson, but just to be sure.*

"Don't worry about Billy," Maggie said. "He's never had much trouble being social. Just like my friend Anne, here."

Anne smiled at her but changed the topic. "Hey, this singer is really good. She wrote the words too."

A group had gathered near them to listen, enjoying her fine voice and lyrics they had never heard before. The audience punctuated the end of the song with loud cheers and applause and encouraged her to sing it again. As she started over, Jimmy's eyes roamed the audience, searching for Billy. *I can see Paul and Walter by the booths, so he's not with them. Maybe he's outside.*

"Excuse me, Anne and Maggie," Jimmy said. "I'm going to go look for Billy."

On his way to the exit, he stopped as he heard Marcy call to him, "Where are you headed, Jimmy?"

"I haven't seen Billy for a while, and I thought I'd check if he's outside."

"Mind if I go with you? I'd like to say goodbye to him before he leaves."

"I'd have thought you'd sooner go in the ballroom and dance," he said curiously. "Didn't you just come from outside?"

"A while ago," she said quickly, "but when you mentioned Billy, I decided I wanted to go with you. You don't mind, do you?"

"No, I like it."

"I mean," she teased, "you weren't just saying you were looking for Billy when really you were planning to meet with one of those cute girls you were dancing with tonight?"

"Yeah, right. Let's go."

Once outside, they passed Officer Grossman as he was coming back in. He seemed to eye them suspiciously, so Jimmy nodded at him and smiled. *Seems like he's looking for someone?* He walked with Marcy toward the dark area of the back of the building, where they found Billy leaning against the outer wall.

"There you are," Jimmy said. "I wondered where you went."

"I've been sitting here enjoying the music."

"All this time! You've missed quite a bit of the dance," Jimmy said.

"In more ways than I can even explain," Billy said. "Marcy knows what I mean. Hey, sit down. Both of you. I could use some company."

As Jimmy and Marcy sat down on either side of him, the dim outdoor lamp mounted high on the pavilion illuminated their faces, and Jimmy saw Billy smile before he continued, "Jimmy, these are the songs of life. And we are in the dance of life. I dropped out for a while, but I'm going to get back in. I know my advice isn't worth a dime, but I advise you to never leave the dance."

"I just stepped out to look for you," Jimmy explained, and he wondered why Marcy and Billy began to laugh.

"No, Jim. I mean the dance of life. Never leave the dance of life. Always stay in it and keep dancing."

"You're talking strange, Bill," Jimmy said, taking a cue from his cousin and dropping the *y* at the end of his name. "Have you been drinking much?"

"Not at all. I'm talking strange because I feel strange. You see, I've absorbed the wisdom that comes with making an unforgettable mistake, one that wounds and scars for life. A mistake that changed the direction of my life. And I'm lucky because I'm okay with it all. Not healed, but on my way."

"You're talking about Anna, aren't you," Jimmy asserted.

"Of course, he is," Marcy said. "It's been quite a day for him."

"Yeah," Billy said. "Hard to digest all the news, really."

"I hope Anna did the right thing by telling you," Marcy said.

They seemed to be talking as if he weren't there. *What are they talking about?* he wondered. *What news?*

"I'm glad she did. She'll have a family before she knows it, but she won't let me help."

Jimmy was about to remind Marcy that he knew Anna was pregnant, but Marcy said quickly, as if to prevent Billy from talking first, "Oh, Billy. Jimmy knows that Anna and *George* are expecting a baby in *December* or so."

"Yeah, Billy. Marcy told me so I would look out for Anna when we stole the bride," Jimmy explained, wondering if the emphasis on *George* and on *December* was meant for Billy or him. But when Billy turned to look at him and paused, as if the wheels of his mind were processing two things while he tried to make them fit together, Jimmy understood. *Why did Marcy tell Mags and me that Anna is pregnant? Just planting a seed about George and her baby? Well, I'll see what happens in December, if I have to wait that long.*

Billy smiled at Jimmy before he said, "Anna thinks of everything. She is an incredible woman. None like her."

"Hey, let's all go back into the ballroom?" Marcy said.

"I'll stay here, but I'd advise you both to go back in the ballroom. I'll be fine, but don't tell anyone where I am. I'll just sit here a while and then go home."

"Are we training tomorrow?" Jimmy asked.

"Hell, yes!"

After Jimmy and Marcy left, Billy leaned back, closed his eyes, and listened to the music as he fell asleep.

CHAPTER 31

LEAVING THE DANCE

Early Sunday morning, June 10, 1956

Jimmy asked Ann Shaurel to dance again near the end of the evening. He wanted to see if she danced as close as she had before, and he was a little disappointed when she didn't. Maybe she felt the same way he did: neighbors attracted to each other, but each a little concerned that spending too much time together would give the other the wrong idea. He was glad when she said, "Jo Anne's waving at me. We're going home. Jane and Albert hit it off. Jo Anne said we're loading his bike in our trunk and taking him home. I can dance another one, though."

Jimmy laughed. "Albert is a nice fella. All he does is work. Glad you kids gave him a good time. I saw you and all your sisters dancing with him before we danced the schottische and the modern tunes."

"Honestly, I was surprised. He looked kind of goofy to me at first when we saw him ride in on his bicycle. But the guy can dance. He was fun for all of us, but Jane is the one who thought he was cute." She added coyly, "I'd sooner dance with you."

Surprised, Jimmy said quickly, "And I'd prefer dancing with you than dancing with Albert too."

Ann playfully whacked Jimmy on the arm. "Oh, you're always kidding."

Jimmy stayed silent till the music stopped, and as they clapped for the band, Jo Anne came up to say, "Let's go, Ann. Good night, Jimmy. We all had fun." She turned to hustle out the door without waiting for her sister.

"Good night, Jimmy." She squeezed his hand.

He felt a wave of warm friendship with this neighbor he'd known all his life, a schoolmate who had been sometimes nice and sometimes not so nice. Tonight she had made the evening special for him, and he wanted to tell her. Surprising himself, he squeezed her hand, pulled her closer, and whispered, "Good night, Ann. Thanks for all the dances. I had fun."

"Me too." She hugged him before she backed up a bit and looked up at him.

Without thinking, he kissed her briefly on the forehead.

She smiled and stretched upward a little to kiss him on the lips, releasing before he could respond. The two of them stepped back and smiled.

"You're even more dreamy than I had imagined, Jimmy, but I think we both know this dream is going nowhere." They both nodded and laughed slightly before she added, "Good friends forever, right?"

"Right. Good friends forever." He felt her hand tighten on his as he squeezed it one more time before she released it and turned to leave. He watched her walk away. *A strange night. Who do we become when the place or costume changes? I guess I can enjoy a girl's company without either one of us being too serious.*

Glad Ann left before the end of the dance—*It could've been awkward*—Jimmy headed back to where his folks were, but as he neared their booth, he spotted Annette, who seemed to be aiming to intercept him.

She talked rapidly, as if he might not let her finish. "Jimmy, I suppose you don't want to talk to me ever again, but I was looking for you. Tony and my friends are waiting outside. Can you just listen a minute, please?"

Jimmy knew it wasn't a question. He was glad to see her, but she continued before he could say anything.

"I'm sorry. I feel so stupid. I know my excuse is lame, but at the drag race I was telling some friends I wanted to stay in touch with you because I really liked you. I saw you dancing with so many girls tonight. I saw you dancing real close with the girl in the low-cut blue dress. And when you didn't ask me to dance during the whole first part, I thought you were ignoring me on purpose. I told my friends at intermission. They said I had to make a move to make you remember me. They told me what to do, but I was too scared, so they suckered me into drinking enough brandy to 'loosen me up,' as they put it. I never drank before that. I'm still a little sick from it. Honestly Jimmy, I'm so ashamed. I don't remember much about what happened in the car with you at all, and I wish I . . . well, I should've never trusted those friends."

"Sometime friends are the last people you should trust, but they were right about one thing—you made me remember you. And all those girls I danced with—they're just my neighbors. Heck, some of them are way too young for me. It was kind of an obligation, you know?"

"I'd like to believe that. But it doesn't matter. The blue-dress girl looked like more than an obligation to me, though."

"Believe me, the dance with you and our time in the car were the highlight of tonight. No, the highlight of my life."

She looked down before she looked up again to meet his gaze. "Nice of you to say. Can we start over?"

"But I don't want to start over. I kind of liked the start we had. Who am I kidding? I loved it."

Annette blushed. "They said I should ask for your phone number."

"Can't give you that." He waited a beat to see the look on her face before he said, "We don't have a phone." He laughed. "I'm even more of a hick than you thought, right? But here's what we'll do." He dug in his wallet for a piece of paper, unclipped a pen from his shirt pocket, and wrote down his address. After he finished writing, he tore a piece off the bottom and gave her the two pieces of paper. "Now, on the blank piece, write down your full name, address, phone number, and give it to me."

"You're a strange guy," she said as she wrote. "Do you always carry a pen and paper?"

"Yes, I do! I don't want to miss out if I get a chance like this."

"Happen often?"

"Would you believe never, until tonight?"

"No, but I want to believe it. You *will* write, won't you?"

"I'll write soon so that when you get the letter you don't say, 'Who the heck is that guy?'"

They laughed. She said with a smile, "You *are* a strange guy."

"Too late to worry about that now." He looked at the address. "I know where you live." Then he read from the paper, "Annette Marie Novotlik." He looked at her and smiled. "Good to know you."

They stood there a long moment before the music started. "Got time for a dance?"

"Yes, but just one. Our car is parked by the ball park, and they told me to be there in five minutes."

"We'll waltz in the direction of the door, and then I'll walk you out. Okay?"

"Yeah." She flashed him that nice smile he remembered from earlier. They didn't talk, but enjoyed the music and holding each other tight.

The music stopped, they clapped, and the orchestra leader announced, "And now for the last dance tonight, we play for you the 'Traveler's Waltz.'"

Turning to face him, she said, "I love this tune, and we should dance the last dance, Jimmy. They'll wait for me."

The lights dimmed, and Jimmy gladly led her into the music, which moved him with its soft, haunting tones. Holding Annette close, he felt ecstatic. *I'm dancing with the prettiest girl in the place, and I just met her a few hours ago.* Unlike most of the night, the dance floor was now only sparsely filled, but the couples all seemed to be sharing a special moment with a special person. Everyone appeared in love with their partner, at least for the moment, as their bodies moved as one with the music. A few couples stopped dancing to kiss passionately, but he and Annette kept dancing, and as the floor cleared, he spied Tony dancing with Maggie. *Ha! Annette's friends will wait for her all right. Tony's here too!* He decided not to tell his partner. The moment was too perfect to break up with talk.

The waltz ended, and the orchestra went into a few bars of "Home, Sweet Home" before the leader announced, "That's all for tonight, folks. Hope you had a great time! We sure did. Good night to everyone!"

"Thanks, Annette. I will remember tonight."

"Me too." She smiled at him before she added, "Look, there goes Tony toward the door. I saw him dancing with Maggie. I wonder where she went?"

"Probably to round up Joey and my folks."

He walked her out the door and to the sidewalk near the trees. Neither of them quite knew how to say good night. Jimmy was reluctant to expect a kiss, despite the fact that they had already kissed earlier. Then he thought, *I'm not a coward!* He drew her in gently and kissed her long enough on the lips for her to respond. Then he stepped back, saying, "You'll hear from me soon."

The spell between them broke when he heard Maggie's strong voice say, "Are you ready to go? Joey's with Mom and Dad. You know Dad's always the last to lea—" She stopped talking when she saw Annette. "Sorry, I didn't see you there."

"I was apologizing to Jimmy. My friends are waiting by the park—we're just leaving. Bye, Maggie. Bye, Jimmy."

She left, and Jimmy watched her run toward the trees.

"She apologized? How did that go? 'I'm sorry for attacking you in the car'?"

"Don't be mean, Mags. She's a nice kid. I'll tell you the story later. Right now, let's see if we can get Dad to go to the car. I'm sure he's explaining how he's drunk but can still drive better than most, especially me."

"I'll look forward to hearing the Annette explanation later. Yeah, Dad was giving the same old spiel. He's drunk but he can drive."

"But we may as well wait here," Jimmy declared. "Better to leave Mom to deal with Dad. If we show up, he'll just get mad."

"Okay." Maggie sat down next to a tree east of the ballroom, near the small drive used to drop off guests at the dance, and made herself comfortable. "Sit down. Tell me about your dances with Ann Shaurel."

"Only if you spill your intimate details about Tony and those other guys I saw you dancing with."

"So, you saw me and Tony, eh?" Jimmy nodded. "It'll be a while before we go," Maggie said. "Dad bought thirty hamburgers. He said, 'People were standing in line ordering one or two, so I just thought I'd save time and order thirty and hand them out as people wanted them.' At a quarter a piece, it cost him seven fifty. Most of the wedding party was gone, but he made some new friends. Especially the cook. He gave him a ten and told him to keep the change."

"Sounds like Dad. He's so generous with Mom's egg money, but it took more than egg money to pay for their part in the wedding—renting my tux, buying your bridesmaid dress, new jacket for Joey, and a new dress for Mom. They shipped Red Bessie to South Saint Paul stockyards because she didn't get bred on schedule. I'm sure the whole check went to the wedding celebration and the gift. They wanted to go there in style. I'm sure he spent a bundle buying rounds all day too."

"Our folks know how to celebrate, that's for sure," Maggie said.

"Now, quit stalling and tell me what Tony said to you."

"Oh, no, I asked you about Annette first. But actually, I'm more interested in all the time you spent dancing with Ann Shaurel. I thought you didn't like her."

"Well, she's a nosy neighbor, but at the dance she was different. She was fun."

"Have anything to do with that blue dress she was wearing? I think I saw that dress on Jo Anne a couple years ago. She had the boobs for it. Ann must've stuffed tissue paper in it."

"Do girls really do that?"

"I wouldn't know, but I've heard they do." Maggie blushed.

"I admit that she danced close and I couldn't see my feet, and the first time I tried to I was a little embarrassed."

Maggie brashly asked, "How about the second and third time you tried?"

Now it was Jimmy's turn to blush. "Well, they were pretty hard to ignore."

Maggie giggled in triumph. "And that was her goal."

They both smiled, satisfied they had exhausted the topic for the moment, each using the silence to scan over the night's wild events.

Under the wide night sky, brother and sister sat back against the gnarly trunk of a short bur oak, he in his rumpled tuxedo and she in her sweaty green bridesmaid dress. Happy to keep their thoughts to themselves, neither one seemed eager to speak until Maggie, after contemplating the overall experience of the evening, quietly voiced a concern.

"I had fun tonight. I really did. But I can't help thinking that it's really always all about you."

Shocked, Jimmy said, "What! How can you say that?"

"With the couples in the wedding party, for just one example, it's the beautiful dresses and the beautiful girls that draw the comments and attention, but with us, it's you."

"That's just not true. Everyone raved about you and your green dress and auburn hair and pretty looks."

"Yeah, maybe a little, but their praise always ended with what a cute couple *we* made, which included you."

"You're being . . . I don't know . . . foolish. Look, Tony came over and wanted to dance with you, didn't he? I mean, here's some hotshot good-looking guy from the big city, and he wanted to dance with you, Maggie the farm kid."

"Not a good example. If I remember right, he said Annette wanted to dance with you and he would be glad to dance with me. You were the big draw."

"You're missing the part where he called you my 'pretty sister.' He came to me because it's the gentleman's way of cutting in. You talk to the guy. You don't just grab the girl and start dancing. Tony is smooth. I put his approach on my mental list of how to talk to girls."

"Is it a long list?" Maggie joked.

"It's the first and only item." Jimmy smiled, glad to know his sister still had her sense of humor.

"Okay, so let me give you more examples. Ann Shaurel and all the neighbor girls just about fell over each other to dance with you. How many neighborhood boys asked me?"

"First of all, how many neighborhood boys can even dance? The neighbor girls wanted to dance with me because I dance. I'm pretty sure I have no reason to get a big head over my . . . local popularity. Besides, all those girls danced with you too. They just wanted to dance."

"Ann Shaurel didn't dance with me."

"Okay, one out of . . . however many. Joe and Tom asked you to dance. Ralph Schoen asked you to dance. He's a good-looking guy. All the Schoen boys are."

"He was really clumsy, poor guy. I tried to help him along, but he got frustrated and quit."

"Now listen, Maggie. He's in your grade, right?" He waited till she nodded before he continued. "Do you realize the courage it took to ask his classmate to dance?"

"Why? It was just me. We used to play together in the country school."

"I can't believe you are not seeing this—here he is, a clumsy fifteen-year-old boy, gearing up the courage to ask Maggie Carlson to dance. She's pretty, she's so smart that it makes his head spin, she talks fast and has a vocabulary like no one else he knows, and here she is in this beautiful dress looking so good it makes his knees weak."

"Is that how you see me?"

"Hell, no, you're my goofy sister." He couldn't resist the chance to joke.

Maggie laughed out loud. "Good to know."

"But lots of boys see you that way. You are a smart, bold, and attractive female. That scares lots of guys. Some of them good guys."

"So, you're saying I should act dumb."

"Hell, no! Never do that. But you did the right thing with Ralph. You were kind and helpful. That's just being you."

"Maybe that's the plight of all girls."

"Maybe, but I hate the sound of me coming off like some expert here. I think of Billy's comment about giving me advice."

"Yeah, and he messed up his own situation."

"Right."

"Another thing—and maybe you don't want to hear this—but I've been thinking about Tony and Annette. She was drunk and without any good sense at the time. But I doubt that he got into the car thinking he was going to push you into allowing him to . . . you know what I mean. You were sitting next to your brother, who would have kicked his butt or at least tried. He had to be aware of that. He got into the car because he wanted to have his arm around you, and one thing led to another. I think he honestly couldn't help himself. I say that because the moment was pulling me in with Annette. I could be wrong, but there it is."

Maggie smiled, looked down, and turned to him. "Actually, Tony came up to apologize. He kind of said the same thing you just did. I forgave him, and we danced."

"I think I know you, but then you never fail to surprise me. Oh, and then there's Robert. He was my friend before he knew I had a sister, so he's not using me to get to you, but he sure does like to show up to drive me home when I have detention. I think he's just itching to get a chance to see you when he drops me off."

"Yeah, to see me in my chore clothes."

"A girl makes the clothes; the clothes don't make the girl. I liked to see Mary. I didn't care what she was wearing."

"So, there is another example of it always being about you. Mary was my friend, but she was your sweetheart first."

"She shared more with you than with me. Right now, if she appeared here after the dance, as B. J. or somebody seems to think she will, she'd want to see you more than me."

"Maybe. But then there's my new friend Anne Busch. I don't think she ever would have talked to me if she hadn't found out you were my brother."

"You don't know that. What you do know is that she is a genuinely kind person. I think she was drawn to you because she seems the type of person who always wants to make friends."

"I'd like to think that is true. She is really nice."

"A dynamic personality! We had so much fun dancing and talking. I met my match at being a smart-ass, that's for sure."

"And you're right about clothes. She looks good in anything."

"Come on, Mags. You do too."

Maggie smiled. "Me too, eh?"

"You too!" The two of them leaned back against the tree to enjoy the night air. "Oh, by the way," Jimmy teased, "what is the dazzling Maggie Carlson willing to pay me to withhold the details of her exploits tonight from her boyfriend and my good buddy, Robert?"

Maggie leaned forward in a flash. "Shut up, Jimmy. You wouldn't tell. Would you? I mean, it was a dance. We have no big commitment to each other."

"I thought that was a guy's line?"

"You'd better not tell—"

He didn't let her finish. "Counterthreats are not a good tactic, dear sister." Jimmy laughed. "Let's just add it to our list of secrets. But you can at least quit telling me to shut up."

"Shut up, Jimmy," Maggie said again before they both leaned back again, smiling.

Maggie stayed silent for a long moment before she carefully said, "You know, Jimmy, the longer the dance went on, the more I started to believe Mary might show up."

"Why do you say that?"

"Katherine is so sure about B. J. knowing what's going on. And Mary took a risk to run away once. She might do it again."

"I'm not so sure," Jimmy said. He glanced toward the dance hall just in time to see Officer Grossman coming toward them. *That's the second time he's shown up when I've been out here. And he's coming directly toward us.*

"Hello, Officer," Jimmy said to alert Maggie to his approach.

"Hi, kids. You two seem to waiting for someone."

"Our folks and our little brother are inside eating hamburgers," Maggie said quickly. "We weren't hungry."

"So we thought we'd wait out here in the cool night air," Jimmy offered for support.

"I've seen you two in and out a lot tonight. I thought maybe you were looking for someone. Or expecting someone."

"No, sir," Maggie said politely.

"Let me know if you need any help," the officer said before he turned to walk back toward the entryway.

Maggie and Jimmy stared at each other, their eyes wild with anticipation. As soon as the officer entered the ballroom, Maggie let out a stifled screech. "The cops are looking for her! They're expecting her! Now I'm convinced Mary is coming!"

"And they suspect that she is meeting us," Jimmy said. "That makes us accessories! Jeez, I'd love to see Mary, but why did she pick such a public place?"

"And why would the cops know about it?"

"Well, they have their ways, I suppose."

Maggie asked, "What should we do?"

"Wait," Jimmy said. "All we can do is wait. Maybe we'll see her and can guide her away from the cops. You know what? I wish Mary would show up right now! We could take her home with us."

"But now," Maggie lamented, "all we can do is wait and hope the cops don't see her first."

CHAPTER 32

AFTERMATH

Early Sunday morning, June 10, 1956

Jack rolled over fitfully, and the smell of his own puke awoke him. Struggling to open his eyes, he panicked momentarily when he saw nothing. He'd been out for hours. Complete darkness had descended on the pits. Once he stood upright, though, the moon gave ample light to lead him to the car. The door was open and the interior light was dim. He crawled into the driver's seat and closed the door quickly, hoping the battery wasn't dead. Keys were in the ignition. After the battery managed a few slow cranks, the engine came to life. *That was close!*

He wanted water fast, but he needed to know the time. Had he overslept? He squinted at the clock on the dash. A few minutes past midnight. The dance would be over at one, but Mary's instructions had told him to wait till the end.

"Hell, I got plenty time to get there." After greedily drinking water from the quart jar, he opened another pint of whiskey and took a drink before he drove carefully out of the pit.

He turned right onto Pit Road and followed the curvy trail south, watching carefully for the gravel road that would take him west to the south end of Lakeland City. *I gotta stay off the tar. Cops might be looking for me and this Caddy by now. I'll come up to the dance hall from the south so cops don't see me.*

"Ah, there's the Torgerson farm on the right. The turn should be coming up," he murmured. His headlights caught the dark intersection ahead, but he braked too late, and as he tried to turn west, his front wheels skidded on the loose gravel, propelling the front of the car over the sharp edge of the road. The Cadillac came to a stop with the front wheels sinking into the small ditch. "Damn!" he screamed as he shifted into reverse and hit the accelerator, but the weight of the Caddy's front half left him short on traction for the back wheels. Feeling helpless, he listened to the engine roar as the spinning back tires spewed gravel across the road. Finally, he shut the engine off, opened the door, and climbed out, noting, *Good thing I'm not too far in the ditch. Another foot or so and I'd be in the water.*

"Damn! Damn! Damn!" Jack yelled at the sky, shaking his fists. *What to do now?*

The answer came to him in an instant. *I'll go get the Torgerson brothers. Sure, it's late, but if I tempt them with cash and a bottle of whiskey, they'll crank up their old Farmall 20 and pull me out.*

When Jack reached the farmyard, the house was dark, but the lights were on in the barn. *Not too unusual to catch these boys milking five hours late. I'm in luck. They've probably spent their money in town and the booze is gone. I've got both money and booze. And if they're milking, they've probably sobered up a little and are thirsty.*

When Jack entered the barn, Magnus was feeding calves while Arne opened the stanchion to let the last cow out of the barn. They were just as Jack remembered them—slim, muscular men with thick mops of light hair tucked under their striped caps. Their faded blue work shirts stuck out of the unbuttoned sides of their striped bib overalls just as they had when Jack had shocked grain with them when he was a kid. They moved slowly even then, but they always seemed to get a lot done.

Magnus, who was in his mid-fifties, spoke in a heavy Norwegian accent. "Christ, if it ain't Jack Drude."

Upon hearing the name, Arne, who was five years younger, said with the same accent, "Holy Moses! I thought the law kept you tied to your folks' farm." His voice had a higher pitch.

Glad that the men were done milking, Jack remarked in a friendly manner, "Hello, boys! Magnus and Arne, how are you guys doing?"

"What are you lookin' for this time of night?" Magnus asked without smiling.

"I thought you had to stay home," Arne said bluntly.

"I'm off for good behavior," Jack lied, "and I came to ask you boys for some help."

"Well, it's pretty damn late, you know," Arne said.

"I got some whiskey and some cash for you if you start up the F-20 and pull me out of the ditch. It'll be an easy pull, and it's just a few yards on the road to Lakeland City." Sensing their reluctance, Jack added, "How about a ten-spot and a pint?"

"I'll take the flashlight and start the Farmall H. No lights on the F-20," Magnus said as he left the barn.

"I'll get the chain," Arne said.

In about twenty minutes, Arne had hitched the chain to the Cadillac's back bumper and to the drawbar of the H, and Jack could hear Magnus talking to the tractor. "Now, I'll tighten the chain slowly, sweetheart. We don't want to jerk. The chain is tight, so now we have to pull. I'll give you more gas, honey, and off we go. Attagirl, you walked that car right out of there."

When Jack noticed Arne eyeing the Caddy, he handed him the whiskey and the ten-dollar bill as he said, "You're right, that is Ziton's car. He loaned it to me for the weekend in trade for some really good hay. And we store the bales until he needs them delivered. It's a good deal for both of us." *Doesn't much matter if they believe me or not. They don't have a phone, so they can't call the sheriff, anyway.* "Thanks again, you guys. See ya!" And Jack climbed in the car and sped off to the west.

Jack looked at the clock in the car and reassured himself, "Twelve forty. Dance will be over at one. I want to be on the east side of the ballroom about quarter after one, just as everyone is leaving. Plenty of time."

Jack took the road north, along the west side of the lake. After he entered the park, he drove along the west side nearly all the way to Main Street before he turned right up a dark maintenance road used to deliver stock to the concession stand. Twenty yards in, he backed into a spot behind a utility building where tall American elms blocked the moon's light. *No one will see me here.* He cut his lights and got out. Then he stripped off his pants and shirt and, using water from the quart jar sparingly, he cleaned his face and hands before putting on clean jeans and a shirt. He transferred Mary's letter to his clean shirt before he wiped the dirty clothes on the grass. Then he rolled them tight and stored them in a corner of the trunk.

After taking a good swig of water, he settled himself in the driver's seat with a quart of whiskey and sandwiches in his reach. He checked the clock carefully. Plenty of time yet to leave for the pavilion.

Alone in the darkness, he began to doubt his plan. He doubted Mary and he doubted himself at first, and if he'd kept on doubting, the alcohol would have worked to depress his mood. But he boosted his own resolve by recalling what he had decided earlier. *There is nothing for me here.* He took the letter out of his shirt pocket and carefully unfolded it. Turning on the interior light, he reread the important part aloud. "Won't we feel good when they see the two of us drive off together in a nice car, never to return. The ultimate revenge! You can live with me." He chuckled as he folded the letter and returned it safely to his shirt pocket. He relaxed but tried to stay awake as he watched the clock, waiting for the right moment to leave.

The silence awoke Billy as he sat against the pavilion. He spent a moment assessing whether or not the talks with Anna and George had really happened. They had. George was pretty amazing. He'd hinted they could be casual friends at family get-togethers. He'd have to stay pretty distant, though. It would work out.

His thoughts turned to others. Did Joey's friend recover from his brief beer binge? *Maybe I should go check on him.* He checked his wristwatch, a gift from his folks. *Fifteen minutes after one. Everyone's left the dance by now.*

He picked himself up from his napping place and stretched broadly. He was in no hurry to leave, so he sauntered slowly into the park, enjoying the cool evening breeze as he walked past the ball field and across the grass. Soon he could see the dimly lit street where he had parked his car. Though he was sad to have lost Anna, he felt a lonely freedom he hadn't felt for years. *My future is full of possibilities, and I'm a bit wiser now.* He smiled as he stepped onto the street and walked toward his car. *I'm sure glad I made peace with Anna and George. They are a couple of great people.*

Jack awoke in a panic. The clock said fifteen minutes past one. *I should make it right on time if I hurry!* He started the engine and sped out of the maintenance road, making a left turn onto the side street that led to the ballroom. Angry that he'd switched on his parking lights instead of his headlights, he looked down as he slammed on the brakes, fumbling blindly for the light switch in the car's dark interior. He hit it and looked up as the headlights illuminated a figure standing in the street alongside the car.

"Jack Drude!" the man exclaimed. "You nearly hit me!" The man swung the door to the Cadillac open, grabbed Jack by his shirt, and began pulling him out of the car. Jack struggled against the man's powerful arms and desperately reached into the front seat, grabbed a half-full bottle of whiskey, and swung it at the man's head. The direct hit sent vibrations through Jack's hand, and the grip on his shirt relaxed before the man fell like a large sandbag to the gravel street.

Still holding the bottle, Jack looked down at the man's bleeding head and still body. "Crazy bastard!" he exclaimed. "I got people to see yet tonight, so I ain't got time to stick around." Jack tossed the bottle back on the front seat, climbed in, and turned left through the park, telling himself, "I can still get to the east side of the ballroom in time."

Jimmy and Maggie had been enjoying watching the crowds exit the dance hall, but now they were a little impatient for their folks to emerge from the crowd to take them home.

"Actually, I'm glad Mom and Dad aren't ready to go home yet," Maggie said. "I'm convinced Mary will show up sometime tonight."

Jimmy replied, "I'd love to see Mary drive up here right now, but you don't think she'd drive the Model A, do you?"

"No, I don't. She's not that stupid!"

"On the other hand," Jimmy teased, "she's done some stupid things in the past. Maybe she has some kind of revenge thing planned. You know, to get even with Jack."

"I wouldn't put it past her," Maggie said as she got up from her spot by the tree to brush herself off.

Suddenly, a black Cadillac zoomed toward them, skidding on the gravel surface and coming to a dead stop just inches away from the sidewalk in front of their tree. The driver's door swung open, and Jack Drude struggled to get out.

In a flash, Maggie was at the passenger door, shouting, "Mary! Mary! Are you okay?" She flung the door open, and as the interior light illuminated only discarded potato chip bags and empty whiskey bottles, she uttered with a mixture of disappointment and relief, "Mary isn't here." Spotting an open envelope among the trash on the car seat, she quickly grabbed it to read the address. *It's addressed to Jack Drude! A letter to Jack Drude!* She fumbled to look inside but found it empty. Taking the envelope with her, she backed out of the car and closed the door to witness Jack Drude staggering toward Jimmy, demanding, "Where is she? Where's Mary Schroedler? Her letter said she'd be here after the dance."

Jimmy remembered Billy's warning about someone who's drunk. *Don't let them get close if they're angry.* "First I heard of it, Jack." Jimmy lied as he stood up and kept his distance. Jack was staggering, but he was always dangerous. Full of anger. Hungry for revenge. But Jimmy relaxed a bit as Jack approached him with a reasonable tone.

"Look, Carlson. Don't bullshit me. I know she prefers you, but maybe when she sees my new car, she'll think again. Ziton loaned it to me. Nice, huh?" He gestured toward the car, edging closer to Jimmy as he spoke. Then, with speed beyond the capability of most drunken men, he stepped forward and put a hard right fist to the side of Jimmy's face, catching him by surprise and knocking him to the ground.

Feeling the full strength of Jack's blow, Jimmy struggled to roll away, but the kicks started as soon as he hit the grass. The tase of blood in his mouth jarred the memory of Billy's advice—*You have to treat every fight like you're in a fight for your life.*

Hands over his face and legs pulled close together, Jimmy continued to roll away as Jack's kicks bit into his stamina and his will. He tried to kick back, but Jack grabbed his foot and lifted it toward him while twisting. Jimmy saw his chance and placed two swift kicks on Jack's left shin, just as he'd practiced with Billy, sending Jack to his knees as he released Jimmy's foot.

Jimmy rolled away, but Jack was up and kicking again before he could stand. But with a lucky reach, Jimmy grabbed Jack's foot mid-kick and managed to hold it long enough to rise to face his opponent. Without hesitating, Jack wildly swung his right fist high at Jimmy's jaw, poking Jimmy's memory of his dad dodging an inebriated Paul several hours earlier. As the momentum of Jack's wild swing carried him forward, Jimmy ducked low and grabbed Jack's crotch with his right hand, and with his left hand he pushed upward on Jack's chest and stomach. Jimmy felt his legs tremble under the weight of his opponent, and he momentarily wished he hadn't initiated the move. Forced to go down on one knee to bear Jack's weight, Jimmy lifted with all his strength as Jack's momentum carried him overhead to slam hard into the rough trunk of the bur oak.

Jack slid down the trunk of the tree and landed on his back. Jimmy saw the opening, and as he kicked hard at Jack's groin, he hollered through the blood in his mouth, "How do you like my pointy dress shoes, Jack?!"

But Jimmy's kick missed the mark as Jack rolled over swiftly, came to his feet, and charged Jimmy, who avoided Jack's punches but also missed his own jabs at Jack's throat.

Suddenly, Jack was no longer standing there. Someone had grabbed him and turned him around to face the other way. Jimmy heard Billy's angry voice yell, "Nail me with a bottle, eh? You'll regret that big time, Drude."

After months of keeping his emotions in check, Billy released his fury on Jack with the force of a runaway locomotive. His first swing connected hard against the left side of Jack's face, crashing him against the side of the Cadillac with a noise that jolted Billy with the reality of his own anger. He paused for just a moment, and instead of ending the fight swiftly with moves that delivered serious injury, Billy elected to punch Jack's body and deliver openhanded slaps to the side of Jack's face, which were less likely to knock him unconscious than closed-fist punches. His flurry of blows bounced Jack against the car, oscillating like a heavy punching bag in a resonant frequency, Billy's superior speed and training rendering Jack helpless to defend himself. Billy did not hesitate to take his anger out on the man who had caused others so much pain.

Maggie came to Jimmy's side and asked, "Do you need to see a doctor?"

"I don't think so," he replied through the blood in his mouth. "I just need to sit here a minute. By the looks of things, Billy is making short work of Jack. I'll spit out the worst of the blood here before I go back into the ballroom to clean up in the lavatory. But when I go clean up, you stay here and watch for Mary. She may still turn up."

They watched as Billy delivered blow after blow until Jack finally fell to the ground. As Jack tried to stand, Maggie saw a folded piece of paper fall from his shirt pocket. Then Billy kicked him hard on the side of his knee and Jack screamed in pain. He lay on the ground, puffing hard, no longer trying to stand.

Billy moved over to Jimmy. "Are you okay, champ?"

"I'm such a dumbass, letting him get in the first punches, but he'd probably beat me anyway."

"Don't sell yourself short. Did you see the way he took those punches I was dishing? He is a tough SOB."

They both looked up as the sheriff's car arrived and the deputy leaped out.

"Gotcha this time, Drude. Berris called us when he found Ziton tied up in his barn. Stealing a car is going to get you some time. And then there's probably an assault charge too." Cuffing Jack, the deputy said, "Can you get up on your own? Your leg looks twisted." Then he turned to Jimmy and Billy and asked, "You guys look kind of bloody. Are you okay?"

"Never better," Billy said.

Jimmy saw blood caked near Billy's eye. "We'd better go inside to clean up before they close the place. We both look like hell."

"Except for the bottle to my head, Jack hardly touched me," Billy said. "Most of my pain is the sore knuckles I got from pounding on him."

While her brother and cousin were distracted with their wounds, Maggie approached the deputy and said, "Thanks. You guys came just in time." Then she casually walked to where Jack had fallen and picked up the folded paper that had dropped out of his shirt pocket. She turned to her brother and said, "Jimmy, you should probably get cleaned up right away before Mom and Dad come outside."

"You're right. I don't want to have a conversation about my bloody looks on the way home."

"Let's go," Billy said as he helped Jimmy to his feet.

"I'll go in to see if the folks are on their way," Maggie said.

"No, stay here and see if Mary shows up. She may be waiting until the cops leave."

"Okay," Maggie said. "If the folks are true to form, they're probably still in the bar saying goodbye and giving away hamburgers."

Jimmy laughed, even though it hurt, and he hurried off with Billy to clean up. Once in the toilet, both men ran cold water on their hands and washed their faces.

Jimmy was curious. "How did he get close enough to you to hit you with a bottle? It looks pretty bad."

Billy briefly explained, adding, "Knocked me out cold for a few minutes, but I woke up in time to catch Drude. Damn him."

"And to save my butt," Jimmy confessed as he attended to the scrapes and cuts on his face. "I hurt all over, but if I move slowly, I'll be fine."

As they left the washroom, Jimmy said, "Let's cancel Sunday afternoon training until further notice."

"Agreed," Billy said.

CHAPTER 33

GOING HOME

Early Sunday morning, June 10, 1956

Jimmy arrived in time to watch the sheriff's car leave with Jack. "Any sign of Mary?" he asked Maggie.

"No." Maggie pointed to the ballroom entryway and added, "Here come Mom and Dad and Joey."

"I don't want to distract them. Better if you help Mom and Dad to the car. I'll wait here a couple more minutes just in case."

Understanding that his presence might upset the dynamic that got Dad to leave the event, he waited until his family was nearly swallowed up by the darkness on the dimly lit path before he caught up to them and suggested, "Hey Dad, I could drive, if you want. It's been a long day."

"Think I can't drive!" Dad bellowed.

"No one thinks that, Martin," Mom said gently. "But Jimmy needs practice driving at night."

"You know, Dad, Jimmy is a good driver," Maggie asserted gingerly.

"I can drive," Dad mumbled. "Sure, I'm drunk, but I'll drive this buggy home."

Jimmy knew he could take the keys from his dad in this drunken state, but not without a tussle that would cause a permanent rift between them. The father-son bond was strong but simultaneously fragile.

The family climbed into the car with Dad behind the wheel as they had many times. No police cars followed Martin, and drunk as he was, he set off slowly but steadily. In the back, the three children slid down in the seat and closed their eyes, trusting their father to take them home safely. But each was filled with their own anxieties—Jimmy worried about leaving Mary behind as he tried to find a position that avoided the worst pain from his injuries; Joey feared the moment his parents would discover the missing beer; and Maggie, also worried about leaving Mary behind, ached to unfold the paper that had fallen from Jack Drude's shirt pocket.

Mom kept up a light chatter with Dad to ensure he concentrated on the road.

"Let's turn off the main road as soon as we can to get on the gravel road home," she advised.

Dad did not respond to her comment. Instead, he ranted against the cars passing him. "Why is everyone in such a damn hurry? They nearly run me off the road!"

"Well, you've driving with the right-side tires on the gravel shoulder, Martin."

"I'm just being careful."

"Yes, and you're doing fine," Mom encouraged, "but you can't blame people for passing. You're only going thirty."

"It's plenty fast. I'm driving fast and straight. Nothing wrong with my driving," Dad insisted.

Mom and the kids had been through this before, and they would have been content for the conversation to continue along the same lines so long as the car continued toward home, even at the slow pace. And it did for another few miles.

"You missed the turn to the gravel road," Mom said bluntly.

"On purpose!" Dad countered. "I hate that dark, curvy trail. I'll turn at the next one in a few miles."

A brief silence followed before the car's interior lit up with the red flashing light of a police car alongside them.

"Jeez," Dad said reluctantly, "I'd better pull over."

No one said a word as the car stopped and the officer strode up to the driver's-side door. Martin rolled down the window as the officer shined a flashlight into the car.

"Something wrong?" Dad asked, his words slurred.

"Driver's license, please," the officer asked firmly.

"Did I do something wrong?" Dad asked again as he clumsily fished out his license from his wallet.

The officer collected Martin's license and aimed his flashlight at the document. "Well, Mr. Carlson," the officer offered, "you seem to be hugging the curb."

Martin replied immediately, "Hell, I'm just trying to stay out of the way of those speeding cars trying to run me off the road."

The officer was silent as he shined the light onto Mary first and then on the kids in the back seat. Finally, he said, "You have a nice family, sir."

Martin nodded.

"Are you and the kids all right, ma'am?"

Mary said evenly, "We are fine, Officer."

"Have you been drinking?" he asked Martin.

"Yes," Martin said,

"Are you drunk?" the officer asked.

"Hell, yes, I am," Martin replied. "I've been drinking beer all day celebrating my niece's wedding. I won't lie to you. I'm drunk. I've been drinking beer since noon."

The officer seemed amused but commanded, "Please step out of the car, Mr. Carlson, and follow me."

Martin stepped out without a word, and a tense silence filled the interior of the car as they saw another officer, a younger man, step out of the police car. The cops ordered Martin to try to walk a straight line along the gravel shoulder and watched his efforts as the Carlson family waited.

"Throw him in the clink," the younger officer declared.

"Get in the back seat of the patrol car," the older officer said to Martin evenly.

Mom hardened her jaw. After a short time, she said, "No telling what will happen now. I just hope he doesn't get belligerent with the cops. He can be a real smart-ass." A moment later, Mom smiled and laughed lightly before she added, "He looked pretty serious when he got out of the car, though. He's no dummy, really, and if he admits to himself the seriousness of the situation, he's in there now talking nice to the police."

"Let's just hope he doesn't start telling them stories," Jimmy said.

Everyone laughed nervously.

"What's going to happen to Dad?" Joey asked. "Is he going to jail?"

"We won't know for a while yet, Joey," Maggie tried to console him. "But it's going to be all right."

"All we can do, kids, is be patient," Mom explained. "Be ready to drive home, Jim. You didn't drink anything, did you?"

"No, I've been saving myself for this moment." He hadn't meant it to be funny, but Mom and Maggie and Joey all laughed nervously before falling silent again.

Fifteen minutes later the older officer brought Martin to the passenger side, opened the front door, and said, "Martin tells me that he has a sixteen-year-old son in the car who has a permit and can drive really good." Shining the light on Jimmy, he added, "Why don't you get in the driver's seat, son. I'll give you the keys. Mrs. Carlson, Martin said that you drive tractors, but you don't drive cars, so could you take your son's place in the back, please? Martin, you take her place in the front seat."

No one said a word as they shifted seats. Then the officer said, "Now, Martin, we're sending you home with your family so you can do chores in the morning." Addressing the kids and Mary, he added, "Martin tells me that the whole family helps with chores. Is that right?"

Feeling a little braver, Joey said, "Sometimes they let me sleep late."

The officer smiled. He turned to Martin again, saying, "Martin, I want you to let your son drive all the way home. Got it?"

"Right!" Martin said seriously.

After closing the door, the officer walked around the car and reached into the open driver's door to give Jimmy the keys. "You know the way home, son?"

"I do, Officer," Jimmy said clearly. "Thank you."

Shining the light on Jimmy's face, the officer asked, "Are you okay? Your face looks a little hammered."

Jimmy paused only briefly before he asserted confidently, "I tripped over a tree root in the park. Too dark to see it. Fell flat on my face. It hurts a little, but I'm okay to drive." *Good thing I washed the blood off my face in the lav.*

"Your dad said you suggested driving home before you left the dance. He said he insisted on driving himself and wouldn't let you drive. Isn't that right, Martin?"

"That's right. My son wanted to drive. I should've let him drive."

"After I close the door, pull out, son. We'll follow for a while, but we'll go straight when you turn off."

The door slammed, and Jimmy wasted no time in starting the car, flicking on the turn signal, and pulling out onto the highway. Nothing was said until Jimmy turned onto the gravel road and the patrol car stayed on the highway. Then Dad said, "If the younger cop had his way, they would've tossed me in the clink and thrown away the key."

No one said the obvious "I told you so." No one wanted to argue, but the family shared a feeling of great relief, as if the car itself sighed, "Whew!"

Less than a mile down the road, Dad began his story about what had happened in the back of the patrol car. At first, he was contrite, an attitude the family had not seen often from their patriarch, but before long he'd swung into storytelling mode, giving himself credit for saying the right things as the officers queried him.

Mom and the three kids all shared the same thought: *By tomorrow morning he will have added it to his list of stories to repeat to all who will listen.* But they were also thinking, *Good to have the old man back.*

"That young guy wanted me in jail. The older guy liked that I admitted I was drunk. He really cussed me out for driving, though, especially when I told him my son could drive. 'You put your family and everyone else on the road in danger,' he told me. When I tried to say something in my defense, he slapped me a good one across the face. He told me to shut up and convinced me I deserved worse. I didn't argue. What he said made sense. I'm glad you're driving now, Jim."

Half an hour later, Jimmy turned slowly into the driveway, and as the headlights illuminated the small yard, Mom chanted, "Home again, home again, jiggety jig." Jimmy parked the car in the grassless area by the house, and everyone slowly opened the car doors, relieved to be home safe.

No one commented on the lovely early morning. Warm, with a cool breeze blowing from the west, the weather was exactly the perfect kind about which any one of them would normally rave. But at this moment, no one took time to notice. Jimmy ran to the house to pull the chains on the lightbulbs on the porch and in the kitchen, and he flicked on the yard light switch to light the way for the other kids, who each walked a little more slowly and carefully than they usually did.

The kids gone from the car, Mom flung the back door open, reached down to the floor, and exclaimed, "What the heck is this?" She picked up a loose can of beer, remarking, "How did this get loose from the rest of the six-pack? Did you break it open, Martin? If so, when? We bought this for tomorrow morning, remember?"

Dad jolted to life at the accusation and denied knowing anything about it. Mom scrounged around on the floor to discover only four of the six cans. Soon the same old accusations flew between the two. As the argument intensified, Jimmy came out of the house, exclaiming, "Hell, you guys can argue here all night if you want to, but I'm going to bed!" But instead of going back into the house, he moved toward the car.

"Don't, Jimmy," Maggie warned.

"Right," Jimmy said, and backed off.

Suddenly, Joey seemed to make a decision. He ran toward his parents, shouting, "Stop! Stop! I took the beer, Mom and Dad. I took the beer!"

His family stared at him in disbelief.

"Ronnie Schoen said it would be great to have some beer, and he bragged about how he could drink beer. I got tired of him bragging, so I said I knew where some was. I took him to our car, and we each opened a can. I knew you always had a can opener in the glove compartment. I took it. I'm sorry, Mom and Dad. Real, real sorry. And I'm not blaming Ronnie. It was all my fault. I'm sorry!"

Jimmy and Maggie listened in awe. Mom and Dad looked at each other as they cooled off a bit, realizing that blaming each other was useless. Mom was the first to laugh. Then Dad. Then Maggie and Jimmy. And finally, as he wiped away tears of guilt, Joey began to laugh too. Mom gathered up the four cans, handed them to Joey, and said sarcastically, "Can I trust my young son to put these in the refrigerator?"

At that, the whole family howled.

CHAPTER 34

PREDAWN MUSINGS

Early Sunday morning, June 10, 1956

The five Carlson family members went to bed about three in the morning after being up twenty-two hours, nearly eighteen hours of which they'd spent celebrating the wedding. But only Martin fell asleep immediately. As tired as they were, Maggie, Joey, and Jimmy found that the events of the wedding day kept their minds too busy to sleep. Joey sat on Jimmy's bed, filling him in on how had Ronnie guzzled the beer and gotten sick.

But it was Maggie who needed to talk. The empty envelope and the folded paper were like a fire burning in her purse all the way home, and only now did she have an opportunity to put out the flame. Once she got to her room, she dug it out, unfolded it carefully, and read the words silently to herself. Astonished at the message, she looked up from the letter. *Mary wrote to Jack? I can't believe it! This will break Jimmy's heart.*

Without regard for being quiet, Maggie ran out of her room and down the hallway to the boys' room, where she was surprised to find both of her brothers awake. But as she saw them in a comfortable state of peace, she was unsure what to do. *Maybe Jimmy doesn't need to know.*

"Hi, Mags," Jimmy said. "I wondered if you were able to sleep. What's on your mind?"

Maggie sat on the floor near the bed. "I don't plan on staying long," she said, stalling. "We're all too tired, but I just have to tell you, Jimmy, you were a totally different person at the dance. I've never seen you so willing to talk to people." *I'll decide whether or not to tell him as we talk.*

"I'm the same guy underneath, but I know what you mean. I look back at the night, and I hardly recognize myself either. I had made up my mind to try to talk to people, but I wasn't sure if I could go through with it. But when you and I danced and Tony and Annette cut in, that's when it started."

"What started?"

"I don't know. It was as if I were a person other than Jimmy Carlson. I was a young man that people sought to be with. When I spoke, I felt good about speaking. And then when so many neighborhood kids wanted to dance with me, I was encouraged to become even more bold."

"Me too," Maggie said. "Boys, and girls too, seemed to see Maggie Carlson differently, and their behavior made me see myself differently. I became a winner instead of a loser. The ballroom became an enchanted place."

"That's it, Mags. You nailed it again. I could never have talked to all those people if it had been anywhere else. I can't do casual talk anywhere to anyone. At a dance, I can just say, 'Let's dance.' And beyond that, I agree the whole place is kind of magical. Romantic."

With her hand over her mouth, Maggie stifled a laugh. "Never thought I'd hear Jimmy Carlson say that. 'Romantic,' eh?"

"I admit it. Dancing with all those girls had an effect on me. I mean, I know my feelings of grandness weren't real—no, they were real for the moment, but not lasting. Not meant to go beyond the magical place of the dance floor. Jeez, I found myself really liking Ann Shaurel, and now I consider her just a good friend."

"I decided I liked Caroline too," Joey admitted.

"Well," Maggie said, "maybe the dance allowed them to be who they really are, and it's daily life where they cover up who they are. Maybe they have just as much trouble with small talk as you do, Jimmy."

"That would mean I have it backward." Jimmy laughed. "I've been wrong before. So, you're saying people want to be that way all the time, but the daily routine prevents them from being who they really are?"

"Something like that."

"Pretty fascinating stuff. Don't you think, Joey?"

"So, that means Ronnie wants to guzzle beer all the time?" Joey asked.

They all laughed lightly before Maggie said, "Not exactly. Maybe it means that he wants to prove something all the time."

"But you had a romantic night, right, Mags?"

"There were some moments. I'll admit that. But they didn't last. Maybe they aren't supposed to."

"Ouch! What does that say about romance?" Jimmy's serious tone indicated he was no longer teasing.

Maggie looked down for a while before she looked up to face her brother. "I don't know for sure. Maybe it means that romance isn't real." *Maybe this will help him deal with the letter.*

"I don't like that conclusion," Jimmy grumbled.

"Me either," Maggie asserted slowly. "But hope is real. And it's romantic to hope. To hope that the guy or girl is who you want them to be or need them to be." *Darn. This just makes the letter harder to take.*

"Jeez! You nailed it again, Mags. And what a night you had! You should feel especially good. And you too, Joey. We all did what we set out to do."

"The question is," Maggie submitted slowly, "will everything go back to the way it was next time we see those people at school or in town or wherever?"

"That may be up to us," Jimmy said. "Right now, my body is screaming for sleep."

"Wait!" Maggie whispered in earnest. "One more thing. You've got to see this." She handed him the letter.

He took the paper from her hands, unfolded it carefully, and silently read the greeting and signature lines. "What! Mary wrote to Jack? I don't believe it!"

"Hard to believe, isn't it?" Maggie said. "I don't think I can believe it."

With mental anguish added to his physical pain, Jimmy scanned the letter and went back to reread a line that caught his eye. "Wait a minute," he said skeptically, "this line is familiar: 'I learned how to type, so I decided to practice by typing a letter to you instead of writing.' When I danced with Katherine O'Keran, she told me that B. J. hated Jack. And B. J. was learning to type because she complained about his bad penmanship; she said he had decided to practice his typing by typing a letter instead of writing to her. And there is no handwritten signature on this letter."

"Right!" Maggie exclaimed. "And no one types their signature! And B. J. was awfully interested in finding Mary, according to Katherine."

Jimmy laughed hard enough that it hurt. "Yeah, B. J. is a person of little imagination, so it might be necessary for him to use the same phrases over and over. I'll bet B. J. wrote the letter and started the rumor that led Jack to steal the car."

"Why would he do that?"

"Revenge on Jack for forcing B. J. to do his dirty work all these years," Jimmy answered.

"Maybe there is some justice for Jack after all," Maggie said, smiling.

"Maybe we'll get to show the letter to Mary one day and have a good laugh," Jimmy said.

"We don't have to tell her we believed she wrote it, though," Maggie urged. "I'm kind of ashamed I believed it."

"Don't be," Jimmy said. "B. J. had a lot of help convincing us. Katherine and Mary Ryan and others seemed convinced. And then all the cops in town! Heck, how were we to know they were looking for Jack?"

"You may be right," Maggie said. "Mary will get a big kick out of it."

"Keep the letter in a safe place, though," Jimmy warned. "We don't want the police to see it. No use incriminating B. J."

After a short pause, Joey said, "I don't understand."

"We'll explain it to you tomorrow," Jimmy moaned. "Right now, let's all get some sleep."

Mary Carlson lay awake, listening to Martin's snore and the noise of her children's voices, though their words were unclear. She could have yelled at the kids to be quiet and nudged Martin to turn over, but her mind's musings wouldn't let her sleep anyway. Not just yet. She had some sorting out to do. *Good that Billy and Anna danced and seemed friendly. Wonder if she told him. No telling how that went. Hope she tells me.*

Glad I told Emma I knew about her lies. I suppose any mother would lie if she thought it was right for her daughter. What wouldn't a mother do for her child? Lie, cheat, kill, steal. Ruin the lives of others. Disparage the names of others? What would I do?

Rose's accusations against Billy and Anna were unacceptable, but maybe Rose was not in control of her own thoughts and actions anymore. Is any mother in control when a perceived threat to her child's welfare grabs her by the throat? To what length will mothers go to control their kids? To prevent them from becoming what they want to be? It scares me.

Fate is an uncaring, cold pendulum that only swings one way, bowling over all things without regard for justice or life or the future. Fate cares for nothing. Mothers care for their children. That's fair enough. What about fathers? Martin said to let Billy and Anna decide. Would he be as open if Billy had been his child? He probably would. He was never obsessed with the belief he was always right. Unlike Rose.

One thing about Martin—he seldom cares if he is right, yet he always tries to do what is right. Not a perfect guy, but I made the right choice when I picked him. I love him for his weaknesses and his strengths. I especially like his unwillingness to force his convictions on others.

And our children? What beautiful, untamed creatures they are! So proud of them today. What lovely, exciting futures they will have. I'll do all I can to give them that future, not by obsessing that they be perfect, but by hoping they do the right thing according to what they know they must do.

And with that thought, Mary's mind relaxed and embraced the deep sleep that contentment provides.

CHAPTER 35

MORNING'S TRUTH

Sunday morning, June 10, 1956

Morning came without concern for anyone's readiness to face the sun. The Shaurel girls got up to milk a little late, expecting their father to rant about their late arrival home. Instead, he just chuckled to himself as he pushed them to finish milking and get ready for mass. Caroline slept in, dreaming of her dances with Joey. And Ann smiled through morning chores as she thought of the time she'd spent with Jimmy, recognizing the night had softened her crush on her neighbor. They had shared many life-changing experiences while attending the neighborhood country school, which had formed a close bond, but there was no romance between them. They were friends. And they always would be.

Miles away, Albert awoke with a new spring to his step, remembering Jane's hugs and kisses and her promise to meet him at the dance next Saturday night. The week of anticipation would pass slowly.

A couple of cousins in St. Paul recalled their time at the country dance fondly, and by noon Annette had already written on a sheet of flowered stationery, *Dear Jimmy.*

Marcella, Helen, Josephine, and Janet eagerly discussed the fun they'd had dancing, and Emma and Joe relished the memory of their oldest daughter's beautiful wedding.

In their bedroom at their farmhouse, George and Anna awoke together, embracing the wonder of marriage. By ten thirty they were eating a hearty breakfast at a truck stop café north of Minneapolis. As they tore into their bacon and eggs, the newlyweds decided they couldn't be happier. In several hours they would arrive at the city of Duluth, where they would spend their honeymoon in a fancy room at the Hotel Duluth, and being together would make everything magical.

Maggie woke early but rolled over to go back to sleep, feeling good about two things. First, she shamelessly admitted to herself that she, Maggie Carlson, had attracted boys who wanted to dance with her and some who had wanted to do even more. And second, she had proved to herself that she had the resolve to say no to temptations that could cause her and her family trouble.

In the next room, Joey slept late, but before he had gone to sleep he'd reveled in the steps he had taken into the world of adults. He had met Caroline head on, and he hadn't backed down. Maybe this girl thing would be okay after all.

Even though Jimmy was dead tired and sore from the fight with Jack, his memory of the beautiful Annette kept him smiling while he did morning chores with his parents, who were happily enjoying the four remaining cans of the six-pack while they worked. They did not argue but talked fondly of the previous day. Dad was not as humble about his bout with the law as he should have been, but he didn't brag of besting them. Instead, he talked of the police with respect, emphasizing, "They liked it when I told the truth about being drunk and celebrating." Jimmy thought that was progress.

Noticing a visitor descending the stairs to the basement barn, Jimmy cheerfully said, "Good morning, Uncle John. What's up?"

Before John could answer, Martin rose from his squat next to a cow and exclaimed, "Never expected to see you this morning! But we can always use the extra help, especially after a whole day of drinking." As he poured the bucket of milk into the shotgun pail, he asked, "Is anything wrong?"

Mary, who had been feeding calves, quickly joined them but said nothing.

John breathed deeply before he stammered, "Billy didn't come home last night."

"Maybe he just slept in the car," Martin offered.

"When I saw him near the end of the dance, he was fine," Jimmy said, deciding not to say anything about Billy's fight with Jack. *Maybe his head wound was worse than I thought.*

"It's just not like him. But I have to tell you that Rose and he and I had a big argument last night before he went to the dance. It didn't end well. He actually said he might not come home. He said he might rent one of Berris's cabins. But just to check, I drove through the parking lot at Crossroads this morning on my way here. His car wasn't there. Maybe I've nothing to worry about, but not coming home is just not like him. It's not like him to worry his folks."

Mom nodded to Dad before she declared, "Go with him, Martin. Jimmy and I can handle morning milking. Maggie and Joey will help with chores after breakfast."

As the two men drove to the Lakeshore Ballroom, Martin speculated, "He was probably just tired and slept in the car. Maybe he had a couple beers and didn't want to drive."

"Honestly," John confessed, "I'm afraid the biggest reason he might not have come home is because of the fight he had with Rose. He actually said he might not come home, but I didn't want to believe it."

Spotting Billy's car west of the ball field, John parked nearby, and they hurried to the scene. John opened the door to reveal Billy lying still in the back seat. "My God, he's not moving!" John exclaimed in a near whisper. "Look at the blood on his face and on his jacket. He's got a cut on his head!" John shook his son's foot gently and said, "Billy! Billy, are you okay?" He turned to Martin to exclaim again, "He's not moving!"

Slowly, Billy lifted his head and turned to see his dad and uncle outside the car. "Yeah. Is something wrong?"

"We were worried about you, son, when you didn't show up for milking. After I finished, I went to get Martin to help look for you. Look at him, Martin! His knuckles are bruised and covered with dried blood!"

"And that cut on his head looks pretty bad," Martin said.

"Yeah," Billy explained, "that knocked me out for a short time, but it quit bleeding and my headache is gone now."

"What happened to your knuckles?" John asked.

"Well." Billy smiled. "When I came to, I found the guy who hit me with the bottle and I used him for a punching bag. He never connected with a punch." Billy sat up slowly. "Sorry to worry you. I was so tired. Instead of driving home I just crawled in the back seat. And honestly, I didn't know if Mom would still be home, and I wasn't looking forward to seeing her at breakfast." Looking at his wristwatch, he said, "I can't believe I slept this late."

John said, "Mom won't be with us for a while. After you left, she called Betty and said it was urgent. I couldn't believe it, but Betty and the pastor picked her up to take her to their place at six this morning. That's over a two-hour drive each way. They had to leave by at three-thirty in the morning to get here and be back by nine so he could do his church service at ten. Rose has some good friends in those two. I'm glad she went there for a vacation."

"I'll miss Mom," Billy said. "But I'll welcome the peace."

"Maybe it will give her some peace too," Martin added.

Many miles away, Mary Schroedler, unaware that her name had been a prominent topic before and during the wedding celebrations, rose with the sun shining into her east attic window. She walked the short distance to the south window, kneeled, and stared at two pillow-sized stones, each with its top painted white. After a moment of reflection, she stood up and declared aloud, "I've held off writing to anyone long enough. Today, I'm going to write to Maggie and Jimmy!"

She moved to her dresser, picked up her tablet, and began. Excited to at last be communicating with her dear friends, she also thought of the risks. *So much has happened! So much I want to say! But I have to be careful not to reveal any clues about where I am.*

She completed her letter in less than an hour and brought it downstairs to give to Dorothea, who promised to mail it the next day.

The End

ACKNOWLEDGMENTS

I thank the entire workforce at Beaver's Pond Press, St. Paul, Minnesota, who have supported us through the publishing of nineteen books. We especially thank my managing editor, Alicia Ester, who kept progress on pace; my editor, Kellie M. Hultgren, who offered many valuable insights to make my novel a better story; and my designer, Dan Pitts, who helped make the book a pleasure to read.

I thank my friends who graciously answered questions about the era, especially my two dear sisters, Joyce Tornio and Judy Malz. I also thank my aunt, Elaine Moss, and my cousin, Janet Mueller, for their valuable input.

I thank my sister Judy for creating the cover artwork for *The Dance*.

Beyond all other measures of gratitude, I thank my dear wife, Nancy A. Fredrickson, who crafted the final maps from my crude sketches, who tirelessly and enthusiastically read many drafts and revisions, and who provided me with the kind of loving encouragement every artist needs to continue to create.

ABOUT THE AUTHOR

Gordon W. Fredrickson was raised on a small dairy farm in Minnesota, served three years in the United States Army after high school, graduated with a teaching degree from the University of Minnesota, taught English to grades nine through twelve, directed high school plays and musicals, and has written nineteen books for children and adults with the aim to enlighten and entertain. His wife, Nancy, coauthored several of the books as photographer and photo editor. For nearly two decades, Gordon performed programs about his books for more than 52,000 children and adults at over 1,000 elementary schools, middle schools, high schools, historical societies, museums, and banquets of all kinds.

Gordon and Nancy have downsized from their hobby farm and now reside in a townhome less than twenty miles from where they grew up. Visit www.GordonFredrickson.com for details and sample pages of their books.

OTHER BOOKS BY GORDON AND NANCY FREDRICKSON

The Dance is the Fredricksons' nineteenth book published with Beaver's Pond Press of St. Paul, Minnesota. Their books include memoir, fiction, nonfiction, children's books, poetry, and fantasy stories. Visit www.Gordon-Fredrickson.com for details and excerpts.

The first two novels of the Discovery series, *Discovery* and *The Dance*, are available now on their website, on Amazon, and in many bookstores. The third novel, *The Search*, will be available in 2025.

Three forthcoming novels will follow the lives of the main characters in the Discovery series to the late 1980s.

WANT TO READ MORE ABOUT THE CHARACTERS IN THE DANCE?

Join them in *The Search,* the third novel in the Discovery series, where nearly everybody is searching for something.

Ride along with Jimmy, Maggie, and Robert as they head west on a road trip to find Mary Schroedler based on clues from a letter in which she pleaded, "P.S. Do not try to find me." On their foolish quest, they encounter Odyssean obstacles and Herculean challenges, forcing them to make decisions contrary to what they had planned, even when their goal is in plain sight.

Meanwhile, their parents travel to seek peace for John and Rose Thorson, only to become entangled with personal issues too deep to resolve.

And Joey stays home to direct a final grand social event for the closing country school before he proves unequivocally that he's "not just a kid."

In *The Search*, the characters face dangerous and difficult challenges to grow and discover themselves on the way to unexpected resolutions.

www.ingramcontent.com/pod-product-compliance
Lightning Source LLC
Chambersburg PA
CBHW020605110726
47899CB00002B/382